DANIEL CLAY is thirty-eight years old and has worked in a succession of clerical and admin jobs before training to become an accountant. His lifelong goal, however, had always been to become a writer, which he has now achieved to great acclaim. *Broken* is his debut novel. Daniel is married and lives in Hampshire.

Shortlisted for the Authors' Club Best First Novel Award 2009. Shortlisted for the Commonwealth Writers' Prize Best First Book Award 2009.

From the reviews of *Broken*:

'There are many good things here: it's bold, prescient, engaging and oddly touching'   *Guardian*

'This is a novel whose plot and vivid, pared-down imagery bravely patrol the terrifying border at which the human blurs into the bestial and inanimate . . . remarkably controlled and disciplined . . . Clay's triumph is in exploring the kindness and love that might heal and restore – and what it is to feel fully alive'   ANITA SETHI, *Independent*

'It's funny and sad and moving . . . and ultimately very engaging'   FRANCESCA SEGAL, *Observer*

'There's so much about innocence and vulnerability in this novel. A lot of it is funny . . . Read this book; don't run away from it'   TOM BONCZA-TOMASZEWSKI, *Independent*

DANIEL CLAY

Broken

HARPER PERENNIAL

London, New York, Toronto, Sydney and New Delhi

Harper Perennial
An imprint of HarperCollins*Publishers*
77–85 Fulham Palace Road
Hammersmith
London W6 8JB

www.harperperennial.co.uk
Visit our authors' blog at www.fifthestate.co.uk

This Harper Perennial edition published 2009
1

First published in 2008 by Harper Press

Copyright © Daniel Clay 2008

PS Section copyright © Daniel Clay 2008, 2009

PS™ is a trademark of HarperCollins*Publishers* Ltd

Daniel Clay asserts the moral right
to be identified as the author of this work

A catalogue record for this book
is available from the British Library

ISBN-13 978-0-00-727014-9

Set in Minion by
Palimpsest Book Production Limited,
Grangemouth, Stirlingshire
Printed and bound in Great Britain by Clays Ltd, St Ives plc

Mixed Sources
Product group from well-managed
forests and other controlled sources
www.fsc.org   Cert no. SW-COC-1806
© 1996 Forest Stewardship Council

FSC is a non-profit international organisation established to promote the
responsible management of the world's forests. Products carrying the FSC
label are independently certified to assure consumers that they come
from forests that are managed to meet the social, economic and
ecological needs of present and future generations.

Find out more about HarperCollins and the environment at
www.harpercollins.co.uk/green

For Alison

'Skunk, Skunk. Wake up, beautiful darling.'

Archie, my father, holds both my hands as he says this. I sense his words rather than hear them:

'Skunk, Skunk. Wake up, beautiful darling.'

I also sense his life now.

It seeps through his palms into my palms. It deadens the blood in my veins. My heartbeat slows. I shudder. Poor old Archie. This is the way that his life is. I see it. I feel it. I know it. Tonight, from midnight through to two in the morning, he will sit all alone in the front room and watch a video of the day I was born. Almost twelve years ago now. There I am. You can see me. A wrinkled pink sack of flesh that does little but lie on its back with tubes feeding into its nostrils. Not a lot different to now then. Here I lie, on my back, with tubes feeding into my nostrils. But tonight I will be a newborn. All that hope. All that promise. Poor old Archie. He'll sit all alone and he'll watch me. He'll drink and he'll think, how did it happen? How did it end up like this? Then he'll go to the bed that he shares with Cerys and listen to her crying. He'll cry a little himself.

Finally, he will sleep and dream that the harsh ringing sound

1

by his bedside is the Royal Hampshire County Hospital phoning to say I am dead. He will sit up, gasping, but it won't be his phone that is ringing, it will be his alarm clock, and it will be time to get up, go to work.

In work, Archie will sit at his desk and recoil every time the phone rings, then he'll rush here to see me.

'Skunk, Skunk. Wake up, beautiful darling. Don't you leave me. Don't you dare.'

All of this will happen. I know for sure it will happen. I know everything now. Especially about Broken Buckley. Poor old Broken Buckley. Hunched over his mother's corpse. Hands pressed to his temples. How and why? Oh how and why? His story started with Saskia Oswald: Broken loved Saskia Oswald. Had. Once. Loved. Saskia. Oswald. But Saskia Oswald never loved him. She just loved his car. She said, Hey, soldier, fancy taking me for a ride? Did he? Oh, did he. Poor old Broken Buckley. He was nineteen years old and a virgin, the sort of guy who spits when he speaks, just little flecks of saliva that hang in the air and distract you from whatever he's saying. Saskia Oswald ate him for breakfast – ate him up and then spat him out. Not enough for her though. She had to tell everyone about it, and that's when it started for him.

'Skunk, please, God, blink, just blink if you can hear me . . . we're here, darling. We're all here beside you.'

It didn't finish there though. It never does with the likes of the Oswalds. They're the family in one of the Housing Association properties on the opposite side of the square. Single parent. Lots of children. Music all hours of the night. Bin bags in the front garden. Portsmouth FC flags hanging from the windows.

*Maori-style tattoos on overdeveloped biceps. This is Bob Oswald.
The father.*

Bob Oswald. The father.

*The first time I saw him hitting someone, I was coming up
ten years old.*

It was summer, hot, and Rick Buckley was washing the car
his father had bought him as a present for passing his driving
test. Skunk Cunningham was skipping on the tarmac drive
that had once been their front garden. Other than Skunk and
Rick, Drummond Square was empty.

The attack happened out of nowhere. Skunk didn't hear
anyone speaking. She didn't hear anyone shouting. The first
thing she heard was the scream: it was high-pitched, like a
horse, and before she knew what was happening, Bob Oswald
had Rick Buckley in a headlock and was twisting him sideways, like wrestling a bull. The two of them staggered out of
the Buckleys' front garden and into the otherwise empty
square. Rick Buckley shouted, Stop it, I haven't done anything
wrong.

Bob Oswald hit him. Not a punch, but a blow with the
point of his elbow. It landed in the small of Rick's back. Rick
collapsed to his knees.

Skunk stood frozen, hot in the sun, her small hands held
up to her mouth. Bob Oswald hit Rick again, and Rick fell
flat on his face. Bob Oswald kicked him in the gut then the
side of the head. Skunk recoiled at the sound of the thud.
Then Bob Oswald took hold of Rick's hair and lifted his head
up. He made a lot of noise dredging his throat clean, then

spat into Rick's face. After that, he studied Rick closely for a moment, then pushed him back down to the ground. Rick lay very still. He was silent. Bob Oswald stepped over him and made his way back into his house. Once inside, the throb of music that had played like a soundtrack in the background rose to a deafening thud.

As far as I can remember, after Bob Oswald left him, Rick stayed on his face in the road. He was sobbing. I wanted to go and get someone to help him, but I was too frightened to move. I stood with my hands raised to my mouth and my heart beating fast in my chest. Maybe as much as half an hour later, Mr Buckley returned from the funeral parlour he managed and helped his son into their house. I sat down on the kerbside and stared at the blood on the tarmac. I don't remember if I cried. I don't remember if I was sick. If I ever asked Jed or Archie about it, I don't remember what they said. In fact, before I fell into this coma, the only thing I really remember about seeing what Bob Oswald did to Rick Buckley was trying to forget it had happened. Even though this is how it all started, I pushed the whole thing from my mind.

The police turned up three days later. The squad car stood out like a beacon as it sat on the Buckleys' front drive. Bob Oswald saw it through his kitchen window and thought about what he should do. Finally, he stepped out of his house and leaned against his jeep. From here, he watched the Buckley house until the policemen let themselves out. Then he marched over towards them.

'You,' he shouted. 'I want words with you.'

The two policemen looked at each other and sighed. The Buckleys had just told them how Bob Oswald had beaten their son up for no apparent reason, but with no known witnesses and no permanent damage done, the officers had convinced Mr and Mrs Buckley to let the matter drop: if what they'd heard about Bob Oswald was true, he was only going to deny attacking their son, and did the Buckleys really want to be involved in a drawn-out court case with someone who lived so close to them? Now Bob Oswald continued towards the two policemen. A huge man, shaven-headed, he yelled, 'I want to report a rape.'

It was his third eldest daughter who had been raped.

She was a skinny slip of a girl with lank blonde hair and an underfed gymnast's body. She never wore many clothes – hot pants, bra tops, stilettos. Her favourite expression was fucker, as in, that fucker over there's giving me the evils, or, that fucker down the road wants to watch herself or I'll do her.

Now that fucker Rick Buckley had raped her.

She told her father this just a few minutes before the fight in the square, though she never said it was rape, she only said it was sex, and she only said it was sex because he refused to believe the real reason she had contraceptives under her bed.

He said, Susan, you're thirteen years old, what the fuck do you want the pill for?

She said, I dunno.

He said, Yes, you do, you want them for having sex.

5

And then he got very angry.

Which made Susan very scared.

So she said that she'd nicked them.

For once, she was telling the truth. She'd nicked them off Mrs McCluskey, who'd made the fatal mistake of leaving an open handbag within reaching range of an Oswald. Mrs McCluskey never did realise they'd been stolen. She just assumed she'd lost them and got another prescription. As teachers go, she was sensible like that. As for Susan Oswald, once she'd nicked them, she didn't know what to do with them. They tasted of nothing and didn't get her going the way her old man's vodka did. What good were contraceptives? She chucked them under her bed and forgot they even existed. Bob Oswald found them six months later when he was looking for a new place to hide his drugs. He yelled, 'Susan. Get up here.'

Susan Oswald sighed. Her old man. He could be a right fucker.

'What?'

'Get your arse up here,' Bob yelled. 'Now.'

Susan climbed the stairs. 'What?'

Bob Oswald threw the contraceptives at her. 'What are these?'

'I dunno.'

'Yes, you do. They're contraceptives.'

A pregnant pause.

'Your contraceptives. I found them under your bed. Susan. You're thirteen years old. What the fuck do you want the pill for?'

'I dunno.'

'Yes, you do. You want them for having sex. Who the fuck are you having sex with?'

Susan Oswald didn't answer. She couldn't. She hadn't been having sex with anyone. Bob Oswald leaned into her face.

'Susan. Tell me. And don't try to give me no bullshit. I know you've been at it with someone. It's written all over your face.'

'Dad, it isn't, I haven't.'

'Then what are you on the pill for?'

'I'm not. Those tablets ain't mine.'

'Yeah. Right. Whose are they? Saskia's? Saraya's?'

'Nobody's.'

'Nobody's?'

'Nobody's. I nicked them. I swear.'

Bob Oswald drew a fist back. 'Nobody nicks the pill, Susan. You get it for free off the state.'

Susan stared open-mouthed at her father's fist.

'Tell me,' he told her. 'Who are you having sex with?'

'Dad –'

'Don't "Dad" me, Susan. Give me a name.'

'But, Dad –'

Bob Oswald punched the wall beside Susan's head. She screamed and fell down on the floor. Bob leaned down above her and pressed his bleeding fist into her face.

'I want a name, Susan. You're gonna give me a name. If you don't give me a name, I'm gonna count to ten, and if I've not got a name by the time I've counted to ten, I'll be punching *you*, not the fucking wall. You get me? I don't want to. You're my daughter. I love you. I'm out to protect you. But if you don't help me protect you, I'll break every bone in your body. Now give me the dumb fucker's name.'

Susan Oswald had never been punched by her father before. Staring into his knuckles, she didn't want to be either. They were huge. His onyx rings would slice through her flesh. She sobbed and screamed that the tablets weren't hers, but Bob drew his fist back and started to count. One, he said, two, he said, three. Susan screamed for someone to help her, but her sisters were cowering on the stairs and there was nobody else who could hear. Bob's voice rose with each number, so it was four, tell me, five, tell me, six, you'd better fucking tell me, SEVEN, right into her face. Then he screamed EIGHT, I'm gonna kill you, I'll break every bone in your body. Give me the dumb fucker's name. NINE. He tensed his fist even tighter. The knuckles were dripping with blood. Seeing it before her, Susan gave up trying to reason. She had to come up with a name. But there was no name she could think of, because there was no one she had shagged. She did know, however, that Saskia, her second eldest sister, had recently shagged Rick Buckley, the weird kid from the other side of the square. Susan knew this because she'd heard Saskia talking about the size of Rick's penis. Saraya, the eldest, had yelled, 'How small? You're like totally kidding me,' then the two sisters had laughed hysterically. Now, just before Bob could scream TEN and start punching, Susan shouted up into his face:

'Rick Buckley.'

'Rick Buckley?' Bob Oswald stared, wide-eyed. 'He's – what – seven years older than you are?'

Rick was six years older. Bob didn't care much for maths.

Susan tried to make the lie convincing: 'We've been doing it in his car.'

'Fucking hell.'

Fucking hell, the two policemen thought. Rape?

They looked back at the house they'd just come from. The Buckleys seemed a nice enough family. The old man was a bit wet and the mum was a bit dull. In keeping with the parents, the boy had seemed a little bit flaky when Mrs Buckley had finally got him to come out of his bedroom and tell them who'd beaten him up for no apparent reason. But rape? He didn't look capable of sex, let alone rape.

Still. An allegation was an allegation.

They radioed it through to the Child Protection Unit, then went for a chat with Bob Oswald. As he filled them in on the details, they looked through the grimy kitchen window at a beaming Susan Oswald. She was doing dance steps with her two younger sisters in a scruffy wasteland of a garden full of swings and beaten-up toys. When one of her younger sisters got her steps wrong, Susan's beam was shattered. You stupid fucking bitch, Sunrise. You do it like this, not that. Sunset, the youngest of Bob's daughters at two years old, looked from one sister to the other, then threw her arms around both. The policemen turned away. Bob Oswald told them Susan's version of how it had happened: Rick Buckley – always a bit of a weirdo, very quiet, very, very creepy – had offered to take her for a drive in the brand-new car his old man had just bought him as a present for passing his test. He had driven her onto

9

the nearby Oak Tree Place development that was currently just a wasteland of unfinished houses and mudflats, held her down, and raped her.

Both of the policemen took notes.

Just over eleven miles away, in Winchester, seven officers of various rank climbed into an assortment of cars and made their way out to Hedge End. Within fifty-six minutes of the allegation being made Rick Buckley was arrested under suspicion of raping Susan Oswald. In the back of a squad car that smelled of burgers and cigarettes, a constable twice Rick's age leaned in close against him and whispered, very thickly, I hope for your sake you didn't do it. Otherwise, you're dead.

The officer on the other side of him said, She's thirteen years old, you wanker.

Back at the Oswalds' place, Susan Oswald was observed as she played with her younger sisters by two highly trained social workers and the Woman Police Constable who would be her chaperone throughout the investigation. All three women noticed the child swung from agitated to content to agitated again. The social workers took notes. The WPC asked some loaded questions. She got some loaded answers. At just after seven thirty, Susan, Bob, the social workers and the police all made their way from Hedge End to the rape suite in Winchester.

In the Buckley home, Mr and Mrs Buckley sat at their kitchen table and watched as officers carried items of Rick's clothing from the house. Mr Buckley put his head in his hands. Mrs Buckley didn't hide her tears. They ran freely down her face and fell to the table from her chin. Upstairs, the discovery of a small collection of porn was greeted with satisfaction.

In the rape suite, Susan was put in a room with a PlayStation and some dolls and pens and paper and jigsaws and brightly coloured walls. The WPC who would be her chaperone sat with her to make sure she was OK. It was at this stage that Susan began to suspect she had done something wrong: people were never this nice to her, and no one ever let her use their stuff for nothing. She said, What's all this about?

The WPC said, Nothing.

Susan was not fooled.

'Is it about what I told my old man about Rick Buckley?'

The WPC said, There's no need to look frightened, honey. You haven't done anything wrong.

Susan Oswald thought, Shit.

It was then that the police doctor came in. She was a very tall, very thin woman who tried her best to disguise the fact she hated children.

'Hello, Susan. How are you?'

Susan said, 'What's it gotta do with you?' She looked from the WPC to the doctor then down at the PlayStation control in her hands. She thought, Shit, shit, shit, shit, shit.

The WPC said, 'This is Dr Mortimer, Susan. Her first name's Susan too.'

'Big fucking deal.'

The WPC smiled. 'She just needs to look at you a moment. Examine you. Make sure you're OK. There's nothing for you to be afraid of. I can stay with you, if you like.'

'Whatever.' Susan stared at the doctor. The doctor stared

at Susan. Then she took a step forward. With the curtains drawn and the door shut, it took a matter of minutes to determine Susan Oswald was a virgin. The doctor stood back and took her gloves off.

She said, 'I'd best go and speak to DS Westbury.'

The police questioned Dr Mortimer for a further half an hour. They said, Even if Susan Oswald is a virgin, couldn't she have been interfered with? Couldn't the act of sexual intercourse have been simulated? Shouldn't we ask her to describe Rick Buckley's penis? The doctor said, For Christ's sake, the child's lying. It's written all over her face.

Bob Oswald had to be restrained when this was put to him. My Susan's many things, but she ain't no fucking liar. Bob Oswald was many things, and he was a fucking liar. Susan lied to him all the time. She got it from her father. He folded his arms and said, That man's been at my daughter. My little baby girl. She's only thirteen years old. How the hell do I get her through this? He took a deep breath. There were tears in his eyes. I want him charged. I want him strung up by his bollocks. Pervert. Fucking creep. If you don't kill him, I will. He's ruined my poor baby's life.

Detective Sergeant Westbury ran his hands through his thick brown hair.

'Look, Mr Oswald. If Rick Buckley has been sniffing around your little girl, I want him off the streets as much as you do. But try to see this from my point of view. I've got your daughter saying she's been raped, and I've got a doctor saying she's a virgin.'

'Then get a second opinion.'

'Well. I'm not so keen to put your daughter through another internal examination. How about we bring her in here and have a little chat with her? Just see if we can clarify things a little?'

Bob Oswald raised his eyes up towards the ceiling.

Fifteen minutes later Susan turned on him and yelled, 'I never said he raped me. I said we had sex. And I only said we had sex cos you made me, cos you wouldn't bloody believe me. I don't even know Rick bloody Buckley. I told you those tablets weren't mine.'

She put her head in her hands and because she knew she was really in trouble this time, Susan Oswald wept.

The adults in the room were silent. Then DS Westbury leaned forward.

'Susan. I want you to listen to me. I want you to listen very carefully. I don't want you to be scared. I don't want you to be frightened. If Rick Buckley's done something, said something, been anywhere near you or exposed himself to you in any sort of way – or even if he hasn't, even if he's just done something to make you feel vulnerable, or threatened, or maybe just suspicious even – I want you to know you can tell us, and whatever Rick Buckley has said to you, or whatever he might have threatened you with, or whatever he might have done to you in the past . . . well, we won't let it happen again. We're all on your side here, Susan. All of us. So feel free to tell us what happened.'

'Nothing, you silly fucker. Nothing bloody happened. Jesus. Jesus Christ.'

Bob Oswald shook his head. He cleared his throat. 'Something must have happened,' he yelled at everyone who was staring at him. 'Look at her. She's terrified. He must have threatened her somehow. She's lying to cover his back.'

The WPC cuddled Susan. She whispered, It's OK, sweetie. You don't have to cry. Susan Oswald cried harder. DS Westbury stood up.

'OK,' he said. 'I suggest a comfort break. Susan. Would you like a game of Sonic the Hedgehog? WPC Davies can get up to level eight.'

Susan was led away. She was given a cup of hot chocolate. She was allowed to play Sonic the Hedgehog. Her tears dried. Her mood brightened. She had learned a valuable lesson: sex was good. It got you attention. It got you affection. It was a good way to get on in life.

And if these things came from just saying she'd done it, she couldn't wait to start doing it for real.

The two Oswalds were dropped off by a squad car at three o'clock the next morning. Caught between charging them with wasting police time and Bob's blind insistence that something had gone on between Rick Buckley and his daughter, the police decided to do nothing. No caution. No slap on the wrist. Free to go.

The same was now true of Rick Buckley. The charges against him were dropped and, as they hadn't been sent to the lab yet, the clothes he had been wearing when he'd been arrested were handed back in a clear plastic bag. In a cold room with bright white lighting, Rick hurriedly dressed in front of two

male constables and a female nurse who watched his shrivelled penis bob as he stepped into light blue Y-fronts and then
pulled up his trousers. Despite his total humiliation, Rick
Buckley did not cry: he finished getting dressed, he put his
watch on, he signed for the loose change that had been in his
pockets. One of the officers marched him down a darkly lit
corridor and out into early morning. It was just after 7 a.m.

No one had told Mr and Mrs Buckley their son was being
released without charge. Rick stood in a dreary drizzle and, as
he had hardly any money and hadn't had his mobile phone
on him when he'd been arrested, started the eleven-mile walk
to Hedge End. Rain saturated his wavy hair and thin summer
cotton T-shirt. He walked with his arms wrapped around
himself. He walked with his head down. He talked as he walked.

On each first step he said, I.

On each second step he said, feel.

On each third step he said, dirty.

He said these words over and over.

I feel dirty. I feel dirty. I feel dirty.

He said them all the way home.

*It was 11 a.m. by the time he got back to Drummond Square.
I don't remember seeing him hurry round the corner and disappear down the Buckleys' side alley, but I do remember Mr Buckley
coming over to our house later that evening. I was pretending
to be asleep in Archie's lap. He had his hands in my hair. I could
hear the depth of his voice through the itch of his polyester shirt.
Mr Buckley's voice was distant in contrast.*

'The police were utterly useless. They ignored what we said

DANIEL CLAY

about Bob Oswald, then took every word he said on oath. You know, after they dragged my son down the station, they stripped him naked and took loads of swabs.'

'They couldn't have done that without his permission.'

'He didn't know what he was agreeing to. Since he took that beating, he doesn't seem to know if he's coming or going.'

'You should have phoned me,' Archie said. 'I really wish you'd phoned me.'

'It all happened so quickly. We didn't know what we should do.'

I looked over at Mr Buckley. I didn't really know him, but I couldn't imagine Mrs Buckley not knowing what she should do. After my father, she was the cleverest person in the square. Sometimes, when she was out in her front garden, I'd go over and ask her about multiplication or spelling and she always knew the right answers. How could she not have known to call my father? She must have known he was a solicitor. I'd told her about loads of his trials.

'That bloody Bob Oswald,' Mr Buckley continued. 'He's reduced my son to a nervous wreck and got away without even a caution.'

'You need to go back to the police, Dave.' Archie's voice rumbled from deep inside his stomach. 'A vicious attack on a nineteen-year-old boy . . . no matter what Bob Oswald thought he'd been up to . . . they have to do something about that.'

Mr Buckley laughed in a way I found scary. 'What like? An ASBO? A caution?'

'It's GBH at least,' Archie said after a moment. 'Bob should be facing prison.'

16

Mr Buckley's voice was high and shaky where my father's was soft and deep. 'You know better than I do he'll be facing no more than community service. What'll probably happen is the police'll decide to charge me with wasting their time. It's been an eye-opener, this has. A real bloody shock.'

A long silence followed. Finally, Archie broke it.

'How's the boy, anyway?'

Mr Buckley's voice went from shaky to jumpy. 'Broken,' he said. 'Utterly broken. He reckons he's never leaving the house again.'

Another silence followed. I was very nearly asleep. It was way, way past my bedtime. Only Archie's voice kept me awake.

'He just needs time,' he said to Mr Buckley. 'Don't worry. He'll be OK.'

But Archie was wrong. Mr Buckley's son was not OK. Just as he'd said to his father, he stayed inside the house. The car he had been cleaning the day Bob Oswald attacked him stood unused on the drive. The curtains to his room stayed shut.

For a time, he was a topic of fascination to me: Has he come out yet, Daddy? Never you mind. What's he doing in there, Daddy? Never you mind. Do you think we should go round and see him? Keep your bloody nose out of other people's business, for Christ's sake, I won't tell you again. Leave the poor Buckleys alone.

Jed was fascinated as well. Why would anyone want to stay in their bedroom when there were so many things to be done? He, being older, got a little more sense out of our father, who told him Mr Buckley's son had suffered a breakdown, and people who suffered breakdowns did things differently to everyone else.

17

Jed still didn't understand though. Why had he suffered a breakdown? Archie shrugged. Some people just do.

This fuelled our fascination. A breakdown? What, like a car? Would a man from the AA come round and jump-start Mr Buckley's son, or tow him away in a tow truck? Eager to see how it ended, we sat on the kerb outside our house. Here, we watched the Buckley place for further developments. As we didn't know Mr Buckley's son's name, we started calling him Broken, as in, any sign of Broken Buckley yet? Nope. Oh. OK. After about an hour of watching, we got bored of just sitting, so we played football while we watched, then rode our scooters up and down the pavement, honking our horns at each other.

'You kids shut that row up,' Bob Oswald yelled as he stepped out into the sunshine. And then, seeing Mr Buckley on his knees in his garden, 'Hey, fuckwit, how's your rapist son healing up?' When he didn't get an answer, he spat in Mr Buckley's direction, then got in his jeep and sped off. The deep thud of bass music echoed in his wake.

Mr Buckley stood with a small trowel in his hand and stared off into the distance. He stood there for a long time, then dropped the trowel and went inside. The slam of the door seemed final, but ten or so minutes later Mrs Buckley came out and picked the trowel up. The Buckleys were tidy like that.

Later, when Bob Oswald pulled up in his jeep, Mr Buckley came out of his house as if he'd been waiting. 'You,' he shouted. 'Yes. You.' Bob Oswald got out of his jeep and turned towards Mr Buckley. 'Yes, you,' Mr Buckley repeated. 'I want words with you.'

Bob Oswald raised his eyebrows. He put on a voice that wasn't his own. 'You talkin' to me?' He was smiling, but he didn't look happy.

Mr Buckley kept right on towards him. 'I don't know how you can live with yourself. My son. He hasn't done anything to you or your family. Now look at him. Your big mouth and your lying bitch of a daughter. You've made him a nervous wreck. You're a wanker. You're complete fucking scum.'

Beside me, Jed sucked his breath in. Even Bob Oswald straightened a little.

'You want to come over here and say that? Or do you want to call the police like last time?'

Mr Buckley kept walking towards him. 'It wasn't my son who shouted rape, was it? Why did you have to go picking on him? Why does it always have to be violence with you? If you had your suspicions, why didn't you just call the police like a civilised human being?' Mr Buckley was in front of Bob Oswald now. Bob Oswald was looking down on him. He had his hands on his hips. His thick black Maori-style tattoos stood out on his arms and his shoulders. Mr Buckley continued. 'My son was just minding his own business. Now he won't even leave his bedroom. All because of your fists and your bitch of a daughter's lies. I don't know –'

Mr Buckley stopped talking when Bob Oswald kneed him between the legs. Mr Buckley cried out and fell down in a heap. Bob Oswald bent low and patted Mr Buckley on the shoulder. Then he made his way back into his house. Drawn out by the sound of raised voices, all five of his daughters were lined up on the front doorstep. They greeted Bob Oswald like he had just done something clever:

Good one, Dad.

That showed him.

The fucker.

Bob Oswald ushered them all inside. As Susan Oswald turned away, she looked over at Jed and smiled. Jed looked down at the ground. I looked at Mr Buckley. He was dragging himself away from the Oswald house, half standing, half on his knees. I felt sorry for him. He looked silly. He looked sad. I shouted, Hello, Mr Buckley, hot today, isn't it? But he ignored me. He went inside.

If Mr Buckley ever tried to have a punch-up with Bob Oswald again, I wasn't there to see it. Come to think of it, the only time I really saw Mr Buckley for a long time after that was whenever he came round to see Archie. I don't think he and my father were friends, exactly, but they were the same age and both supported Southampton, so at least they had that in common. Three or four times a year Mr Buckley would come over with a four-pack of Carlsberg and the two men would swear at the widescreen. Jed would watch as well, so even though I hated football I'd often drift in to join them. As an aside, once Southampton had been beaten, Archie would ask after Mr Buckley's son, who he never referred to by name. How's the boy? Or, how's he doing? Or, any news? But, finally, Archie stopped asking, and I can't really blame him. It's not like he ever got a straight answer. Mr Buckley would shrug and say something like, oh, you know, or, no change, or, same as ever, really. The last time I ever heard Archie ask him, Mr Buckley said nothing. He put his hands over his face and shook his head. When

Mr Buckley's shoulders started to shake, Archie gave me and Jed a tenner to go and buy chips for our tea. As far as I can tell, neither of them mentioned Mr Buckley's son after that. It was as if he no longer existed. He did though, in his bedroom, and one day he would come out.

It wouldn't be for more than a year, though.

This year was long and hard for the Buckleys. Although all charges had been dropped, and although everyone outside of the Oswalds' accepted Susan had been lying, her accusations somehow stuck. This was mostly due to the other Oswald girls, who would scream *rapist* across the street every time they saw a Buckley moving about in broad daylight. Once in a while, minor acts of vandalism occurred – Broken's car had its tyres slashed, and some eggs were thrown at the house that Halloween. Rubbish was tossed into their garden, and cigarettes were stubbed out on their UPVC window frames. Nothing to call the police for. Just enough to make life unpleasant.

If Bob Oswald ever saw Mr Buckley in the street, he would always shout something, but Mr Buckley would never respond. One time, Archie Cunningham intervened on Mr Buckley's behalf. He had just taken Jed and Skunk to see *Revenge of the Sith* at the Odeon in Port Solent, and Mr Buckley was carrying some shopping into his house. Bob Oswald was standing on his doorstep with his huge hands cupped around his huge mouth. 'How's your prick of a son doing, Buckley? Still touching up the kiddies?' Mr Buckley hurried into his house and slammed the door behind him.

Archie said, 'Stay in the car,' then got out and walked to

the edge of the drive. Jed and Skunk wound down the windows so they could hear what the adults were saying.

'Hey, Bob,' Archie shouted. 'You up to speed on your libel laws?'

Bob Oswald turned his gaze from the Buckley house to Archie Cunningham.

'What the fuck's it gotta do with you?'

'Well, if Dave or his son wanted me to represent them, I'd be happy to do it for free. Open-and-shut case, considering the police dropped all charges. Like taking candy off a kid, taking money off you.'

Bob Oswald stared at Archie Cunningham. 'Answer me one question, Cunningham. You let your kids go over the Buckleys'?'

'More often than I let them go over yours.'

Bob Oswald said nothing.

Archie took a steady step forward. 'You watch your big mouth in future. And if you ever want legal aid again don't come running to my firm. Get me?' He stared at Bob Oswald, then turned and ordered Skunk and Jed inside. 'I don't want you playing with the Oswalds any more,' he said as they took their coats off. Skunk and Jed raised their eyebrows: like they ever played with the Oswalds. All of the Oswalds were mental. But so, too, was Broken Buckley: he crouched down by his bedroom window and watched his father scurry away from Bob Oswald, then watched Archie Cunningham shout Bob Oswald down in the street. Fearing Bob Oswald might look up and see him, Broken moved away from the curtains and sat down on the edge of his bed. Hunching his shoulders forwards, he tormented himself with memories of the day Bob Oswald attacked him. Then he remembered the policemen coming to get him after Susan Oswald accused him of rape. These memories were nothing compared to the day Saskia Oswald came on to him and then laughed at the size of his penis. Why did she have to go and do that? Why did she do that to him? Broken didn't know. He couldn't understand. Still, though, he went through it over and over, hidden away in his box room, curled on his side on his bed. Sometimes, he stared through a gap in the curtains. If he ever saw Bob Oswald, he relived the day of his beating. If he ever saw Saskia Oswald, he stepped quickly away from the window and paced up and down his small room. Outside of his bedroom, the world continued without him. Time passed without him emerging: days and weeks and months. He didn't just refuse to come out – he refused to open the windows or the curtains or even the bedroom door. He went to the toilet in a bucket and brought it out when Mr Buckley was at work and Mrs Buckley was out shopping. For the rest of the time he lived in a strange world of curtains, shadows and dread. His parents were despairing. Mrs Buckley, on the landing:

'Rick. Rick. Are you in there, Rick? Can you hear me? Can I come in? Love? Please? Love? Please?'

Silence. A chair wedged under the handle. If Mrs Buckley listened, she could hear him, breathing. If she came home unexpectedly, she could hear his footsteps, scurrying, up the stairs. Late at night or in the small hours of the morning, she could hear him moving about in the kitchen, making himself something to eat. She would nudge Mr Buckley awake.

'David,' she'd say. 'David. Wake up. Quickly. He's down there. Listen. He's downstairs. He's moving about.'

Mr Buckley wouldn't answer, though he hadn't been asleep. He had been listening too. And thinking. And trying not to cry. In the daytime, he tended dead bodies at the funeral parlour he managed. He sat and watched the bereaved deal with death. He held out tissues. He powdered dry cheeks. He lifted the limbs of virgins and put the corpses of babies in boxes. He applied make-up where coroners cut. And at night-time, in the dark times, he lay on his back and he listened to the ghost of his son scrape around in the kitchen.

His wife said, 'We have to do something.'

'I know. But what can we do?'

'I don't know. But we have to do something.'

'I know. But what can we do?'

Mr Buckley knew what he had to do. He just didn't want to do it. He didn't want to go to the doctor. He didn't want to sit down before a man who was two years younger than he was, a man he remembered from school as a corn-sheaf of a child who would sit at the back of the assembly with a stupid blank expression all over his dim empty face. He didn't want to say, my one son is mad.

My one son is mad.

He never actually said this.

What he said was:

'It's Rick. He's having some problems.'

Dr Carter sat back in his chair and looked at the under-taker with dry biscuit eyes through lashes of dust. He thought about his golf swing.

'Uh-huh.'

Mr Buckley nodded. 'He's not acting himself.'

'Uh-huh.'

Mr Buckley did not say any more.

Dr Carter stared at him. Finally, he relented. 'In what way has he not been acting himself?'

Mr Buckley cleared his throat. Then he shut his eyes. As he talked, he thought of Rick sitting on a swing on an autumn day that had never existed. On this autumn day that had never existed, Mr Buckley was pushing Rick – who was five – higher and higher and higher. Rick was clinging to the thin grey metal chains that held the swing to its rusty old frame. A sharp, dry breeze was blowing leaves into a sandpit and the rest of the playground was empty. *Faster, Daddy, faster.* The sound of laughter. The scrape of leaves. The glint of sunshine through a darkness that hadn't quite fallen. Mr Buckley said, 'He won't leave his room. He won't eat any food that we cook him. He compulsively washes his body. He isn't acting himself.'

Dr Carter shrugged. 'Why don't you tell him to pop down? I'll have a chat.'

'He won't leave his room, let alone the house.'

'Is he being aggressive towards you?'

'No.'

'Then tell him to pop down. I'll have a chat.'

'Doctor. He won't leave his room. Let alone the house.'

Dr Carter shrugged. 'If he's not being aggressive towards you, I can't come out to see him. He's a grown man, Mr Buckley. He has to come here of his own accord.'

Mr Buckley sighed. 'Look,' he said. 'Doctor. We've asked

him to come down and see you, but he won't listen to us. Can't you please come out and see him?'

'Only if he's posing a danger to himself or the general public.'

Mr Buckley rubbed his eyes. 'Doctor. I'm not sure I'm making myself clear here. This is a situation I really struggle to talk about. But my son, Rick, who you've treated all his life, has been through a hard time lately. Ten months ago, he was beaten senseless by a total nutter and then falsely accused and arrested for rape. Since these events have happened, he's hardly left his bedroom, let alone the house. He's lost his job. He's lost contact with his friends. He's become moody and uncommunicative with his mother and myself. I'm worried about his mental health and his physical safety. I've asked him to come and see you, but, as I've already mentioned, he won't leave his room, let alone the house. So, clearly, he's suffering some form of mental illness. So, please, won't you come out and see him?'

Dr Carter blinked. 'I'm sorry, Mr Buckley, but I can't go out and see your son on your say-so unless he's being aggressive or posing a danger. Is he being aggressive or posing a danger?'

Mr Buckley said, 'No.'

'Then I'm afraid I can't come out and see him. You'll have to get him to come here.'

Mr Buckley said, 'Christ.'

Dr Carter blinked. 'There's no need to be aggressive.'

Mr Buckley left.

*   *   *

Poor old Mr Buckley. He came in to the hospital to see me last night and stood with his head bowed and his hands clasped before him. He didn't speak, but I knew he was wishing me better.

Mrs Buckley never came with him. Obviously. She's dead.

Even after everything that's happened, I feel sorry for the Buckleys. All they ever did was love their son. And they used to buy me stuff for birthdays and Christmas. Mrs Buckley used to talk to me while she did the weeding in her front garden. In fact, before Jed got me too scared of axe-murderer-psycho-killers to go anywhere near their side of the square, I used to spend ages following her around and asking her questions. Unlike my father, she was never too busy to answer, and, unlike Cerys, she never shouted she was busy, Jesus, get out of my face. Sometimes, now, lying here, I wonder if I could have helped them: Broken Buckley only ever wanted someone to be kind to him, someone to make him feel better. I could have done that. I could have been his friend. Archie sees it differently. He sits and he holds my hands and I feel his thoughts flooding through me: Fucking Rick Buckley. Bastard. Fucking bastard. I should have had him put away. But Archie could never have done that, because once Mr Buckley stopped talking about Broken, Archie never gave Broken a second thought. Once the novelty of his situation wore off, none of us did. We all just stopped thinking about him. We all just got on with our lives.

Then, suddenly, he reappeared.

It happened towards the end of the summer holidays fourteen months after Bob Oswald attacked him. Jed was thirteen and Skunk had just turned eleven. They had spent most of that summer holed up in Jed's bedroom playing *Star Wars* on Xbox, but, occasionally, they would venture out so Jed could smoke. As Drummond Square – with its four sides of houses facing in on each other – didn't have anywhere to hide his habit from Cerys (whose cigarettes he was stealing), the best place for Jed to smoke was down Shamblehurst Lane South, a long, winding overgrown path that ran from the One Stop to the train station via the Hedge End Household Waste Recycling Centre. Archie once told Skunk that the only reason the houses on the far side of the square were Housing Association and not privately owned like the rest of the square was because their gardens backed on to the Recycling Centre. Skunk hadn't known what Housing Association meant. She asked Archie to explain. He said Housing Association properties were rented dirt cheap to people who couldn't afford to buy their own houses, and the reason the planners had made these properties Housing Association was because no one in their right mind would buy a house that backed on to a rubbish dump.

Across the room, Cerys had laughed, which was unusual for Cerys. Skunk asked why she was laughing. Cerys nodded in Archie's direction and said no one in their right mind would buy a house opposite a row of Housing Association properties that could be rented dirt cheap to scum like the Oswalds.

Skunk had thought they were both talking rubbish. The dump was cool, and so was Shamblehurst Lane South. There were always loads of fallen branches to use in light-sabre battles with Jed, and people often walked their dogs there, which meant she sometimes got to pet one. It was also where she and Jed met Dillon.

He was riding his bike, but it wasn't his bike, it was a bike that had been left outside the One Stop. It was far too big for Dillon, so he was weaving all over the path. He nearly ran Jed over.

'Watch yourself,' Jed told him.

'Watch yourself yourself,' Dillon said, and then fell over. Skunk couldn't tell if he'd ripped his jeans when he'd fallen, or if they'd already been ripped. They were so big on his hips that they practically hung off his buttocks. His Calvin Klein boxers were worn like a badge of pride, as was his pale pink hoodie. Glowering from underneath it, Dillon had scraggy blond hair and bucky-beaver teeth. His skin was freckled and greasy, and his knuckles were bleeding from falling over. He held them out towards them. 'Look what you made me do.'

Jed blew smoke out through his nostrils. 'Didn't make you do anything. Not my fault you can't ride your bike.'

'Not my bike. I nicked it.'

'Stealing's bad.' Skunk knew this. Archie had told her. Cerys had told her. And she'd been taught it at school.

'Shut your face, dick-splat.'

'You shut your own face, twat-head.'

'Both of you shut your faces.' Jed stepped closer to the bike. 'Where'd you nick it?'

'Just outside the One Stop.'

'Aren't there cameras at the One Stop?'

'Duh. That's why I put my hood up.'

Jed nodded his approval, then offered Dillon a drag on his cigarette. Dillon said cheers and took it. Skunk could tell Dillon didn't smoke much, because he didn't take it all the way back the way Jed said you were meant to: he just sort of inhaled, kept his mouth shut for a second, then puffed out a big grey cloud. Jed took his cigarette back, but Dillon's blood had stained the filter, so Jed heeled it and put his hands on the bike's handlebars. 'Couldn't you nick one more your size?'

'Didn't nick it cos I wanted it. Nicked it cos I could.' Dillon wiped his knuckles on long grass. 'Who're you, anyway?'

'My name's Jed. And this is Skunk, my little sister.'

'I'm Dillon,' Dillon said. 'Skunk's a crap name for a girl, though, ain't it? What happened? Did she stink when she was a baby?'

'No,' Jed told him. 'Our mum liked Skunk Anansie.'

'And anyway,' Skunk said to change the subject, 'Dillon ain't much better. Where's Zebedee and Florence?'

'Yeah,' Jed laughed. 'Where's your roundabout and Dougal?'

Dillon looked from one Cunningham to the other. 'What the fuck are you two on about?'

Jed took the bike from Dillon and tried to pull a wheelie before Skunk could admit they both watched *The Magic Roundabout* on Children's BBC. It was then that the bike's owner saw them.

'Oi. You little wankers. Give me my fucking bike back.'

He was a big bloke with a shaved head. He was running towards them. His belly heaved with the motion, and his two bags of shopping knocked against his legs.

'Give it back,' he yelled. 'I'll kill you.'

Before Skunk knew what was happening, Jed had climbed off the bike and was running in the direction of the Shamblehurst Barn Public House. She turned round to ask Dillon where Jed was going, but he had run off as well. In their absence, the bike remained standing of its own accord for a second, then fell over on its side. Its owner kept sprinting towards Skunk.

'You stay where you are, you little fucker.' His face was all red and there were sweat stains under his armpits. Skunk felt her legs turn to jelly. The man was going to kill her. She could see it in his eyes. He was going to grab her by the throat, pick her up and smash her to bits on the pavement.

Possibly he would have, but his shopping bags split before he reached her, and cans of Stella spilled all over the path. His charge towards her was halted and she turned and ran off as well. Ten minutes later, she found Jed and Dillon hiding out in the bus shelter by the train station. This is where they got to know each other. Jed told Dillon his and Skunk's ages and about their dad who was called Archie and their live-in au pair who was called Cerys. He didn't mention their mother, but, then, since the day she'd done a bunk to Majorca, nobody ever did. Dillon, in turn, told them he was a Gypsy. He was fifteen years old and this was the eleventh county he'd lived in since his mum, dad, two brothers and younger sister had all been killed in a fire started by another Gypsy who had caught Dillon's older brother having it away with his wife. Dillon had only escaped because he'd been arrested that after-noon for trying to rob a sausage roll off the deli counter in the Great Yarmouth branch of Asda. Now Dillon lived with his aunt and uncle outside the old Halfords store that had shut down the previous winter. Even though he was older than Skunk and Jed, he couldn't read or write anywhere near as well as they could, but he did have the ability to steal from a sweet counter with the shopkeeper staring straight at him, and the shopkeeper would never know. His ambition was to rob a house. Jed's ambition was to be a professional footballer. Skunk's ambition was to get married and have lots of babies and never ever leave them, so she asked Dillon back to play Xbox, which Dillon thought was cool, because all the other kids he'd met in Hedge End so far had called him a stinking pikey and left him to play on his own. As they made their way back to the Cunninghams' house, two police cars sped down Drummond Road and screeched into Drummond Square. Thinking the bike's owner had dobbed them in for stealing, Skunk turned and started to run, but Jed grabbed her by the shoulder. 'They're not looking for us, Skunk. They're parking outside the Buckleys'.'

Skunk turned back and looked at the police cars. Mrs Willet from Drummond Primary had once got a policeman to come into school and tell them stealing's bad, but he'd come on a pushbike, so this was the first time she'd ever seen them with lights on and sirens wailing other than on the motorway. Now, close up, they were huge and gleaming and there were two policemen in each one. All four of them got out and ran towards the Buckleys'. The front door was already open and Mrs Buckley was standing under the porch roof. Her house was a giant behind her, the biggest in the square, and Archie looked at it dreamily each time he got in his car. Unlike the Cunningham place, which just had a double driveway, it was set back from the road and partially screened by swaying horse chestnuts that had recently lost their blossom and would soon start to lose their leaves. Mrs Buckley looked much the same as the trees; a tall woman with auburn hair that was greying, her face looked haggard and bloodless. She ran towards the policemen and the five of them formed a huddle. Skunk, Jed and Dillon moved as close as they dared and they listened.

'It's my son . . .'

'. . . his name?'

'. . . Rick. Rick Buckley . . . he hasn't been acting himself . . .'

'. . . have you called social services?'

'. . . how long has he been like this . . .'

'. . . you say your husband's in there with him?'

'. . . please . . . he's my son . . .'

Snippets. Maddening snippets. The three children were so engrossed in the conversation they didn't notice Cerys's presence until she took hold of Skunk's and Jed's ears. The two of them were dragged back to their side of the square. In an impressive show of allegiance that made Skunk instantly love him, Dillon crossed the road to be with them. Here, they joined a swelling gaggle of neighbours and passers-by who had come out to witness the Buckleys' shame. Mrs Buckley was crying openly now. It wasn't the first time Skunk had seen an adult cry – Archie had cried after Euro 2004 and the World Cup in 2006, and Cerys cried each time another man dumped her – but it was the first time she had seen one cry the way a child cries. Mrs Buckley's face screwed up and she lost the breath that she needed to speak with. The policemen seemed scared of her emotion. They sneaked off into the house. Mrs Weston from number 12 went to Mrs Buckley and put her arms around her. Mrs Buckley sobbed in Mrs Weston's arms. The house, in contrast, stood silent.

Skunk said, 'What's going on?'

Jed said, 'Their son's gone mental.'

Cerys said, 'You shut your mouth. I'll give you mental,' and clipped Jed around the ear.

Behind them, people Cerys could not beat into silence spoke on . . .

'. . . Poor Veronica and Dave . . .'

'. . . it's the kid I feel sorry for . . .'

'. . . shouldn't be out anyway . . .'

'. . . a danger to himself . . .'

'. . . a danger to us all . . .'

'. . . that Bob Oswald's a bastard . . .'

. . . in hushed, excited voices that reminded Skunk of Christmas. These voices only quietened when an ambulance and two more police cars pulled up outside the Buckley house. As they tried to find spaces to park in, three of the four policemen came out with a man Skunk hadn't seen for what seemed like forever. She didn't get much of a look at him now. He was huddled with his head down and he had his hands behind his back. To Skunk, he didn't act like he'd gone mental. Sunrise Oswald at school was mental; she smoked roll-ups in the playground and called lezzer after female teachers. This man did nothing like that. He simply got in the back of one of the police cars and a policeman got in beside him. The car pulled away with its lights off and siren silent.

Really, it was quite dull.

Then Mr Buckley came out.

They didn't carry him out, but a medic stood either side of him and Mr Buckley had one arm in a sling. It looked like

34

he had been bleeding – there was blood on his shirt and his trousers. Mrs Buckley ran to him and said, Oh David, David, but he snapped, Get off me, Veronica, and got in the ambulance without her. Again, it drove away without sounding its sirens. Mrs Buckley stood all alone on the pavement while the remaining policemen talked among themselves. Across the street, the crowd gossiped on.

'. . . that's the last we'll see of him then . . .'

'. . . I didn't even know he still lived there . . .'

'. . . I'd almost forgotten they had a son . . .'

Skunk had forgotten as well. Somehow, in the past fourteen months, Broken Buckley had slipped from her mind. Sure, she and Jed had been fascinated for a short time, but then Jed got an Xbox for his birthday and *Star Wars* took over their worlds. She turned and looked up at Cerys. 'What's he been doing in there?'

Cerys shrugged. 'How the bloody hell would I know?'

'He's probably been murdering people,' Jed said speculatively. 'Like Fred West or the Yorkshire Ripper.' The only books Jed ever read were about serial killers. He was an expert on the subject, and Skunk bowed to his superior knowledge. 'Mr Buckley probably found a head in his fridge and asked Broken what it was doing there and that's why Broken attacked Mr Buckley. Mr and Mrs Buckley are lucky to be alive.'

'Right,' Cerys said. 'That's it. Inside.' She took hold of Skunk and Jed and ushered them up the drive. Dillon followed behind. 'And where do you think you're going?'

'To play Xbox.'

'Uh-o. I don't think so.'

'I am so,' Dillon insisted. 'They asked me up to play.'

'Did they indeed.' Cerys's tone was even frostier than normal, but remembering the way Dillon had crossed the road to stay with them earlier, Skunk stepped forward in his defence.

'Cerys,' she said, 'this is Dillon. He's coming upstairs to play Xbox.'

'No he's not,' Cerys said firmly. 'Bye-bye, Dillon. Off you go now, back to your mum and dad's lay-by.'

Dillon looked at Jed and Skunk for assistance, but they knew better than to mess with Cerys. He hid his face by pulling his hood up and made his way out of the square. Cerys didn't wait till he was out of earshot:

'I don't want you playing with pikeys. They'll rob the shirt off your backs.' She pushed Skunk and Jed into the house and slammed the door behind them. Skunk was going to tell her how Dillon had already robbed some bloke's bike, but Jed stopped her by raising his eyebrows. The two of them went up to Skunk's bedroom. Outside, the square was empty again. Jed pointed towards the Buckley house.

'I reckon he's been killing babies.'

'Who? Dillon?'

'Nah. Broken Buckley. I reckon that's what the police wanted him for. They'll come back in a minute and put up a tent in the garden. Then they'll start digging up bodies.'

Skunk stared over the road. 'There'll be TV cameras,' she said.

'And helicopters,' Jed told her.

She put her hand to her bedroom window. 'Wonder if it was anyone we knew?'

Jed shrugged. 'The Oswalds are missing.'

'They're at the seaside.'

'So we think.' Jed put his hands on Skunk's shoulders. 'Wouldn't it be brilliant if Broken Buckley's murdered the Oswalds?' He paused a moment, then relented. 'Maybe not Susan Oswald. But all the others. Wouldn't that be cool?'

Skunk had to admit the idea had its attractions. Sunrise Oswald was in her form class at Drummond Primary. Skunk, like the rest of the class, had been paying her two pounds fifty protection money each week. In return for this protection money, Sunrise made half-hearted attempts to keep her sisters at bay: two of them – Saskia and Saraya – were too old for school now, but that didn't stop them hanging around the school gates and robbing pupils as they made their way home. Even worse than Saskia and Saraya, Susan Oswald often broke into the playground from the secondary-school playground next door. Protection money or not, if Susan Oswald decided to rob you, fighting back was stupid, and complaining was suicidal.

They discovered this at the start of the spring term in 2002, when Fiona Torby complained.

Fiona Torby, who had just started at Drummond Primary because her mum and dad were spending the money they had set aside for her private school fees on a divorce, complained when Susan Oswald nicked the iPod Fiona's dad had bought her to say sorry for leaving her mother. Distraught by the theft of her iPod, Fiona Torby told Mrs Willet, who, as one of the more sensible teachers, ignored her. Unimpressed with Mrs Willet and refusing to be a victim, Fiona Torby told her mother, who was already in a foul mood because her bastard husband had left her.

Mrs Torby complained to the headmaster, Mr Christy, a thin, balding dust jacket of a man who reminded Mrs Torby of her bastard soon-to-be-ex-husband. She slammed the door on her way into his office, then slammed a fist down hard on his desk. 'What sort of school are you running here?' she demanded. 'You've had my happy, balanced daughter for less than a week and she's an emotional wreck already. You'd better sort this situation out, you balding little man, or I'll have your bollocks for earrings, and that's nothing compared to what the PTA will do to you once I've finished. I'll have you out of this job before you can say unfair dismissal. And you won't get another. Not after the mess you've made of this one.'

Mrs Torby made several other threats, then slammed the door on her way out. It was the happiest she'd felt in weeks. Mr Christy, on the other hand, took umbrage at being threatened in his own office, and took it out on Mrs Willet.

'What sort of class are you running there? You've had that happy, balanced little girl for less than a week and she's an emotional wreck already. You'd better sort this situation out or I'll ... I'll ... I'll ...'

He never actually thought of anything to do, but Mrs Willet got the picture. The Oswalds were picking on one of her pupils. She had to be seen to do something. Being an adult of more than average intelligence, she ran down the list of Oswalds she could complain to and went for the weakest one. In front of a form class of terrified Year 2 students, she called Sunrise Oswald to her desk and asked her to turn her bag out. Sunrise did so.

There was an iPod in her bag. It was Fiona Torby's. Sunrise had no idea what an iPod was or what it did, but on a scouting expedition under Susan Oswald's bed, Sunrise had seen this bright and shiny thing and decided that finders were keepers.

Mrs Willet picked the iPod up. Engraved across the back were the words, *Dear Fiona, just because I don't love your mother any more doesn't mean I don't love you. The music's never ending. Dad.*

'Fiona. Is this your iPod?'

Fiona Torby looked at Sunrise Oswald and remembered the way Susan Oswald had threatened to kill her if she didn't hand over her fucking iPod. Suddenly grasping the consequences of getting an Oswald into trouble – all of the Oswalds would kill her – she decided losing her iPod to the Oswalds wasn't as bad as being murdered by them.

'No, Miss. I don't think so.'

'Yes it is. It's got your name engraved on the back. Come up here and get it.'

Fiona Torby went up and got her iPod. Mrs Willet turned to Sunrise Oswald.

'Do you think stealing's clever?'

'No.'

'Do you think stealing's big?'

'No.'

'Do you think it's big or clever to be a thief? Mrs Torby's ex-husband worked hard to afford this iPod for Fiona. Do you think it's fair that you just came along and took it?'

'Nuh-nuh-no.'

'I beg your pardon?'

'No, Miss. It ain't fair.'

'No, it isn't fair, Sunrise. It's cowardly and it's wrong and let me tell you that older children who steal get taken away from their families and locked up in horrible prisons and terrible things get done to them. Is that what you want to happen?'

'Nuh-nuh-no.'

'I beg your pardon?'

'No, Miss. It ain't.'

Sunrise started to cry. Mrs Willet pounced.

'Well, then, everybody. Look at the big brave thief now. Not so clever now, is she? Not so big now, is she? Sunrise, I want you to write some lines for me. A hundred lines. I want you to write, *I will not be a thief.* Now sit back down and stop crying.'

Sunrise Oswald sat down but she didn't stop crying. She went home in tears. Bob Oswald said, Jesus, baby, what's the matter with you? Sunrise Oswald told him. Bob Oswald said, She called you a thief? Sunrise Oswald nodded. Bob Oswald bent down before her. Honey, he said, I'm going to teach you two words now, and if anyone ever calls you a thief again, I want you to stand up straight and look them in the eye and use them. These two words are, Prove it. You get me? Prove it. You think I'm a thief? Prove it. What did I tell you to say?

Prove it.

That's my girl. Prove it. Now, give me a hug, then get me a pen and some paper. I'll write your lines out for you. Don't you worry about a thing.

*   *   *

The next day, Sunrise Oswald handed her lines in. Mrs Willet paled.

'Sunrise. Come to the front of the class. Right now.'

Sunrise got up and approached the front of the class.

'What's the meaning of this?' Mrs Willet held the lines up. The handwriting was huge and spidery, but all the words were joined up, so it was obvious Sunrise hadn't written them. Sunrise stared at Mrs Willet.

'My lines, Miss.'

'You didn't write these lines.'

Sunrise folded her arms and gazed at Mrs Willet and followed her father's instructions. 'You calling me a liar?'

Mrs Willet hesitated, then opted to sit on the fence. 'I'm saying you didn't write these lines.'

'Prove it.'

Mrs Willet stared. To her right, the classroom door swung open and Bob Oswald entered the room. 'Which of you fuckers has got my little girl's iPod?'

Bob Oswald was a big man in the real world. In a room full of little desks and little people, he seemed to be a giant. His shaven head gleamed. His tattoos rippled. His smell of cigarettes and sweat pervaded. Fiona Torby stood up like she was on springs.

'I told Miss it wasn't mine.'

'OK, sweetie. Bring it here.'

Fiona Torby did so. Bob Oswald took her iPod from her and handed it to Sunrise.

'There you go,' he said. 'And you,' to Mrs Willet. 'You think it's big and clever to bully little children?'

Mrs Willet said, 'No. Of course not. But I didn't bully your daughter, Mr Oswald. I simply asked her to empty her bag out.'

'Yeah. Right. Sure.' Bob Oswald walked towards Mrs Willet's desk. 'So how many other kids did you get to empty their bags out?'

'Well, none, Mr Oswald. But I knew –'

Bob Oswald yelled before she could finish, 'I said, how many other fucking kids did you get to empty their bags out?'

Mrs Willet shrivelled back in her chair. She said, 'None.'

Bob Oswald leaned over towards her. 'So. You think it's big and clever to bully little children?'

Very quietly, Mrs Willet said, 'No.'

'What did you say?'

'Nuh-nuh-no.'

'What?' Bob Oswald leaned closer. Mrs Willet leaned back. 'What did you say to me?'

'No, Mr Oswald. Sorry.'

'Sorry?'

'Sorry.'

'Well,' Bob Oswald said, and a wisp of Mrs Willet's hair shifted under his breath, 'you better be sorry. This is my little baby I'm trusting you with. You ever send her home to me in tears again, you won't just be sorry. You'll be very fucking sorry. You get me?'

'Yes, Mr Oswald.'

Bob Oswald straightened. He ruffled his daughter's hair. 'And you,' he said in a harsh parade-ground bark, 'stand up for yourself in future. Don't be so bloody soft.'

'No, Dad. Don't worry. I won't be.'

'Good girl.' Bob Oswald looked over his shoulder and scowled at the petrified Year 2 pupils behind him, then turned and walked out of their world. Sadly, for Skunk, the council moved him and his family into their current Housing Association property soon after Mrs Oswald died giving birth to Sunset, and the Oswalds became the curse of her home life as well as the curse of her school life. It would not be a bad thing if Broken Buckley had murdered them all.

Now she turned to Jed and she said, 'How do you think he'd have done it?'

Jed considered the question. 'With a knife, or maybe an axe. Most likely with an axe, though, and I bet he slaughtered Mr Oswald first, then Saraya, then Saskia, then I reckon he'd have done away with Susan, before, finally – chop, chop – Sunrise and Sunset.'

'But why do you think he did it?'

'Serial killers don't have motives, Skunk. That's what makes them so difficult to catch. In fact, I bet Broken Buckley wasn't content with just slaughtering the Oswalds. I bet he's been watching you too.'

'Jed,' Skunk said, 'shut up.'

'No, Skunk. Think about it. If that's Broken Buckley's bedroom at the front there, he can see right into your room from his room. I bet that's what he's been doing since he slaughtered the Oswalds – watching and thinking and waiting. I mean, what else would he have been doing? He's been locked away in that house for almost forever. That's classic serial killer behaviour, that is – they hide away, but they're not hiding, they're watching, and while they're watching, they're working out who to kill next and what to do with the bodies.' Jed dropped his voice to a whisper. 'Some cut them up and store them in bin bags. Others eat them – Jeffrey Dahmer did that – and some hide them away under floorboards. There was even this one in America who turned his victims into furniture. He shot his last victim in the head and made a lampshade out of her skin. I bet you'd make a cool lampshade. I bet that's what Broken Buckley's been thinking. You're lucky he got caught when he did. Let's hope he never escapes.'

'Jed,' Skunk yelled. 'Shut up.' And then, even louder, 'Cerys, Jed's trying to scare me.'

'Ain't trying,' Jed yelled proudly. 'Doing.'

Skunk punched him on the shoulder. 'Ain't scared of no mad axeman,' she lied, and fled, sobbing, down the stairs.

In the hallway, Cerys was crying even harder than Skunk was. She wasn't just crying, though. She was chasing Mike Jeffries down the hallway and hurling insults at his back: Wanker. Tosser. Scum. Skunk wasn't all that worried by this behaviour. Mike and Cerys were always arguing. It was because of the things they wanted. Cerys wanted to buy a house and get married and have children. Mike didn't. Now, sick of not being proposed to, Cerys hurled her cigarette lighter as hard as she could at the back of Mike's head. It hit his shoulder and bounced back to where she was standing. Before she could grab it and throw it again, Mike yanked the door open and fled. Cerys yelled after him, 'Go on then, fuck off. And don't even think about coming back here because I won't be here waiting. I'll find someone who loves me. I'll find someone who cares.' Silence for an answer. Cerys curled her fists up. 'I know you're out there, listening. I know you're not really leaving.' The sound of Mike's car driving into the distance seemed to drain her. She spoke without looking around. 'Go upstairs, Skunk. Go play Xbox.'

'Have you and Mike split up?'

'Skunk, what did I just tell you?'

'You told me to go upstairs and play Xbox.'

'Go on then. Bloody go upstairs. Jesus. Fucking hell.' Cerys fumbled a cigarette into her mouth and grabbed her lighter off the floor. It fell apart in her hands. She stared at it a moment, then went through to the kitchen and slammed the door behind her. Skunk stood all alone in the hallway. She knew Cerys was crying because she could hear the hoarse sound of her tears. She sat down on the stairs and carried on crying herself. She didn't want to be killed by Broken Buckley. She didn't want to be turned into a lampshade. Even more than these things, though, she didn't want Mike and Cerys to split up. She loved Mike. He was the best boyfriend Cerys had ever had. None of the others had ever remembered her birthday or bought her presents at Christmas. Now she would probably never see him again. He would go the same way as all the other men Cerys had ever been out with. It wasn't fair. Mike was dead good-looking and dead cool and almost half good at Xbox. Secretly, Skunk had dreamed of marrying him herself when she was older. Now this would never happen. She felt deserted. Betrayed. She sat on the stairs and tried not to think about Mike or Broken Buckley. She sat on the stairs and tried to think about Dillon instead: she remembered his smile and his freckles and decided he might be the best alternative for her affections now Mike had departed the scene. She wondered when she would see him again.

It turned out to be the next day, but that would be the last time she saw him for ages.

He was running out of the One Stop with a sausage, egg and bacon sandwich in one hand and a bottle of Sprite in the other. The lady behind the counter was giving chase. Although Dillon was faster than she was, an old man with a rolled-up newspaper grabbed him by the hood of his pale pink hoodie. Dillon cried as they dragged him back into the store. Behind him, very slowly, the automatic doors slid shut. Jed and Skunk stared at the sign that was stuck there. ALL THIEVES WILL BE PROSECUTED.

Jed sighed and said, That'll teach him. Then he took Skunk home to play Xbox. Outside, it started to rain. Summer was nearly over. It seemed incomprehensible to Skunk. She didn't know where it had got to. Not knowing what else to do with the last few days of the holiday, she moped around the house while Jed tried to do six weeks' worth of homework in just under five and a half days. Skunk wished she had homework to do. Instead, all she had was the vague worry of starting her first term at Drummond Secondary School. According to Jed, older children flushed your head down the toilet on your first day while teachers stood back and did nothing. Skunk didn't want to have her head flushed down the toilet almost as much as she didn't want to be murdered by Broken Buckley. She sat at her bedroom window and stared out on the street. Today, it was very quiet. It was never usually so quiet but every summer the Oswalds went to live by the seaside and have a good time. Skunk wished her family could go and live by the seaside every summer and have a good time. She phoned Archie on his mobile and asked him why they couldn't. He said it was because he had to work to keep a roof over their heads. Skunk said, Doesn't Mr Oswald have to work to keep a roof over their heads? Archie said, morosely, That lazy bastard's on benefits, Skunk, so doesn't have to struggle like we do. Now bog off. I'm trying to work.

Skunk hung up and returned to staring out the window. Across the way, life seemed to be back to normal. Mrs Buckley was on her hands and knees in the front garden and Mr Buckley's car wasn't on the driveway, so he was most likely at work. Skunk didn't know where Broken was. Jed had several theories: A, he was in an asylum; B, he had been locked up for murdering babies; C, he had been locked up for murdering babies, escaped, and was now living rough in the fields behind Botleigh Lakeside. Skunk wanted to go over and ask Mrs Buckley where Broken had got to, but was put off by Jed's theory D: Broken had been locked up for murdering babies, escaped, and was now being sheltered by Mr and Mrs Buckley who – in a desperate attempt to keep him from butchering them in their sleep – were keeping him supplied with eleven-year-old girls to be slaughtered and turned into lampshades.

In truth, Broken Buckley was sharing a small room in a secure unit with three other men who were broken the same way Broken was broken. Each day a male nurse would inject him in the left buttock and he would lie down and drift off to sleep. Or stare. Or sob. In the evenings, Mr and Mrs Buckley would phone the centre and ask to speak to Rick. As the phone was in the residents' common room, quite often, nobody answered. On the few occasions when somebody did answer, he or she failed to grasp they were using a phone. They picked it up, they stared at it, then let it drop and shuffled away. The mouthpiece hung limp on its cord. Hello? Hello? Hello? Eventually, Mrs Buckley would crack and hang up. She would turn her back on her husband. She would sob in the palms of her hands. Mr Buckley would stand helpless beside her. At night, they would lie in bed without speaking and worry themselves sick about Rick. How was he doing? How was he coping? Was he being well fed? Mrs Buckley imagined him sobbing. Mr Buckley imagined him slowly getting better as psychiatrists and social workers discovered the things that were wrong in his head. Please, he kept thinking, please let them discover the things that are wrong in his head. Mr Buckley had tried to do this himself after his trip to see Dr Carter, but it had proved to be beyond him. 'Son,' he would say on the landing outside Broken's bedroom door. 'Son? Can I come in? Can we talk?' No answer. Mr Buckley would rattle the handle. The chair on the other side would hold firm. 'You can't stay locked away in there forever,' Mr Buckley would say. 'You'll have to come out in the end.'

No answer. Never any answer.

Never any response at all.

One time, Mr Buckley retreated down the stairs and waited. At 3 a.m. the following morning, his patience was finally rewarded when Broken shuffled out of his bedroom and made his way down to the kitchen. Mr Buckley stood in darkness and watched his son make his way to the fridge and stand with his hands pressed flat against its white surface. Broken stayed that way for a long time, then quietly pulled the door open and began to pick from the plate of food Mrs Buckley had left there in the hope he would come down and eat it. In the yellow glow of the fridge light, Mr Buckley felt sick at how pale his son was and the scratch marks on his face and his arms. Oblivious to the fact he was being studied, Broken continued to eat. A cold sausage, a boiled egg. He drank milk. After a few minutes, the cool refrigerated air began to remind him of fresh air, and this, in turn, reminded him of the day Bob Oswald attacked him. No longer hungry, Broken dropped the ham sandwich he'd been eating and pushed the fridge door shut. He put his hands to his face. Inside, whispered, breathless, he said, over and over, I feel dirty, I feel dirty, I feel dirty, but he didn't make any sound. In contrast, Mr Buckley said, 'Son?'

Broken froze at the suddenness of the voice. A sick giddiness swept through him. He said nothing, did nothing, was still.

'Son,' Mr Buckley said. 'It's OK. I just want to talk to you. That's all I want to do.'

Broken stayed huddled in darkness. Behind him, out of more darkness, Mr Buckley said, 'I just want to know how you are. That's all. I just want to know how you're doing.' His voice was shaking. He didn't know why. It was only his son he was talking to. Mr Buckley stepped forward. 'Son, please. Just tell me. What's going on in your head? Why are you hiding away in your bedroom? Is there anything I can do to help? Is there anything anyone can do to help? Anything at all?' He took another step forward. Broken didn't hit him. He just screamed and flung his arms out. Mr Buckley jumped back and banged his hip against the work surface. A cup rolled off the edge and smashed to bits on the floor. Above their heads, there was the sound of sudden movement, then Mrs Buckley came running down the stairs and into the kitchen.

'What's going on?' She switched the light on. 'Rick?' she said. 'Rick? Are you OK? Is everything OK?' She held her arms out and stepped towards her son. He screamed in her face and pushed her away. Mrs Buckley stumbled backwards. Broken ran past her. His footsteps pounded the stairs. His bedroom door slammed. Silence fell. Mr and Mrs Buckley stood helpless within it, he with shards of china glittering all around him, she staring at the half-eaten sandwich Broken had dropped on the floor.

Finally, she said, 'He was eating, David. He was eating. You know how little he eats these days. Why couldn't you leave him alone?'

'We've left him alone for too long, Veronica. Look at the state he's got into.'

'He is not in a state. He's going to be fine.'

'He is not going to be fine. How can you say that?'

'Because, David, he is.' Mrs Buckley picked the ham sandwich off the floor and fed it into the waste disposal unit, then went back up to bed. Mr Buckley used a dustpan and brush to throw the shattered cup away then went upstairs to join her. The two of them lay together, alone, and stared into darkness from different directions. Neither wished the other goodnight.

The next day, Mr Buckley stayed up again, but Broken remained in his bedroom. And the next day. And the day after that. Scared that his son was starving to death, Mr Buckley tried to get into his bedroom once more, but a chair remained wedged between the floor and the handle. As Mr Buckley pushed and pushed against it, Broken lay on his side with the knife he had taken from the kitchen soon after Bob Oswald attacked him. He held it in a tight, sweaty palm with the blade rising up at an angle. Sometimes, he pointed this blade towards the window. Sometimes, he pointed it towards the door. Other times, during the worst times, he turned round and round in a circle, because he was frightened of being attacked from behind, without warning, but couldn't see all ways at once. Broken was always afraid now. He couldn't make sense of it all. He had only been washing his car. Why had Bob Oswald attacked him? Broken didn't know, Broken couldn't imagine, so he clutched his knife and lived in fear of Bob Oswald while, outside, Mr Buckley tried to get into his room.

'Son? Son? Open this door. I'm not going to hurt you. I just want to know how you are. Please, son, please. I'm worried sick about you. Your mother's worried sick about you.' Mr Buckley stood back. He shook his head. Mrs Buckley was standing behind him. She said, 'You'll have to go back to the doctor.'

'What's the point in going back to the doctor? Carter's useless. A bloody fool.'

'Yes. I know. But you'll have to go back to him, David.' She nodded towards the shut bedroom door and dropped her voice to a whisper. 'I don't think he's eaten in days.'

'I know that, Veronica, I know that, but I don't think starving yourself to death constitutes aggressive behaviour, do you?'

The two of them stared at each other, then Mrs Buckley began to cry. Mr Buckley said sorry and put his arms around her. She stiffened and pushed him away. 'He's our son,' she said. 'He's our son.' Mr Buckley nodded and went out to the garage. He carried his toolbox back into the house. He took an electric screwdriver out and used it to remove the screws from his son's bedroom door handle, then pulled the casing away and twisted the bolt around and around while he pushed at the door with his shoulder. It didn't make any difference. The chair on the other side held firm. Still, Mr Buckley kept trying. He didn't know what else to do. Behind him, Mrs Buckley kept crying. She didn't know what else to do. Inside, Broken Buckley curled tight on his bed with his knife clutched in his hands. He whimpered each time Bob Oswald tried to get into his bedroom. Go away, go away, go away. But Bob Oswald wouldn't go away. The door shook as he kept pushing against it. The chair holding it slipped slightly. Broken sat up in his bed. His narrow shoulders hunched over. Go away, go away, go away. The door shook again. The chair slipped a little further. Broken made himself get to his feet. He held the knife out before him. His whole arm was shaking. Ahead, his bedroom door was shaking. The chair was juddering, inch by inch, across the carpet. Very soon, it was going to fall. Broken made himself walk towards it. He put a palm to the door. It shook beneath his touch. The chair slid, and then hit his legs.

A gap appeared between the door and the door frame. Broken plunged his knife between it. When he pulled it back, it was bloody. He screamed and dropped the knife to the floor. He put his hands to his face. He stared at the door and waited for it to crash open. As he did so, Mr Buckley cried out. Blood dripped through his fingers, which were clutched to his left arm, where the knife had slid in and then out. Seeing what her son had done to her husband, Mrs Buckley screamed and stepped backwards and almost fell down the stairs. Mr Buckley grabbed her. 'Call Carter, Veronica. For God's sake, he has to come out this time. Telephone Carter.'

So Mrs Buckley telephoned Carter.

Carter telephoned social services.

Social services telephoned the police.

And the police took Broken away.

Mr and Mrs Buckley never heard from Carter again. For a short while, they heard nothing at all. Then, eight days after their son had been sectioned, the police came out to take statements, but as Mr Buckley didn't want to press charges, and as social services had sectioned Broken indefinitely under the Mental Health Act, they dropped the case like a hot brick. Social services, on the other hand, passed Mr and Mrs Buckley around from one department to another. Once in a while they managed to get hold of a social worker who would say things like, Rick? Rick who? Rick Mutley? Not Mutley? Can you spell it? B-U-C-K-L-E-Y – Buckley? Rick Buckley? Give me a minute, will you? Hold on. Oh. Yeah. Rick. Rick Buckley. He's doing great, responding to medication, he'll be home in a matter of weeks.

Neither Mr nor Mrs Buckley could imagine their son coming home. It was as if he no longer belonged to them. In a way, he didn't. Broken Buckley was a patient of the state now. He became one the second he climbed in the back of that police car with his hands cuffed behind his thin back. Bewildered and exhausted, he stared out on streets he had known as a child. Everything seemed to be huge. Everything seemed to be threatening. Broken made himself small by pressing himself into the fabric of the car seat and pulling his legs into his stomach. In his head, the sound of birdsong roared, as did the blood in his ears. He shut his eyes and buried his face in his knees. Oblivious to his terror, the policemen drove him away from all he knew and talked between themselves about football and telly. Broken didn't listen. He hummed to blank out their voices. He didn't see where they were taking him, either. He kept his eyes shut and his face pressed into his knees. When they finally arrived at the secure unit social services had referred him to, they led him across a shingle car park and in through double doors. Inside, people were waiting. Somehow, they all knew his name:

'Just come through here, Rick.'

'Hi, Rick. How you doing?'

'Rick. We're taking these cuffs off.'

'That's it, Rick. Nice and calm.'

'Rick. Take it easy. Lie down.'

Women's voices. Men's voices. Hands on his shoulders. Voices behind him. 'His name's Rick. He attacked his father this morning. No. He seems very calm.' Footsteps. Another voice. 'Go and get Dr Gerrald. OK. Let's get him booked in.'

Doors opening. Doors closing. More hands on his shoulders. More voices, soft, in his ear.

'Roll over, Rick. On your back.'

'That's it, Rick On your back.'

'Rick. Do you know where you are? Do you know why you're here, Rick?' This question, repeated. Broken ignored it. The admissions nurse said, 'Rick, we need you to get undressed now. We need you to get into this gown.' Broken looked up. People were staring down on him. One of them was Saskia Oswald. She was standing between two orderlies who were dressed in lawn-green hospital uniforms. She had her hands on their shoulders. She had a glint in her eye. Broken reached down and covered himself up. The admissions nurse persisted: 'Calm down, Rick. We're not going to hurt you. We just need you to put this gown on. You can't wear your clothes on the ward.' She smiled. Broken shook his head. He kept his hands cupped over his privates. 'Rick. I'm telling you. Be good now. Come on, Rick. Don't be a pain.' Hands reached out towards him. Broken slapped them away. The orderlies stood back with their palms raised. Broken breathed in through his nostrils. He had no spit in his mouth.

More footsteps. Clipboards. A man wearing glasses. A woman with grey in her hair. More questions from the admissions nurse: Hello, Rick, do you know why you're here? You attacked your father this morning. Do you remember? Rick? Do you remember? No answer. Just silence. Gritted teeth. Wide flaring nostrils. Tears in the whites of his eyes. The woman with grey in her hair said five milligrams. The man with the glasses leaned forward. 'Hello, Rick. I'm Dr Gerrald. We're very worried about you. You're tired. You're hungry. You're confused. We're going to give you an injection. It's going to send you to sleep.'

It took four of them: two orderlies took hold of his arms; two took hold of his ankles. Broken bucked. He writhed. He bared his teeth. After they got the needle in him, their faces became blurred and unfocused; Broken became blurred and unfocused. The fight went out of his body. His head lolled back and then sideways. Darkness overtook him. It was like running into a wall. It was like being sucked down a plughole. Broken swirled. Faces from his past flecked the darkness. He threw his hands out for something to cling to, but there were no sides anywhere near him. He went down and down and down.

When he came out the other side, Saskia Oswald was sitting on his chest. She was chewing gum and laughing. *Fancy taking me for a ride?* Broken blinked. She disappeared. He tried to sit up so he could see where she had got to, but he had been strapped to his bed. 'Where am I?' he shouted. 'Where am I?' He fought against the binds across his body. He tried to lift his head and look around. 'Where am I?' he shouted. 'Where am I?' He thrashed his feet up and down. The bindings around him held tight. 'Help me,' he shouted. 'Help me. Where am I?' The door to his room was pushed open. A nurse stepped in and approached him. Broken said, 'I want to go back to before.' The nurse injected him in the left bicep. The force of it was like a punch from Bob Oswald. Broken swirled down once again.

Over the next ten weeks, this became a pattern: Broken

would wake up. He would get frightened. He would shout. They would put him to sleep. If anyone ever spoke to him before these injections, he could never remember. If anyone ever spoke to him after these injections, he could never recall. A needle would go in, the world would turn black, he would sleep. Later, sometime later, he would wake up face down on his bed or slumped in an armchair in the common room. One time, it was the sound of the telephone that woke him. Broken turned his head towards it. He stared and stared and stared. Finally, another patient picked it up and let it drop and shuffled away. Hello? Hello? Hello? Eventually, Mrs Buckley put the phone down and turned her back on her husband. He stood beside her and felt utterly helpless as she sobbed in the palms of her hands. Later, they lay side by side without speaking and worried themselves sick about Rick. Mrs Buckley imagined him staring off into the distance and missing his mum. Mr Buckley imagined consultants talking to him about his mood swings and working out ways they could help. As the summer turned into the autumn, they tried to pretend things were normal. Sleepless nights. Silent meals. The TV masking the sound of their breathing. On the few occasions anyone bothered to ask about Rick, they always said he was fine, oh yes, thank you, he's just fine.

Everything's just fine.

Across the road, in the weeks between Broken being committed and Broken being released, the Cunninghams were oblivious. Jed crammed homework. Skunk stared out the window and worried about her new school term. Cerys mourned the death of her relationship with Mike by pouring her heart out to Archie during long nights spent on the sofa: He was the love of my life. I miss him so badly. I want him back. I just want him back. Archie, in turn, admitted he had been relieved when his wife finally left him: We married too young. We had kids too quick. She never bonded with them and she never really loved me. They shared wine and cigarettes and, one Sunday evening at the start of September, they shared each other in Cerys's bedroom. After, they lay side by side in awkward silence and stared off in different directions, then Archie made his excuses and headed back to his own room. As he crept across the landing in his boxers and his T-shirt, Skunk came out of the bathroom. He kissed the end of her nose and wondered if his breath smelled of wine or cigarettes or Cerys. He said, Go back to bed, Skunk. I love you, little darling. Skunk climbed in beside her Snoopy Dog and pulled her Jedi Knight duvet up under her chin and said what she always said before sleep-time, softly, under her breath: Goodnight, Daddy; Goodnight, Jed; Goodnight, Cerys; and finally, silently, without even breathing in case Archie should hear her, Goodnight, Mother. Sleep tight. Sweet dreams. I miss you.

The next day was the first day of the new school term. Skunk brushed her teeth and showered and dressed in her brand-new uniform, then went downstairs to open negotiations for an increase in her pocket money. She sat opposite Archie at the breakfast table and pulled his cigarettes towards her: 'Smoking Causes Cancer.'

'Yes,' Archie said. 'I know that.' He pulled the cigarettes

away. Skunk made a grab for his lighter. He pulled that away as well. 'Skunk,' he said. 'What do you want?'

'More pocket money please.' She looked at him and nodded. 'I'll need much more than fifteen pounds a week at secondary school. Jed says there's a tuck shop.'

'OK,' Archie said. 'Fifteen pounds fifty.'

'Daddy. Fifty pence is nothing. I can't do much with that.'

'Yes you can,' Archie said. 'You can save it. Fifty pence a week is two pounds a month. Two pounds a month is twenty-four pounds a year. Twenty-four pounds a year is a lot of money. That's a bigger rise than I got this year.'

Skunk frowned. 'What's a rise?'

'It's what your daddy's taking out of you.' Cerys buttered toast and put it on the table, then put her hands on her hips and looked at Archie. 'Why don't you just give her what she wants? That's what you normally do.'

'God,' Archie said, 'you sound like . . .' he was about to say 'her mother', but stopped himself in time. Instead, he said, 'She needs to learn the value of money.'

'Make her work for it then. That's what my mum and dad did with me. I had a list of chores to do. If I did them, I got money. If I didn't, I got bugger all.'

'But I already pay you to do the chores,' Archie said.

'I'm not saying she has to do household chores,' Cerys lied. 'Get her a paper round. That'll teach her the value of money.'

'She's too young to do a paper round. You have to be twelve or thirteen. She's only just turned eleven.'

'You sure about that?' Cerys asked. 'Sunrise Oswald's the same age as Skunk, and she's got a paper round. I've seen her dumping what she can't be bothered to deliver down Shamblehurst Lane.' Cerys was only part right here: although Sunrise Oswald did a paper round, it wasn't actually her paper round. It was Susan Oswald's paper round. Susan subcontracted it to Sunrise because she hated getting up in the mornings.

Sunrise had agreed to take on responsibility for Susan's paper round because she needed Bob Oswald to know she had a regular source of income.

Sunrise needed Bob Oswald to know she had a regular source of income to explain the fact she always had money.

Sunrise always had money because everyone in her form class paid her two pounds fifty a week to stop her sisters from killing them. From today though, now they were in secondary school, rumour had it Sunrise would be putting this charge up to a fiver.

Which was the reason Skunk needed more pocket money.

She said, 'I'm only asking for twenty pounds a week, Daddy. Fiona Torby gets thirty.'

Archie sighed. 'Seventeen pounds. Final offer.'

Skunk took a moment to consider. 'Not fair,' she said. 'Jed gets twenty.'

'Of course Jed gets twenty. He's older. And he has to put up with you.'

'But,' Skunk said bitterly, 'seventeen pounds is nothing.'

'It's much more than I get,' Cerys lied. 'And I have to put up with all three of you.'

'Seventeen pounds,' Archie repeated, trying to ignore Cerys.

'Twenty,' Skunk said.

'Seventeen.'

'Daddy, you're a tightwad.'

'Call me what you like. Seventeen pounds is my final offer. Going . . . going . . .'

Skunk reluctantly accepted Archie's final offer, then set off for school with Jed. Her first day at Drummond Secondary School was quieter than she had expected. This was partly due to the fact the Oswalds were still at the seaside. It was also partly due to the fact no one seemed remotely interested in flushing her head down any of the toilets. These weren't the only brilliant things about her first day at Drummond Secondary: her form teacher turned out to be Cerys's ex-boyfriend, Mike. Skunk walked into Class 7D and there he was, perched on the edge of his desk. Hi, Mike, she said, how's it going? To which he said, It's Mr Jeffries in school, Skunk, not Mike, to which she said, It's Miss Cunningham to you, Mr Jeffries, not Skunk, and he looked at her the same way Jed did whenever she'd said something really stupid.

Skunk liked her new school, but not the playtimes. At home, when Cerys was trying to have a calm-down smoke and Skunk was making too much noise, Cerys would yell, For fuck's sake, Skunk, go play something, will you, and Skunk would go play Xbox, which was fun. Playtime at Drummond Secondary, however, was not fun. It was a case of dodging marauding gangs of older children who were on the lookout for brand-new mobile phones. Skunk had seen enough of this behaviour through the railings of Drummond Primary's playground next door to know how dangerous playtimes at her new school were going to be, and spent both the morning and afternoon breaks with her back to a wall and her mobile phone hidden deep in her satchel. A couple of Year 7 students who had been to Berrywood Primary – which, unlike Drummond, didn't have a secondary school anywhere near it – lost their mobiles within minutes of playtime starting. Another ex-Berrywood Year 7 student had brought a skipping rope with her. She lost that as well. Skunk went over and told her she was lucky Susan Oswald was still at the seaside: she would have throttled her with it, not nicked it.

After school, Skunk walked home with Jed. When the two of them got there, Cerys was supposed to make sure they did their homework, but an arrangement existed here where all three of them could tell Archie they had done this, and it wouldn't be classed as a lie. Jed sat watching telly and Skunk went up to play Xbox. Cerys sat in the kitchen and smoked. As Archie was hoping for a repeat of the previous night's performance with Cerys, he got home from work earlier than usual. The four of them sat down to eat dinner together. Jed questioned his dad about work:

'Did you get any mass murderers off today, Dad?'

'Nope.' Archie forked his lasagne. 'All I did today was meet with tosspot partners who don't know their elbows from their arses. Fucking place.'

'Fuck's a bad word,' Skunk told him.

'Only when you and Jed use it,' Archie said. 'It's like cars, Skunk. It's OK for me to drive a car because I'm old enough and suitably trained, but it's not OK for you to drive one because you're too young. Swearing's exactly the same. OK?'

Skunk nodded. Beside her, Jed was impatient.

'So what *did* you do today, Dad?'

'I told you. I met with tosspot partners who don't know their elbows from their arses.'

'Oh. OK.' Jed looked down at his dinner plate. Skunk pitied him sometimes: he wanted to be a solicitor when his professional football career was over, but it was obvious to Skunk he was too easily thrown from his subject. She took over his line of enquiry:

'And why did you meet with tosspot partners, Daddy?'

'Good question, Skunk. I'm still trying to work that one out for myself.' Archie looked over at Cerys. 'Can you believe it?' he said in a tone that he tried to keep casual. 'I'm a specialised criminal solicitor. David Jefferson's a specialised personal injury solicitor. Brent Phillips is a specialised probate solicitor. We're all in charge of departments that are working well and performing to target. So what does Simon Trewster want to do? Lay off two accounts clerks and get us doing our own invoicing. In six weeks' time, I'll be spending more time looking at spreadsheets than defending my clients.'

Cerys looked at Archie with an air of total boredom. He pretended not to notice.

'Sometimes I despair of that place. I really do despair.'

'Never mind,' Cerys told him, and carried plates out to the kitchen.

'Nice meal,' Archie called after her. 'Thank you.' He looked sideways and watched as she bent to load the dishwasher, then hid behind the *Daily Express*. Across the square, Mrs Buckley did much the same with the telly: *Coronation Street*, *EastEnders*,

The Bill, Inspector Morse, Inspector Wexford. Anything not to have to think. Mr Buckley sat beside her and stared at the sky through the window. When the evening was over they went up to their bedroom and lay in silence, not sleeping. The next day, Mr Buckley got up and faced sobbing mourners and ghost-white bodies and made phone calls to crematoriums and arranged the digging of graves. He sent drivers to hospital morgues and care homes and people's houses. He smiled. He shook hands. He was pleasant. And all the time, he thought Rick, oh Rick, oh Rick. And, as he thought Rick, oh Rick, oh Rick, Mrs Buckley pruned flowers and dusted and hoovered the house through on soft moist September mornings and all the time she thought Rick, oh Rick, oh Rick. How are you doing? How are you feeling? How did it all come to this? In the evenings they watched telly and made their phone calls and it was always Mrs Buckley who cracked and hung up and stood sobbing in the kitchen with her hands up to cover her face.

A world away, in Brighton, the Oswalds were having a great time. Bob had his fortnightly social security payments and a job down the seafront selling helium-filled balloons to gawping Asians and sulking Australian barmen who were out to impress dumb wispy English girls. The kids had an endless supply of stones to throw at the sea or distant tourists who posed no immediate threat. The weather was glorious and the days were careless. The only shadow was thrown by their landlords, a prim middle-class couple who reminded them of the Buckleys. Their names were Mr and Mrs Hateley: in their early fifties, neither of the Hateleys could understand the world that Bob and his daughters had come from. The laziness. The dirtiness. The endless tirade of foul language. The Oswalds were alien to them, and they wished they would go back to where they had come from.

Twice, Mr Hateley asked Bob Oswald to leave, but Bob Oswald was a hard man to boss around. Twice, Mr Hateley relented, and the Oswalds were allowed to stay. These reprieves, however, were fleeting. At the beginning of October, Bob's social security payments were stopped as he'd used up his holiday allowance. A trembling girl in Brighton's Mill Lane post office explained his options to him. He could find a permanent address in Brighton, make the 120-mile round trip to Hedge End's post office once every other week in order to pick up his benefits or, preferably, go home.

Bob Oswald, being a lazy bastard, took his family home.

Just over three weeks later, on a dismal, damp Wednesday morning towards the end of October, Skunk was pushed to the floor and punched in the small of her back. Her pockets were searched and eight pounds twenty was taken. Her face was rubbed in the dirt and her mobile phone was snatched from her satchel, placed on the floor and stamped on. A letter from social services had forced Susan and Sunrise back into school. The quiet start to the school year was over.

Mr Jeffries said, 'Been dragged through a hedge backwards, Miss Cunningham?'

Skunk said, 'I dropped my mobile, Mr Jeffries.'

Sunrise Oswald sniggered.

Mr Jeffries sighed but did nothing. Skunk didn't mind, though. Now he was her form teacher, her crush on him was stronger than ever. Cerys, on the other hand, hated him. When Skunk said, Mr Jeffries says hi, Cerys looked up from Archie's ironing and said, You can tell that prick to go fuck himself. Mr Jeffries gave Skunk a thousand lines: *I must not swear in class. I must not swear in class.* Cerys laughed. She said, I always knew that prick was an arsehole. But she wouldn't do Skunk's lines for her the way Bob Oswald had once done Sunrise's: Skunk had to write them out all on her own. She was just over halfway through when she heard a sudden commotion outside. She looked out the window and saw Sunrise and Saskia Oswald chucking eggs at Mr and Mrs Buckley's front door. Sunrise was doing most of the throwing. Saskia was giving directions.

'Go for the bedroom window. Fucking ace shot. Now lob one at their front door. Get the cars. Get the cars.'

Sunrise was a good shot. Egg after egg cracked on the windscreens of Mr Buckley's beige Mondeo and Mrs Buckley's green VW Beetle. Broken's unused car was covered by an old green tarpaulin. Three eggs were smashed against that. Saskia howled with laughter. Sunrise laughed with delight. Mr Buckley came running out.

'What the hell do you think you're doing?' He half ran down the path, then turned and looked at the mess the two Oswalds had made of his house. 'You . . .' he shouted. 'You . . .' But he didn't seem able to think of a good enough word to call them. 'You wait till I speak to your father. He'll sort you out about this.'

Saskia laughed and gave him the finger. 'He'll kick your head in, like he did your mental son.'

'Don't you talk about my son. Don't you dare.'

'Oh fuck off, you old prick.'

'What? What did you say?'

'You heard,' Saskia told him, and then, to Sunrise, 'Come on. This is boring. Let's go home.'

The two Oswalds retreated across the street. Mr Buckley stared after them, then turned and stared at his house. He was still staring at his house when Skunk became aware there was someone standing behind her. She turned round. Archie was staring at her neatly written out lines.

'Skunk, what have I told you about swearing?'

'That it's like driving. Can I have a new mobile?'

'No. You didn't look after the last one.' He came and stood next to her at the window. Together, they watched in silence as Bob Oswald came out of his house, walked across the road, picked up one of the eggs Sunrise hadn't got round to throwing, and hurled it at Mr Buckley. Unlike Sunrise, Bob's aim was awful. The egg sailed over Mr Buckley's head and smashed against the Buckleys' lounge window. Mr Buckley ran inside.

Bob Oswald picked up the final egg and threw it at the Buckleys' front door. Then he, too, went inside. Archie shook his head sadly. 'That man,' he said. 'That man.'

Skunk said, 'Why can't I have a new mobile?'

'Because you can't go around breaking your old phone and just expect me to buy you a new one.'

Skunk hadn't told Archie the Oswalds had broken her mobile: she was scared he would complain to Mr Oswald. As much as her father sometimes annoyed her, she had no desire to send him to war with the Oswalds, so she started a war of her own: Please can I have a new mobile? Please can I have a new mobile? Please can I have a new mobile? She followed him around the house: Please can I have a new mobile? Please can I have a new mobile? Please can I have a new mobile? On the second day it actually backfired. Archie sat at the breakfast table reading the paper and saying very loudly from behind it, no you can't have a new mobile, no you can't have a new mobile, no you can't have a new mobile. It was maddening. But Skunk couldn't give in. She upped the ante. Five days after Archie first said no, she sat in the garage reading *Harry Potter* till nearly midnight in an attempt to frighten him into submission. Then she let herself in through the front door. At first, it seemed her efforts had been wasted: Archie wasn't even home. Cerys was, though: she smacked Skunk hard on the backside and said, Don't you dare do that again, you selfish little bitch. You think about your father. All he ever does is put you kids first. She shook Skunk hard by the shoulders, then gave her another smack. Skunk was sent to bed, sobbing. Cerys then texted Archie to tell him his daughter had turned up safe. Ten minutes later, Archie pulled up in the driveway. After phoning around Skunk's schoolmates to see if she was with any of them, he had been driving around Hedge End in an effort to find her. Now he went straight up to her bedroom. He didn't turn her light on, but Skunk heard him climbing the stairs and saw his silhouette in the doorway. He said, very gently, 'Skunk.'

She said, 'Go away. Leave me alone. I hate you. I want my mummy.'

'Don't say that, little darling.'

Skunk immediately regretted using her mother to upset her father. She lay very still, very quiet.

Archie remained in the doorway a long time, then gently pulled the door shut. The next day was a Saturday. He took Skunk into Southampton and bought her a brand-new mobile phone with a camera and Internet connection on the solemn understanding she wouldn't bankrupt the household by sending texts or making unnecessary phone calls to premium-rate chatlines. She hugged him very tightly and said, I don't really hate you, Daddy. He laughed and said he knew. Then he drove her home.

By the time they pulled into Drummond Square, Skunk had used her brand-spanking-new car-charger to charge her brand-spanking-new mobile enough to call Jed on his pathetic-stone-age mobile that only sent texts and made phone calls. She said, 'You'll never guess what I got.'

'Not a video phone?'

'No.' Skunk wanted to say 'It's better than a video phone', but it wasn't, so she couldn't. She felt suddenly deflated. Then she saw something that brightened her mood. 'Broken Buckley's back.'

He was sitting in the back of his father's car. He had his hands in his lap. He was resting his head against the back of the driver's seat. He was refusing to move.

'Please, Rick,' Mr Buckley was saying. 'Please. Just come inside.'

'Not until it's dark.'

'Dark? But it's only 11 a.m.'

'Not until it's dark.'

Mr Buckley scratched his head. He stepped away from the car. Mrs Buckley watched from the kitchen window. When Mr Buckley raised his arms in exasperation, she had to turn away. Mr Buckley went inside. Broken Buckley lifted his head from the back of the driver's seat, took a look around him, then put his head forward once again. Jed said in Skunk's ear, 'No he isn't.'

'Yes he is. He's sitting in the back of Mr Buckley's car.'

There was the muffled sound of movement. Skunk looked up at her bedroom window. Jed was staring down.

'See.'

'Yeah,' Jed admitted. 'He is.'

A hand rested on Skunk's shoulder. 'Inside,' Archie ordered.

She ended the call to save credit and hurried on into the house. Then she ran up to her bedroom. From here, she and Jed watched as Archie crossed the square and knocked on the Buckleys' front door. Mr Buckley answered. He had been on the phone trying to get through to social services. He desperately wanted to talk to someone about his son's behaviour during the car journey home. After Mr Buckley had picked him up, Broken had insisted on walking from the secure unit to Mr Buckley's car under the cover of Mr Buckley's coat. Once inside the car he had barked baffling instructions at his father such as, turn left here, stop at these lights, don't go round that corner. Mr Buckley had ignored him. Broken had then put on his seat belt and said, He's going to find me. Mr Buckley had said, Who's going to find you? to which Broken had said, I can't say in case you tell him. Mr Buckley had sighed. Then he had felt a sudden jarring sensation in the centre of his back. He had looked in the rear-view mirror and seen his son had taken off his seat belt and was pushing his head into the driver's seat. Neither of them had talked again until Mr Buckley pulled up on the drive and Broken refused to get out.

Now Mr Buckley stood in his hallway and tried every telephone number he'd been given by the social worker who'd contacted him last Wednesday and told him Rick was well enough to come home. Each number was engaged. As Mr Buckley dialled the first one over again, the doorbell rang. Hoping his son had changed his mind about staying in the car until it was dark, Mr Buckley rushed to open the door. Archie stood on the doorstep.

'You OK, Dave?'

Mr Buckley felt his cheeks redden. 'Oh yes, fine, fine.'

'You sure?'

Mr Buckley looked at Archie Cunningham. He thought, Archie, I know you mean well, but there's nothing you can do, so why don't you leave me alone?

'Yes,' he said. 'Everything's fine.'

Archie Cunningham looked at Mr Buckley. He thought, Jesus, I know I mean well, but there's nothing I can do, I wish I'd just left this alone.

He said, 'Well, OK. But if there's anything I can do, we're only across the square.'

'Thanks, Archie. You're a pal.'

Archie nodded and made his way back home. As he walked

past Mr Buckley's car he ducked his head a little. 'Hi, Rick. Good to see you home.'

Broken Buckley shivered and covered his face up. Archie kept on walking. Jed and Skunk stayed at Skunk's bedroom window for the next twenty minutes, but when nothing of interest happened they went to Jed's room and played Xbox. As Skunk's Obi-Wan Kenobi slaughtered Jed's Darth Vader, Jed whispered, as an aside, 'Sleep with your windows locked tonight, Skunk.'

She glanced at him then back at the light-sabre battle before her. 'What? Why?'

'Broken's back,' he told her. 'Who knows what'll happen.'

'Why should anything happen?'

'He's an axe-murderer-psycho-killer, remember.'

'No he isn't.'

'Yes he is.'

'No he isn't. The police never came out and put tents up. The Oswalds came back from the seaside. Broken Buckley never killed anyone.'

'Yes he did,' Jed insisted. 'But he's the worst kind of axe-murderer-psycho-killer there is, Skunk – the type who only kills people he doesn't know, like the Yorkshire Ripper, or Jeffrey Dahmer, or Dennis Nilsen. It took the police ages to catch them, yet Dr Crippen only murdered his wife and they caught him before he could cross the Atlantic.'

Skunk took another look at Jed. He kept staring at the screen. He talked quietly, with total belief.

'I reckon the police have been questioning Broken about tons of missing people, but they can't pin anything on him, so they've had to let him go, even though they know he's an axe-murderer-psycho-killer. The problem is, Skunk, now Broken knows they're on to him, he's going to start getting reckless. That's why you need to watch out. Your bedroom window's virtually opposite his room.'

Skunk was openly staring at Jed now. Her stomach felt greasy and empty.

'You think he's likely to kill me?'

'More than likely. In *The Silence of the Lambs*, the killer started with a woman who lived over the road. He weighed her body down with stones so she wouldn't be the one the police found first. It took Jodie Foster nearly two hours to figure that one out, and then only with the help of another axe-murderer-psycho-killer.' Jed had seen *The Silence of the Lambs* when Archie got drunk one night and forgot to send him to bed.

Now Skunk's throat was dry and her hands felt sweaty. She hadn't looked at the TV screen for nearly a minute. Jed let out a sudden shriek of delight.

'Gotcha, sucker.' He threw his control down. Skunk turned and looked at the telly. Her Obi-Wan was a smouldering heap of rags before Jed's Darth Vader, who was heavy-breathing over the corpse. Jed punched Skunk's shoulder in triumph. 'Loser! Loser!'

'Stupid game,' Skunk shouted, and threw her own control down. 'And you're stupid too. Broken Buckley isn't an axe-murderer-psycho-killer. You're full of shit and I'm not playing with you any more.'

She stormed out of Jed's room.

Inside her own room, she stared nervously out of the window. Broken was still in the back of his father's car. His face was pressed against the headrest of the driver's seat. Although Skunk couldn't see it, his hands were turning in his lap and his lips were moving as well. No sounds were coming out of his mouth but, in his head, Broken was clinging to an image: it consisted of a field sloping gently southwards. Broken had no idea where this image had come from, but for a few days after each injection he was able to go to this field and find some sort of relief. It was always peaceful in the field. Instead of the sound of Saskia Oswald's laughter and the sound of Bob Oswald's fists hitting flesh, there was only ever the sound of birdsong and wind in the trees. Broken felt safe in the field. Outside of the field, in broad daylight, Saskia Oswald might come on to him and laugh at the size of his penis. Bob Oswald might attack him. Inside of the field, neither of them could find him; neither of them could hurt him. Broken sat in the back of his father's car and felt at least he was safe.

Across the square, Skunk continued to stare down on him from her bedroom window. Her throat was dry. Her palms were sweaty. She felt total and utter terror: if Jed was to be believed, this man was going to kill her. He was going to sneak into her bedroom in the middle of the night and chop her to bits with an axe. Taking deep breaths, she tried to tell herself Jed was talking rubbish: Broken Buckley didn't look like an axe-murderer-psycho-killer. But, then, what did an axe-murderer-psycho-killer look like? At school, they talked about Stranger Danger, but what did a stranger look like? Bob Oswald looked strange with his swirling tattoos and shaven head, but he wasn't a stranger. Right now, sitting over the road in the back of Mr Buckley's Mondeo, Broken Buckley looked even stranger than Bob Oswald, but, still, he wasn't a stranger. He wasn't an axe-murderer-psycho-killer. Was he? Skunk didn't know. She couldn't be sure. To take her mind off things, she went back to play Xbox with Jed. This worked for half an hour, but then, with her Darth Vader close to destroying Jed's flying green Yoda, Jed started to chant, very softly, almost under his breath, Broken's gonna getcha, Broken's gonna getcha. Skunk fled back to her room. Broken was still in the back of his father's car. He hadn't moved at all. He didn't move all day. Skunk didn't watch him constantly. She flitted around the edges. An hour spent reading *Harry Potter*, half an hour for lunch, a whole twelve minutes reading the manual for her brand-new mobile phone. The afternoon dragged on and nothing much happened until three of the Oswald girls – Sunrise, Sunset and Saskia – stalked across the square in the direction of the One Stop. Skunk waited with bated breath for them to spot Broken Buckley and cause chaos, but the Oswald girls didn't see him. They went off to cause grief someplace else.

Finally, the sun set.

And Broken went into his mum and dad's house.

It would be the last time Skunk saw him for more than four months. Outside of Mr and Mrs Buckley, a social services community psychiatric nurse, Sunrise Oswald and Dillon, it would be the last time anyone saw Broken Buckley for more than four months. Now she put her hands to her mouth and watched him make his way from the car to the house. He was

a tall man with messy blond hair, a very slight frame, a sideways way of walking, sort of hunched, looking back over his
shoulder, waiting for Bob Oswald to pick up on his move-
ments and attack him. When he finally disappeared inside the
Buckley house he eased the front door shut so quietly behind
him that, even with the window open, Skunk didn't hear any
sound. She sat and stared out of her bedroom window and
had no idea he was climbing the stairs to his bedroom, shutting his bedroom door, falling down on his bed. She had no
idea he was curling up onto his side and tucking his knees
tight into his stomach. All she had was her imagination: Did
he have an axe in there? A gun? A bomb? She stared at the
closed curtains of the room she had always assumed to be
his: they stayed very still, very closed. She watched them for
any sign of movement until Cerys yelled up the stairs it was
teatime. Skunk hesitated a moment – starvation or surveillance, starvation or surveillance – then went downstairs for
some food.

Eating helped Skunk forget about her fear of Broken
Buckley. So did sitting in the front room with Archie and
Cerys and Jed while they watched *Finding Nemo* on DVD. It
was only after, when Archie refused to let her stay up any
longer, no matter how much she begged, that her terror
returned. Across the front room, behind Archie's back, Jed
made slashing, axe-like motions with his hands as Skunk was
bullied towards the stairs with threats of having her brand-
new mobile phone confiscated.

Upstairs, in her bedroom, she checked the window was
locked. Then she shut the curtains. Then she turned on the

light. Then she got into bed. Then she thought, Oh my God, the light, he'll be able to see the light from his bedroom window. So she got up. She turned the light off. She lay down all alone in the dark. She stared at her bedroom curtains. What was going on behind them? Was Broken Buckley watching her darkened window from the darkness of his own room? Was he standing, bloodstained axe in one hand, machine gun in the other, watching the darkened street, wondering who to kill first?

Oh please let him murder the Oswalds. Please let him murder the Oswalds.

Or was he making his way down Mr and Mrs Buckley's stairs, out of their front door, across the street, up the Cunninghams' drive, and climbing the ivy that led to Skunk's bedroom window?

It was the not knowing she couldn't cope with. She got up. She opened the curtains. She stared out on the street. Very dark and totally silent. She pulled the stool from under her vanity unit and sat with her chin in her hands. She watched the street and she waited.

It must have been Archie who put her to bed. One minute she was staring out on the darkened street and fearing for her life, the next she was waking up on a bright, cold Sunday morning with the sun streaming in through the curtains and the idea of Broken Buckley being an axe-murderer-psycho-killer seeming stupid inside her head.

Archie didn't say anything over breakfast. He rarely did on a Sunday. He slumped behind the *Sunday Express* and tutted if Skunk or Jed or Cerys made too much unnecessary noise. For pity's sake, it's Sunday. Later, he watched rubbish politicians lie on stupidly repetitive television programmes. Then, suddenly, after lunchtime, he wanted to be a good dad: Football on the Xbox, kids? As the sun was still shining, they had to shut the curtains to see the screen. Archie was Southampton. Jed and Skunk were Brazil. Obviously, they beat him. They almost always did.

Sitting in shadows in Jed's bedroom, hunched between Jed and Archie, with a single slice of sunlight forcing its way through a gap in the curtains, the idea of night-time and Skunk's terror of Broken Buckley seemed a billion light years away. Come bedtime, though, her fear had returned. That night she fell asleep by the windowsill again. The next morning she woke up exhausted for school. She showered and dried and got herself dressed, then straightened her hair, put her favourite pink bow in it, and went downstairs to get breakfast. After eating her cornflakes, she got her stuff ready for school. It was then that she saw her pocket money was missing.

She said, 'Where's my pocket money?' It was always with her sandwiches. Seventeen pounds, every week.

Archie said, 'What pocket money?'

Skunk said, 'What do you mean, what pocket money? My pocket money. The pocket money you give me.'

'Ah,' Archie said. 'That pocket money.'

'Yes,' Skunk said. 'That pocket money.' She checked inside her lunch box and under her can of Diet Fanta. It definitely wasn't there. Archie put his own lunch in his briefcase and looked at Skunk very sternly.

He said, 'It's been stopped.'

'Stopped?' Skunk said. 'What for? What have I done?'

'What have you done?' Archie mocked her. 'You've broken a perfectly good mobile phone. You've stayed out way past your bedtime, causing me untold worry and grief, and I've just had to spend ninety-five quid on a new phone that you wouldn't have needed if only you'd looked after your old one, so, no pocket money for the next . . .' he pretended to consider . . . 'oh, let's say, six months?'

'Six months? That isn't fair.'

'Life,' Archie said, 'isn't fair.'

'But . . . but . . . but . . . Daddy. I need that money.'

'Need?' he said. 'What for?'

Skunk thought, but did not say, To stop Sunrise Oswald letting the older Oswalds kill me.

'Er,' she said.

'Er indeed,' Archie said.

And went to work.

So Skunk needed five pounds. And she needed it fast.

Jed said, 'A fiver? Why? What's it for?'

Skunk couldn't tell him what it was for. It would have shamed him to realise his little sister was being bullied by Oswalds, but instead of protecting her himself, he would have given her a slap for being a loser, then left the Oswalds to finish her off.

Skunk said, 'To buy *My Little Pony*.'

'But you don't read *My Little Pony*.'

'Look,' Skunk said, 'will you give it me or not?'

'Yes,' he said. 'But there's interest.'

'Interest? What's interest?'

'I give you a fiver. You owe me fifteen pounds.'

'Jed,' Skunk said, 'that isn't fair.'

'Life,' he said, 'isn't fair.'

Refusing to be ripped off by Jed, Skunk turned to her final option, but Cerys wouldn't lend her five pounds either. She trotted out her usual line that Archie paid her less than seventeen pounds a week as it was, and said it would do Skunk good to see how the other half lived. Knowing there was no one else she could turn to, Skunk went off to school and her doom.

Collection days were usually Monday mornings, so she spent the morning break hiding in cubicle three of the second-floor toilets, and lunchtime in cubicle four of the ground-floor toilets. There was no escaping, though. Twenty minutes into a lesson that involved the whole of Class 7D reading in silence while Mr Jeffries marked homework for one of his other classes, Sunrise whispered, *Hey, fatso.*

Skunk had never been called fatso before, so didn't think Sunrise was talking to her.

Till Sunrise jabbed her in the ribs.

'Oi. You deaf as well as fat, bitch?'

'Er. I'm not fat,' Skunk said. 'Or a bitch.'

Sunrise considered this answer. 'You calling me a liar?'

'No.' Skunk started to gather her things up. It was time to go hide in the toilets. At the front of the class, Mr Jeffries was still busy marking homework. He either didn't see her raised hand, or saw it and chose to ignore it.

Sunrise whispered beside her, 'Where you going, lardy? You owe me some money.'

'Toilet. 'S'cuse me, Mr Jeffries, sir? Sir?'

Mr Jeffries looked up. 'Miss Cunningham?'

'Need to go to the toilet.'

'Then cross your legs till home time.'

This drew the expected laughter from the rest of the class. Sunrise put her hand up.

'She can't cross her legs cos they're so fat.'

Mr Jeffries sighed and put his red pen down. He rubbed the bridge of his nose. 'Sunrise,' he said, as if talking to an idiot, 'I'm sure you've spent enough time hanging around McDonald's to know Miss Cunningham isn't fat, so why don't you say sorry to her before I give you a thousand lines? And no. I won't accept lines written by your father – yes, I know about that little trick – I'll expect you to sit in here through your lunch breaks while I watch you write them yourself.'

Skunk looked at Mr Jeffries in horror. Then she looked at Sunrise. Sunrise looked at Skunk. Skunk knew this look. She was dead.

'Well, Miss Oswald,' Mr Jeffries said. 'Apology or lines. You decide.'

Sunrise mumbled sorry.

'Good,' Mr Jeffries said. 'Now, Miss Cunningham, just to prove Sunrise wrong, why don't you cross your legs till home time? It's only ten minutes away. OK?'

'OK.'

'Good girl.' Mr Jeffries smiled, then got on with his marking. Stunned by his behaviour, Skunk continued to stare at him in horror. Beside her, very gently, Sunrise Oswald whispered, I want that money, fatso. Today. Or you're dead.

The rest of the lesson passed in a blur. After, there was a brief chase that ended when Fiona Torby – who, after the iPod incident in Drummond Primary, had realised her best chance of surviving school was to become best mates with Sunrise Oswald – caught up with Skunk and pinned her to the wall by the ground-floor toilets until Sunrise caught up and took over. The fight itself was a quick one. Skunk didn't fight back. She just covered her face and told herself she'd be OK so long as there were no marks on her face. Her reasoning went something like this:

So long as there were no marks on her face, she wouldn't have to tell Archie she'd been in a fight.

So long as she didn't have to tell Archie she'd been in a fight, she wouldn't have to tell him who she'd been in a fight with.

So long as she didn't have to tell Archie who she'd been in a fight with, he wouldn't go over Bob Oswald's and get himself beaten to death.

Surprisingly, being beaten up by Sunrise Oswald wasn't all that bad. It was nothing compared to the hidings Cerys sometimes dished out, and these, in turn, were nothing compared to the beatings Skunk took from Jed every once in a while. The worst thing was it happened in front of the rest of the class: they all stood around shouting fight, fight, and cheering Sunrise on as she punched Skunk again and again. Even this humiliation didn't last long – it ended when Mr Jeffries grabbed Sunrise and Skunk by the shoulders and marched them back into room 7D. He slammed the door behind him and sat on the edge of his desk.

'Miss Cunningham,' he said, 'that was the most pathetic display of self-defence I've ever seen in my life.'

Skunk said nothing. Mr Jeffries glared.

'I know you can fight,' he said. 'I've seen you fight with your brother. I bet he punches a lot harder than Miss Oswald here. Why weren't you fighting back?'

Still, Skunk didn't answer. Mr Jeffries stared at her for a long time, then he turned his gaze back to Sunrise.

'Miss Oswald,' he said, 'why do you think Miss Cunningham wasn't fighting back?'

'Because she's a stupid fat loser?'

'That's not quite the answer I was looking for,' Mr Jeffries said. 'It's not even one I'm particularly impressed with, A, because Miss Cunningham isn't stupid – her marks are the best in this class and close to the best in the year; B, because for the word fat to be applied to an individual said individual has to be overweight, and I would say if anything Miss Cunningham is slightly underweight and could do with filling out a little; and, C, the dictionary definition of loser is a competitor who doesn't come first. Miss Cunningham wasn't competing. She was letting you win.'

Sunrise gazed at Mr Jeffries with blank, uncomprehending eyes. Mr Jeffries sighed.

'Sunrise,' he said, and lowered his face towards her, 'I haven't known you very long, but I have heard a lot about you. And your sisters. And your father. Let me tell you what I think happened today. I think that, when you woke up this morning, you got it into your head that you would bully someone for no apparent reason, and that someone turned out to be Miss Cunningham. I don't know why. I don't think Miss Cunningham knows why, and, if I'm perfectly honest, I don't think you even know why yourself. Am I right?'

Sunrise stared but said nothing.

'No answer? Cat got your tongue?'

No answer.

'OK. Fair enough. Say nothing.' Mr Jeffries rearranged himself on the edge of his desk. 'But I've got my eye on you, Sunrise Oswald. You'd better believe me. And unlike Miss Cunningham here, I'm not scared of your dad or your sisters, which means I don't have to hold back in my dealings with you. Do you understand what I'm saying?'

Still Sunrise didn't answer.

Mr Jeffries sighed. He turned to Skunk. 'Miss Cunningham, you can run along home now. Miss Oswald will be right along behind you once she's promised not to bother you or anyone else in this class ever again. Should she renege on this promise, I'll be arranging for her to join her two layabout sisters on the outer fringes of the playground for the rest of the term and possibly longer. I'm sure she'll find that rewarding in her own sad twisted way.'

Skunk stared at Mr Jeffries. She had no idea what the word renege meant, but got the gist of what he was saying: he was going to bully Sunrise Oswald into no longer bullying her. She left the classroom thinking it wouldn't work, and completely expected to be killed as soon as Mr Jeffries had finished with Sunrise Oswald. Not prepared to hang around until she was murdered, she headed home as fast as she could. After telling Cerys she had an upset stomach – which was sort of true; the upset was caused by terror – she fled to the relative peace of her bedroom and tried to work out what to do.

The way she saw it, she had three options: she could run away; she could throw an indefinite sickie; or she could go to school and face her doom. The three options seemed to work out something like this:

Running Away:

She would have to find somewhere to live. She would have to find someone other than Archie to give her pocket money and food. She would have to find someone to dress her and pay for her phone credits. She would probably be caught within days, given a good hiding by Archie, and sent back to school and her doom.

Throwing an Indefinite Sickie:

She would have to pretend to be ill. Jed would assume she was lying and try hard to get her caught out. Cerys would assume she was lying and try hard to get her caught out. Archie would assume she was lying and make her life hell until she caved in and said she felt better, but until she caved in and said she felt better, her temperature would be taken once an hour and she would be bombarded with questions – Where does it hurt? What sort of hurt is it? Have you been sick? Have you been to the toilet? What did it look like? How did it smell? – and banned from eating her favourite foods or watching her favourite programmes or, even worse, playing Xbox.

Once her deceit had been seen through she would get a good hiding from Archie and be sent back to school and her doom.

Facing Her Doom:

All of the Oswalds would beat her until she was dead.

Of all her options, facing her doom was the worst, but as all her options seemed to lead back to facing her doom, Skunk decided to get it out of the way as soon as she could.

This wasn't as easy as it sounded. As the long dark hours ticked past her, she considered each of the older Oswalds and the harm they were likely to do:

Saskia Oswald was the most dangerous, even though she wasn't the eldest. Rumour had it her right hook could kill an adult with one blow.

Then there was Saraya, who was the eldest. She liked to bite, now she'd had her braces removed. The fresh imprint of her teeth was a common sight around the school playground.

Susan Oswald was the maddest. One minute she was all calm and sunny, the next she was spitting and screaming and trying to claw your eyes out. Out of all the Oswalds, she was the one Skunk feared the most.

Sunrise wasn't anywhere near as vicious or scary as the older Oswalds, but she was still more than happy to kick and gouge a victim once the older three had shattered that victim's resistance.

Skunk didn't think about the harm Sunset Oswald was capable of inflicting because she expected to be dead at the hands of the other Oswalds long before Sunset was old enough to join in the slaughter.

She lay awake fretting all night.

But the next day no beating happened. Instead of being beaten, she was given a note by Fiona Torby that said, *Pay double what you owe by two weeks on Monday, fatty, or you and your family are dead.*

As Skunk sat and read the note over and over, Mr Jeffries strode into class, sat on the edge of his desk, and said, 'This lesson has been cancelled.'

There was a sharp intake of breath. The last time Skunk remembered a lesson being cancelled it had been because a half-inch of snow had fallen overnight and brought Drummond Primary to a halt: everyone had been sent home to cause chaos. Today, however, a quick glance out of the window confirmed it was just another dreary, wet November morning – there wasn't a snowflake in sight, let alone half an inch of the stuff. Mr Jeffries got up off his desk and strode purposefully towards the whiteboard. On it, in faint blue pen, he wrote: LIFE.

And then he turned round and stared at Class 7D.

'Guess what today is,' he said.

The class stared back at him in silence. Mr Jeffries sighed and then continued:

'Today,' he said miserably, 'is my birthday.' And then added, even more miserably: 'Guess how old I am?'

Again, he got no answer. The whole class just stared at him as if he was mad.

Again, Mr Jeffries sighed. 'Sunrise,' he said. 'What are two tens?'

Sunrise counted up on her fingers. 'Twenty.'

'Correct. Patinda. What do two and five make?'

'Seven.'

'Seven,' Mr Jeffries nodded. 'And Jason. What is the sum of twenty and seven?'

Jason Hopkinson stared open-mouthed at Mr Jeffries.

'It's not a trick question, Jason.'

'Twenty-seven?'

'Correct. I am twenty-seven years old today. And who can tell me what twenty-seven plus twenty-seven is?'

It took three attempts, but Patinda got there in the end. Twenty-seven plus twenty-seven was fifty-four.

'Good,' Mr Jeffries said. 'And a gold star to the first person who can tell me what fifty-four plus twenty-seven adds up to . . .'

He let them guess for about five minutes before putting them out of their misery, but instead of telling them the answer, he wrote it up on the whiteboard:

Fifty-four plus twenty-seven was . . .

DEAD, PROBABLY.

Skunk, along with the rest of Class 7D, stared. She didn't understand what Mr Jeffries was trying to tell them. She doubted any of the other eleven- and twelve-year-olds around her understood it either. Mr Jeffries smiled.

'It's a joke,' he said. 'But it isn't really funny, so it's OK that nobody's laughing. What I'm trying to say, in my own sad twisted way, is that when you get to my age, you start to think about life differently to the way you do at your age.' Mr Jeffries underlined the word LIFE on the whiteboard, then said, 'I was thinking about life last night. My life, mainly. I was thinking about where I was going. I was thinking about where I'd been. Did any of you know that, before I decided to become a teacher, I used to be an accountant?' Mr Jeffries put the lid on his pen and looked at Class 7D very sternly. 'Kids,' he said, before any of them could answer his question, 'if anyone ever tries to convince you to become accountants, don't listen to them. It is the dullest, most stupid profession ever invented by man.'

Skunk put her hand up.

'Miss Cunningham?'

'My dad says the dullest, most stupid profession ever invented by man is being a solicitor.'

Another hand went up on the other side of the class. 'Mine says it's being a salesman.'

Someone else said, 'My mum says it's being a cleaner.'

Mr Jeffries held his own hands up. 'Well, irrespective of what your parents might think, I got it into my head that being an accountant was the dullest, most stupid profession ever invented by man. That's why I decided to be a teacher. And you know what? These days, I sometimes wonder if being a teacher is the dullest, most stupid profession ever invented by man. At least when I was an accountant I had formulas and rules that made sense and a half-decent pay packet. Now all I've got is you lot and an overdraft.' He walked back to the whiteboard and drew a graph. 'That's why today's lesson is cancelled. What I'm going to do today is tell you all something I wish I'd been told at your age. You probably won't want to hear it. You probably won't understand it. But if you've got any sense, you'll listen, you'll remember, and, in twenty or thirty years' time when you've all messed up your own lives, you'll think, that Mr Jeffries who took me in Year 7, I should have listened to him.'

The graph he drew had a left-hand vertical line and a right-hand horizontal line. The left-hand vertical line was labelled ASPIRATIONS. The right-hand horizontal line was called TIME. Working along the right-hand line, Mr Jeffries wrote 0, 5, 10, 15, 20, 25, 30, 35, 40, 45, 50, 55, 60, 65, 70 and DEAD, PROBABLY. Then he drew a line on the graph. It shot up at an alarming rate just past 10, kept on rising over 15, peaked at 20, dipped at 25, and flatlined above the bottom right-hand line just past the number 30. Somewhere between 70 and DEAD, PROBABLY, it joined with the bottom line.

'Hands up who knows this word?' Mr Jeffries tapped ASPIR-ATIONS. Patinda said ASPIRATIONS cured headaches. Mr Jeffries laughed. 'If anything, they cause headaches. ASPIR-ATIONS are things you want to achieve, and this graph shows the relationship between your chances of achieving something and how old you are when you decide you want to achieve it.' Mr Jeffries waved his hand over the whole of the graph. 'These two lines here,' he said, 'are called axes. Over the next couple of years, people who have been boring you silly with times tables and multiple division will send you crazy with axes and other such rubbish, but for now, all you need to know is that the bottom line represents your age and the left-hand line represents dreams.' He looked at the class over his shoulder, then tapped the line he'd drawn in the shape of an arc. 'This line here repre-sents the way your lives will most likely work out. From the ages of nil to five and five to ten you're all getting to grips with the basics. Craig? Stand up and walk to the front of the class, please.'

Craig, a chubby boy who liked to play kiss-chase but only with other boys, got up and walked to the front of the class.

'Right,' Mr Jeffries said. 'Excellent. Craig, the same as the rest of you, has spent the years nil to five learning how to walk and talk and eat and get himself to the toilet and understand basic instructions – thanks, Craig, you can sit down now. Then Craig, the same as the rest of you, spent the years five to ten learning how to read and write and send text messages to like-minded individuals. In terms of ASPIRATIONS, there's not really a lot going on in your heads. This is only right. You are, after all, children. You should be having fun. Experimenting. But, at the same time, you need to be aware – like I wish I'd been aware – that the years between eleven and eighteen are when you really need to start deciding what the rest of your lives will consist of. Anyone know why?'

None of them knew why. Mr Jeffries continued.

'You need to start deciding because by the time you get to this age – fifteen to twenty – and then this age – twenty to twenty-five – your chances of realising your ASPIRATIONS get smaller. And by the time you get to this age – twenty-five to thirty and beyond – they all but disappear. This isn't because you no longer have any ASPIRATIONS. I do. I have greater ASPIRATIONS now than I ever did at your age. It just gets virtually impossible to do anything about them. You get stuck in what adults call a rut. Yes, Miss Torby?'

'My dad left my mum because he thought he was stuck in a rut.'

'I'm very sorry to hear that, Fiona. The sad fact is, though

– in this day and age – that if your relationship is in a rut, you can fix it by walking out. If your career is in a rut, however, it can be a little bit harder to change it. The reason for this is MONEY. At your age, you have a distorted view of money. That's because your parents give you all the money you need. But, mostly around about this age,' he tapped 15–20 on the graph, 'this source of income dries up. You have to get either a student loan or a job. The job you get will be very poorly paid in relation to the trade you are in. So, say you get a job as a trainee teacher – don't look like that, Patinda, somebody's got to do it – then your salary in relation to a head teacher will be absolutely pathetic. So you work your way up. And as you work your way up, you get more money. What do you do with this money? Well, probably, for a few years, you'll go out drinking every night. Once or twice a year you'll go on a cheap package holiday to Spain or Greece or Turkey. Then you'll buy a car. Then you'll decide you're too old to live with your parents and rent a flat or take out a mortgage. Now you're utterly broke, and what you need is more money. How do you get more money? You put in more hours at work. You work your way up the ladder. But the higher you get up the ladder, the more debt you seem to get into. Your car's a total old banger, so you buy a new one on finance. The flat you're renting isn't big enough, so you take out a lease on a house or get a bigger mortgage. Heaven forbid you get married and have children. So now, where are you? You're in your late twenties. You're in debt right up to your eyeballs and you're halfway up the career ladder at work. But what if you're unhappy?' Mr Jeffries tapped his graph. 'What are you going to do if you can't stand your job or the people you work with? Get a new job doing the same thing somewhere else? That's an option. But then, when you've done this three or four times and you're still unhappy, you'll start to realise it's not the people or the place that's making you unhappy. It's what you're actually doing. So you want out. You don't want to be a teacher or whatever it is you're doing any more. You want to do something different. So you look around. And that's when it finally hits you. If you want to do something different, you have to go back to the level of salary you were on when you first started work. But you're in debt up to your eyeballs. You need more money, not less. So you can't do anything different. You're only in your late twenties, and yet somehow you've got yourself trapped. What you're doing today is what you're going to have to do right to the day you drop dead of exhaustion or retire into bitter old age.' Mr Jeffries paused. He stared at his class. He clasped his pen tight between both his hands. 'That's why the five or six years directly in front of you now are going to be the most important of your lives. Right now, right this minute, anyone in this class can be anyone they want to be. Take Gordon Brown, for instance. He sat in a classroom like this once. He wasn't anything special. He was just a little kid like you lot. Now he's one of the most powerful men in the world. One of you could do that. One of you could be a film director. One of you could be a computer operator on a film like *Shrek*. Or a disc jockey on Radio 1. How cool would that be?' Mr Jeffries turned back to his graph. 'But the hard facts are, if you don't make the right choices in these years here,' he underlined 15–20 with his pen, 'then whatever you are by the time you reach twenty-five is what you will probably always be.'

He turned back to his class. He smiled.

'Hands up anyone who understands what I'm on about?'

Skunk started to put her hand up, then let it drop down again. She didn't have a clue what he was trying to say.

Two desks further over, Sunrise Oswald put her hand up.

'Miss Oswald, as you're the only person here who understands what I'm talking about, can you please translate for the rest of the class?'

'Yeah. You're saying what my dad says. He reckons there ain't no point in him getting a job now as they'd take our house and our benefits away. He says it's how life is.'

Mr Jeffries sighed. 'Sort of, Miss Oswald, thank you. What I'm really trying to say, though, is think about what you want to be when you grow up. Not in terms of being a footballer or a pop star or an actor – dream the dream, by all means, I'm not saying none of you could be a footballer or a pop star or an actor, I'm just saying it's unlikely – but in terms of being a biochemist or a plumber or an accountant or a teacher. Start to get it into your heads that when you walk out of school or college or university you'll need to get some sort of job, and you'll be pretty much stuck with this job or a variation of this job for the next forty or fifty years. Forty or fifty years. Forty or fifty years. Can you imagine doing something you hate over and over and over for forty or fifty years? Is that what you want with your lives?' Mr Jeffries glared at the eleven- and twelve-year-olds before him. His eyes were wide and unblinking. Skunk noticed he was sweating. Something in his expression reminded her of Broken Buckley the day the police came and took him away. Thinking of Broken Buckley, she suddenly realised what was happening. Mr Jeffries was having a breakdown. Right there. In front of her eyes.

This was confirmed to her just after her bedtime.

She had lost the daily battle to stay up half an hour later than normal and was lying in her bedroom wondering how she could pay off Sunrise Oswald when the doorbell rang. It was Archie who answered.

'Oh. Hello. What do you want?'

'I'd like to speak to Cerys.'

It was Mr Jeffries. His voice sounded thick and slurred.

Archie said, 'I'm not sure she wants to speak to you.'

Mr Jeffries shouted, very suddenly, 'Cerys! Cerys! You in there? Are you in there?'

Archie shouted across him, 'Look. I think you should go home. You smell like a bloody brewery.'

'Cerys! Cerys! I love you. I bloody do.'

And, suddenly, Cerys, from the hallway: 'Well. You've got a funny way of showing it. Where the hell have you been? I've been waiting nearly three months for you to call me. I was beginning to think you were dead.'

Archie said, 'I'll go on inside then, shall I?'

'Yes,' Cerys said. 'Thank you, Archie.'

Skunk got out of bed and went over to the window. It was too dark to see anything but from the sound of Mr Jeffries' voice, he and Cerys had stepped off the porch and moved sideways, so they were standing right underneath her window.

She could hear every word, but they didn't speak much at first. There was just this sort of funny wet sound and then a rustling sound and then a very long drawn-out sigh. Finally, Mr Jeffries said, 'God. I've missed you. How could I have been so stupid?'

'Yes. How could you have been so stupid?'

He said, 'I think I just got scared. Commitment. Mortgages. Settling down. I'm not old enough. You're not old enough. Why can't we just have fun? What's wrong with just having fun?'

Cerys's voice sounded dismal. 'Life's not about fun, Mike. You know that as well as I do. Look at the houses around us. Go on. Take a look around you. The Oswalds' house is the only one that might sell for less than two hundred grand if it wasn't Housing Association, and that's only because they've butchered it. Two hundred thousand pounds. That's nearly ten times what you're earning, for fuck's sake, and it's twenty times what I get in cash. Where's the fun in that?'

'I know, I know, but . . .' another silence was punctuated by that peculiar wet sound that reminded Skunk of Gollum eating a fish in *The Two Towers*, '. . . let's not talk about it tonight. Let's go upstairs. I've missed you.'

'Ah-ah-ah,' Cerys said. 'What's this? Any old port in a storm? You're a little bit drunk and a little bit lonely so you make your way round here for a leg-over? You can fuck right off.'

'No, wait, don't.' There was the sound of what might have been a struggle. Then a further burst of wetness. Then Mr Jeffries said, 'Listen to me. I'm not saying never. I'm saying, yes, I want the fitted kitchen, I want the block-paved driveway,

I want the patio and the sunlounger and the power shower and the en suite and the all-inclusive holiday twice a year and kids and all that shit, and I want these things with you, and I want some of them sooner rather than later, but right now, right this minute, I just want to fuck your brains out and be inside of you again.'

There was another burst of wetness, then the front door opened, then the front door slammed shut, then there were footsteps on the stairs, then Skunk heard Cerys's bedroom door slam, and then everything went quiet. She got back into bed and listened for any further sounds, but nothing seemed to be happening, so she shut her eyes and went to sleep. In the room next to Skunk's, however, Archie Cunningham lay wide awake and listened to the sound of Mike Jeffries making love to Cerys. He shut his eyes and thought of the one time he had made love to Cerys. He remembered the springy texture of her nipples and the way her buttocks had felt in his hands. Then he imagined the two of them together: Mike, young, energetic, his whole life before him; Cerys, spread out underneath him, thinking, how could I have done this with Archie Cunningham? I must have been out of my mind.

Archie put his forearm across his eyes and wondered how he'd face them at breakfast.

Skunk didn't think anything of it. She said, Hello, Mr Jeffries, will lessons be cancelled today? Mr Jeffries shook his head and took his cornflakes up the stairs. Skunk ate her cornflakes alone and started to think about ASPIRATIONS. A lot of what Mr Jeffries had said yesterday had left her feeling slightly confused. He seemed to be saying a person could only have one set of ASPIRATIONS: a footballer or a pop star or an actor; a biochemist or a plumber or an accountant. Skunk had always thought you could be whatever you wanted, and had planned to be a nurse and a guide-dog trainer and someone who rode lots of horses. She had also planned to be a policewoman and a brilliant inventor and a presenter on Children's BBC. Sometimes, she planned to be lots of other things as well, such as an artist and a dance instructor and a solicitor – the same as her father was now. Obviously, she had also intended to get married and have babies. Now, all of a sudden, she realised ASPIRATIONS weren't like that. Mr Jeffries was only a teacher. Archie was only a solicitor. Out of all her choices, which one should she be? Looking for some pointers, Skunk went upstairs to ask Jed what his ASPIR-ATIONS were. He said he wanted to be a professional footballer and then a solicitor, like Archie. Being a girl, Skunk knew she couldn't be a professional footballer, so – as being a solicitor had been one of her original ASPIRATIONS – she left Jed checking for zits in the mirror and took herself back downstairs to ask Archie if he was happy being a solicitor. He snorted and said, Are you mad? Skunk said, What else are you going to do with your life then, Daddy? Archie was quiet for a long time, then told her to stop depressing him and pulled his newspaper close to his face. Skunk went back upstairs to ask Cerys what she wanted to do with her life. Mr Jeffries hid under the duvet. Cerys yelled at Skunk to get out. Skunk went back to her bedroom. She stared out the window. The world seemed different today, pre-school, on a damp November

Wednesday. All these houses. People had bought them. They had to be paid for: how much were they worth? Cerys had said hundreds of thousands of pounds. How did people afford them? Skunk only got seventeen pounds a week pocket money (and she didn't even get that at the moment, thanks to her tightwad father). How would she ever afford one? How did Bob Oswald afford one? Archie had said he was on benefits so didn't have to worry about a mortgage. Skunk had asked him what a mortgage was. Archie had said, It's a worry, Skunk, a huge, huge, horrible worry. Could Skunk get a job on benefits and live in a house without a mortgage? And, if so, would she get trapped on benefits in a house next door to a family like the Oswalds? Would she end up bitter and twisted, thirty years old, wanting to do something different with her life but suffocated by debts and unable to change?

Maybe she should just narrow down her original ASPIR-ATIONS to getting married and having babies? Or was having two sets of ASPIRATIONS a little too ambitious? Maybe she should just concentrate on babies: that's what the McCafferty twins in Year 10 were doing, and Sarah Watson, and Nicola Harvey. Peter Wilson's mother, according to Peter Wilson himself – who was the scruffiest boy in Skunk's class – had got pregnant with him at thirteen and been given a flat by the council. Now she was given extra money for each new baby she had, and only needed one more to get a brand-new house that was bigger than this one. A brand-new house! That was bigger than this one! Skunk would make an excellent mother. But who could she have babies with? She considered the boys in her class:

Jason Hopkinson was a no-no. He was too stupid and slow.

Craig Andrew was a no-no. He only played kiss-chase with boys.

Peter Wilson was a no-no. He was the scruffiest boy in Skunk's class. And Cerys said his mum was a lazy cheap whore.

Roger Fenney was a no-no. He touched his testicles in class.

Carl Usher was a no-no. His hair was too greasy. And his clothes smelled of pee.

All of them, for one reason or another, were useless.

The only real option was Dillon. But Skunk didn't know where Dillon was. Dillon had been taken from her way back in August, and she had no way of finding out where he had got to or what he was doing.

And then, that very morning, he came back into her life.

In the playground round the back of the Science Block.

Where he'd been wasting the majority of his schooldays since serving several weeks for the One Stop theft.

Skunk rarely went anywhere near the playground round the back of the Science Block because it was where Susan Oswald hung out. On this particular morning, though, Skunk knew Susan Oswald was skiving school because she'd seen her get in the back of a van with two men selling drugs. Deciding it was safe enough to risk it, she crossed the playground on her way to double science. As soon as she saw the pale pink hoodie, she ran over and pulled Dillon's hood down. He glared at her, then realised who she was. Still, he said, 'What d'you want?'

Skunk didn't say babies. It would have been impolite.

'Nothing. D'you like my phone?'

''S OK. Where'd you nick it?'

'Didn't nick it. Bought it.'

'Where'd you nick the money to buy it?'

'Didn't nick the money to buy it. Archie bought it for me.'

'Archie? Who the fuck's Archie?'

'Archie's my old man. Remember? And fuck's a bad word.'

'I know. That's why I use it. And if your old man gave you the money to buy that phone, then you didn't buy that phone, your old man bought that phone, which means it ain't your phone cos the next time you piss your old man off for no particular reason, he'll tell you to give him his phone back. And anyway, it doesn't take videos, so it ain't no good. Here. Have a look at mine.'

Skunk had a look at his. It was better than hers. She gave it back without saying a word.

'I nicked it out of Woolies. The next time I'm in Woolies, I'll nick one for you as well.'

And he did, partly because Skunk never called him pikey the way everyone else did, and partly because her smile reminded him of his dead sister. It came in a box and everything.

It seemed rude to refuse it, so Skunk took it and kissed Dillon's cheek. Chad Radleigh saw her do it and shouted PAEDOPHILE at Dillon. This was a word Skunk didn't know. As soon as she'd hidden Dillon's gift in the back of her wardrobe – in the hope her father wouldn't find it and send her to prison for stealing – she asked Archie what it meant. He retreated behind the *Express*. She went back upstairs to ask Mr Jeffries. He put his hand on Cerys's shoulder and said, 'Leave her, she's doing no harm,' then said, 'Yes, Skunk, how can I help you?'

Skunk said, 'Why am I Skunk here and Miss Cunningham in class?'

Mr Jeffries looked sideways at Cerys. 'Because in class I'm your teacher, and here I'm just your friend.'

'Oh.' Sometimes, Mr Jeffries talked nonsense. Skunk remembered why she'd come up here. 'What does the word paedophile mean?'

Mr Jeffries stared at her a moment, then looked at Cerys again. 'Er. That's a good question. Why don't you go downstairs and ask your father?'

'I already did. He's hiding behind the *Express*.'

'Ah. Right. Is he now. Well, er . . .'

'Oh for God's sake,' Cerys snapped. 'Men. You're all bloody useless. Skunk, a paedophile is a bad man. Where did you hear that word used?'

Skunk said, 'I kissed Dillon in the playground and Chad Radleigh shouted out that word.'

Cerys frowned. 'Dillon? Not that little pikey you and your brother were hanging around with in the summer? You shouldn't be kissing pikeys, honey. They've got more fleas than hedgehogs.' Cerys put her cigarette down and pulled herself into a sitting position, then, when she saw Skunk's eyes widen, covered her breasts with the sheet. 'How old is he? Fourteen? Fifteen?'

'Fifteen, I think – but he's only in Year 8 because the social workers all think he's slow –'

'Because he's missed a lot of schooling,' Mr Jeffries said quickly.

'Well,' Cerys said, 'whether he's slow or lazy, he's too young to be a paedophile. A paedophile is a full-grown man. You remember Stranger Danger, and how you mustn't get into cars or go for a walk with any adult you don't know? That's because of paedophiles. They like little children in a different way from normal people. They like to do things to them. They're horrible and nasty. That's all you need to know. Now do me a favour, sweetheart? Go downstairs and tell Archie what a paedophile is, because, obviously, he doesn't know. And, in future, if you want to come in here, knock and then wait to be asked in.' She dug Mr Jeffries in the ribs, very hard. 'Don't they teach manners in schools any more?'

Mr Jeffries said, 'Inflicting manners on little people is a violation of their human rights. And, Skunk, Dillon isn't a pikey. Don't go using that word in school.'

Skunk didn't know what a pikey was. She still wasn't sure what a paedophile was. It was all very confusing. Dillon was confusing as well. He was ignoring her in school, but out of school he was her boyfriend. Whenever they were alone, he held her hand and told her that he loved her. Once or twice, he kissed her cheek. Other times, he pushed her on the swings at Botleigh Lakeside and said things like, Skunk, when we're older, we'll run away to Ireland. We'll live by the side of a stream. It was Dillon's dream to go to Ireland. No one would call him a pikey in Ireland, because the Irish were all pikeys themselves. No one would call him a paedophile either, because Skunk would be older by then. Right now, though, she was too young for him to be seen with. Chad Radleigh had said so: Find someone your own age, you fucking paedo, and make sure she ain't fucking local. We don't breed with pikeys round here. Dillon was scared to death of Chad Radleigh. He was a psycho, a total nutter, which was why, when some kids from school turned up to cadge roll-ups, Dillon acted like Skunk wasn't there. She hated the fact he could do this, but it did prove Cerys was right: Men. They were all bloody useless. Archie wouldn't answer her questions. Jed wouldn't listen to her questions. Mr Jeffries would listen *and* answer her questions, but she couldn't work out what he was on about. In terms of sensible answers there was only Cerys she could turn to, but Cerys could be very moody. Sometimes, Skunk stood outside her bedroom door for ages, waiting to be let in. Inside, Cerys would lie with her head on Mr Jeffries' hairy chest and trace a single finger around one of his nipples. She would say, You've got to do something about her. He would say, What can I do? The kid lives here. She's got more right to be here than I have. At this stage, Cerys would pounce. Let's get a place of our own then. Mr Jeffries would sigh. We've been through this already. We can't afford it. Not yet. Cerys would say, We can't keep carrying on here. It isn't fair on Archie. Mr Jeffries would point out, What's wrong with him lately anyway? He always seemed to like me before. The two of them would fall silent. Then Skunk would knock again. 'Can I come in now?' Yes, they would both say, come in.

At school, the rumours were flying. This was because of the Oswalds. Susan Oswald, to be precise. She saw Mr Jeffries leave the Cunningham house just after six one Tuesday morning. She wasn't up early. She was coming home late. She'd been out with Chad Radleigh. He and his mate Darren had stolen a Rav 4 from outside the Shamblehurst Barn Public

House and taken Susan for a spin down the small lanes out at Durley. As a reward for their friendship, Susan gave each of them a blow job round the back of PC World. Then the three of them went to McDonald's, which was shut, and met up with a load of Chad and Darren's mates. In the dark litter-strewn car park, an assortment of cars raced each other round and round and round. At intervals, they stopped, and Susan climbed from one car to another. She lost track of it all in the end. Who and why and what. The scream of engines. The wailing of tyres. The bounce of laps and the smell of sweat and cigarette butts and spitting it out into tissues. After, the boys smoked dope in the shadows of the drive-thru while Susan sat tucked up among them and felt at least she was liked. They left her to walk home on her own.

As she climbed back in through her bedroom window, she saw Mr Jeffries. He was heading down the Cunningham drive in the same clothes he'd worn to school the day before. He looked bleary-eyed and crumpled. Susan Oswald shouted out the window, Mr Jeffries is fucking Skunk Cunningham. He's a paedo. A dirty old perv. Then she ducked behind the curtains. Mr Jeffries looked around, saw no one, and made his way back to his flat.

Mr Jeffries' flat was in a suburb of Southampton that was slowly falling apart. There were tower blocks and car parks and halal butchers and kebab shops and a couple of open-all-day pubs. There were Jews and Muslims and Christians and Hindus and heathens. There were crackheads and smack-heads and little old people scared to go out day or night. The police drove through with their lights on and sirens wailing, just to get in and out as fast as they could. Mr Jeffries hated it. He wished he could live in Hedge End in a house like Archie Cunningham's with a woman like Cerys and kids like Skunk and Jed. Poor old Mr Jeffries. He had enough problems already. He didn't need Susan Oswald spreading the rumour he was fucking Skunk Cunningham all over school. Luckily for him, though, it didn't stick. For a start, Mr Jeffries was more popular than Susan Oswald. And secondly, he was the best looking male teacher in school, so no one really accepted the idea of him going out with a scrag-ended runt like Skunk Cunningham. On top of this, it was widely believed Mr Jeffries was fucking Mrs McCluskey. Bizarrely, this was also down to Susan Oswald. Because Susan Oswald had once stolen Mrs McCluskey's contraceptives, the whole school knew Mrs McCluskey was sexually active. And as Mrs McCluskey was married, and as married people never seemed to do it with the people they were married to (based on the evidence of the parents of most of the pupils, who were all separated or getting their ends away with people they shouldn't have been getting their ends away with), the whole school assumed she was getting it elsewhere. Hence, she was getting it off Mr Jeffries. Skunk brought this up with Cerys.

'What would you do if Mr Jeffries was seeing someone else?'

Mr Jeffries covered his eyes and then hid under the duvet.

'I'd cut his wotsits off,' Cerys told her.

'What are wotsits?'

'What's what, what?' Mr Jeffries said from under the duvet. 'What?'

'What?'

Skunk gave up and went to her room. It was raining outside. The street was empty. She stared over the road, at Broken Buckley's window. She thought she saw movement behind the closed curtains, but she must have been mistaken: Broken Buckley wasn't by his window. He was lying on the floor by the side of his bed. He'd not long had his monthly visit from the community psychiatric nurse. The pinprick was still visible in his left buttock. Pain flared, and then faded away. Life faded away. It faded into a field that sloped down to the south. Broken lay naked within it, arms spread, face turned to the sun, no sense of danger, no panic. Broken sighed. He felt happy. Broken sighed. He felt sad. This was the way of his life now. Sleep. Dream. Wake up. Come down. Stare at the ceiling. Oh no. Not you again. Saskia Oswald, laughing. Saskia Oswald, pointing. Sometimes, he imagined her walking towards him. Her short skirt. Her bare feet. Her low-cut top. Her cleavage. *Fancy taking me for a ride?* Broken felt his pulse race. Even with the sound of her laughter, he still loved Saskia Oswald. Always had, from a distance. Three years younger than he was. The age gap meant nothing to him.

For Dillon, it wasn't so simple.

He said, 'You're so fucking dumped, Skunk.'

And then he said, 'Don't worry, though. I still love you. When you're older, we'll get back together. We'll run away to Ireland and get married. We'll live by the side of a stream.'

Skunk was far from impressed. 'If you want to marry me,' she said, 'and if you want to run off with me when I'm older, then why am I so fucking dumped?'

107

Dillon pulled his hood low. 'Don't swear, Skunk. I hate it when you do that.'

'I wasn't swearing. I was repeating what you said.'

Dillon sighed. He shrugged. With his hood low and the wintry light all around him he looked like Emperor Palpatine off of *Star Wars*. He sounded weary with the grief of it all. 'Skunk,' he said, 'it ain't you. It's them. All of this. It's all them. They keep going on at me. They say you're too young. They say you're just a kid. They say I'm a stinking paedo pikey and they'll do me if I don't dump you. I don't want to dump you, you know I don't want to dump you, but it's hard enough for me around here as it is. If I keep going out with you, I'll be in traction by the end of the week. Chad Radleigh reckons he'll break my legs if he sees us together again. And Chad Radleigh's a complete fucking psycho. I don't want no trouble with him.' Dillon paused. He saw the look on Skunk's face. 'Don't,' he said. 'Come on. We'll be OK. I still love you. You still love me. One day we'll be together. Trust me. For now, though, we'll just keep it secret.'

'Archie says, trust no one.'

'Archie? Your old man? He got that off a film.'

'What film?'

'I don't know. Some film. You want a smoke?'

'No. Smoking Causes Cancer.'

'I know that.' He lit one. Then some kids from school turned up to cadge roll-ups. Dillon put space between Skunk and himself. Skunk ached. It wasn't fair. But, still, she was allowed to stay with him because Jed was with him, so it wasn't like she was with Dillon, though he winked whenever he could from the darkness deep down in his hoodie. After a while spent kicking a ball around and cadging Dillon's roll-ups, everyone drifted off to hang around by the cash machine outside the One Stop. Dillon hesitated, then followed. Skunk, in turn, followed him. There were eleven or twelve of them in total, though the gang was forever changing as some of them went home and others came out for a smoke. Skunk was the youngest there. The eldest was maybe twenty. All three of the older Oswalds were there: they had come out to escape their old man, who was drunk and playing the Bangles version of 'Hazy Shade of Winter' at full volume on repeat. The sound of it echoed around Drummond Square as Bob Oswald played air guitar in his front room. Archie could hear it as he sat reading the *Daily Express* and trying not to dwell on what Mike Jeffries and Cerys were doing upstairs in her bedroom. Mike Jeffries and Cerys could hear it as they lay in Cerys's bedroom and tried to work out if they could afford a one-hundred-and-eighty-five-thousand-pound mortgage on a combined income of thirty-two thousand pounds a year and debts of just over eleven. Broken Buckley could hear it as he lay in his room and tried to block the grating scrape of Saskia Oswald's laughter from his poor tired aching mind. *Why did she have to go do that? Why did she do that to me?* The kids outside the One Stop couldn't hear it. They were too far away. But even if they had been able to hear it, they wouldn't have been able to hear it, because they were making too much noise of their own. The lady who was so poor she had to work the eight-till-late shift at the One Stop as well as the early shift at McDonald's said so.

'You kids. Stop making so much noise. And stop hanging around the shop doorway. And you,' she pointed at Dillon, 'I've already told you. Don't even try to come in here.'

'Fuck off, you old bitch.'

'Swivel.'

'Suck my cock.'

And this, from one of the Oswalds:

'Lick my clit, you stupid old biddy.'

The lady who worked at the One Stop threatened to call the police. The kids hung around for most of the hour it usually took the police to turn up, then headed off into Hedge End Village. There were retirement flats there. They rang the security bells and threw stones at some of the windows. Then they ran off to the police station, which was no longer twenty-four-hour, and sat on the steps in the darkness. Some of them smoked and some of them kissed and Susan Oswald disappeared around the back with one of Chad Radleigh's mates who had heard she was good for a blow job. Chad Radleigh shouted encouragement – go on, my son, get in there – until he realised no one was paying attention, then started throwing his knife at the police station's front door. As he walked over to pull the blade out, he asked Dillon where he was going to live when the council finally got round to forcing him out of his car park. Dillon shrugged and said nothing. Jed stared off in the direction Susan Oswald had gone in and then said to Skunk, 'Come on. It's time to go home.' Dillon went with them as well. As they made their way towards the shut-down Halfords, Skunk asked Dillon what it was like to live in a car park. He said it was OK in the summers, but in the winters it got too cold to sleep. Jed said he'd steal Dillon a duvet from out of their attic. Dillon's reply was disdainful. If I want a duvet, I'll nick one myself.

Dogs barked as they approached the small ring of caravans. Dillon muttered, Seeya, and merged into the night. His pale pink hoodie glowed where he had been.

Skunk and Jed walked on. It was a cold, bright night. Despite being the end of November, there were fireworks going off. Sporadic explosions. Jed took hold of Skunk's hand. He said, 'Skunk. Don't you go falling for Dillon. He won't be around here for long.'

Skunk said, 'Mind your own business. You don't know anything about it.'

'Well. Don't say I didn't warn you. Chad Radleigh's right. The council are bound to move them on sooner or later. No way he'll stay in touch with you after that. Watch yourself. That's all.'

They walked the rest of the way in silence. The square was now quiet and still. Bob Oswald was slumped at his kitchen table, a whisky bottle in one hand, photographs of the late Mrs Oswald spread out all around him. Archie was asleep as well, but there was no picture of Jed and Skunk's mother clutched to his chest, just the Sky+ remote control. In the kitchen, Cerys and Mr Jeffries were having a row about whether they should book a package holiday or start saving for a deposit on a flat: Cerys wanted to start saving; Mr Jeffries wanted to go skiing over Christmas. Skunk and Jed went up and played Xbox, but Jed's heart wasn't in it. He hated it when Cerys rowed with Mr Jeffries. It reminded him of when Archie and his mother used to row. He kicked Skunk out around midnight and she went through to her own room. Later – much, much later – she heard her bedroom door open. Archie looked in on her as he always did then went on to his bed. He lay in darkness and listened to the sound of Cerys and Mr Jeffries making up for their earlier row and told himself he wasn't bothered. He shut his eyes and he drifted. The whole house was asleep now, all except for Skunk, who lay awake in her bedroom and thought about life and ASPIRATIONS and who to have them with if the council moved Dillon on like Jed had said they might. She didn't think about Broken Buckley. He had completely slipped from her mind. She didn't think about Mr Jeffries either, because she knew he belonged to Cerys, and, therefore, could never be hers. She didn't even think about the fact she owed Sunrise Oswald three weeks' worth of double protection money, and the deadline had already passed. It wasn't until the next morning that she remembered she was in danger, and by then, well, it was too late.

There were three of them waiting when Skunk left for school – Saskia, Susan and Sunrise. They waited out of sight until Skunk was out of Drummond Square, then tailed her up Drummond Way and past the One Stop. As she continued towards Wildern Lane, Sunrise Oswald shouted, Where's my money, fatty.

Skunk looked over her shoulder and felt a wave of terror. This was the worst-case scenario. No Jed. No Archie. No schoolteachers. No toilets to run to and lock herself in. No way to get back to the house and Cerys. Archie was miles away, at work. By Skunk's reckoning, she was at least an eight-minute sprint from the playground. She could run for it. She might just make it. All the Oswalds smoked and lived off McDonald's and McCain's Crinkle Cut Oven Chips. There was a good chance she could outrun them.

But if she didn't . . .

If they caught her . . .

She didn't have any money.

And even if she did, they would kill her anyway. She knew this, because things were different outside the playground. Skunk didn't understand why. She just knew they were. Even the Oswalds who had left school treated a fight inside the playground as a fight between little children. Outside, it was a fight between adults. She might only be eleven years old, but what did that matter to Saskia Oswald? What did Saskia Oswald care if she was seven years older than Skunk Cunningham was? She would pick her up and snap her without thinking if it was fair. Skunk had no choice but to run for her life.

She took a couple of very deep breaths, hooked her bag over her shoulder, and legged it.

For the first ten or so steps she thought they weren't going to bother chasing her. Everything was very quiet behind. Then a stone sailed past her shoulder and bounced off the wing of a parked car. Saskia Oswald shouted, Get her, the fat little fucker. The sound of six rapid-action stilettos was like a cavalry charge behind her. The Oswalds were going to war, and Skunk was the target nation. She screamed in terror and ran as fast as she could. Her hair flew out behind her. Her satchel banged against the small of her back. She reached the first corner and ran across the main road without looking. A couple of car horns sounded. Another stone narrowly missed her shoulder. Someone shouted, Watch where you're going, why dontcha? An Oswald screamed, Watch out yourself, you stainer. Skunk reached another corner. The sound of stilettos seemed closer. Her lungs were bursting with the effort. It wasn't fair. They weren't fitter, but their legs were longer than hers were. They only needed one stride to her two or three. They were going to catch her. Outside of the playground. God knew what would happen. She was fully prepared to be killed. This realisation stunned her. There was a good chance she was going to die in the next three or four minutes. Someone had to be the Oswalds' first ever fatal beating. It was an accident waiting to happen. The thought seemed to exhaust her. The air seeped out of her lungs. The energy drained from her legs. Behind, a hand landed on her shoulder. She was spun round and smacked in the face. Then she was kicked in the leg. A heel came down on the big toe of her left foot. She was pushed to her back on the floor. Then they dragged her along by her satchel. She twisted. She turned on her front. Gravel grazed her face and her shoulder. Her mouth filled with bits of dirt. Above her, the Oswalds were all laughing. Susan Oswald tried to kick out her teeth.

And then, thank God, it was over.

She had no idea at first who had stopped them. An adult. His voice thundered: You girls. You girls. Stop that. Alone, it wasn't enough. He could have stood on the other side of the road shouting stop that, you girls, stop that, until the moment Skunk was dead. Luckily for her, he didn't: he put himself among them. Saskia was forcibly pushed off her. She stumbled and fell to the ground. This calmed Susan and Sunrise enough to allow Skunk to get to her feet. Mr Jeffries put a hand on her shoulder. 'It's OK, Skunk. It's over.' She looked up at him. He smiled. Then he turned on Saskia Oswald. 'What the hell do you think you're playing at? You're a grown woman, for God's sake. A grown woman. Haven't you got any brains?'

Saskia got up to her feet. 'Fucking touch me again, I'll kill you.'

'Come near my pupils again, I'll call the police. That goes for you and Saraya. If either of you so much as set foot in the playground again I'll be dialling 999. And I'll be calling the *Sun*'s Shop a Benefit Fraudster Hotline. You can't be looking for jobs if you're hanging around the school gates every day of the week. Now get out of my sight, or I'll call the police right now. I've never seen anything so disgusting in all my life. Beating up little kids. You're a disgrace, even for an Oswald. You want to get yourself a life.'

Saskia brushed herself down. 'Fucking paedo. Fuck off. You fucker.'

Mr Jeffries got his mobile phone out. He tapped out 9, 9, 9.

Saskia Oswald ran off.

Mr Jeffries switched his phone off. He turned on Sunrise and Susan.

'You two don't know what trouble is. Clear off into school now. I'll see you both in the headmaster's office. Go on. Now.'

Skunk had never heard anyone sound so angry in all her

life. She doubted the Oswalds had either. They actually did what Mr Jeffries told them: they turned round and headed for school.

Mr Jeffries watched them into the distance, then turned and looked down at Skunk. Now his voice was soft and concerned. 'Skunk,' he said, 'I'm so sorry. Are you OK?'

She said, 'Yeah, I'm fine.'

She was as well. Being saved by Mr Jeffries was worth a near-death experience at the hands of the Oswalds. Her face was all flushed with excitement and her mind was replaying the scene. Even though she hadn't seen him run over to save her, she could imagine his hair flying backwards, his jacket flapping, his jaw set firm and strong. No wonder Cerys loved him with all of her heart. Skunk's own heart was pounding. Totally oblivious to his effect on her, Mr Jeffries bent down and looked at Skunk's wounds. The worst one was the big toe of her left foot. A sharp heel had split the nail down the middle. Blood was soaking through her sock and filling her shoe. Mr Jeffries couldn't see this, so his gaze was drawn to her grazes. There was one on her cheek and another on her chin. Skunk could feel the flesh on one side of her neck stinging, and both her elbows, and the palms of her hands.

'Those girls,' Mr Jeffries said. 'Those bloody girls.' And then, 'Do you want to go home?' Normally, Skunk would have jumped at the chance to go home, but she guessed today would be a good day to be around Mr Jeffries. Lots of attention. Lots of sympathy. She put on her weakest voice:

'No. I don't want to fall behind on my lessons.'

Mr Jeffries laughed. He patted Skunk's shoulder (she

winced, but not too much). He walked her the rest of the way to school. Skunk felt like a princess, walking so close beside him, her small hand wrapped in his big one. As they walked, he asked Skunk if she enjoyed his lessons. She told him that she did, but admitted she couldn't decide which ASPIRATION to choose. Mr Jeffries suggested she looked in the job pages of the *Echo* every Thursday to see if she could see any careers that she fancied. This wasn't the answer Skunk had wanted. She said, 'Mr Jeffries, what about yours?'

'My copy of Thursday's *Echo*?'

'No. Your ASPIRATIONS. You said you still had them.'

'I do,' he said. 'I do.'

'Well,' Skunk said, 'what are they?'

He shook his head. He sighed. 'They're more dreams than aspirations, Skunk. They sound silly, said out loud.'

'You said dream the dream.'

'I told you and the rest of the class to dream the dream. I'm too old for all that.'

'Daddy says you're never too old.'

'Daddy's talking rubbish.'

They reached the school gates. Skunk felt him trying to let go of her hand. She gripped his hand even tighter. He took her to the school nurse then went off to murder the Oswalds. They were sitting in the headmaster's office, drinking glasses of squash the headmaster had poured them. Mr Jeffries said, 'What the hell's this?'

Mr O'Driscoll stared at Mr Jeffries. 'What the hell's what?'

'This,' Mr Jeffries snapped, and grabbed the beakers from Sunrise and Susan. 'These two and one of their halfwit sisters have just tried to murder one of your brighter pupils in broad daylight, and you've poured them beakers of squash?'

Mr O'Driscoll watched Mr Jeffries slam the beakers down on his desk, then folded his fingers and regarded Mr Jeffries with cold dry eyes. Mr Jeffries turned on Susan and Sunrise.

'So,' he said to them. 'Come on then. How far was it going to go?'

Susan Oswald heard the words *how far* and thought about sex and giggled. Mr Jeffries slapped his hands together in front of her face. The blast of air pushed her hair back and stopped Susan Oswald from laughing.

'What?' Mr Jeffries said to her. 'You think violence is funny?'

Susan Oswald said nothing. Mr Jeffries put his face very close to her face so his eyes filled up her whole world. His breath smelled of toothpaste and mouthwash.

'Susan,' he said, very gently, 'you're fifteen years old. That's four years older than Skunk Cunningham. If I saw you in a fight with her on your own, I'd be disgusted with you. To see you, an eighteen-year-old and a twelve-year-old all ganging up on a lone eleven-year-old together . . . I'm sorry, but that just makes me feel sick. And it wasn't like that fight was childish. There was real violence going on there. You and Saskia were doing your level best to inflict real harm. I saw you try to kick Skunk in the face. It was only the fact Saskia's foot got in the way that stopped you from doing real damage. Do you know what would be happening now if your foot had made contact with Skunk Cunningham's face?' Mr Jeffries paused. He looked sideways at Sunrise. 'You listen to this as well, Sunrise, because I hold you just as responsible for this as your sisters. What would be happening now is that Skunk Cunningham would be in hospital. You two and Saskia would be down the police station. You and Sunrise might get off with cautions, but Saskia's old enough to be charged with GBH now – or attempted murder. Do you know how long you can be jailed for either of these offences? Ten years? Twenty? I'm not sure. But I'm sure of one thing: Skunk Cunningham's father is one of the best criminal solicitors in Hampshire, and he'd be jumping all over the police to make sure full charges were brought. On top of that, he'd be preparing a water-tight case against this school and your father for lack of parental and moral control. He'd sue the school for every penny it had. And that's nothing compared to what he'd do to your father. You think times are hard now? You haven't seen the half of it. Did you know your father could go to prison for what you did, even though he wasn't there? Did you? Did you know that?'

Susan Oswald said, No.

'Sunrise. Did you know that?'

Sunrise said, No, then started to cry. Susan put an arm around her. Mr Jeffries stood up.

'OK. I want both of you to go outside now. I'm going to talk to Mr O'Driscoll about whether we're going to expel one or both of you. Do you understand me? We're going to talk about expelling you for violence and criminal intent. You're lucky we're not simply calling the police. Now get out of my sight.'

The two Oswalds walked out of the office. Mr Jeffries slammed the door shut behind them. As the sound of it echoed to silence, Mr O'Driscoll went mad.

'What the hell do you think you're playing at? Threatening little children like that? What's going on in your head? Don't you know who their father is? You'll be dead by lunchtime. Jesus Christ, man. I knew it was a risk giving you a job here, what with your lack of experience, but I never thought you'd be this bad. You can't talk to pupils like that.'

Mr Jeffries held his hands up. 'Terry,' he said, very calmly, 'if you'd seen what those nasty little bitches were up to, you'd have done well not to throttle them yourself. Believe me. I was restrained.'

'Restrained? It was total bollocks. How can what sounded like a silly little scuffle lead to a charge of attempted murder? How can Bob Oswald be sued for what his freaky little daughters have done? I hope you talk more sense when you're teaching. I hope to God you do.'

'Oh for fuck's sake, Terry. I was just scaring the two of them. That's all people like the Oswalds understand, a bit of fear and loathing, not a glass of squash and a group hug. We'll leave them to sweat in the corridor for ten minutes, then call them in and tell them they've got detention for the rest of the term. While we're at it, we'll warn the little buggers they'll be expelled if anything like this ever happens again.' Mr Jeffries sat down. He looked at Mr O'Driscoll. Mr O'Driscoll looked at him. The ten minutes passed in uncomfortable silence. Then Mr Jeffries got up and opened the door and called Susan and Sunrise back in. Neither Oswald came. Mr Jeffries looked out of Mr O'Driscoll's office. The corridor was empty of Oswalds. They had fled home to complain to their father. They knew he'd be at home. Bob Oswald was always at home. His days were spent looking after Sunset and selling soft drugs to professional people who thought it was cool to be high. That morning, as Sunrise and Susan were sprinting across the school playground and as the school nurse was sending Skunk Cunningham back to her lessons, Bob was teaching Sunset to cook her own breakfast so he could spend longer in bed in the future. As he did, he looked over at Saskia and said, 'You what? This bloke just pushed you over in the street?'

'Yeah. Just ran across the street and pushed me.'

'What were you doing? You must've been doing something.'

Saskia looked down at the floor. 'Wasn't doing nothing.' She lit a cigarette and blew smoke out through her nostrils. 'The fucker. I think he's a teacher.'

'A teacher?' Bob Oswald picked Sunset up off the floor and put her on a chair so she could see into the frying pan. 'What's the world coming to? Teachers running around going crazy? Bloody tosspot liberals. You recognise his face?'

'Reckon I would. Most likely.'

'Well. Once little madam here's done cooking, maybe we'll take a walk down that school and see if we can see him.'

Bob Oswald had no need to do this. Sunrise and Susan were home ten minutes later. Sunrise was still sobbing. Bob Oswald pulled her in towards him and hugged her very tightly. He kissed the top of her head. Susan Oswald told him an abridged version of what had happened. It went something like this:

That bitch Skunk Cunningham over the road with the jumped-up dickhead dad who's screwing that stupid thick Welsh slapper with the big tits n saggy fat arse has been bullying Sunrise for weeks, Dad. Well. Me n Saskia ain't having it, are we? The fucker. We saw her going into school n we just wanted a word. So we's just having a word with the jumped-up little fucker n this dumb-prick teacher comes running out n starts having a go at Saskia n threatening to call the police, so Saskia goes, Chill, I ain't doin nothing n I don't want no trouble, n she just turns round n comes home, n Sunrise goes to this teacher – who just happens to be a friend of the Cunninghams so it's like there ain't no surprises there then is there – I'm sorry, Mr Jeffries, sir, but Saskia was only here cos Skunk Cunningham's been stealing my pocket money for the past few weeks, n this Mr Jeffries just slaps Sunrise around the face n tells her to keep her big fat mouth shut or there'll be more where that came from. The fucker. Said he'd get her expelled.

Bob Oswald stared at Susan. He said, 'Susan, is this more of your bullshit?' But Saskia shook her head on Susan's behalf: No, Dad, really, it's gospel. Bob Oswald felt a vein twitch in the side of his head. He pushed his chair out from under the table.

'Saraya. Watch the kids.'

Saraya was watching *Trisha* on the plasma in the front room. 'Leave it out, Dad. Do I have to?'

'Yeah. You fucking do.'

'Jesus Christ. This family.'

'Just shut up and look out for your sisters. I'll be back in less than an hour.' Bob Oswald got up from his chair. He stubbed his cigarette out. He walked out of the house. He walked past the Buckley house. He walked past the Cunningham house. He walked out of the street and up the main road. He turned left at the One Stop. He crossed the road by the VW garage and followed the curve of the path into Wildern Lane. Here, he walked past Drummond Primary School then vaulted the waist-high gate that barred his route into Drummond Secondary. He appraised the school grounds for a moment, then made his way across the tarmac playground. When he reached the nearest door he found it was locked. He raised a fist and pounded on it, hard. 'Open this door,' he yelled. 'Open this door. Open this fucking door.' Within minutes, a teacher came running. It was Mrs McCluskey.

'What do you want?' she shouted.

'Sunrise Oswald. My daughter. Her little sister just died.'

'Oh my God. I'm so sorry.' Mrs McCluskey reached out and tapped in the door code. The lock released. Bob Oswald barged the door open and grabbed Mrs McCluskey by the throat.

'Jeffries,' he screamed in her face. 'I'm after a teacher called Jeffries.' He shook her, hard, then pushed her away. Mrs McCluskey staggered backwards and collapsed in a heap on the floor.

'Class 7D,' she managed. 'It's that way.'

Bob Oswald stepped over Mrs McCluskey and walked in the direction she had pointed. It led him down a corridor. When he reached the end of this corridor, a sign pointed left towards rooms 1D through to 9D. Bob Oswald turned left. He walked past rooms 1D, 2D, 3D, 4D, 5D and 6D. The door to room 7D was now on his left. He turned and kicked it open. Then he stepped into the room. Skunk Cunningham's mouth went dry when she saw him. He was wearing a pair of dirty green combats and an old white vest he'd got too fat for. His arms looked as powerful as ever. His tattoos were still tight to his muscles. He strode across the classroom and punched Mr Jeffries in the face. Mr Jeffries fell over. Bob Oswald stamped on his head. Then he stamped on his stomach. Then he tipped Mr Jeffries' desk over. It crashed down. Marker pens scattered. Skunk hid her face in her hands. The children around her were screaming. Bob Oswald was shouting and swearing. He was punching Mr Jeffries over and over. Over and over. Over and over again. Skunk was crying. She was whispering stop it, stop it, stop it. It was the worst fight she had ever seen, much worse than the one between Bob Oswald and Broken Buckley, because she hadn't known Broken Buckley and she hadn't loved Broken Buckley. She loved Mr Jeffries. And Bob Oswald was killing him. Dead.

She thought he was dead.

Even when the beating was over, she really thought he was dead.

The whole thing was worse than a nightmare.

Teachers came. None of them intervened though. They just crowded around the doorway. Bob Oswald paid them no attention. He kicked and punched Mr Jeffries. Mr Jeffries looked like a rag doll, flopping and falling and flailing. He writhed each time he was kicked. Bob Oswald towered above him. Bastard. Fucking bastard. I'll kill you. I will kill you. He kicked Mr Jeffries' face so hard his boot came away wet with blood. Skunk looked over at the teachers in the doorway. Do something, she thought, one of you, do something, but the teachers showed no signs of moving. They just stood there, huddled together. Mrs McCluskey had tears in her eyes. Skunk looked back at Bob Oswald. He was still kicking Mr Jeffries, throwing punches, yelling and screaming. Mr Jeffries tried his best to evade him, huddled with his back to his overturned school desk, his arms raised to keep off the blows. Then Bob Oswald stamped down on his ribcage, and Mr Jeffries went limp on the floor. Totally unopposed now, Bob Oswald started punching his face. Skunk screamed at him to stop it, to leave him alone, then got up and threw herself at him. Her arms barely circled his waist. She ducked down and tried to bite him through his thick greasy-tasting combats. Getoffhimgetoffhimgetoffhim. Bob Oswald raised an open palm. He brought it crashing down towards her. At the last minute, he pulled it away. Something seemed to leave him. He gently prised her arms from his midriff and guided her away from his body. Then he walked out of the room.

It was Mrs McCluskey who took over, even though Mr O'Driscoll was standing right there beside her. 'Phone an ambulance,' she ordered one of the other teachers, and then she added, 'Make sure the police are on their way as well.' Then she stepped into the room and clapped her hands together. 'OK, 7D. Everyone out. Let's go next door and do some reading till break time. Come on. Out you all get.' Skunk's classmates slowly got to their feet. They filed out of room 7D. As they did so, they looked down on Mr Jeffries' still form. Skunk looked down on it as well. The tears came suddenly and quickly. 'Don't be dead,' she whispered. 'Please, please don't be dead.'

A hand rested on her shoulder. 'He's not dead, honey, don't worry.' Mrs McCluskey bent down and put her arms around Skunk's shoulders, then guided her out of the room. In the distance, sirens were wailing. The whole school seemed to be talking or crying or screaming. Skunk was led back to the nurse's office. The nurse checked the bandage she'd put on Skunk's toe earlier, then gave her a cold drink of water and told her to rest on the bed. The next thing Skunk knew, Cerys was shaking her awake. She didn't know what time it was. She didn't know where she was being taken. She didn't even know that Cerys could drive. Archie drove them everywhere. Today, though, the whole world was different, and today it was Cerys who drove. She cried quietly as she did so; just tears – she made no sound, she said no words. Skunk wanted to ask her about Mr Jeffries, but she was too scared of hearing the answer, so she sat in the passenger seat and stared at the closed glove compartment and the jumble of cigarettes and cough sweets and two-hour parking permits that formed a mess all over the dashboard of Mr Jeffries' car. Finally, they arrived. Cerys led Skunk across a busy car park and into a tall cold building and sat her down on a hard plastic chair like a school chair but bigger and with grey buckled legs. Cerys wiped her eyes dry. She blew her nose. She said, 'Fuck, I could murder a fag.'

'Fuck's a bad word,' Skunk mumbled.

'I know,' Cerys agreed.

Bob Oswald was arrested at noon. Social services turned up at one. There was very nearly a pitched battle when they tried to collect minor Oswalds and take them all into care. Then

Saraya Oswald signed some papers to say she would look after the children, and social services melted away.

As Bob Oswald was being led into the cells at Eastleigh Station, Cerys and Skunk were walking down a narrow corridor that smelled of bleach and empty vases. They reached heavy double doors and pushed through into a ward that was dark and cold and full of old people. Mr Jeffries was in the bed furthest from the doorway. He was sitting up. There were bandages around his chest and his head. One of his arms was in plaster. He tried to raise the other in greeting, but gave up and squeezed both his eyes shut. Cerys and Skunk stood before him.

Cerys said, 'What a mess.'

Mr Jeffries smiled. Skunk began to sob. She couldn't help it. He wasn't dead. Mr Jeffries wasn't dead. He didn't even look that badly beaten up. Maybe Bob Oswald fought the same way Sunrise Oswald fought – a lot of punches of little substance. Obviously, she was wrong: Bob Oswald fought like a psychopath. He was capable of murder. Mr Jeffries was not hurt as much as he could have been because instead of trying to fight back he had curled up into a ball and protected the most vulnerable parts of his body. Even when Bob Oswald was stamping on his head, Mr Jeffries was covering himself with his arms. This was why his left arm was in plaster. Still, despite the efforts he had made to protect himself, both his eyes were deep purple and his lips were a thickening mess.

Skunk said, 'Sunrise Oswald is dead. I'm going to kill her.'

Mr Jeffries made a snorting sound that may have been laughter. Cerys put a hand on Skunk's shoulder. 'You let grown-ups deal with the Oswalds. You keep your little nose out.'

'But –'

'No buts, Skunk. Butt out.' Cerys pulled up a chair and sat Skunk down. Then she mother-henned Mr Jeffries. Had he had enough to eat? Had he had enough to drink? Did he have any clean underwear? Mr Jeffries either nodded or shook his head. Cerys wrote out a list of all the things she thought he needed. It all seemed a bit cold to Skunk: Mr Jeffries had nearly been murdered, and Cerys was writing a list that included shaving foam and razors. Within ten minutes the list was complete. Cerys told Mr Jeffries she loved him and that she'd try to pop back later that evening. Then she said, 'Come on, Skunk. Let's get you home.' As the two of them stood up to leave, a nurse walked up and said Mr Jeffries would have to go home with them because someone else needed his bed. Cerys threw the list in the bin and helped Mr Jeffries get dressed. Then she helped him out to the car. When they got there, it had been clamped.

Mr Jeffries looked more pained paying the sixty-five-pound release fee than he had when Bob Oswald tried to kick him to death. Even so, he didn't look as pained as Archie Cunningham did when he got home and found Mr Jeffries in a makeshift bed on his sofa. He put his briefcase down in the hallway and went through to the kitchen. 'What the hell happened to him?'

Cerys looked up from the soup she was heating for Mr Jeffries. Before she could answer, Skunk ran in and said, 'Daddy, Mr Jeffries saved my life. Then I saved Mr Jeffries' life. I've asked him back for his tea.'

Archie looked down at his daughter. She looked up at him.

There was a graze on her cheek and another under her chin. She also had bruises around her throat and scratch marks on her arms and her neck. 'Jesus,' he said, 'what the hell happened to you?'

Skunk and Cerys told him. Mr Jeffries filled in the gaps. Archie sat on the edge of his armchair and listened. As he listened, he watched Cerys. She was sitting with Mr Jeffries' head in her lap. Tufts of Mr Jeffries' hair were sticking out of the bandages wrapped tight to his forehead. Cerys was curling them in her fingers, then she was smoothing them flat. Archie looked down at his daughter. 'What I don't understand,' he said, 'is why the Oswalds were trying to beat you up in the first place. What had you done to them?'

Skunk said, 'I hadn't done nothing.'

'You hadn't done anything,' Mr Jeffries corrected.

'Sorry, Mr Jeffries.'

'But anyway,' Jed continued for her, 'you don't have to do anything to the Oswalds. All the Oswalds are mental.'

'Jed,' Mr Jeffries said, 'don't say mental. That's not a very nice word.'

'Mike,' Archie said, 'this is my house. Not your classroom.'

'Sorry,' Mr Jeffries said.

'Daddy,' Skunk said, 'Mr Jeffries is your guest.'

'No he's not. He's your guest.' Archie stood up and ruffled Skunk's hair, then walked over to the window. Behind his back, Mr Jeffries looked quizzically at Cerys. Cerys looked down at the floor. Totally oblivious, Archie stared across the square towards the Oswald place. 'Where's Bob Oswald now then?'

Mr Jeffries said, 'Who knows?'

Cerys said, 'Who cares?'

Archie looked back at Skunk. His eyes were drawn to the scratches on her arms and the bruises around her throat. He imagined her being chased by three older girls, then thrown to the floor and punched and kicked and scratched. He said, 'Which of the Oswald girls attacked you?'

Skunk counted them off on her fingers: 'Sunrise. Saskia. Susan.'

'Right,' Archie said. 'I'm not having this. I'm going over there to sort that lot out.'

'No,' Skunk shouted. 'Daddy. Don't. Mr Oswald will kill you.'

Archie turned and put his hands on Skunk's shoulders. 'Don't be ridiculous, Skunk. No one's going to kill anybody. I'm just going over there to talk to him. That's all.'

'But . . . but . . .'

But he was gone. Out of the house and across the square and over towards the Oswalds'. Poor old Archie Cunningham. He didn't have a clue what he was letting himself in for. Within minutes of Bob Oswald's arrest, Saraya Oswald had been hard at work in the kitchen, making a cake out of Bob Oswald's stash. Saskia and Saraya had eaten half this cake between them while Susan, permanently on a diet, had helped herself to a thin but potent slice. Saskia and Saraya had then finished off what was left before encouraging Sunrise and Sunset to lick the pan clean of cake mix thick with weed. Sunset, being only three years old, tripped out first: the plasma rippled and the head of a dinosaur burst through. Sunset staggered backwards and screamed. Saraya and Saskia collapsed in stitches as the three-year-old weaved and ducked in an attempt to escape the non-existent predator. Then she fell over and couldn't get up. Sunrise, distressed by the state of her little sister, went running over to help her but overshot and knocked herself out on the coffee table. Saraya howled. Saskia howled. Susan, who hadn't had as much cake as the others, went to answer the door.

'Where's your dad?' Archie Cunningham demanded.

'What's it gotta do with you?' Susan Oswald responded.

Before Archie Cunningham could think of an answer, Saraya Oswald yelled: 'Who's at the door?'

Susan Oswald shouted back over her shoulder: 'Skunk Cunningham's old man.'

'What the fuck does he want?' Saraya shouted.

'I don't know. I can't remember.' Susan Oswald looked back at Archie Cunningham. 'What the fuck do you want?' she asked him.

Archie felt his cheeks burn. 'I want to speak to your father.'

Susan Oswald looked back over her shoulder and did a good impression of Archie Cunningham's voice: 'He wants to speak to our father.'

Saraya and Saskia looked at each other, then got up and headed for the front door. 'What do you want to speak to him for?' Saskia asked him.

'I want to complain about you lot attacking my daughter.'

'Well, here we are,' Saskia said. 'Go on then. Complain.'

'Yeah,' Saraya echoed. 'Here we are. Go on then. Complain.'

'You fucker,' Susan added.

Archie tried hard to keep his composure. 'Look,' he said. 'I'm not willing to get in a slanging match with you three. I want to speak to your father.'

'Well, tough,' Saraya told him. 'He ain't in. But even if he was in, he wouldn't want to speak to a silly old tosser like you. So fuck off. Sling your hook.'

'Yeah,' Saskia snapped. 'Fuck off, you old fucker. And while you're at it, tell that daughter of yours she's dead next time I see her. The jumped-up little bitch.' She glared at Archie Cunningham, then pulled Susan away from the door and slammed it in Archie's face. Immediately, the doorbell started ringing. The Oswald girls ignored it and retreated to the front room where Saskia and Saraya collapsed on the sofa while Susan fell into an armchair that smelled of cigarettes and hairspray. Before them, Sunset and Sunrise were still comatose on the floor. The three older Oswalds looked at each other in silence while the doorbell continued to ring, then Saskia said, 'There's somebody at the door. There's somebody at the door,' and all three of them started laughing, though Susan had no idea why.

When the doorbell eventually fell silent, Saskia, Saraya and Susan fell silent as well. The three of them sat staring into space, their mouths open, their eyes wide and vacant. Then, suddenly, Susan got the munchies. She turned to her older sisters. 'Is there any more of that cake left? I am like totally starving.'

There wasn't any cake left. Other than two tins of beans and an out-of-date tin of spam, there wasn't any food in the house at all. Saraya, Saskia and Susan started searching for money instead. In a plastic bag under what was left of Bob Oswald's stash of marijuana, they found just under a thousand pounds. Susan was sent to the One Stop. She returned with frozen pizzas, frozen chips and twelve bags of Walkers Sensations. The three elder Oswalds ate and tripped out and smoked more dope. The two younger ones slept through the night. By seven o'clock the next morning, their sisters were unconscious as well.

Totally ignorant of this fact, Skunk Cunningham buttoned her school blouse with trembling fingers. Today, surely, the Oswalds were going to kill her. Not only had she still not paid any protection money, she had now attacked their father in front of Class 7D. As if that wasn't enough to be going on with, there would be no Mr Jeffries to save her today: he was bed-bound in the box room. Skunk had looked in on him earlier to say good morning. With his black eyes and swollen lips he had looked like something off of *Plastic Surgery Nightmares Gone Wrong* on Living TV. As she prepared to leave the house she silently mouthed *I love you Mr Jeffries thank you for trying to save my life what a pity your efforts were wasted* then shut the front door behind her and made her way off to her doom. It was a cold grey day. The first day of December. Potential Oswalds lurked around every corner. Skunk's heart pounded in her chest. Today, she was going to be murdered. It wasn't a question of if. It wasn't a question of when. It was simply a question of how: kicked to death? strangled? drowned in one of the toilets? Whichever. Whatever. She would be dead before lunchtime.

She knew this for sure. It was fact.

But she was wrong.

The school was empty of Oswalds.

It was also empty of Mr Jeffries. He lay in Cerys's box bedroom and gave a statement to two uniformed policemen while a supply teacher took his class and prattled on about nothing anywhere near as interesting as LIFE or ASPIR- ATIONS. Skunk's morning drifted on in a haze of boredom and daydreams.

In Drummond Square, however, the morning drifted on in a haze of flashbacks and nausea. Sunset put her head over the toilet and threw up for the umpteenth time. Sunrise put a hand on her shoulder. Downstairs, the older Oswalds were having a party. It was just after 11 a.m. They had been awake for nearly an hour. Saskia had just got back from Sainsbury's, where she'd spent a large wad of Bob's drugs money on crisps and cakes and lager and vodka and gin. Music pumped from each of the three stereos in the house. Susan sat smoking a joint.

'All this food and drink and weed isn't a bad way to spend a Friday,' she said, 'but what we really need is some boys.'

'Boys?' Saraya shook her head. 'You're boy mad, you are, Susan. A right little slapper.'

'Yeah,' Saskia said. 'How many men have you slept with?'

'I don't sleep with men,' Susan said proudly. 'I chew them up and spit them out.' She got her mobile phone out. Saraya chucked half a milk-chocolate Hobnob at her head.

''S nothing to be proud of. You're only fifteen years old.'

'So what if I am? You were at it when you were thirteen.'

'I was going through a stage.'

134

'I'm going through a stage.'

'You're going through most of Hampshire.'

'Fuck off, you fucker.' Susan got back to sending her text. It said: PARTY. SSN'S HSE. NOW. DITCH SKOOL. ALL INVTD. It went to the best-looking boy she could think of. His name was Jacob Lester. He was captain of the Year 11 football team. Within seconds of Susan sending it, he felt the message vibrate in his pocket. He pulled out his mobile phone, read Susan's text, then forwarded it to three of his mates. They forwarded it to their mates, who then sent it on to their mates. The message was sent on and on.

It was Jed who forwarded it to Dillon. It was Dillon who forwarded it to Skunk.

It was 3 p.m. by this time. Dillon was drunk on Special Brew. He had been at the party since lunchtime. Skunk read his message then texted him back: CAN'T GO TO OSWALDS. THEY WANT ME DEAD. Dillon texted back: OSWALDS WASTED ON BOOZE N WEED. BE COOL. Skunk texted him back once more: WHO ELSE AT PARTY? She got this reply: ME N JED N HALF OF SKOOL. It was true. The school had grown quiet since lunchtime. Skunk had wondered where everyone was. Now she knew. Nearly everyone had gone to the Oswalds'. Jed was there as well. He was drunk on Stella Artois. He liked Stella Artois. It tasted beautifully fizzy. It made his head feel all fuzzy. Before Susan Oswald got him started on Stella Artois, Jed had been pretty wound up. He'd kept saying, over and over, 'I can't be at this party, my old man's gonna kill me, especially after you lot tried to murder my sister. It's all right for you lot. Your old man's in prison. Mine's

135

not. He's a fucking nightmare. You lot. You don't know how lucky you are. It's an easy life being an Oswald.' Susan Oswald opened a can of Stella and sat down close beside him. She put a hand on his knee. 'Chill out, for fuck's sake. All you ever do is go on.' Jed refused to chill out, though. 'What were you doing beating my sister up anyway? For fuck's sake. She's only eleven years old.' Susan Oswald laughed and passed him her can of Stella. 'Look, you miserable fucker. I'm sorry we beat up your sister. All right? I won't let it happen again. Now, for fuck's sake, drink up, shut up, and chill.' Jed was totally chilled now. He'd had at least four cans. Dillon had drunk even more. Special Brew tasted like syrup. The Oswalds' party was cool. Everyone was too wasted to call him a pikey. It almost felt like he belonged. He drank some more and shut his eyes and wished Skunk was here to savour the moment. Around him, the room was a fog of smoke and writhing bodies. Three songs collided from the three stereos that were playing. The air smelled of weed and sweat and a spilled carton of chicken korma that was eating its way into the carpet. A hand landed on Dillon's knee. 'Why don't we go upstairs where it's quieter?' Dillon opened his eyes. Susan Oswald wasn't just talking to him. She was talking to Jed as well. She took both boys by the hands and led them up the stairs. The stairs were bare of carpet. There was no wallpaper on the walls. Saskia Oswald was passed out on the landing. Sunrise and Sunset were having a water-fight in the bathroom. Susan led Dillon and Jed into the wasteland of Bob Oswald's bedroom. It was the largest room in the house. There were guitars hanging on the walls and pictures of Hell's Angels around campfires or riding off into cherry-red sunsets that looked like fake tans sprayed on grey skies. A tatty old leather jacket with DEATH Tipp-Exed across the shoulders was nailed above the bed like the carcass of something Bob had killed. Susan shut the door and led the boys to the bed. She went and shut the curtains. In shades of filtered sunlight, she danced to an echo of the music downstairs. The boys stared at one another, then they stared at her. Jed said, 'What sort of bed's this then?'

'It's a waterbed. Do you like it?'

Jed nodded. Susan Oswald smiled, then walked over to the rocking chair in the corner. Her old man liked to sit here and play acoustic guitar. Susan sat and played with the rings on her fingers. She looked at the two boys before her. 'Ever played strip poker?'

Jed felt a stirring within him. He looked at Dillon, whose expression was swamped in the swathes of his pale pink hoodie. Across the room, Susan rocked gently backwards and forwards. 'I could teach you, if you wanted.' She tucked her hair behind her ears then got out of the rocking chair and walked towards the wardrobe with her shoulders back and her arms folded beneath her breasts. In a shaft of sunlight that was bursting in through the drawn curtains, she searched through a mess of Bob's T-shirts and jeans and boxers until she found an old deck of cards peppered with specks of cocaine. She took them to the bed and sat down between Jed and Dillon. 'Aces high. Dealer goes first. Winner takes nothing off. Lowest hand has to remove one item. He who busts loses two.' She shuffled the cards. She dealt the first hand. Jed stared at his cards. In his chest, his heart was pounding. His penis was rock hard. Completely massive. It felt like all the blood in his body had made its way into his Y-fronts. His heart was struggling to beat on a regular basis without it. He took a deep swig of his Stella.

Beside him, Dillon drank nearly all of his Special Brew. 'Twist,' he said, and then, 'Bust.' Dillon kicked off his trainers. Both his socks had holes in. One sock was red. The other was green. Susan looked at Jed.

'You sticking?'

Jed stared at his hand. He had a king and the nine of spades. 'I'm sticking.'

Susan looked at her hand. 'Twist,' she said, and then, 'Twist,' and then, 'Twist,' and 'Twist,' again. She kept looking at her hand. She was frowning. Jed noticed her eyebrows met in the middle. The hairs there were quite thick and wiry. Her eyelashes were thin. She looked up. She saw he was staring. She stared straight back and said, 'What does a two, a three, a three, a seven, another two and a four make?'

Jed frowned. 'More than twenty-one, I reckon.' He counted it out in his head: Two plus three was five and five plus three was eight. Eight plus seven was nine ten eleven twelve thirteen fourteen fifteen, plus another two was seventeen, and seventeen plus four made, 'Twenty-one, you jammy bitch.' Jed kicked off a trainer. Susan whooped and picked the cards up. She shuffled. She dealt out fresh hands. This time, Dillon stuck on nineteen, Jed stuck on eighteen, and Susan won with twenty. Jed took off his other trainer. When he and Dillon bust on the next hand, Dillon took his socks off. Jed removed his as well. In the back of his mind, he tried to work out how many items of clothing he had in the bank: one pair of school trousers, a pair of boxers, his school shirt and a loosely knotted tie. If he bust twice more, he would be naked. Oh God, he thought, oh fucking hell. He stole a glance at Dillon. Sockless, Jed guessed Dillon had boxers on under his trousers, which made two items. But what was under that hoodie? Jed could only guess. A shirt? A vest? Layer after layer of clothing? Jed had no idea. He turned his gaze to Susan Oswald. She was wearing stilettos, hot pants and a bra top. He wondered if the seven or so necklaces dangling around her neck counted as items of clothing. He was going home if they did.

Beside him, Dillon drained his Special Brew. He said, 'Anyone up for another drink?'

Susan said, 'Grab us a bottle of vodka. And see if there's any joints left.'

Jed said, 'I'll have another Stella.'

Dillon got off the bed. His movement sent ripples under the surface and nudged Jed and Susan together. Suddenly Susan kissed Jed on the neck, then the lips. She said, 'I read this magazine article once on how you can tell if someone loves you. They salivate when they kiss you. What does salivate mean?'

Jed had no idea. He kissed Susan Oswald again. Her breath stank and her spit tasted bitter. She probably hadn't brushed her teeth in days, but there was a certain mustiness about her, like the taste of an overripe banana, or coffee with too many sugars. The more Jed tasted it, the more he liked it. And Susan's body felt warm. Jed had never been this close to a girl in this way before. He had never kissed a girl in this way before.

Fourteen years of age, he was like a dog straining on a leash. The whole thing felt electric. It sent spasms up his spine. These spasms pushed him closer to Susan. She yielded. She lay down on the bed. Jed eased down beside her. The waterbed moulded a new shape underneath them and wrapped them up closer together. Jed put a hand on Susan's stomach. It was very flat. Her muscles were hard and springy. Jed moved his hand very slightly in a tiny, tentative circle. He wanted to move his hand upwards, he wanted to know how her tits felt, but he didn't quite have the nerve. Susan sighed. She pressed herself against him. She was all hands and hips and teeth and tongue and saliva and legs that got wrapped up in his legs. It was like kissing an eel. Then it was like kissing nothing, because Dillon was back in the doorway, and he had his arms full of booze.

'Look,' he said. 'I got vodka. And whisky. And Stella. And Special Brew. Special Brew's wicked. I like cough mixture, too.' He threw the drinks down on the bed. 'There ain't any drugs left. There's a bloke downstairs lighting farts.'

Susan sat up. She straightened her hair with the palms of her hands. 'What does salivate mean?'

Dillon frowned. Susan Oswald scared him. She had narrow eyes and her eyebrows met in the middle. The older Gypsy women at the campsite said girls with narrow eyes made terrible mothers. Skunk Cunningham had lovely wide eyes. Dillon wished she was here at the party. He opened his can of Special Brew and drank heavily while it foamed, then searched the pockets of his hoodie for his mobile. Beside him, Susan drank vodka like it was water. Jed sipped at a fresh can of Stella. He wished Dillon wasn't here. He wished it was just him and Susan Oswald, even though Susan Oswald made him feel slightly sick. Beside him, Susan dealt out the next hand. She and Jed drew with nineteen each. Dillon twisted till he bust, then kicked his trousers and his boxers off. Susan Oswald stared, but there was nothing much to see. Dillon might have been fifteen or sixteen, but he was so undernourished he could have been ten or eleven. And anyway, the swathes of his pale pink hoodie covered whatever he had to hide. What did Susan Oswald care though? Dillon was just a teeny baby pikey, sitting on the edge of the bed, wearing nothing but that ridiculous pale pink hoodie, sending texts to God knows who, drinking Special Brew like gone-flat Coca-Cola. She turned her attentions to Jed. He was cute. Quite tall. Not too spotty. He had well-cut hair and his clothes were well up with the fashion. She liked his eyes. They were blue, but not baby blue – they were a sky blue that made Susan dreamy and wet. There were other things making her wet: when Jed had laid down beside her, she had felt the length of his erection. It hadn't been huge, but it had been vibrant. Now, eager to see what it looked like, she dealt another hand. Jed twisted, he twisted, he stuck. Dillon stared at his hand for ages, then slowly toppled sideways and passed out on the bed. Jed shook him, but it was hopeless. Six or more cans of Special Brew had sent Dillon to the side of a stream in Ireland. Skunk was sitting beside him and they were skimming stones across the stream's surface. I love you, Skunk Cunningham. I love you, Dillon O'Hanlon. Sunlight glistened off the water. Beside him, back in the real world, the game carried on regardless. Jed lost another hand. He took his tie off. Then he lost another and took his shirt off. He felt self-conscious and stupid with his nipples on display and a tent pitching up in his trousers. He wanted to get up and run. He wanted to lie on his stomach and grind himself off on the mattress. But then Susan twisted, she twisted, she bust. Jed felt his heart start to hammer. He had never seen breasts before. Not real ones. Not live ones. Not perky little ones with nipples as hard as small stones. He sat very still in anticipation, then thought, no, she'll take off her shoes first . . . I'm just going to see her bare feet . . .

But Susan Oswald didn't take her shoes off. She slipped her bra top over her head then stepped out of her hot pants. She wore no knickers. Jed almost fell off the bed. Susan Oswald, naked, before him, except for her high heels and her pants hanging limp in her hands. She smiled. She opened her legs wide. Jed stared open-mouthed at her body. She threw her hot pants at his gawping face and then she threw herself at him. The two of them fell backwards. The waterbed jellied beneath them. They sank into its depths. Susan slipped a hand into Jed's trousers. She wriggled it into his boxers and took hold of his erection. Jed spasmed beneath the touch of her fingers. He felt hot, fluid sperm erupt from inside him. Susan Oswald laughed. She said, 'You did a bum's rush, you fucking prick.' Jed didn't know what a bum's rush was. He didn't care. It didn't matter. He kissed Susan Oswald's mouth that tasted of ripe bananas and coffee and put his hands on her tits. They were hard, unyielding. He soaked her nipples with saliva. Her hand was still stuck down the front of his trousers. Her fingers were dripping with semen. She tried to pull it out, but the angle of Jed's body wouldn't let her. And, anyway, why would she want to? Jed's erection hadn't faded. If anything, it had got harder. Susan Oswald felt her breath catch. This was different to blow jobs in McDonald's car park with tyres screeching and the smell of burgers and chips in her nostrils. This was a waterbed. This was a teenage boy, a rampant teenage boy, tongue on tits and hands on arse and hips thrusting away like Elvis Presley on speed. Susan used her other hand to undo his trousers. It was hard getting his boxers over the tip of his dick. It was hard keeping Jed still long enough to get his dick in her mouth. Once it was inside, though, he grew very still. He was speared like a fish on a hook. He eased to his knees on the waterbed with stinky-mouthed Susan Oswald bobbing up and down on his penis and her hands digging into his hips. Two feet away, Dillon lay comatose in nothing but his pale pink hoodie. Jed shut his eyes. He put his hands in Susan's hair. He made a soft, soft sound that was moaning but was never a moan. He thrust gently backwards and forwards. Susan's technique was fantastic. Her tongue. Her teeth. Her soft lips. Her hands massaging his balls. Oh God. This day was fantastic. Jed felt the sudden lightness of teenage boys when sex finally confronts them. Jesus, he thought, oh Jesus, I can do this. Except, he didn't know how to do this, so he sat back and let Susan Oswald blow him with his hands in her hair and his dick in her mouth and a stupid grin all over his face. After five or so minutes, Susan grew hungry for more. She rose up from her knees and pushed Jed down flat on the mattress. She kissed his mouth and as she kissed his mouth she got on top of his body and as she got on top of his body she slid down and slipped him inside her and Jed was swept into velvet darkness, soft tight wet velvet darkness, and Susan Oswald was happy because this was the way to be happy, with her hands on her hips and a boy buried deep down inside her, and the sensation of being needed, wanted, desired, spread an orgasm deep inside her and she yelled and tilted her head back and this was when Skunk walked into the room.

I stood frozen in the doorway. Neither of them saw me. Dillon didn't see me either. He couldn't have. He was unconscious. I was glad of that: he looked so stupid in his pale pink hoodie and no trousers that I couldn't bear to look at him. I looked at Susan Oswald instead. She was bent forwards on top of my brother so her back was hiding his face. I could see everything else though: she was rising up and then pushing down, rising up and then pushing down. Standing there, staring at them, I felt shivers running up and down my spine, and I felt cold, numb and cold, and dirty, and sick, and guilty; though I wasn't sure what they were doing, it looked like what they were doing was wrong. Not wanting to be anywhere near them, I turned and walked out of the room. They didn't see me leaving. They didn't see me arriving. They were totally oblivious to the fact I had been there. We all went our own separate ways.

In an attempt to forget about what she had seen, Skunk fled back over the road and rushed upstairs to play Xbox. As the computer's Darth Maul slaughtered her Anakin Skywalker, Jed continued to fuck Susan Oswald. He fucked her good and proper. Then he fell asleep. Susan Oswald lay breathless between Jed and the unconscious Dillon. She lit a cigarette and smoked it. Then she put Bob Oswald's tatty old dark blue kimono on and went downstairs for some food. Saskia Oswald stood and watched her make a crisp sandwich. She said, 'What's up with you?'

Susan said, 'Nothing.'

Saskia said, 'If nothing's up, why are you grinning?'

Susan took a bite from her sandwich. 'I've just had the shag of my life.'

'Not another one, Susan. Bloody hell. Who with this time?'

'Jed Cunningham. God. He's electric.'

Saskia lit a cigarette. 'Jed Cunningham? What? Not little Jed from over the road?'

'Little Jed's not little.'

Saskia took a sudden interest. 'Not like Rick Buckley . . .'

'Definitely not like Rick Buckley.'

'Really? How big we talking?'

'This big.' Susan held her hands apart. She exaggerated a couple of inches. Saskia remained unimpressed.

'That's not big. It's just normal. The barman down the Shamblehurst's hung like a horse compared to that.'

'It's not his size. It's how he used it. We did it for over an hour. Then, straight off, we did it again.'

Saskia relented. 'That,' she agreed, 'is impressive. Most of the blokes around here can't keep it up for five minutes.'

Susan finished her crisp sandwich then took a cigarette off Saskia. Around them, the kitchen was a mess of bottles and party food and unwashed pots and pans. A group of boys from Year 10 were slumped around the breakfast bar. A quarter-full bottle of whisky and two empties stood like monuments between them. Music pumped in from the lounge.

Teenagers sang along, a rabble of rising and falling voices orchestrated by Saraya Oswald, who was playing *Karaoke Hits Volume 3* and strutting her stuff with a microphone made out of a hairbrush that was full of loose strands of greasy blonde hair. The sink smelled of vomit and cigarette ash. Susan dragged on her cigarette and shut her eyes. 'There's nothing quite like a shag and a smoke.'

Saskia shook her head. 'You're such a fucking slut, Susan. I hope you've been using condoms.'

Susan looked at her sideways. 'Did you use one with Rick Buckley?'

'God, no. A thimble would've swamped him, let alone a condom. The loser.'

Susan took another drag on her cigarette. 'You know, Saskia, you've got a bloody nerve calling me a slut. At least I don't go around shagging losers.'

Saskia laughed out loud. 'Leave it out, Susan. I didn't shag him because I fancied him. I shagged him because Saraya bet me I wouldn't.' She pulled herself up on the work surface and lit a fresh cigarette off the butt of her last one. Good dope and a fair amount of gin had made her reflective and mellow. 'Whatever happened to Rick Buckley?' she asked no one in particular. 'I haven't seen that freak in years.' Saskia had no idea. No one had any idea. Not even Mr and Mrs Buckley had any idea. Poor old Mr and Mrs Buckley. They lived in the same house as a man who was rapidly falling to pieces, yet no one would tell them what treatment he was being given, what analysis he was being given, or what care he was being given. Once a month a community psychiatric nurse would come out to their house and ask to go upstairs to see him. Broken would let the CPN into his bedroom because some part of him grasped the link between his injections and the peace the field always offered him. The CPN would inject him in the left buttock then make his way back down the stairs. This was the one contact Mr and Mrs Buckley had with Broken's carers. Desperate for information, they would trail him down the stairs and out of the front door.

Mr Buckley: 'How's he doing?'

The community psychiatric nurse would shrug.

Mrs Buckley: 'Do you think there's been any improvement?'

Again, the community psychiatric nurse would shrug. Then he would start to walk faster. How the hell should he know how Rick Buckley was doing? How the hell should he know if there had been any improvement? He came out to these people who had become undone, unhinged, unstable, and he injected them in the left buttock and then he went home to a tower block in Portsmouth and sat watching TV through a Freeview decoder while he missed his mum and his dad back in South-East Asia. It wasn't his job to see how these people were doing. It was his job to make sure they were too drugged up to cause any harm to themselves or the general community. This seemed mad in itself to the community psychiatric nurse, but this was the way the English liked it. They made no attempt to cure these people. They made no attempt to understand what these people were going through. They made no attempt to help them recover. The policy was restrain, disarm and move on. This left the community psychiatric nurse with no answers except drugs, drugs and drugs, and as the community psychiatric nurse had no answers, the community psychiatric nurse answered no questions. He cited patient confidentiality and made his way back to his car.

Mr and Mrs Buckley stared helplessly after him, then went back into their house. Here, Mrs Buckley watched the omnibus edition of *EastEnders* while Mr Buckley dreamed about running away.

As they sat all alone in their front room, Broken Buckley lay in a field that sloped southwards and drifted through the sound of Saskia Oswald's laughter and an evening down the Shamblehurst Barn Public House two days after she had come on to him. Lying on his front in his bedroom, Broken remembered the barman grinning as he pushed his way through the large double doors.

'Hiya, fella. How ya doin?' A glint. Some sort of gleam in his eye. An occasional lover of Saskia Oswald's, the barman was just glad it wasn't *his* sexual dimensions being texted all over the south. As he poured Broken the pint of lager-shandy he had ordered, the barmaid working beside him said under her breath, Is that him? Is that Rick Buckley? Oh yeah, the barman said. That's him. Poor fucker. The barmaid suppressed a giggle. Poor *small* fucker. The barman gave Broken his drink. Broken drank it in silence. He caught snatches of conversation. He glanced at people who had never really been his friends but had never really felt like his enemies the way that they felt like his enemies today. Now, less than two years later, he lay on his side and he shivered. He remembered the whispers and sneers, the pinprick of tears. He remembered the message scrawled out by some wit with a marker pen above the urinal in the gents' toilets: *What's the difference between a pin and Rick Buckley? A pin's prick has a point!!!* Broken Buckley shut his eyes. He felt the breeze in the field all around him. He buried his face in dry grass. He had been sick for eighteen months now. It seemed like only yesterday. It seemed like earlier today. The taste of Saskia Oswald's saliva. The lilt of her voice as she said, *Like the car, soldier. Fancy taking me for a ride?* Why did she have to go and tell everyone? Why did she do that to him? Broken cupped his hands to his groin. *I feel dirty. I feel dirty. I feel dirty.* He wished it could be like before. But what was before? What had he been like before?

Innocent. Before Saskia Oswald, Broken Buckley had been innocent, a child, just the same as Skunk and Jed Cunningham from over the road were children. Sometimes, Broken saw them getting into their father's car, or making their way to school, or just hanging around in the sunshine. He watched them through a gap in the curtains. He wished he could be like them: just go back in time, be a child, be happy, be free. Poor old Broken Buckley. It was the closest he had to a dream.

Bob Oswald was released on bail at six fifteen that evening. A police constable he sold dope to on a regular basis dropped him off in his squad car. As the squad car pulled away, Bob Oswald stood before the tangled mess of his front lawn and stared up at his home. He sighed a huge sigh of relief.

It was good to be back. Better than good, fantastic. His own bed. His own supply of soft drugs. He started up the front path toward the front door and hummed along with the music blaring out of the house.

In the front room, Saraya sang along with it. As she sang along with it, she strutted her stuff through a mess of empty bottles and fag burns and vomit and crusts of half-eaten take-away pizza. The carpet was stained with spilled Indian food. Half-full cartons of Chinese bean sprouts slowly congealed where they sat. Saraya waltzed through this mess with a hair-brush in one hand and her hair held up in the other. Bob Oswald watched her from the doorway. God. She was a good-looking woman. Twenty years old. Big tits. Narrow hips. Lovely hair. She reminded him of her mother – God rest her poor drunken soul. Bob waltzed into the front room and joined in singing as well. Saraya whooped and threw her arms around him. Bob twirled her around a couple of times then went to check on the rest of his daughters. Saskia was asleep in the kitchen. Sunrise and Sunset were on the rusting old swings in the back garden. Susan had passed out face down on her bed. Bob stood over her and smiled. During his one night in a police cell, he had been worried sick about his daughters. What would they do without him? How would they cope? How would they survive? Did they have what it took to get by? Now he had found out the answer. His daughters hadn't simply survived, they had flourished. They had smoked all his dope and spent a fair wedge of his drugs money. They had thrown themselves a party and got drugged up, boozed up and virtually wrecked the whole house. Bob didn't have any complaints. They had acted as he would have acted. He wasn't annoyed with them. If anything, Bob Oswald was proud.

To celebrate this new-found sense of pride – and the fact bail hadn't cost him a penny – Bob Oswald threw an impromptu party that not only rivalled the one thrown by his daughters, it totally blew it away. By eleven o'clock that evening, Drummond Square was a mess of heavy, shiny motorbikes that littered the pavements and blocked up the road. Music didn't just blare out of the open windows, it pumped, and the sound of laughter and swearing and screaming rang out of every room. By two o'clock in the morning, seven separate phone calls had been made to the local police station, which was no longer twenty-four-hour. These phone calls were routed to a central switchboard and then bounced around the country until they were lost. Bob's party rolled seamlessly on until four o'clock Saturday afternoon. Then there was a bit of a lull. Then it kicked off again until the early hours of Sunday. As 'Ace of Spades' roared out for the sixteenth consecutive time, Mr Jeffries sat up in bed and said to Cerys, 'You know what, I wish he'd killed me. At least I wouldn't have to lie here and listen to this.' Cerys said, 'Just shut up and go back to sleep.' But Mr Jeffries couldn't sleep. No one in the square could sleep. The sound of the music was deafening, but there was much more than that to upset the neighbours: leather-clad rockers kept throwing up in people's gardens, or urinating in the middle of the square. Skunk was so scared by the noises crashing in through her window that she went and slept with Archie for the first time in nearly five years. He lay like a brick beside her and thought about Cerys next door with Mr Jeffries. Two rooms down the hall from his room, Jed was restless as well. He was sitting up playing Xbox and thinking about Susan Oswald. His stomach turned with elation and guilt and shame and desire. The noise of Bob

Oswald's party echoed through his head. It echoed through the whole house. It echoed through every house in the square. Some of the neighbours tried to phone the police again. Some of them put on headphones. Some went to stay with relatives or friends. A few of the younger, more stupid ones from the other Housing Association properties actually went over and joined in the party. In the Buckley house, however, the sound of the party was mostly ignored. There was another sound screaming out of the darkness that filled them with terror. It was the sound of Broken Buckley shouting WHY DID SHE HAVE TO GO TELL THEM? WHY DID SHE HAVE TO GO TELL THEM THAT? WHY? WHY DID SHE DO IT? WHY? WHY DID SHE DO THAT TO ME?

The high twist of his voice sent shivers up and down Mr Buckley's spinal column.

Mrs Buckley couldn't stand it either, but instead of lying on her back like her husband, she got out of bed and ran out to the landing. 'Who, Rick?' she called through his bedroom door. 'Who are you talking about, love?'

WHY DID SHE HAVE TO GO TELL THEM *THAT*?

'Tell them what, Rick? What?'

'Oh for God's sake,' Mr Buckley said from behind her. 'He doesn't know what. He doesn't know what he's talking about.'

'Shh,' Mrs Buckley snapped. 'He'll hear you.'

'How the hell can he hear me?' Mr Buckley snapped back. 'With that racket going on over the road? And what would it matter if he did hear me? He's as mad as a bloody hatter. It's not like he'll understand.' He stared at his wife. She stared at him. Then Mr Buckley shook his head and went back to bed.

Mrs Buckley stared after him, then sat down on the landing and put her back to her son's bedroom door.

'It's OK,' she said, very quietly. 'Listen to me, love. Listen very carefully. I don't know who *she* is and I don't know what's going on in your head, but I love you, Rick. I love you so very much.' She shut her eyes and said to him, 'I don't know what's the matter with you. I can't even start to imagine. But I want you to know that I love you and I will always love you. You're my son. I remember the night I conceived you. I remember the minute the doctor told me you were inside me. I remember telling your father I was pregnant with you and I remember the hug that he gave me and the tears that streamed down our faces when we realised that you would come true. Both of us love you as much now as we did then, Rick. Despite everything that's happened, despite what your father just said, both of us really do love you so very much. I want you to know that. I need you to know that.' She put the back of one hand against the door frame. She pressed her flesh to the grain. In his bedroom, Broken lay on his bed and pulled his pillow tight over his head. That music. God. That music was incessant. And the laughter. The sound of laughter. WHY DID SHE HAVE TO GO TELL THEM? I NEVER DID HER ANY HARM. These words were yelled into his pillow, which muffled them, killed them dead, but inside, where it mattered, these words echoed, just as the sound of Saskia Oswald's laughter echoed, just as the sound of breaking glass and revving engines and the duh-duh-duh of the bass line on the stereo across the square echoed on into the morning, when, finally, everyone at Bob's party except those who were too strung out to fall asleep fell asleep, and those who were too strung out to fall asleep found themselves sitting in silence around the kitchen table smoking joints and drinking whisky and staring into nothing without fully understanding there was nothing before them to stare at.

The dregs of Bob Oswald's party were gone by Monday evening. Life slowly returned to normal.

But, really, what was normal?

For Jed Cunningham, it was lying in his bedroom thinking of Susan Oswald's breath and the pit that was her vagina. It was listening to Mr Jeffries groan as he rolled over and felt his broken arm hurt. It was going to school and wanting to see Susan Oswald but not wanting to see Susan Oswald because he thought deep down inside that he was in love with Susan Oswald but couldn't quite understand why. It was hope and fear and pointless recrimination even though he had done nothing wrong.

For Bob Oswald it was getting legal aid from his solicitor and not really giving a fuck. So what if he had a court case pending? It meant nothing to him. ABH. GBH. Magistrates' court. Crown court. For fuck's sake. They couldn't even get their dates right; one week he was due to be called up in February, the next it was put back to March. Whatever. Whenever. As if Bob Oswald cared. Irrespective of whether they ever got around to prosecuting him for attacking Mr Jeffries, he doubted he'd end up in jail. And even if he did end up in jail, what was he likely to get? Six months at the most? That meant he'd be back home in three. Twelve weeks

away from his daughters? Wow. Big fucking deal. Bob Oswald
didn't care. He knew his daughters could look after themselves. He knew they'd get by without him. So he smoked his
dope, he threw his parties, and, if he ever saw Mr Jeffries
hobbling about in the street, he cupped his big hands to his
big mouth and he yelled: Next time I'll fucking kill you.
Harassing my fucking daughters. You're lucky you're not dead
already. And then he strolled into his house.

Mr Jeffries, on the other hand, glanced over his shoulder
in Bob Oswald's direction then hurried back into Archie
Cunningham's house. Normal for him was feeling drowsy
from painkillers. Normal for him was being cooped up in a
box room. Normal for him was watching daytime TV and
being waited on by Cerys: a cup of tea, a sandwich. She made
their bed. She washed his clothes. Mr Jeffries moped around
the house and read novels written by dead people. He planned
lessons for when he would be fit enough to go back to school.
He played solitaire or dozed afternoons away in an armchair.
He gave Cerys a frightening glimpse of what he might be like
to live with. Archie Cunningham, on the other hand, battled
his kids at Xbox. He laughed out loud at the telly. He stood
on the landing at 7 a.m. every day and stretched his big frame
and shouted, Good morning. He seemed to have something
about him. Cerys had never seen it before. But, then, she had
never really been looking. Even in the summer, when they'd
shared that drunken fumble, she had never really taken any
notice of him. He was in his forties. He was her employer. He
was getting fat and getting bald and he wasn't the sort of man
she thought she wanted. She wanted a man like Mr Jeffries.

She loved Mr Jeffries. Mr Jeffries was more her age. Mr Jeffries had a great body. Mr Jeffries was the man of her dreams. But now Mr Jeffries was in her bed every night and every morning and under her feet every day, Cerys suddenly wondered: What's so special about Mr Jeffries? She began to think, nothing much. He was quiet. He was moody. His arm hurt. His ribs hurt. He was bored. He was boring. As the winter dragged into December and Mr Jeffries' injuries kept him confined to the box room, she found herself spending less and less time in there with him. She had to make the dinner. She had to make Jed and Skunk's sandwiches for the next morning. She had ironing to do. She had shopping lists to write. She had Archie come on to her when they were watching the widescreen. It happened two weeks before Christmas. Mr Jeffries was asleep – as ever – upstairs. Jed and Skunk were in Jed's room playing Xbox. It had fallen to Cerys and Archie to put the Christmas decorations up and then drink three bottles of wine between them. Archie had been thinking about making a move on her all night. Whether it was the wine or the fact she was wearing a low-cut black top that really enhanced her cleavage, he wasn't quite sure, but as they bent down and reached up and passed each other baubles, he kept catching glimpses of her and remembering how good she had felt and how good she had tasted and wondering if he was in with a chance. Finally, when they were side by side on the sofa watching a rerun of *Porridge* on UKTV Gold, he made himself lean towards her. Part of him didn't want to. He didn't want to upset her. He didn't want to go behind Mr Jeffries' back. He especially didn't want the humiliation of being knocked back by a woman twenty years younger than he was who spent her nights in bed with another man in the room that was next to his room. In the end, though, he just couldn't help himself. He moved his mouth towards her and felt a surge of lust and hunger when she didn't pull away. He put his tongue in her mouth and then put his hands on her tits. She put her hands on his face and then pushed her body against his. The two of them tumbled sideways. Their mouths locked. Their hands pulled at each other's clothing. Then they were on the floor. His jeans were down. Her legs were in the air. He was pushing himself inside her: Oh my God, I've missed you. Fucking hell, I've missed you. It was quick. It was dirty. It was great. After, they rearranged their clothing and sat on the sofa in breathless sweaty silence. They shared Cerys's last cigarette. Then they both went up to their separate bedrooms. Archie lay on his back in cold darkness and thought fuck, fuck, fuck, fuck, fuck. Cerys lay next to the snoring Mr Jeffries and thought fuck, fuck, fuck, fuck, fuck. What a mess. What a terrible mess.

It was enough to drive a person insane.

As was Broken Buckley's illness.

Mr Buckley was beginning to glimpse this. His son's illness might well drive him insane. What was there in his life now? He lifted cold limbs. He dressed dry corpses in the clothes that their relatives brought him. He handed out tissues to those who had loved and had lost. And he thought, you lucky bastards. Go on. Enjoy it. Your funeral. Your wake. Your time of grief and remembering. Your sandwiches cut into triangles and your kind words from all those who love you. Go on. Go on and do what you need to. Put up your gravestones. Put up your pictures. Have your chats about the good old days when so-and-so was still with us and life seemed better and easier and death didn't seem quite so close. Have your moment of self-indulgence and grieving. I don't begrudge you at all.

And then he went home to his thinning wife and his son who was as dead to him as a corpse but not buried, not remembered, not grieved for, just haunting all the things he did, all the things his wife did, all the things they never did any more, and it was these things they never did any more that destroyed him, poor old Mr Buckley. His life became awful routine. He ended his working days by switching lights off on stiff corpses and then went home to do what they did, just lie and go cold and do nothing. Then, finally, one night, as Mrs Buckley sat across from him and strained to hear any sounds of movement floating down from upstairs, Mr Buckley studied her profile. He thought, my God, Veronica, you look so sad and so weary. Do I look so sad and so weary? He shut his eyes and he dozed. He woke up and it was bedtime and Broken was shouting WHY DID SHE HAVE TO GO TELL THEM? These days, Broken often did this, though sometimes all he did was sob loudly, and sometimes all he did was be silent, utterly silent, and at other times he did all of these things in rapid succession, and, every once in a while, he did none of these things at all. His madness had no pattern. It came out in different ways. Mr Buckley couldn't take it. He had to get away, if only for a short while. He said to Mrs Buckley, 'We should book ourselves a holiday. When was the last time we went away?'

Mrs Buckley snorted. 'It was three years ago last Easter. You and me and Rick went to Perranporth. Do you think he'd agree to come now?'

She stared at him. He said nothing.

'No,' she said. 'I don't think so either. And I'm not going without him. So why don't you go on your own?'

Mr Buckley said, 'I might do that.'

She nodded. Her lack of resistance was like a cold hard slap in the face.

Mr Buckley said, 'If I go, then I'm not coming back.'

And Mrs Buckley said, 'If you go, I wouldn't want you to.'

A stretch of silence followed. It was punctuated by the sound of sobbing from upstairs. Finally, Mr Buckley sighed. 'Well, then. That's that, Veronica, isn't it?'

Mrs Buckley said nothing.

Mr Buckley sighed once again. 'I'll move into the flat over the funeral parlour. It's been sitting there empty since Dad died.' He stared at her. She stayed silent. He stood up. He stretched his arms. He cracked his knuckles. He went upstairs and he packed. Mrs Buckley sat on her own in the front room. She did not cry. She did not feel angry. She did not feel sad. Maybe she felt disappointed, but if she felt disappointed, then disappointment felt normal. Life was disappointing. To her, it always had been. Disappointing teeth, disappointing breasts, disappointing parents who had failed to mask their disappointment in her. A disappointing career that had failed to reward her for all the effort she'd put in at university, in a field that had advanced so rapidly she hadn't been able to get another job after Rick had started school. A disappointing marriage in a disappointing house with disappointing neighbours who had pretty much cold-shouldered her since Rick's troubles had started. All topped off by a disappointing husband who shut the door very quietly as he left and never came back. Mrs Buckley sat all alone and she trembled. Even the manner of Mr Buckley's exit had been disappointing. He could at least have slammed the door.

Upstairs, Broken was silent. She looked up towards the ceiling. She said, 'Son, now it's just you and me.'

Very soon, this became normal. She cooked his meals. She left them to go cold on the landing. Broken never ate them. He sneaked out of his bedroom in the small hours of the morning and scraped meals together then. Mrs Buckley didn't care. While the meals that she cooked went uneaten, she sat on the top step of the staircase and talked to her son very softly. *Do you remember that time you went missing? You probably don't. You would have only been three years old. We had the whole square out looking for you. Things were different then. No Oswalds. A family called Perkins rented the Oswalds' house back then. Nice people. Very private. Liked to keep themselves to themselves. Still. They came and helped us look for you. Everyone came and helped us look for you. I was panic-stricken. I was sobbing in the middle of the square. Your father was beside himself. Everyone was so kind though. Even when we found you curled up asleep in the spare room, nobody said anything bad. They seemed to think it was a bit of a giggle. People carried you around on their shoulders, like you were a cup they had won.* Story after story. Day after day after day. And, yards away, all alone in his bedroom, Broken sat and stared in the mirror, or lay on his back on his bed, and heard these long-ago days whispered to him from under the doorway in fragments of sighs and hushed sadness.

Listening very carefully, he thought, it wasn't so bad being me once then. Once, being me was a good thing to be. And he tried to think, when was it? And then he thought, and when did it stop? And when did it change? And why? And how? And what for? Maybe with Saskia Oswald? Maybe when Bob Oswald beat him up in the square? Broken didn't know. He couldn't work it out. But in a fog of injections that suppressed his anger and distorted his psyche, he listened to his mother's invention of glorious, innocent childhood, and thought, if I could just get back to the way I was when I was younger, if things could just go back to the way that they were, if we could all just somehow go back through time . . .

Maybe I'd be OK then.

And these feelings. They became normal.

And that's what normal was, then.

It was the way that things were.

But normal, to Skunk, was the last Monday in January, when Mr Jeffries came back to school.

Maybe because he had virtually been living in their house for the majority of the time he had been off sick, she never really appreciated just how much she had missed him till he came back. She had though. She had really missed him. And so had the rest of his class. School just hadn't been the same without his off-the-cuff lessons and his way of talking that left them all wondering just what the hell he was on about.

161

DANIEL CLAY

That's why, almost two months to the day after Bob Oswald beat him to a pulp in front of their eyes, they gave him a standing ovation as he limped back into the classroom. Patinda had even bought him some flowers. He kissed her cheek, then held them up. 'Class,' he said, 'this is called a posy. This is what you buy for your mother on Mothering Sunday, or on occasions like this, when a friend needs a bit of support. Boys, on Valentine's Day, never buy a girl you want to impress a posy. Buy her roses. Twelve red roses. And when someone dies, you buy lilies. These things are called traditions. Traditionally, traditions were referred to as customs. Does anyone know why this changed? No? Well. I don't know why either. It's just the way things are.' Skunk stared at Mr Jeffries. How on earth did he do it? School had been like dry dirt in her mouth since he'd been gone. Now she wanted to learn once again. It seemed they all did – all with just one exception. That little trog Sunrise Oswald sat glowering at poor old Mr Jeffries. She didn't join in the applause when he limped in the door. She didn't heckle him either. She just sat there and bided her time.

Time.

It had not passed kindly for Sunrise. With Saskia and Saraya staying well clear of the playground, her power base had eroded, and as she could no longer use them as a threat when she demanded protection money from her form-mates, one by one, they stopped paying. Due to her total lack of pocket money, this rebellion was unwittingly started by Skunk. In the corridor where Sunrise had first attacked her, she was made to turn out all her pockets. 'If I ain't got it, you can't

162

have it.' Sunrise tried to think up a clever answer. When this proved to be beyond her, she punched Skunk in the face. It wasn't a very hard punch, but before she could stop herself, Skunk punched Sunrise back much harder, and was left staring in horror at what she had done. Sunrise stood holding the left side of her face and said, You're so fucking dead, Cunningham, but she didn't try to hit Skunk back. Instead, she stalked away with Fiona Torby trailing behind her. The rest of the class watched in silence, then filed back into class. Not a single one of them said it, but Skunk knew what they were thinking: she would be dead by the end of the week.

Thinking the same as the rest of the class, Skunk spent the next few days hiding out in toilets and classrooms, waiting for older Oswalds to kill her. Her evenings were spent trying to work out when they were most likely to do it, and praying they would at least make it quick. Somehow, though, it just never happened. With Saskia and Saraya keeping their distance, Sunrise only had Susan to turn to, but Susan wouldn't help her. She had problems of her own to deal with. Big problems. Big, ugly, adult problems. At 7 a.m. on the day after Mr Jeffries limped back into the classroom, she sat alone in the Oswalds' downstairs toilet and watched a pregnancy test turn blue. Her heart beat hard in her chest. Her spit went dry in her mouth. Oh Jesus. Oh Jesus Christ. Susan couldn't believe it. She hadn't even thought she was pregnant. It hadn't even been her pregnancy test. It had been Mrs McCluskey's pregnancy test. Poor old Mrs McCluskey. After sixteen years of taking the pill and desperately praying she wouldn't fall pregnant, she was now desperate to be a mother. She and her husband had been trying for almost a year; every weekday evening and four or five times every weekend. It didn't do any good, though. Despite all their very best efforts, Mrs McCluskey kept getting her periods. Then, one month, it didn't arrive. Mrs McCluskey couldn't believe it. She couldn't really be pregnant. A little baby. A little human being. A perfect beautiful angel of a baby. Growing. Inside her. She tried to contain her excitement. She waited a little while longer. Five weeks. Five and a half weeks. Still, she hadn't come on. Still, she couldn't believe it. She waited and waited and waited. Six weeks. Seven weeks. Eight. Then nine. And then, pressurised by her husband, she drove into Hedge End one Monday lunchtime and bought a pregnancy test from the same chemist she used to get her pill from. In her little blue Ford Fiesta she sat tight-breathed and read the instructions. For best results, these instructions told her in small white text that was almost impossible to read, do the test first thing in the morning. Mrs McCluskey told herself patience was a virtue and put the pregnancy test away in her handbag. Then she drove back to school and dreamed her way through afternoon lessons. A little blue line. That's what she wanted. Angela McCluskey for a girl. Adrian McCluskey for a boy. And, as she dreamed her dreams of blue wallpaper for a boy and pink wallpaper for a girl, Mrs McCluskey never noticed Susan Oswald's hand reaching into her handbag; she just felt a twinge, the slightest twinge, and by teatime the twinge was an ache, and by 7 a.m. the next morning Mrs McCluskey had woken to find her period had started. She lay on her back in soft darkness and cried all alone while her husband slept fitfully beside her. Poor old Mrs McCluskey.

She never did notice her pregnancy test had been stolen. Thanks to her monthly menstruations, she didn't need it again.

Across Hedge End, in the Oswalds' downstairs toilet, Susan Oswald did the test for a giggle, and found herself staring at a very strong blue line.

She thought, what's a blue line mean?

She looked at the hard-to-read small white text.

Oh, she thought.

Oh fuck.

Oh fuck, fuck, fuck, fuck, fuck.

She put the pregnancy test in the bin and pulled up her tracksuit bottoms. She flushed the toilet. She splashed her face with water. She walked out of the toilet. She didn't think, my God, I'm pregnant, even though she knew she was pregnant. Instead of thinking, my God, I'm pregnant, she pretended nothing had happened. Her reasoning went something like this: if she pretended she wasn't pregnant, then maybe she wouldn't be pregnant.

Deep down, she knew this plan was flawed. Susan wasn't stupid. She had half paid attention in sex education and she had seen enough episodes of *Trisha* to know unprotected sex caused HIV and babies. But, at the same time, Susan knew pregnancy tests could be wrong. It said so on the packet: 99.9% accurate. She thought about doing another, but according to the crumpled sticker on the thin edge of the box, the test had cost Mrs McCluskey eleven pounds fifty. Susan Oswald could get two packets of Benson & Hedges for less. She laughed as she smoked her way through them. Her. A mother. What a joke. What a total doss. For God's sake. She was only fifteen years old. Her old man still got child benefit for her. Parenthood could wait till these payments got stopped.

But, despite Susan's attempts to pretend otherwise, deep, deep down inside her, a tiny little foetus curled itself into a ball the same way Broken Buckley curled himself into a ball and tried hard to make himself smaller. The voices and the laughter and the incessant pressure were steadily getting worse. Broken didn't know why. He couldn't understand it. He couldn't seem to stop it. Mr Buckley couldn't stop it. He had left. The community psychiatric nurse couldn't stop it. He no longer administered injections. He had been transferred to another team within social services that dealt with sex education for the under-thirteens. In his place, a woman called Nadine Campbell took over responsibility for Broken Buckley's monthly injections. At the time Broken's file was passed over, Nadine was on long-term sick leave. Broken's file sat in a pile on the corner of her desk and dust gathered and madness strengthened and Mrs Buckley felt the brunt of it one Saturday afternoon as she sat on her knees on the landing and told a tale of a summer's day that had never happened when everyone had come up and told her what a beautiful baby her little Rick was. The door to his room swung open and Broken Buckley stepped out and grabbed Mrs Buckley's hair and screamed WHY DID SHE HAVE TO GO TELL THEM? I DIDN'T DO HER ANY HARM. Flecks of his spit hit her face. He put his hands on her throat. Mrs Buckley tried not to scream though she was hurting and she tried not to feel fear though she was frightened and she tried not to fight back though she knew that she should. Broken stared and stared and stared and then he called her a fucking whore and shook her by the throat and threw her across the landing and ran back into his bedroom. The slam of the door killed all sound.

Mrs Buckley stood all alone on the landing and took thin, shallow breaths. She put a hand to her chest, which was heaving. Then she straightened her clothing and sat down where she had been sitting before her one son had attacked her.

'It's OK,' she said very quietly. 'Mummy loves you, Rick. Mummy loves you so very much.' She put her head in her hands. She took deep, deep breaths. She said, 'Everything's OK.'

And everything was OK. Everything was normal. Oblivious to the Buckleys' problems, the people around them lived their day-to-day lives: Bob Oswald played his music and smoked his dope and did whatever he wanted. Saskia and Saraya Oswald watched daytime telly while they got out of their heads on the cider they bought with their social security payments. Sunrise Oswald did sporadic elements of Susan Oswald's paper round then dumped what was left down Shamblehurst Lane South. Mrs Weston from number 12 walked her dog. Skunk Cunningham played Xbox and thought about Mr Jeffries. Archie Cunningham drove home at lunchtimes and had sex with Cerys. Cerys waited for him under his duvet, naked, expectant, guilty, needing him in her again. After, the two of them lay side by side and smoked cigarettes and stared at the ceiling and didn't talk about where this was going. Then Archie got dressed and went back to work and Cerys showered and scrubbed and bathed her body in perfume while she fretted about Mr Jeffries. She had no wish to hurt Mr Jeffries, but she no longer loved Mr Jeffries. Now that his injuries had healed, she let him stay over less and less. On the few occasions he managed to persuade her, Archie lay all alone in his bedroom and hated the sounds that they made. In the room on the other side of Cerys's box room, Jed lay and listened to the sound of them together and jerked himself off over the memory of shagging Susan Oswald. At school, they all had their jokes about her. Bike. Slapper. Slut. Whore. Susan Oswald ignored them just the same as she ignored the cramps that she got in her stomach. She put the vomiting down to too much Tennent's Extra. She pretended she wasn't pregnant in the hope that it might go away.

Dillon had much the same attitude.

He tried his best to ignore Skunk in the hope that she might go away.

Because if she went away, the taunts might go away.

Paedo. Pikey. Paedo pikey cradle-snatching bastard.

And if she went away, the threats Chad Radleigh kept making towards him might go away as well.

Still, though, in solitary moments, he told her that he loved her. He held her hand and gazed in her eyes and said, Skunk, one day we'll run away to Ireland and get married and live by the side of a stream. But Skunk couldn't wait forever. And his version of love, well, it wasn't enough. She was at that age now – eleven, coming up twelve – where she wanted more than snatched moments whenever his so-called mates weren't around, so hour by hour, day by day, their love fell apart at the seams. It was slow and it was painful, but by the time Valentine's Day was upon them, their romance was a chaos of silence – hardly a romance at all – and, by the end of the last full week in February, when Dillon disappeared forever, Skunk hardly noticed he had gone.

Nobody in school did. Not the kids who had called him a dirty stinking paedo pikey bastard. Not Mr O'Driscoll. Not Mr Jeffries. Not Mrs McCluskey. Not even Jed, who was the last one to see him alive.

His aunt and his uncle noticed, though. Where is he? Where the hell has he got to? He could at least let us know that he's safe. They sat up in the cold winter shadows of Halfords car park and waited for him to come home. When, after a couple of days, he didn't, they put the word out that Dillon was missing. The fact no one had seen him hardly came as a surprise. The group was such an ever-shifting collection of caravans, motorhomes, transits and VW campers that Dillon could have gone off with anyone, anyone at all. Dillon's aunt and uncle tried to tell themselves he'd moved in with some other relative and busied themselves with worrying about their own children: one had just been arrested for theft, another was on the run for assault, and the rest were being investigated by the Department of Social Security for various benefit scams. Every now and then they would look at each other and shrug. Inconsiderate little bastard. Didn't he know they'd be worried? What was there they could do, though? They'd asked everyone they could think of, and there was no way they could go to the police, given the police were already looking for most of the people who lived on the site. They just had to sit and wonder.

Seven days after Dillon's disappearance, the Gypsies were served notice by Hampshire County Council that retail parks were not authorised traveller sites: move on within fourteen days. Not being overly bothered about fighting for their right to remain in the shadow of a shut-down Halfords, the Gypsies packed up the next day. As the last of the caravans pulled into the traffic queuing for the M27, Dillon sat wide-eyed in darkness. He breathed rapidly through his nostrils. An old pair of socks robbed his mouth of all sound. Hunger and thirst and terror and hatred made him feel empty and weak. Dillon made this sound: Nnnnnn. Nnnnnn. Nnnnnn. If Mrs Buckley ever heard him, she thought it was Broken Buckley, chanting, or mumbling some sort of prayer. She sat down on the landing and said, *I don't suppose you remember but a Gypsy woman once stopped me in the street when you were a baby and said you'd grow up to do brilliant things.* Behind her, the sausage and mash and onion gravy she had cooked for his dinner went cold and then stale and then hard. Beyond it, inside Broken's bedroom, Broken sat and stared into the wardrobe. Dillon sat in and stared out. He was tied in a huddled position under hanging suits and shirts and trousers Broken hadn't worn in almost two years now. Dust drifted down from them like a thin haze of nuclear snow. Broken rocked backwards and forwards. He said, very quietly, 'I was once like you. Things never used to be quite so painful. WHY DID SHE HAVE TO GO TELL THEM? I NEVER DID HER ANY HARM.' And Dillon stared narrow-eyed into madness and made this sound: Nnnnnn. Nnnnnn. Nnnnnn.

And Jed said, I told you so.

Skunk stared at the empty car park and piles of rubbish and dog shit and a stark blood-red spray-paint message that said GYPPOS FUCK OFF HOME. She said, 'He could have at least said goodbye.'

Jed said, 'I told you not to get involved. I said they'd be moving on soon.'

Skunk said, 'He could have at least said goodbye.'

I tried to pretend I wasn't bothered. I tried to tell myself Dillon was just a little pikey waste of space who looked dumb in his pale pink hoodie. I tried to convince myself I was better off without him. And, anyway, I loved Mr Jeffries. He made school time fun. Each day he told me something new, something I would never have imagined till he explained it to me. I never knew, for instance, that people used to believe the earth was flat, or that the UK used to own America, or that one man's terrorist is another man's freedom fighter. I never had a clue, until Mr Jeffries told me.

Things are different now, though.

I know everything now.

For instance, I know Broken Buckley never abducted Dillon. Poor dumb helpless Dillon. He went and abducted himself.

Dillon abducted himself while he was waiting for Jed to bring him a duvet.

He was waiting for Jed to bring him a duvet because it was freezing in the caravan and Dillon was sick of being cold through the long winter nights with nothing more to warm him than the swathes of his pale pink hoodie. Obviously, he had tried to steal himself a duvet, but he hadn't appreciated the sheer size of the average duvet – even a thin single summer duvet couldn't be hidden in the folds of his pale pink hoodie.

Instead of stealing himself a duvet, Dillon robbed five Xbox games out of Dixons and offered to swap these for Jed's duvet.

Jed, to his credit, hadn't quite been stupid enough to give away his own duvet. He went up to the attic and took one of the spare ones. Then he hit his first problem: Cerys was in the kitchen, smoking cigarettes and cooking dinner. Jed had to think of a way to distract her before he could get the duvet out of the house. Unable to think of a way to distract her, he played Xbox until Cerys went through to the lounge and sat down to watch *Weakest Link*. With her back turned to the front door, Jed took the spare duvet down the stairs and out into the street, where he had agreed to meet Dillon.

But Dillon was nowhere to be seen.

Dillon was nowhere to be seen because he was inside Broken Buckley's bedroom.

He was inside Broken Buckley's bedroom because he had noticed the Buckleys' front door was wide open.

The Buckleys' front door was wide open because Mrs Buckley had gone to the One Stop.

Mrs Buckley had gone to the One Stop because she had forgotten to buy eggs for Rick's tea.

Mrs Buckley needed eggs for Rick's tea because she was making him egg and chips.

Mrs Buckley was making egg and chips for Rick's tea because, as a child, Rick had loved egg and chips. He had especially loved to dunk his chips in the unbroken yolk of his egg. Mrs Buckley had peeled the potatoes and sliced them into chip shapes and put them in the chip pan and got out the frying pan for the eggs when she suddenly looked up at the ceiling and put both her hands to her mouth. She had completely forgotten to buy any eggs. She was just so forgetful these days. What on earth was the matter with her?

Pressure. Pressure was the matter with Mrs Buckley. She was tired. She was on edge. She missed Mr Buckley. She was worried sick about Rick. It was no wonder she was forgetful.

But Mrs Buckley didn't think this. She only felt annoyed with herself. Rick must have eggs for his tea. She shook her head and took off her apron and got her purse and made her way to the One Stop. Preoccupied with why she was getting forgetful, she forgot to shut the front door. Leaving it open behind her, she stepped out of the house and walked out of Drummond Square and up Drummond Road and crossed Shamblehurst Lane South to the One Stop where she exchanged small talk with the woman who was so poor she had to work the eight-till-late shift as well as an early shift at McDonald's. Wasn't it cold today? Would this rain never end? By the time Mrs Buckley got home, the front door was no longer open. Dillon had shut it behind him as he entered the Buckleys' dark hallway. *Hello? Anybody home?* Dillon got no answer. He went through to the kitchen and the dining room and the living room and then he checked out the conservatory and the downstairs toilet and then he made his way up the stairs. His heart was beating fast as he did this because he was thinking he might not have to swap the computer games he had stolen from Dixons for Jed's duvet after all. He was thinking he could steal himself a duvet from the Buckleys'.

Dillon felt almost excited. It had always been his ambition to rob a house. His dad had been a housebreaker. And his dad's dad. And his dad's dad's dad before him. As well as feeling excited, Dillon also felt slightly embarrassed. It seemed a bit sad to be robbing his first house of nothing more exotic than a duvet. It was hardly the sort of thing he could impress the other kids at school with. But needs must, and Dillon needed a duvet. It was freezing in the caravan. He hadn't slept properly in weeks.

And, besides, there might be other stuff he could take once he'd got himself a duvet. Money. Jewellery. Credit cards. Ornaments. A video player or DVD. Anything he could carry. He could spend the money on some new clothes. He could give the jewellery to Skunk to show her how much he loved her. His aunt and uncle could fence the rest for a share in the profits. First, though, he had to get hold of a duvet. He opened the door to Mr and Mrs Buckley's bedroom and took a good look at their duvet. It was huge – king-sized at least. Dillon would take it if he had to, but he wanted to check the other duvets in the house first. He cast a quick glance towards the jewellery box on the dressing table, then backed out of Mr and Mrs Buckley's bedroom and went into the next room. The bed in there was stripped bare, as was the bed in the next room. Dillon made his way towards the last but one room on the landing. Unlike the other rooms, this door wasn't shut. Also unlike the other rooms, there was a plate of sandwiches on the floor. All of them were uneaten. Dillon stared at them for a moment, then stepped into the room. It had a peculiar smell of confinement. Shadows overlaid the crumpled pillows and the duvet Dillon had already decided to take with him – it was single, the same as his bed was, and looked heavy and comfy and warm. Dillon stepped eagerly towards it and gathered it up in his arms. It was then that he heard the sound of a toilet being flushed, followed by the sound of a door being opened. Dillon dropped the duvet and turned to run, but there was already somebody standing in the doorway, tall and gangly, with long tangled hair and wide wet weary eyes. The man stared at Dillon, then took a step forwards and screamed without saying a word. Dillon stumbled backwards. His legs hit the bed and he fell. He turned and tried to rise up, but felt two long, thin arms grab at him from behind. A weak voice whispered, 'Who are you? Did he send you?' Dillon tried to scream, but a hand clamped over his mouth. Dillon tried to kick, but instead of being lifted, he was being pushed, face down, and he had no power to kick with, only terror, raw terror, and hot oily panic, like heartburn, in his throat.

Again, Dillon tried to scream, but the full weight of a grown man was pushing down upon him, and any sounds he made were muffled by the duvet that had been his reason for coming here in the first place. Still panicked, he tried to struggle, to break free, but the man was too strong. All Dillon could do was lay trapped underneath him. Beyond that, he just couldn't think.

Neither could Broken Buckley. He sat on top of the young boy he had pinned underneath him and didn't know what he should do. This was a frightening development. Other than the CPN, no one ever came into his bedroom any more. It was his place. A safe place. A sacred place. A place where Bob

Oswald couldn't attack him. Now, though, it had been invaded. Now, though, Broken felt invaded. He couldn't think what he should do. He sat very still on top of his attacker and decided it was best to do nothing. But then, he realised, he had to do something. There was a young boy in his bedroom. Broken didn't want this young boy to be in here. The young boy didn't seem to want to be in here: he struggled; he kicked; he sobbed. But despite the fact Broken didn't want the boy to be in here, and despite the fact the boy didn't seem to want to be in here, Broken could hardly let him go. The boy might go and tell Bob Oswald where he was. Broken shivered. He shuddered. He couldn't let the boy do that. He had to keep the boy here.

Acting without thinking, Broken made a fist out of his hand and punched the boy in the back of the head.

The boy screamed. Broken gasped. The pain in his hand was immense. He lifted it high. He let go of the boy. The boy made a run for the door, but he was dizzy and groggy and breathless. Still, though, he very nearly made it. Broken was jerky and twitchy and rusty from hiding away in his bedroom. His thought process was slow and confused. For instance: his hand hurt. Why on earth did his hand hurt? It hurt because he had hurt it. How on earth had he hurt it? That's right. Now he remembered. He had hurt it by punching that boy in the back of the head. What boy? That boy. That boy in his bedroom. What boy in his bedroom? Ah. *That* boy in his bedroom. The one stumbling sluggishly towards the door.

Suddenly remembering, Broken leapt at Dillon. He caught him a blow to the shoulder.

Dillon twisted. He fell sideways. He hit his head on the

door handle. A dull smudge of blood appeared on the dusty brass plate as the door gently swung shut behind him.

Slowly, Dillon slid downwards.

Broken stood frozen above him. He was suddenly transported to a hot summer's day. Bob Oswald was standing above him. Bob Oswald was dredging up phlegm. Broken flinched. He covered his face up. He yelled through his fingers: WHY DID SHE HAVE TO GO TELL THEM? I DIDN'T DO HER ANY HARM. The pain and the pressure swelled in him. I DIDN'T DO HER ANY HARM. Broken staggered. He turned. He threw himself down on his duvet. He buried his face in dry grass. A gentle breeze caressed the back of his neck. Birdsong. So calming. It soothed him. No strange boy in his bedroom. No thoughts of Bob Oswald's anger. Nothing but soft grass and breeze. Broken felt warm. He felt safe. Then he heard the slam of the front door. His mother shouted, *I'm home*. The sound of her feet in the kitchen dragged Broken back out of the field. He lay all alone in his bedroom and heard an echo of Saskia Oswald's laughter. *I could have more fun with my little finger*. The hard mocking tone in her voice: *You could fuck my belly button with that*. Broken yelled bitterly into the duvet: WHY DID SHE HAVE TO GO DO IT? WHY DID SHE DO THAT TO ME? The duvet muffled his words and his pain and his anger. He curled his knees tight into his stomach. He lay very still on his side. Deep breaths. Deep breaths. Birdsong. The breeze. The smell of grass. Like a dream. Too thin to sustain him. The sound of Saskia Oswald's laughter. Oh no. Not you again. Broken sobbed. He shook. He quivered. He rolled over onto his front. The field sloped southwards before him. Dillon lay unmoving within it. Broken stopped moving as well.

Downstairs, completely regardless, Mrs Buckley fried eggs and cooked chips and carried this food up the stairs.

'Rick. Your dinner's ready. Egg and chips. Your favourite. Rick? Your favourite.'

No answer.

Just silence. Just woodgrain.

Mrs Buckley placed the plate on the carpet.

She sat with her back to the door.

And, gently, she started to talk:

I don't suppose you remember when you used to play for Hedge End Under-Fourteens . . .

A pause here. A moment of silence. Mrs Buckley folded her hands in her lap and continued.

Do you? Do you remember? Oh, me and your dad were so proud. We used to go down and watch you play. One time, I remember, you had to play up front, because the normal striker was injured. Three goals you scored. A hat-trick, your dad called it. Oh Rick . . . we were so proud . . . we are, love. We're both still so proud of you . . .

Mrs Buckley smiled. She shut her eyes. She talked very softly, very gently, about things that had never happened, times that had never been, and Broken lay curled in a ball in his bedroom and thought, maybe it wasn't so bad once, maybe it was OK to be me . . .

And then he thought, when was that?

And then he thought, when I played for Hedge End Under-Fourteens.

And then he thought, how old would I have been then?

And then he thought, well, I must have been twelve or thirteen.

And then he sat up and looked down on Dillon.

Dillon looked twelve or thirteen.

His face was very smooth and his shoulders were narrow and underdeveloped.

Lying in Broken's bedroom, curled up in the corner, Dillon looked peaceful, at one with the world.

Like Broken, when Broken had been twelve or thirteen.

Untroubled. Unbent by the world.

Broken got up off his bed. He moved cautiously over to Dillon. He knelt down close beside him. Dillon didn't move. He was breathing like he was sleeping – gently, in and out. Broken could smell his breath. It smelled sweet. Dillon's face looked sweet. There was no anger to it. There was no nastiness, either. There was no shadow of Bob Oswald's violence or Saskia Oswald's laughter.

Broken wished he could feel the way Dillon looked: peaceful, untroubled, relaxed.

Broken wished he could change places with Dillon.

He wished he could go back to a time when he didn't feel like he felt now.

Without thinking what he was doing, Broken put his mouth to Dillon's mouth and drew Dillon's innocence out. Dillon's breath tasted as sweet as it smelled. Broken sucked it deep down inside him, then squeezed Dillon's nostrils shut and blew his own misery in. This breath was a long, hot, drawn-out one. It may well have gone on forever, but a lack of air

DANIEL CLAY

forced Broken to end it. He sat back. He breathed in very deeply. Then he stared down on Dillon. He felt a connection between them. A bond. An unbreakable force. Dillon was what it had been then, to be Rick, before Rick became Broken.

Broken sighed. He shivered. He reached out. He touched Dillon's shoulder. He pulled Dillon close in towards him. He sucked Dillon's innocence out. He blew his own misery in. And, gently, as he did so, the breeze whispered through the meadow and the sun grew strong in the sky. The sound of birdsong strengthened. The sound of unhappiness receded. Gently, it faded away.

And this, then, was salvation.

To suck innocence in.

To breathe misery out.

Broken sensed it. He knew it. He had the solution. Here it was, in his bedroom. He just had to keep it nearby. He just had to keep it from slipping away.

Gently, ever so gently, he eased Dillon back down to the carpet, then searched through the mess of his bedroom. He took the cord from his pyjamas and the sash from his pale blue bathrobe. He used these to secure Dillon's ankles and hands. Then he forced a rolled-up pair of socks into Dillon's mouth. Dillon snorted. He snuffled. Broken lifted him into the wardrobe. It was at this stage that Dillon woke up. He tried to struggle, but it was useless. His hands and his feet were tied. Around him, the darkness was stifling. Dillon screamed. Nnnnnn. Nnnnnn. Nnnnnn. Broken stared down on him. He said, It's OK now, she can't laugh at us any more. Dillon screamed. Nnnnnn. Nnnnnn. Nnnnnn. Broken pushed the wardrobe doors shut. He laid himself down on his bed. From underneath his doorway, Mrs Buckley's voice droned on. From outside, in the square, there was the sound of cars and pushbikes and the tinkle of an ice-cream van. Broken lay and listened to these sounds. Dillon sat and listened to these sounds. Skunk sat and listened to these sounds as well: she was maybe a few hundred yards from Dillon, eating, sleeping, breathing, yet she had no idea he was missing. Once she had accepted the fact he had left her, she didn't give him a second thought. Nobody gave him a second thought. They all had their own problems: Archie with his rabid desire for Cerys that made him feel guilty and grubby; Jed, with his task of getting the spare duvet back into the attic and his love for Susan Oswald; Skunk, with her homework to do when all she wanted to do was play Xbox and dream about Mr Jeffries; and, most of all, Mr Jeffries, whose heart was about to be torn into two.

It was about to be torn into two by Cerys.

Which was ironic, really, because Mr Jeffries was just starting to want all the things Cerys had always wanted: marriage, a place of their own, and babies. Over the past few months, the desire for these things had ambushed Mr Jeffries completely. Part of the reason for this was the amount of time he was spending with children. Mr Jeffries couldn't believe how much he now loved being a teacher. Sure, the curriculum was stifling, the paperwork was exhausting, some of the kids could be shits, but the feeling he got from explaining something new to a kid like Patinda Patel or Skunk Cunningham was electrifying. It made him feel new and alive.

Surviving Bob Oswald's attack had also left Mr Jeffries feeling new and alive. Sometimes, he relived standing by the white-board as the classroom door flew open and Bob Oswald came charging towards him. He had thought he was going to die. He hadn't died, though, and survival had opened his eyes: where was his life going? Twenty-seven years old, renting a flat in a crappy little suburb of Southampton, no roots, no long-term plans for the future: was this a good way to be living? Mr Jeffries had once thought so, but, suddenly, he wasn't so sure.

The final persuader had been convalescing at Archie Cunningham's house. Mr Jeffries had never lived in a nice house before. He had never lived with young children before, either. Jed was a really nice kid, but Skunk – well, if Mr Jeffries could choose the sort of child he would father himself in the future, it would be a clone of Skunk Cunningham. She was smart, bright, questioning, interested in everything, consid-erate, a pleasure to teach, lovely to be around, and, what's more, she had mainly been brought up by Cerys. Although Mr Jeffries knew he couldn't have Skunk Cunningham for a daughter, he did know he could have the woman who had moulded her for a wife. It was the logical next step for him. He began to trawl jewellers' shops in his lunch break.

But each day, as he did so, Cerys removed her jeans and her T-shirt and knickers and slipped under Archie Cunningham's duvet and waited for him to sneak home in his lunch break and make love to her. Archie Cunningham sneaked home as fast as he could and slipped his key in the door and slipped out of his suit and then slipped himself into Cerys. The days of drunken fumbles were over. They made love in leisurely silence, their tongues probing, their finger-tips stroking, their bodies comfortable with the rhythms they had learned to enjoy. Cerys bit Archie's shoulder whenever she climaxed. Archie said her name softly into the cleft of her neck and her shoulder. And, after, as the last rain of winter hit hard against the windows or the first sunshine of spring flooded in through the net curtains, they lay side by side and talked about how much they wanted to be together and what they were going to do about Mr Jeffries. At night, on the few occasions Cerys relented and let Mike stay over, she lay fretting beside him as he slept on unaware. She had never dumped a lover before. She didn't know how to go about doing it. What was she meant to say? How was she meant to bring it into a conversation? She didn't know. She had no idea. She only knew she was dreading doing it and, the more she dreaded doing it, the more snappy she got with Skunk.

'Come on, Skunk. You're late. Get a move on.'

Skunk was late because she'd been up all night playing Xbox.

She'd been up all night playing Xbox because it was the one thing that stopped her from thinking about Mr Jeffries. Ever since he'd saved her from certain death at the hands of the Oswalds, Skunk had thought about nothing but Mr Jeffries. Only playing Xbox took her mind off Mr Jeffries, and when she wasn't playing Xbox, thoughts about Mr Jeffries roared like a whirlwind inside her, just going around and around in her head. She felt tense and jittery and sick. She was sub-merged in all things Mr Jeffries, which meant she never thought about Dillon, tied up in a wardrobe, and she never thought about Broken, sat in a heap before Dillon, saying, I'd like to be young again, and she never thought about Archie, all alone in his bedroom, dreaming about his future life with Cerys, and she never thought about Cerys, lying sleepless beside Mr Jeffries, dreading finishing it with Mr Jeffries, and she never thought about Susan Oswald, getting too swollen for her combats, throwing up in the mornings, craving more Bensons than she could nick from the One Stop.

She never thought about anything except Mr Jeffries and Xbox.

Which meant she got good at Xbox.

Which meant Jed got mad because Skunk kept beating him at *Star Wars* – not just beating him, but trouncing him, completely. One Wednesday evening two weeks after Dillon disappeared, Jed threw his Xbox control at her and yelled, 'For fuck's sake, Skunk, you're cheating.'

She threw her Xbox control at him and yelled, 'Fuck's a bad word, and how the fuck could I have been cheating?'

They stared at one another, then Jed yanked the door open and shouted, 'Get out. Just cos you're missing Dillon.'

And she shouted, 'I ain't missing Dillon. You're just in love with Susan Oswald.'

And Jed punched her, properly punched her, really hard in the small of her back.

Skunk staggered from Jed's bedroom and went through to her own room and lay on her front and she sobbed. Jed stayed in his room and lay on his back and he sobbed. Cerys and Mr Jeffries pretended they couldn't hear them as they lay side by side after making love for the very last time. Mr Jeffries sighed with contentment. Cerys felt she'd just cheated on Archie Cunningham in the way she used to feel she'd cheated on Mr Jeffries. She cleared her throat and said, 'Mike.'

'Wait,' he said. 'Don't say a word. Just close your eyes.'

'What? No. I don't want to.'

'Go on,' he insisted. 'Close your eyes.'

She looked at him. He was leaning up on one elbow. His hair was all in his eyes. He had a boyish grin on his face. Cerys knew this was the moment: no more putting it off, no more dodging the issue. She took a deep breath and tried to find the words she needed to end it.

But, before she could do so, Mr Jeffries took hold of her left hand and slipped a ring on her wedding finger.

'Cerys, will you be my bride?'

She shut her mouth. She stared at him. Then she stared at the ring on her wedding finger. It sparkled like freshly shed tears. Mr Jeffries grinned and leaned forward to kiss her, then frowned as she pulled away.

'Mike,' she said. 'I'm sorry.'

'Sorry?' he said. 'Why are you sorry?'

'I'm sorry. The answer's no. I don't want to get married to you.'

He stared at her a moment. She watched his frown turn into a scowl. 'You don't want to get married to me?'

'I don't want to get married to you.'

'But . . . but I thought you wanted to get married. I thought that's what you wanted. A wedding. A place of our own. Some kids. That's what I'm saying, Cerys. I want us to do all these things.'

'I know what you're saying,' she said. 'And I'm sorry.' It seemed to be all she could say.

'Fucking hell, Cerys.' Mr Jeffries sat up. He pulled on his boxers. He sat with his elbows on his knees and his chin in his palms. His hair hung in his eyes. Cerys couldn't stand to look at him. She rolled over and stared in the opposite direction. The two of them wallowed in silence. Finally, Mr Jeffries got up and began to get dressed. He said, 'I'm going home.'

She said nothing.

'I'll come back tomorrow evening. We'll talk about this some more.'

She stayed silent. She kept her eyes fixed on the wall. Finish it now, she thought. Tell him it's over. Tell him it's finished. But she didn't have it in her to do it. She shut her eyes and listened to the sound of his leaving. It seemed to take him forever. He couldn't find his socks. He couldn't do his shoes up. His hands were shaking too much. Finally, he was ready. He looked down at her from the doorway. She was lying with her hair spread over the pillow and her hands raised to cover her eyes. She was still wearing the engagement ring he had slipped onto her finger. It looked good on her. It suited. Perhaps, tomorrow, she would accept it. Perhaps, tonight, his proposal had come as a shock. She had panicked. She had refused out of fear. Or maybe she just didn't want him? Mr Jeffries sighed and pulled the door shut. He made his way down the stairs. He let himself out of the house and made his way to his car, which was parked in the lay-by to the left of the Buckleys'. He stood outside it for a moment with his head in his hands. Why didn't she want to marry him? What had happened? What had changed? Poor old Mr Jeffries. He thought his life was in turmoil. He didn't have a clue. Dillon's life. That was in turmoil. Poor old Dillon. He battled. He struggled. He fought. And, as he fought, he thought: Do I breathe? Do I beg? Do I scream? What's happening to me? What have I done to deserve this? Oh Skunk. Oh Auntie. Oh Uncle. Somebody. Anybody. Please. I'm starving. I'm starving to death.

But no matter how hard he fought – no matter how hard he thought – he sat in the dark, he grew cold, he grew starving.

And, slowly, he began to starve towards death.

It was a long drawn-out process. Sometimes Broken fed him. Sometimes Broken held a glass of water to his lips. These times were sporadic. The gaps between them grew longer as Broken fell apart more and more. Dillon sat tied in the wardrobe. His body ate up the meat in his muscles. His throat robbed his tongue of saliva. Darkness deepened. Fear grew. Steadily. Minute by minute. All alone in the wardrobe. Drifting. Dreaming. The sound of fast-running water. Thirst, unquench-able thirst, a thirst that left Dillon blinking and dozing and waking up by the side of a stream. He stared down on clear cool fast-running water. He dipped a hand into its flow. He lifted it. He licked his fingers. So cold. So perfectly cold. Dillon's head nodded forward. He picked at soft warm bread. He chewed it and chewed it and chewed it. He drank from the stream once again. He looked up at clear blue sky. Was this Ireland? Had he made it to Ireland? He took a closer look at his new surroundings. White clouds. Cows grazing. Skunk on his left. His sister on his right. They talked across him, like he wasn't there. Hello? Hello? Can you hear me? Am I real? Do I exist? His tongue felt too thick to speak with. He swallowed. He gagged on his thirst. Around him, the sound of fast-flowing water. The sun shone bright off its surface. If Dillon could just move his lips to the water . . . But he couldn't move his lips. Or his head. Or his hands. Or his feet. He was tied. Dillon was tied. He was gagged. He opened his eyes. He found himself back in the wardrobe. No dead sister. No Skunk. No nothing. No nothing at all.

And he went, Nnnnnn. Nnnnnn. Nnnnnn.

He pulled hard on his bindings.

He sobbed weakly, very quietly.

He kicked feebly.

His head spun.

His throat ached.

His body shuddered.

And Mr Jeffries said, 'Class, I'm not feeling very well today so I want you all to sit quietly and write me an essay. The title of this essay will be "What I Want To Be When I Grow Up". And, as I'm not feeling very well, you're all going to write this essay in total silence. I'm not going to hear a peep from a single one of you. Have I made myself clear?'

Class 7D looked nervously at each other, then opened their exercise books and started to write – even Sunrise Oswald. Mr Jeffries sat back and watched them for a moment, then leaned forward and put his head in his hands. He stayed that way for the rest of the lesson, then stayed in the same position while the class filed out of the room. Those who had finished their essays put their exercise books on his desk. When, finally, the classroom was empty, Mr Jeffries sat up and pulled the essays towards him. He flicked through them with growing disdain. Sunrise's read: *When I grow up I wanna go on the social.* Patinda's said she wanted to be a biochemist, the same as her mum and her dad and her brothers. Fiona Torby wanted to work for Relate. A few of the boys wanted to be footballers or cricketers or singers in a boy band. Two girls wanted to be nurses. The rest wanted to be contestants on *Big Brother*. In contrast, Skunk Cunningham's essay read:

When I grow up I want to be a schoolteacher because I want to be thought of like I think of Mr Jeffries who's the best teacher in the world because I never thought about what I wanted to be before he came along and now he's made me think about the things that I could be doing with my life instead of just beating Jed on Xbox. I love Mr Jeffries. He makes school time FUN.

Mr Jeffries read Skunk's essay over and over. Then he read it over again. Then he pinched his eyes shut and rubbed them until they were dry. Then he stared at the empty desks and pushed-in chairs and the spaces his class all worked in before putting his head in his hands once again.

When, finally, the day was over, he returned to the Cunningham house and led Cerys up to the box room their relationship had died in.

He said, 'Why don't you want to marry me?'

She looked at him. She took a deep breath. Last night – after Mr Jeffries had left her – she had crept into Archie's bed and the two of them had discussed what she would say when this conversation took place. Now she sat on her bed and took a deep breath and said, almost by rote: 'I'm sorry, Mike, but it's more than not wanting to marry you. I don't want to be with you any more either.'

Mr Jeffries stared, stunned. Cerys took another deep breath.

'I'm sorry,' she said again. 'But it's over. We're finished.' She reached into her pocket and pulled out the engagement ring he had given her the previous night. She held it up between her thumb and her forefinger. 'I'm sorry,' she said yet again, as if there was nothing else she could say.

Mr Jeffries reached out and took the ring from her. 'You're dumping me?'

'Please,' she said, 'don't say it like that.'

'But why?' he asked her. 'Why?'

Again, she and Archie had discussed this part of the conversation. They had decided diplomacy was best: 'I don't love you any more,' she said as gently as she could. 'I don't know why. I just don't feel the same as I used to.'

'You don't love me any more?' Mr Jeffries held the ring up to the light, then looked back at Cerys. 'Why not? What's happened? What's changed?'

'I don't know,' she lied. 'I just feel . . . I feel like we've grown apart . . . I'm not happy . . . it's . . . this isn't . . . I don't know.' She took a deep breath. She clenched her hands into fists. 'This just isn't what I want any more.'

Mr Jeffries shook his head. 'This isn't what you want any more? This isn't what you want any more? Jesus, Cerys. All you've ever wanted since I met you was to get married and buy a house and have a family. You used to go on and on about it. Over and over again. That's why I walked out on you last summer. It used to drive me insane. But now I'm saying I want all these things with you and you're telling me it's not what you want any more? What's happened? What's changed your mind?'

'Mike,' she said. 'I don't know what's happened. I don't know what's changed my mind. I just know that I want you to go.'

'Cerys . . .'

'Please. This is hurting too much.' She blinked several times, then turned her back on him and put her face in her hands.

From behind her back he said, 'I still love you, you know.'

She said, 'I know.'

'Don't you love me?'

'Don't do this, Mike. It's too painful.'

'Tell me you don't love me.'

'Mike,' she said, 'just go.'

Mr Jeffries sighed. He took a step towards her, then turned and walked out of the room. He made his way down the stairs. He made his way out of the house. The door echoed when he slammed it behind him. Outside, in his car, he gripped the steering wheel and started the engine and drove out of the square. He drove with his windows down and his music loud. Rain lashed. Tyres turned. The lights of a roadside Tesco proved too bright for him to drive past. He stopped and bought eight cans of super-strength lager and a bottle of cheap single malt whisky. Then he drove the rest of the way home and let himself into his flat. It was cold and damp and lonely. He slammed the door behind him and dumped his booze down in the kitchen. It smelled of chip wrappers and yesterday's unwashed plates. Mr Jeffries sat at the falling-down shelf that passed as a breakfast-bar-cum-table and drank and looked at the damp patch behind the boiler and listened to the sounds of night-time through the window and three and a half hours later he woke up to find himself all on his own.

But that was nothing special.
We were all on our own.

Dillon in the wardrobe, Broken on his bed, Mrs Buckley on the landing, Mr Jeffries reaching for another can of super-strength lager, Skunk Cunningham dreaming of Mr Jeffries and, most of all, Susan Oswald, sitting in her bedroom, cradling her bump in her hands.

People were starting to see now. Comments had been shouted at school: Fatso. Lard-arse. Slutty gutty whore. Soon, her sisters would notice. Then her old man would find out. Then she would really be for it. Bob Oswald was going to kill her. He wasn't just going to kill her. He was going to rip her apart limb from limb. He'd said it time and again: If any of you little bitches ever get pregnant, I'll kill the fucker who did it, then I'll break your necks as well. You're my beautiful little daughters. Not some slutty little slappers. Keep your legs shut. Show some pride.

Her old man. He could be a right fucker.

Fucker or not, though, he was going to kill her. Susan Oswald lay awake and fretted all night. She felt utterly desperate. She didn't want to have her father trying to kill her. She didn't want a stupid little baby. She was fifteen years old, for Christ's sake. She didn't want that sort of responsibility. She didn't want that sort of hassle. What Susan Oswald wanted was drugs and sex and a few years on the social before she started to worry about crap like that.

She also wanted an abortion.

But she didn't know how she could get one.

So she decided to ask Mrs McCluskey.

But Mrs McCluskey was sick.

On this particular Friday morning, Mrs McCluskey was lying in bed with period pains rippling through her. These pains were unpleasant, unwelcome, but, physically, they caused her no harm. The real harm came in the knowledge that, once more, she had failed to fall pregnant. Mrs McCluskey was sick to death of not falling pregnant. She was sick to death of her life. Work and sex and sleep. Work and sex and sleep. Time of the month. Disappointment. Do it all over again. She really needed to fall pregnant. But how was she meant to fall pregnant? She was always tired. She was always in a hurry. Her life was just work and sex and sleep, work and sex and sleep. No wonder she never fell pregnant. She was too uptight. Too on edge. What she needed was a break. She pulled herself free of the duvet and telephoned Mr O'Driscoll. She told him she was sick.

At the exact same moment Mrs McCluskey did this, Mr Jeffries woke up and considered doing the same. He, unlike Mrs McCluskey, was sick to the point where he had to run to the bathroom and throw up before he'd even managed to switch his alarm off. He didn't call in sick though. For a start, his illness was self-inflicted. And, secondly, what was he going to do if he didn't go into school? Sit and drink and think about Cerys? What was the point in that? Mr Jeffries drank three pints of water then showered and dressed and made his way to school. Once there, he helped himself to several cups of coffee in the staffroom then set off for a double English lesson with a class from Year 9. Too hung-over to do any teaching, he let them read *Much Ado About Nothing* for the first period and *Macbeth* for the second. While the class stared blankly through dog-eared copies of Shakespeare, Mr Jeffries stared blankly into space and thought about Cerys: her breasts, her lovely soft buttocks, the fact she no longer loved him. He wondered if he would ever see her again. He decided he probably would. One day. Some day. They'd bump into each other as they walked down a drizzly high street in some obscure little English town. She would have kids by some paunchy balding accountant and he would be a dusty old Mr Chips type with whiteboard marker-pen ink on his fingers and droopy, tired red eyes. Not a lot different to today, then. Mr Jeffries' eyes looked like piss-holes in the snow. Last night, he had drunk all the super-strength lager he'd bought in Tesco's, then drained nearly all of the single malt whisky. Now his stomach lurched as if he was starving, but the idea of food made him feel sick once again. What he needed more than a meal was an alcoholic drink. He might have to sneak off to the Shamblehurst in his lunch break, or maybe the Botleigh Grange. And tonight, he might have to go for a curry – a curry and a couple of pints. Now, that's what he needed to cheer him up: a spanking hot plateful of curry and three or four chilled Cobra beers. Mr Jeffries brightened. He could do this sort of thing now Cerys had dumped him. In fact, now Cerys had dumped him, Mr Jeffries could drop all this nonsense about getting married and having children and lumbering himself with a 100 per cent mortgage and get on with living his life. The thought made him feel almost happy. It was a Friday, he was single, he was relatively affluent and, as it was the end of the lesson, he could finally go for that drink.

He stood up to follow his class out, and that's when he saw Susan Oswald. She was hanging around by the doorway, all greasy hair and bare legs. Her school blouse was unbuttoned to show the frayed lacy tops of her bra. She looked like she wanted to speak to him. Mr Jeffries sighed. He said, 'Hello, Susan. What do you want?'

Susan Oswald said, 'Nothing.' And then, 'Sir. Can I have a word?'

Mr Jeffries felt his good mood melt. 'Yes,' he said. 'Come in. Sit down.' He rubbed his eyes as Susan Oswald approached the side of his desk. This close, she smelled of cigarettes and perfume. Her lips glistened the same bright red as the chipped paint on her fingernails. Mr Jeffries was reminded of the scratch marks on Skunk Cunningham's face. He made himself say, 'OK, Susan. How can I help you?'

Susan Oswald said, 'I'm pregnant.'

Mr Jeffries said, 'What?'

Susan Oswald said, 'I'm pregnant. I want an abortion.'

Mr Jeffries said, 'You want an abortion?'

Susan Oswald said, 'I want an abortion.' She stared at him.

He stared at her. She was chewing gum. Her hands were clasped in her lap. Mr Jeffries saw how tightly they were knotted and realised her fingernails weren't chipped, they were bitten. A couple had recently bled. He wasn't just reminded of the scratch marks on Skunk Cunningham's face now. He was also reminded of the fact Susan Oswald was only fifteen years old. The unbuttoned blouse, the short skirt, the stilettos suddenly seemed childish, not sluttish.

'Susan,' he said, very gently, 'are you sure you want an abortion?'

Susan Oswald stared down at the floor. 'I dunno. What else can I do?'

Mr Jeffries said, 'You could keep it.'

Susan Oswald said, 'No I bloody couldn't. I don't want no stupid baby.'

'Fair enough,' Mr Jeffries said calmly. 'That's your decision. But what about the father? What does he think you should do?'

'The father?'

'Yes, Susan, the father. What does he think about you being pregnant?'

'I dunno. I ain't really talked to him since.'

'Since? Since what? Oh. Don't tell me. Since *that*.' Mr Jeffries rubbed his temples. 'Come on, Susan. Don't you think he's got a right to know you're carrying his baby?'

'No,' Susan Oswald said. 'Cos I ain't carrying his stupid baby. I'm getting his stupid baby aborted. And anyway, I ain't really sure whose it is.'

'Susan,' Mr Jeffries said, very clearly, 'it is not a stupid baby.

It's a little human being. It's got fingers and toes. It's got eyes. You can't just toss it away without thinking it through.'

'But I have thought it through. And I want an abortion.'

'You may think that now. But what about in five years' time? What about in ten years' time? What if your mother had decided to have you aborted? Where would that leave you now?'

Susan Oswald said, 'Not here. Not bloody pregnant,' and laughed at her own razor wit.

Mr Jeffries slammed his hand down on his desk.

'Susan. This isn't funny.'

Susan Oswald stared. Mr Jeffries leaned forward.

'Look,' he said. 'I'm sorry. I didn't mean to shout. And it's not my place to tell you what to do. But if you know you want an abortion, why are you telling me you're pregnant?'

'Because I don't know how to get an abortion.'

'So?'

'So I want you to tell me. You can, can't you? I mean, you're a teacher. You must know how I can get one.'

'Yes,' Mr Jeffries said, 'I do know how you can get one. I can even put you in touch with a social worker who'll give you a lift to the clinic. I won't, though. Not today. Because if I'm going to help you, I want you to think – and I do mean think – about what you're doing, because when you have an abortion, a doctor goes inside you and scrapes out a living baby. It's not a picnic, Susan. It's an incredibly hard thing to go through.'

Susan Oswald stared wide-eyed at Mr Jeffries. She didn't just look young and childish now. She looked young and childish and scared.

Mr Jeffries softened his tone.

'OK, Susan. What I want you to do is take yourself home and have a long hard think about what I've just said. If you still want an abortion when you wake up Monday morning, come and see me. If you feel it can't wait till Monday, give me a ring on this number over the weekend. I'll help you in any way that I can – whether you want an abortion or not. OK?'

Susan Oswald nodded. 'OK.'

'Good girl. Here.' Mr Jeffries wrote his mobile number down on a slip of paper and gave it to Susan Oswald. She put it in her pocket. She walked out of the classroom. She made her way to the swings at Botleigh Lakeside. Here, she sat smoking Bensons in the drizzle and thought about what she should do. She didn't know what she should do. Kill a baby? Have a baby? Smoke another Benson? Her hands shook as she lit it. Smoke curled, then drifted away. Dillon drifted as well now: out of the wardrobe and out of Broken Buckley's bedroom and into the first bedroom he had searched. He crossed to the jewellery box he had seen there and opened up the lid. He reached inside and rummaged through rings and bracelets and earrings until he found a string of pearls at the bottom. He pulled them out. They were heavy, pale. They seemed more solid than he was. He turned and gave them to Skunk. She held them to her chest then looked at Dillon and smiled. Its warmth was like a cloak settling over his shoulders. He pulled it close around him and stepped towards Skunk to say thank you, but his mouth was full of balled socks. Dillon snorted. He started. His tongue felt so dry in his mouth. His heart beat so loud in his ears. Oh Skunk. Oh Auntie. Oh Uncle. Help me. Please. Somebody. Please. Help me. Help me. Please.

Dillon made a faint noise. An echo. Soft. Nnnnnn. Nnnnnn. Nnnnnn. Skunk's smile faded, then slipped from his mind. Dillon sat numb in the dark. Susan sat numb in the park. She imagined abortions, creations, a baby being scraped out of her stomach, a baby, alive, in her arms. She felt sick and scared and lonely. She felt too young to make this sort of decision. She needed somebody to make this decision for her, but Susan Oswald had no one. Her mother was dead, Mrs McCluskey was pulling a sickie, and Susan had no friends of her own. She only had her father and sisters, and she couldn't talk to her father, because he would go mental and kill her – rip her apart, limb from limb.

Seeing she had only one option, Susan stubbed her fag out and got off the swing and made her way out of the playground. She made her way past Berrywood Primary School. She made her way up Drummond Way. She made her way into Drummond Square and past the Cunningham house and past the Buckley house and up the drive to her own house. Inside, Bob Oswald was smoking a joint in the kitchen, Sunset was standing on a stool and washing up yesterday's dishes, Saskia was preening herself in the bathroom and Saraya was watching *Trisha* on the plasma: *My sister slept with my lover.*

Knowing better than to interrupt an episode of *Trisha*, Susan went up to the bathroom and said, 'You'll never guess what's happened to me.'

And Saskia said, 'I don't give a fuck what's happened to you.'

So Susan said, 'Well, I'm pregnant.'

There was a pregnant pause.

Then Saskia said, 'No you're not.'

And Susan said, 'Yes I am.'

So Saskia said, 'You silly bloody slapper, Susan. What did I tell you about using a condom? What the fuck are you gonna do?'

Susan said, 'I dunno what I'm gonna do. I'm bricking it. Totally freaking.'

Saskia put her eyeliner down, then turned and stared at her sister.

'You're totally freaking? Imagine how Dad's gonna be. He's gonna go fucking ape.'

Susan put a hand on Saskia's shoulder. 'Not if we don't tell him. Not if I get an abortion.'

'Don't be so stupid, Susan. You can't get an abortion without telling Dad. It'd kill him if he ever found out.'

'Yeah, but, Saskia, if I tell him, he's gonna kill me.'

'No he won't. He'll just go a little bit mental. You know what he's like. He blows his top and then he calms down. Once he's calmed down, he'll help you decide what to do.'

'He won't help me decide what to do. He won't have to. He'll have killed me. You know what he's always said about us getting pregnant.'

'He's not going to kill you,' Saskia insisted. 'That's just talk because of what happened to Mum.' She put her hands on Susan's thin shoulders. 'Look,' she said. 'If you're bricking it that much, lock yourself in here for a couple of hours. I'll go and tell him for you.'

'No, Saskia. Don't. Not now . . .'

But Saskia was past her and out of the bathroom and down

the stairs and into the kitchen before Susan could think what was going on.

And by the time she reached the kitchen herself, Bob Oswald already knew.

And he went fucking ape.

'Pregnant? You stupid little slapper. Pregnant? I'll fucking kill you. I'll kill the father. Who's the fucking father? That little bastard is dead. And you. You're dead as well, you stupid little scrubber. Come here. I'll fucking kill you, Susan. Get your arse over here.' Bob Oswald lunged towards her. Susan Oswald ducked out of his way. She pulled the kitchen table between them. Bob Oswald grabbed it and overturned it. Plates smashed. Cutlery scattered. Saskia yelled at him to calm down. She tried to get in between them. Bob Oswald took hold of Saskia's shoulders. He threw her out of the way. 'Who's the father?' he shouted at Susan. 'I want a name. I want an address. I'm gonna fucking kill him.' He made another lunge for her. Susan Oswald ducked out of his reach and fled up the stairs to her bedroom. Again, Saskia tried to get in between them – calm down, Dad, fucking hell, calm down – but Bob Oswald barged her aside and charged up the stairs. Sunset and Saraya crept halfway up and stood cowering as he pushed his shoulder against Susan's bedroom door. By the time Saskia had picked herself up and joined them, he wasn't just pushing himself at the door, he was throwing himself at it, giving it bloody great whacks with his shoulder. It crumbled like bits of balsa. Bob fell into Susan's bedroom. Susan hit him with a pink fluffy slipper. Bob grabbed it and slapped Susan's face with the flat of his palm. She fell backwards onto her bed. Bob Oswald jumped on top of her. He took hold of her throat. WHO'S THE FATHER? WHO'S THE FATHER? WHO'S THE FUCKING FATHER? Behind him, in the doorway, Sunset started to cry. Saraya guided her downstairs. Saskia stayed in Susan's bedroom doorway and screamed, Dad, get off her, get off her, get off her, but her words were drowned out by the sound of Bob Oswald shouting WHO'S THE FATHER? WHO'S THE FATHER? Susan lay screaming beneath him. WHO'S THE FATHER? WHO'S THE FATHER? WHO'S THE FATHER? Susan couldn't tell him. She didn't know. She had no idea. There were so many boys she could choose from: Jed, Jason, Simon, Stuart, Billy, Andy, John – and these were just the boys from her year. There were others. So many others. Too many for her to think of. Too many for her to remember. But she had to think of something. Bob Oswald's hands were squeezing. She was finding it hard to breathe. She was finding it impossible to think. Bob Oswald kept on shouting: WHO'S THE FATHER? WHO'S THE FATHER? WHO'S THE FATHER? His spittle splashed her face. Susan squeezed her eyes shut. She gasped, 'You'll kill me if I tell you.'

'I'll kill you if you don't.'

Susan kept her eyes shut. She thought, I should have just had an abortion. I should have just got rid. Bloody Mr Jeffries. Bloody do-gooder tosspot twat. Why did I listen to him?

Bloody Mr Jeffries . . .

An idea. Just a glimmer of hope. Susan opened her eyes wide. Bob Oswald screamed in her face,

'Tell me . . . fucking tell me . . .'

'I can't, he made me do it.'

'You're not telling me he raped you? I won't fall for that one again. We've been through that one before . . .'

'No, not rape . . . but . . .'

A loosening of the fingers. The closeness of Bob's face. Susan gasped. She blurted out words.

'But I didn't know . . . what I was . . . doing. He's older . . . he's pushy. Dad. Please . . . stop . . . squeezing . . . my . . . throat . . .'

'A name,' Bob Oswald demanded, and squeezed her throat even harder. 'Tell me the fucker's name.'

Susan Oswald said, 'Mr Jeffries. From school.'

Bob Oswald stopped squeezing her throat.

Susan sucked a lungful of air in, then spoke in a huge hurried rush: 'Mr Jeffries. From school. You know. Sunrise's teacher. The one who got you arrested for kicking his head in. He'd been on at me for ages. I'm telling you, Dad, he wouldn't give it up. The dirty fucker. *Please, Susan. You're so nice. You're so sexy. You turn me on when you smile.* He's a right dirty old bugger, Dad. I didn't want to do it with him. I didn't want no mucky old perv stuffing his hands down my knickers. But he kept on offering me lifts. He kept on giving me money. He kept on buying me clothes. He said I reminded him of an old girlfriend he used to have once. He said he'd slap Sunrise if I didn't give him a blow job. He made me do it in his car. He said he wouldn't put it in me. Then he changed his mind. I didn't like it when he did it. He forced me, Dad, he forced me, though he didn't threaten me or nothing. He was just dead forceful and I didn't know what he was doing. I mean. I'd never done it before. And I've not done it since.

But look at me. Look at me. I'm pregnant, bloody pregnant. What the fuck am I gonna do?' Susan sucked more breath in. Bob Oswald stared wide-eyed at her. Behind him, Saskia yelled, 'It's the truth, Dad, she told me when it happened. I told her to tell you, but she was too scared cos she knew you'd go off on one. And look at you, she was right. You're an idiot. An animal. Fucking hell. Let her go.' Saskia ran over to Susan. She pulled Susan into her arms. Susan accepted her embrace. She shut her eyes. She sobbed. She sobbed the same way Dillon sobbed, though he sobbed alone in pitch darkness, tied up and gagged in Broken Buckley's wardrobe, thinking, oh Skunk, oh Uncle, oh Auntie, oh somebody, oh anybody, oh please, and his head spun, his stomach ached, his hunger roared, while across the square, oblivious, Skunk and Jed put their knives and their forks down and let huge plates of curry go cold.

And Archie said, 'We're in love.'

Cerys looked at him. She nodded. She smiled.

'We're in love,' Archie said again. 'Aren't we, Cerys?'

'Yes,' she said. 'Yes. We are. It's taken us a long time to see it. But yes. We are. We're in love.'

'So,' Skunk said, 'what about Mr Jeffries?'

Archie said, 'What about Mr Jeffries?'

Cerys said, 'Mr Jeffries and I are still friends, Skunk. And he's still your schoolteacher. That's all there is to say.'

Skunk looked at her. She said, 'Does this mean you're still our cleaner?'

'Cerys was never our cleaner,' Archie said very calmly. 'As you know full well.'

Skunk shrugged. She didn't say anything. Jed didn't say anything either. He pushed his plate away and went upstairs to play Xbox and think about Susan Oswald. Skunk pushed her plate away and went upstairs to cry all alone in her bedroom. Archie and Cerys stayed downstairs and tried to pretend the reaction hadn't bothered them: Be careful what you wish for, Archie said ruefully. Me, a bloody cleaner, Cerys said with a slightly forced smile. It was a long, awkward weekend. It seemed to drag on forever. Bob Oswald pacing and ranting and raving. Susan Oswald sobbing and smoking cigarette after cigarette. Saskia, Saraya, Sunset and Sunrise sitting with their arms around her, then drifting off to watch telly. Dillon breathing, staring, gasping, Broken cross-legged before him, the field sloping down to his left: WHY DID SHE HAVE TO GO DO IT? WHY DID SHE DO THAT TO ME? And, from the other side of his doorway, on a cold damp Sunday evening, Mrs Buckley said, I love you, son. I always have. I always will. Please come out. Eat your dinner. She turned. She looked at the egg and chips on the landing. Minutes passed. Hours passed. The weekend passed.

And everyone just kept on moving, in the direction that brings us to now.

Now. In darkness. Sadness. Silence.

This is how we all got here.

Minute by minute. Hour by hour. The sun rising. Alarm clocks ringing.

The start of another new week.

*   *   *

It started off badly for Sunrise Oswald.

The lady who was so poor she had to work the eight-till-late shift at the One Stop as well as the early shift at McDonald's had swapped shifts to help out a colleague. She was ready and waiting when Sunrise turned up to collect the papers she was due to deliver that day.

'You,' she snapped at Sunrise Oswald. 'I want words with you.'

Sunrise glared at her from under the baseball cap she was wearing. 'What?'

'If I get one more complaint about your papers not being delivered, you're finished here. You hear me?'

Sunrise continued to glare from under her baseball cap. 'I hear you.'

'Good. Now get going. You're late.'

Sunrise picked up her bag full of papers and made her way out of the shop.

The lady who was so poor she had to work the eight-till-late shift at the One Stop as well as the early shift at McDonald's smiled as she watched Sunrise stalk off into the dawn mist. It had felt good, treating an Oswald like that.

As Sunrise set off to deliver Susan Oswald's papers, Mr Jeffries woke face down on the breakfast-bar-cum-table in his kitchen. Empty cans of Kestrel Super lay scattered all around him. The sink smelled of vomit. His body smelled of cigarette smoke and sweat. He dragged himself into the shower then dressed and made his way into school. By the time he arrived there he felt almost human. It was a bright warm day and blossom was blowing in the breeze. The long dark of winter was over. It was the first day of the rest of his life.

Skunk was surprised at his manner: despite the fact Cerys had dumped him only last Thursday, Mr Jeffries seemed happier than he had done in weeks. He wrote the word CHOICES up on the whiteboard and said, 'Class, who understands choices?' They all thought they understood choices. For example, Skunk had chosen to wear pink socks that morning and Patinda had chosen to have cheese and pickle in her sandwiches. Mr Jeffries shook his head. Sure, these things were choices, but they weren't the choices he was talking about. He was talking about CHOICES, the ones that directed people's LIVES. Not in the little ways Skunk and Patinda had mentioned, like would they wear pink socks or would they eat cheese and pickle sandwiches at lunchtime, but in the big ways that made a huge difference, such as the way they all acted towards each other. For instance, would they be nice to the people around them this morning, or would they be nasty? Mr Jeffries looked around for Sunrise Oswald as he said the word nasty, but Sunrise Oswald wasn't in school today. On this particular Monday morning, the school was empty of Oswalds.

Except for Bob Oswald's voice.

It rang out in Mr O'Driscoll's ear.

'I want to make a complaint.'

Mr O'Driscoll shut his eyes. He could feel the beginnings of a headache.

'What sort of complaint, Mr Oswald?'

'A complaint about one of your teachers. He's been sticking it to one of my daughters.'

Mr O'Driscoll sat up a little straighter. 'That's a very serious allegation, Mr –'

'It ain't no allegation,' Bob Oswald yelled into the mouth-piece. 'It's the fucking truth. That prick Jeffries has been sticking it to my Susan, and now my Susan's pregnant. Pregnant. Bloody pregnant. And don't say to me, are you sure, because, yes, I'm bloody sure. In fact, I'm fucking certain. I've had her do a test. She did it Saturday morning. Eleven pounds fifty it cost me. Eleven pounds bloody fifty. You can add that to the damages. And yes, there will be damages, because you can bet your arse there'll be a lawsuit, and where there's lawsuits, there's damages, you fucking jerk. My beautiful daughter's pregnant. What the fuck are you playing at in that school? Teachers impregnating pupils? What the fuck's been going on?'

Mr O'Driscoll sat speechless. Bob Oswald continued to rant.

'I want that Jeffries sacked. Until you tell me you've sacked him, I'm keeping my kids out of school. And I'm going to the papers. This is a scandal. A national scandal. My poor little baby. I sent her to your school to get educated, not violated. Fifteen years old and pregnant. Pregnant. At fifteen years old. It's a disgrace. A fucking outrage.'

Mr O'Driscoll recovered a fraction of his composure. 'Mr Oswald,' he said, 'this is a very serious matter. I want to assure you we'll be investigating it as thoroughly as we can, but when you say Jeffries, do you mean Mike Jeffries – the teacher you're presently on bail for attacking?'

'Of course I mean Mike Jeffries,' Bob Oswald yelled. 'How many other perverts have you got working up at that school?

And I'll tell you this for nothing. He's fucking lucky I didn't know about this last November, because he'd have got more than just a kicking. In fact, he's fucking lucky I'm not coming down that school right now to finish off what I started. I should have caved his fucking skull in. My little girl's in bits. You know how her mother died? Giving birth to our youngest. What if that happens to Susan? I tell you. My little girl is in bits.'

'OK,' Mr O'Driscoll said hurriedly. 'OK, Mr Oswald. Please. Try to be calm. I understand why you're so angry. I also understand what you're saying about not returning your daughters to school while Mr Jeffries is employed here. However, there are procedures I have to follow. There has to be an investigation. I can't – I won't – contemplate sacking Mike Jeffries until a proper investigation has been carried out. You can rest assured, though, that until any investigation has been completed, he won't be allowed to set foot in this school. Now. Susan's fifteen, isn't she? Yes? Well, that means she's under the age of sexual consent, which makes this an even more serious matter than the breach of pupil–teacher trust. Have you contacted the police?'

No. Bob Oswald had not contacted the police. He had made several phone calls to see how much something like this might be worth in terms of damages, but calling the police hadn't crossed his mind. It was, therefore, Mr O'Driscoll who contacted the police, and it was the police who came and took Mr Jeffries from his classroom halfway through the last lesson of the afternoon. As he was led from room 7D he said, Class,

I'll be back in a couple of minutes. But he was wrong. He was lying. He was gone.

There was a brief gap between Mr Jeffries being taken away and a supply teacher coming in to take charge of his class. With no one to tell her not to, Skunk ran over to the window and peered out on the car park. After a couple of minutes, she saw Mr Jeffries being led towards a blue car. She didn't realise it was a police car until she saw one of the men put a hand on Mr Jeffries' head and ease him into the back of the vehicle. The action reminded her of the police taking Broken Buckley away the previous summer. Skunk felt her stomach lurch and reached for her mobile phone. As she speed-dialled her father's number, Mr Jeffries sat in the back of the unmarked police car and looked at the two men sitting before him. He said, 'Am I under arrest?'

DS Jenks looked at Mr Jeffries over his shoulder. 'We just want to talk to you down at the station.'

Mr Jeffries repeated a question he had already asked several times: 'Why?'

DC Carson said, 'As if you didn't know.'

DS Jenks said, 'Because there have been serious allegations made against you, Mr Jeffries, sir.'

DC Carson repeated what he'd just said: 'As if you didn't know.'

The rest of the journey passed in silence. Once they arrived at Eastleigh Station, Mr Jeffries was booked in at the front desk and led through to an interview room. A tape was put into a cassette recorder and DC Carson said for its benefit who was present in the room. Then he looked at Mr Jeffries and asked him to describe his relationship with Susan Oswald. Mr Jeffries felt a thrill of indignation as it suddenly occurred to him what had happened. He leaned towards the two policemen and said, 'Has Susan Oswald accused me of getting her pregnant?'

DC Carson leaned forward as well. He and DS Jenks had interviewed Susan Oswald earlier that afternoon. During this interview, Susan, with her father sitting beside her, had accused Mr Jeffries of pursuing her in an aggressively sexual manner throughout October and November of last year, and insisted that full sexual intercourse had taken place in the back of his car on the twenty-second of November between seven and eight in the evening. Both Carson and Jenks suspected the girl was lying, but an allegation was an allegation and they had to be seen to be doing their jobs. Now DC Carson fixed Mr Jeffries with a stare and started to work his way down a list of pre-prepared questions: How long have you known Susan Oswald? Mr Jeffries said, Less than a year. Is Susan Oswald in any of your regular classes? Mr Jeffries said, No. How would you describe your feelings towards Susan Oswald? Mr Jeffries said, Right now, scornful. So you regret having sexual intercourse with Susan Oswald, then, do you? Mr Jeffries stared at DC Carson and laughed out loud in his face: You can't really believe I had sex with Susan Oswald? That's ridiculous. Completely insane. His laughter was met with silence. Mr Jeffries sat back in his chair and shook his head. DC Carson stared at him. DS Jenks stared at him. There was a knock at the door.

'Mr Jeffries' solicitor is outside, sir.'

DS Jenks looked from the desk sergeant in the doorway to Mr Jeffries. 'When did you call a solicitor?'

Mr Jeffries looked confused. 'I didn't call a solicitor. I don't even have a solicitor.'

DS Jenks looked back at the desk sergeant. 'OK,' he said. 'Send him in.' The desk sergeant nodded and went to get Mr Jeffries' solicitor. Moments later, Archie Cunningham walked into the interview room and sat down next to Mr Jeffries. He said, 'What are the charges against my client?'

DC Carson said, 'Rape.'

Mr Jeffries felt a thrill of fear. Archie Cunningham showed no emotion. He said, 'In what capacity?'

DS Jenks said, 'Unlawful sex with a minor. He's got a fifteen-year-old girl pregnant.'

'Have you arrested him?'

DC Carson said, 'No. He's helping us with our inquiries.' He looked sideways at DS Jenks, who nodded imperceptibly. The questions began again: Where were you on the evening of twenty-second November last year? What do you mean, you don't know? Come on, Mr Jeffries, it was a Wednesday. It was between seven and eight o'clock. DC Carson rested his chin on his fists. Come on, Mr Jeffries. You must remember where you were. You were in your car having sex with Susan Oswald. Archie Cunningham looked at Mr Jeffries. Mr Jeffries shook his head. I wasn't, he said, I wasn't. Well, DC Carson said, where were you then? Between 7 and 8 p.m.? On the twenty-second of November? Mr Jeffries spread his hands. I was probably round my girlfriend's. Probably? Probably? What do you mean by probably? Mr Jeffries said, I mean that's where

I was spending most of my evenings back then, but I can't remember for sure. I could have been at home on my own. DC Carson said, Well, that's too bad for you. There was a pause, a moment of silence, then it began again: What's the name of this girlfriend? Where does she live? How's she going to feel when she finds out you've been sleeping with underage girls behind her back? What? You're no longer with her? Well. At least you won't have to explain what you've been up to. A wry smile. A sudden change in direction. What sort of car do you drive? A Rover? That's exactly what Susan Oswald said. Well, Archie Cunningham interjected, it's hardly surprising she knows what car he's got, is it? He drives it to school every day. The two policemen paused for a moment, then Carson began yet again. Do you think it's OK to have sex with your pupils? How did you know Susan Oswald was pregnant? Why do you think she came to ask you about getting an abortion? Why not another teacher? Mr Jeffries sighed. He said, I don't know. DC Carson persisted: Why not one of her school friends? Mr Jeffries sighed. He said, I don't know. Again, DC Carson persisted: Why not one of her sisters? Mr Jeffries shook his head. I don't know. I don't know. I don't know. DC Carson raised his eyebrows. How many times did full sexual intercourse take place? Mr Jeffries shook his head, nonplussed. The questions began again. Let's go back to the beginning. How would you describe your relationship with Susan Oswald? What did you find attractive about Susan Oswald? If you didn't find Susan Oswald attractive, why did you have sexual intercourse with her? Well, if you didn't have sexual intercourse with her, why is she saying you did? A shake of the head.

Silence. Off they went again. What were you doing on the night of twenty-second November last year? How many times did intercourse take place? Prove to us it didn't. Well, if you can't prove to us it didn't, why should we believe you when you say it didn't? Someone's been having sex with her. She's nearly four months pregnant. Around and around. Over and over. Until, finally, Archie brought the charade to a halt: It's her word against his. Either charge him or let him go home.

'It's not as simple as that, Mr Cunningham.'

'It never is with the Oswalds.' Archie leaned towards DS Jenks. 'Do you know for a fact she's pregnant?'

DS Jenks shrugged. 'We've no reason to believe she isn't.'

'So you don't know she's cried rape before?'

The two policemen gave nothing away.

'No,' Archie said. 'I didn't think you'd have checked.' He looked sideways at Mr Jeffries, then turned his gaze back to the two policemen. 'She accused a kid called Rick Buckley of raping her two years ago. Susan's father – who, incidentally, is on bail for attacking my client and landing him in hospital – beat the poor kid to a pulp, then had you lot arrest him. Rick was held in the cells over at Winchester till it turned out Susan was a virgin. So, considering the father's got a grudge against my client and the girl's a proven liar, let my client go. Either that or arrest him so we can take this matter further when her story falls apart. And, believe me, it will fall apart. You can bet your next promotions on that.'

The two policemen stared at Archie then at each other then had Mr Jeffries returned to the cells so they could continue their investigation. Archie felt helpless as he watched the desk sergeant take Mr Jeffries away. He felt even more helpless that evening when Skunk bombarded him with questions as soon as he walked through the door.

'What has Mr Jeffries done, Daddy?'

'Nothing, sweetheart.'

'Why has he been arrested then, Daddy?'

'He hasn't been arrested, sweetheart.'

'Why was he taken away by the police then, Daddy?'

'Over a misunderstanding, sweetheart.'

'What sort of a misunderstanding, Daddy?'

'Skunk. For God's sake. Leave it alone.'

She went to her bedroom without eating and curled on her side and fretted about Mr Jeffries. What had he done? Why had he been taken away? Where was he now? Was he OK? Would he be back tomorrow? What did the police want him for? When were they going to release him? Skunk didn't know. No one seemed to know. Archie couldn't tell her. Cerys couldn't tell her. The relief teacher who had come to take over Mr Jeffries' class couldn't tell her. The school secretary couldn't tell her. No one seemed able to tell her. Skunk lay and fretted all night. Downstairs, Archie sat on the sofa with Cerys.

She said, 'Did he ask about me?'

'No,' Archie said. 'He didn't.'

'Did you tell him about us?'

'No,' Archie said. 'I didn't.'

Cerys put a hand on his shoulder. 'Thanks for going to help him. That can't have been easy.'

'No,' Archie said. 'It wasn't. I felt a right bloody Judas. Sitting there like I'm helping him out when really I'm –'

'Don't,' she said. 'Don't.'

The two of them looked at each other, then Archie pulled himself to his feet.

Cerys said, 'Where are you going?'

'To get last year's diary. If we can find out what he was up to last November, we can sort all this mess out.' He came back down five minutes later. The two of them pored over his diary: Fireworks night on the seventh. A PTA meeting on the twelfth. Children in Need on the seventeenth. Southampton reserves played Reading reserves on the twenty-third. Nothing, though, on the twenty-second. The day was a total blank. Archie's mind was a total blank. So, too, was Cerys's. She couldn't remember a thing, not a thing, except that a week to the day after Mr Jeffries was supposed to have got Susan Oswald pregnant, Bob Oswald tried to beat him to death.

Finally, they gave up. They didn't know what Mr Jeffries had been doing that night any more than Mr Jeffries knew what he'd been doing that night. The two of them sat in miserable silence until Cerys said, 'So what happens now?'

Archie sighed and looked up at the ceiling. 'The police can hold Mike for twenty-four hours without charging him. If they don't charge him in those twenty-four hours, they have to let him go. As things stand at the moment, I don't think they'll charge him – Susan can't prove he had sex with her any more than he can prove he didn't, so it's simply a case of her word against his, and she's too unreliable to trust – so what they'll probably do is release him on police bail until the baby's born, then do a DNA test to see which one's telling the truth. If the baby's Mike's, they'll arrest him and charge him with rape. If it's not, I'll do everything I can to make sure they press charges against Susan Oswald for wasting police time – yet again. In the meantime, I'm going to speak to Terry O'Driscoll tomorrow and try to make sure Mike's job is kept open till his name's cleared.'

'What the hell do you mean? Till his name's cleared?'

Archie looked from the ceiling to Cerys. 'Look,' he said, 'I'm no employment law expert, but as far as I know, the best Mike can hope for while this is hanging over his head is to be suspended on full pay.'

'Archie. You have to be joking.'

'I wish I was.'

Cerys shook her head. 'You're telling me he's not going to be able to work until Susan's had her baby? Even though there's not a chance in hell it's his?'

Archie sighed. He nodded.

She stared in the general direction of the Oswald house. 'That family,' she said. 'That fucking bastard family.'

For about half a second after he woke up, Mr Jeffries couldn't remember where he was or why he was there.

Then it all came flooding back.

'Fucking hell,' he said. 'Fucking hell.'

He sat up and pushed a blanket that smelled of somebody else's urine away from himself. Outside, in the corridor, there was the sound of shouting and banging and footsteps. Mr Jeffries held his head in his hands. He stayed this way for the next hour and a half, until Archie Cunningham stepped into his cell.

'Come on,' Archie said. 'Let's get you out of here.'

Mr Jeffries said, 'They're letting me go?'

Archie shook his head. 'You're being released on police bail. You need to report back here once every eight weeks until there's more substantial evidence one way or another.'

'What does that mean?'

'It means there's nothing anyone can do now until Susan gives birth to the baby. Until then, you're free to go.'

Mr Jeffries stared up at Archie Cunningham. He said, disbelievingly, 'I'm free to go? Just like that? It's all over?'

'Well, until Susan's had her baby and they can do a DNA test, yes.'

Mr Jeffries laughed. 'But Archie,' he said, 'a DNA test is only going to prove one thing: that baby's not mine.'

'I know,' Archie said. 'I know that.'

'Which means it's over,' Mr Jeffries said happily. 'I can go back to work. I can put all this behind me.' He put his head in his hands and laughed out loud again. 'You'll never believe how worried I've been through the night. I've never felt so scared in all my life. I kept thinking, how am I going to prove I never touched her? What's going to happen to me if I can't? Am I going to be stuck in here till she has that bloody baby? Jesus. Jesus Christ. I've been driving myself mad. At least now I can go back to work while I wait for the DNA test to prove she's lying.'

Archie hesitated a moment, then made himself shake his head. 'I'm sorry, Mike, but you can't go back to work. Not when you're a schoolteacher on police bail for something like this. I've spoken to Terry O'Driscoll already. You're going to be suspended on full pay until Susan stops lying or DNA tests prove you haven't fathered her baby.'

The smile disappeared from Mr Jeffries' face. 'I can't go back to work till she gives birth to the baby?'

'You're under suspicion of rape,' Archie said gently. 'You can't really blame the school. They have to consider their pupils.'

'But I didn't do anything. I've never been anywhere near her.'

'I know,' Archie said. 'I know that. And anyone who knows you knows that. But no one can actually prove it.'

Mr Jeffries hunched forward. 'But she's a liar, Archie. And she's a total slut. I mean, for God's sake, we're talking about Susan Oswald here. She's had it away with most of the school.'

Archie held his hands out. 'I believe you, Mike. Honestly, I do. But Susan Oswald says she's had sex one time, and one time only, and it was in the back of your car with you. Until we can prove she's lying, all we can do is wait.'

Mr Jeffries took a deep breath. 'OK,' he said. 'OK. If all we need to do is prove she's lying, why can't we find someone who's had sex with her to come forward? That would blow her whole story apart.'

'Mike,' Archie said gently. 'She's fifteen years old. Anyone who admits to having sex with her would be putting themselves in a worse position than the one you're already in. Who the hell's going to do that? An adult who'll end up on the sex offenders register? A schoolboy who'd have to be accompanied down here by his parents? For God's sake. The question's not even worth asking.'

'What about witnesses then? Everyone knows she's a slapper.'

Archie rubbed his temples. 'You're talking about personal opinion and rumour. Unless you can find someone who's actually seen Susan Oswald having full sexual intercourse with someone and is able to come forward and say who it was with, where it took place and exactly when it happened, the police aren't going to be interested, and the school aren't going to be either. I'm sorry, Mike, really, I am.'

Mr Jeffries sighed. He shook his head. Archie carried on talking.

'I really hate to say this, but without an alibi for the night Susan says you had sex with her, I think you're totally out on a limb.'

'But everyone knows she's a liar,' Mr Jeffries said desperately. 'She lied about Rick Buckley. She's lying about me. And her dad's on bail for beating the crap out of me. How the hell can anyone believe them?'

'No one believes them, Mike. But it's not about who believes who at the moment, is it? It's about who can prove what. Until someone can prove beyond reasonable doubt that you never touched Susan Oswald, Terry O'Driscoll has to put the reputation of the school first. And so would you, if you were in his shoes.'

'But if I'm suspended,' Mr Jeffries said, 'I'm going to look as guilty as hell. People will think I've actually done something wrong. What about innocent till proven guilty?'

'Mike,' Archie said wearily, 'what about it?'

Mr Jeffries put his head back in his hands. 'Fucking hell,' he said. 'Fucking hell.'

* * *

Sixty minutes later Mr Jeffries stepped into sunlight and sat wearily on the brick wall outside the station. Like Broken Buckley before him, he felt dirty and sick and ashamed. He refused Archie's offer of a lift and walked to the taxi rank outside the train station. As soon as it dropped him off outside his flat he let himself in and listened to the message Mr O'Driscoll's secretary had left on his answerphone confirming what Archie had already told him: he had been suspended on full pay until further notice. Mr Jeffries played the message five times then stripped and got in the shower. After, he tried to eat some breakfast, but it was no good; he didn't feel hungry. All Mr Jeffries felt was dirty. He stripped his clothes off again and got back under the shower, then scrubbed and scrubbed and scrubbed. It didn't do any good, though: no matter how hard he tried to scrub himself clean, his feelings just wouldn't wash out.

As Mr Jeffries tried to scrub himself clean, we gossiped for all we were worth.

Why had the police marched into our classroom and taken our favourite teacher away?

The more popular rumours went like this:

Mr Jeffries was a murderer.

Mr Jeffries had sexually assaulted Mrs McCluskey.

Mr Jeffries had been downloading music illegally on the Internet.

Mr Jeffries wasn't really Mr Jeffries at all! The real Mr Jeffries had spent the whole term tied up in an attic with a pair of tights stuffed into his mouth. The false Mr Jeffries was really a down-and-out tramp who had grown sick of living in doorways and taken over the real Mr Jeffries' life.

This, out of all the rumours, made the most sense to me. The false Mr Jeffries was too young to be a teacher. He was too good-looking to be a teacher. He talked too much sense to be a teacher. Now, though, he wasn't a teacher. He was a criminal. What would become of him? Again, there were tons of rumours. The playground was buzzing with them. For once, though, I didn't join in. I was too gutted to gossip. In just a few days the man I loved above all others had gone from living in the box room across the landing and teaching me at school to having no part in my life at all. What if he never came back? What if he disappeared just like Dillon? Or my mother? I was desperate to know what had happened, but I wasn't interested in rumours. I needed to find out the truth.

And then I found out the truth.

And it was too stupid for words.

'He never slept with your sister.'

It was Patinda who said this. She curled her top lip with disdain.

'Yes he did,' Sunrise Oswald insisted. 'And now she's pregnant. We're getting compensation.' She glared at her classmates with an odd mixture of defiance and pride. 'He's a dirty fucker. He's gonna end up in jail.'

'Yeah, right,' Patinda said. 'Like he'd sleep with your slutty sister.'

'My sister ain't slutty.'

'Yeah she is. She's a right old slapper. She's slept with most of the school. Even my brother's had her, and my brother's a right geeky twat.'

'My sister ain't no right old slapper. And she ain't slept with your geeky twat of a brother.' Sunrise curled her fists up. The rest of the class waited for the fight to begin – all except Mrs McCluskey, who stood at the front of the class and pretended that nothing was happening. Sunrise lowered her voice. 'And anyway,' she said, 'it wasn't like Susan wanted to sleep with Mr Jeffries. Mr Jeffries *forced* her.'

This drew a burst of mocking laughter. The idea of Mr Jeffries forcing anyone to do anything was bizarre enough in its own right, but the idea of Mr Jeffries – nice kind Mr Jeffries – forcing Susan Oswald to sleep with him – well, that was too stupid for words.

'He did. He did. He forced her.'

Patinda leaned in close to Sunrise. 'You're full of shit.'

'Well, so what? You're full of curry.'

'I'd rather be full of curry than full of shit.'

Sunrise tried to think of a witty response. When this proved to be beyond her, she tried to punch Patinda in the stomach, but Patinda caught Sunrise's fist and twisted it behind her back, then took Sunrise by the hair and banged her head against her desk. After that, she walked back to her own desk. Sunrise sat with her head in her hands and she sobbed. The two of them didn't speak for the rest of the lesson. Skunk didn't speak to anyone either. She sat in stunned silence and tried to digest what she had just heard: Mr Jeffries had slept with Susan Oswald. Susan Oswald was pregnant. It was rubbish. Complete and utter rubbish. There was no way

Mr Jeffries would sleep with Susan Oswald. Susan Oswald was lying. Skunk said so to Archie that night.

He said, 'I know, Skunk. That's what I think, too.'

'Then why isn't Mr Jeffries being allowed back into school?'

'Because, right now, no one can prove Susan's lying.'

'But everyone knows she's a liar, Daddy. And everyone knows Mr Jeffries would never have slept with her. Patinda Patel said so to Sunrise today. She said Susan Oswald's a right old slapper who's slept with most of the school.'

Archie drew his breath in. 'That's neither here nor there, Skunk. It doesn't matter if Susan Oswald's a liar, the same as it doesn't matter if she's a right old slapper who's slept with most of the school. All that matters at the moment is the fact we can't prove she's lying about Mr Jeffries getting her pregnant. Can you or Patinda do that?'

'We could tell Mr O'Driscoll we know she's a liar. We could tell the police or a judge.'

Archie sighed. 'That's not proof, little darling. That's just what you think.'

Skunk stared at him a moment, then started on him again. 'But if everyone knows Susan Oswald's a liar, Daddy, why does anyone need proof?'

'Because.'

'Because why?'

'Because that's the way that it works.'

'But that's stupid.'

Archie spread his hands. 'I don't make up the rules.'

'But, Daddy. You're Mr Jeffries' solicitor. Why can't you prove she's lying?'

Archie opened his mouth and then shut it.

'Because,' he said. 'Just because.'

This wasn't the answer Skunk had been looking for. She went upstairs and lay on her bed and wished there was some way she could make Susan Oswald stop lying. A Chinese burn, or a kung-fu kick. She wished she had a light-sabre. She also wished it was Sunrise Oswald who was lying, because Skunk wouldn't need a light-sabre to sort out Sunrise Oswald. She'd be able to do it with her fists. Susan, though, was a different proposition. Even with a light-sabre, fighting her would be suicidal. Susan Oswald was mental. She'd scratch your eyes out for blinking. Skunk lay awake and fretted all night and was exhausted the next morning at school – exhausted and excited, because Mr Jeffries would be back today. How on earth could he not be? Some adult somewhere would have seen through Susan Oswald's lies by now, and Mr Jeffries would be back in the classroom. It would seem like he'd never been gone.

But Mr Jeffries wasn't back in his classroom. He was drunk on his sofa. Empty cans of Kestrel Super Strength lay scattered all around him. While Skunk sat and fretted about where he was and whether he was safe and how on earth she could help him, he slept with his head tilted back and his arms spread out wide. At the same time that he did this, Broken Buckley sat in front of his wardrobe and rocked gently backwards and forwards, gently backwards and forwards. Before him, Dillon's mind reeled from one subject to another. Darkness. Light. Time. Space. Egg and chips and nothing. The sound of skipping didn't reach him. It was

Susan Oswald who was skipping. Sunrise was standing beside her, clapping out a beat as the rope whirled round and round. Cerys watched from Archie's front-room window and imagined Mr Jeffries during his one night in a police cell. She wondered what he was doing now, suspended, drifting, helpless. Bitches, she thought, evil little bitches. She looked at that day's copy of the *Echo* and shook her head in disgust: *Schoolgirl pregnant. Teacher suspended.* Skunk didn't read it when she saw it. She ran straight up to her room and threw herself down on her bed. Just over three hours later, Cerys took a cheese and pickle sandwich up to her. She said, 'Darling, are you OK?'

Skunk was exhausted from worrying about Mr Jeffries. She said, 'I'm not hungry.'

Cerys said, 'Well, how come? You love cheese and pickle sandwiches.'

Skunk said nothing. She stared at the wall.

Cerys sighed. 'Skunk,' she said, very gently, 'is this about Mike? Or me and your dad?'

Skunk kept her face to the wall. She said, 'Cerys, why can't anyone prove Susan Oswald's lying about Mr Jeffries?'

Cerys sighed. 'They can, Skunk. And they will. It's just going to take a long time.'

'Why?'

Cerys said, 'It's complicated, Skunk. Don't you go worrying yourself about it. It'll all sort itself out. OK?'

Skunk didn't answer. She kept her face to the wall.

Cerys left the sandwich on Skunk's bedside cabinet and went downstairs to see Archie. He was holed up in his study, making notes on Mr Jeffries' file. She put a hand on his shoulder. 'Archie,' she said, 'go and talk to your daughter. That poor kid's breaking my heart.'

Archie sighed and went upstairs to see Skunk.

'Sweetheart,' he said, 'what's the matter?'

Skunk kept her face to the wall. She said, 'Why can't you prove Susan Oswald's lying?'

Archie sat down beside her.

'It's complicated, little darling. Right now, we don't have any proof that Susan Oswald's lying. But we'll get proof in the end. Don't you worry about that.'

'How will you get proof, though? And why can't you get proof today?'

Archie sighed and then said, 'When Susan's had her baby, there's a test that can be done to prove whether Mr Jeffries is its father or not. It's called a DNA test.'

'What's DNA stand for?'

'I don't know, Skunk. But once they've done this test, we'll have proof Susan Oswald's a liar and Mr Jeffries will be able to go back to school.'

Skunk looked at Archie over her shoulder. 'When will Susan have her baby?'

'Sometime in the summer. Maybe July or August.'

'That's forever away.'

'It's not so long, Skunk. It'll come round soon enough.'

'Mr Jeffries won't be my form teacher any more then. I'll hardly ever see him again.' Skunk stared up at her father, then hid her face in her pillows because she was scared she was going to start crying. Archie stared down on her, then buried his face in her hair. He stayed that way for a long time, then finally made himself straighten.

'Skunk,' he said, 'please try not to worry so much. What's going on with Mr Jeffries will sort itself out. In a few months' time, he's going to be back at school and it'll be like he's never been gone. In the meantime, you've got to stop worrying about him. Mr Jeffries wouldn't want you to. OK, little darling? OK?'

Skunk kept her face in the pillow.

The next day Mr Jeffries woke on the floor in his front room with no idea how he had got there. As he dragged himself to his feet he realised he had no real idea of where the last two days had got to, either. The only clue he had came in the shape of the empty cans of lager strewn all over the floor. He made himself walk around with a bin bag and gathered up thirty-seven of them. He dumped the bin bag in the kitchen, then went and fetched another can from the fridge. He stared at it for a moment, then pulled the tab and started to drink. As the fluid hit the back of his throat he reflected that he wasn't drinking because he was guilty; he was drinking because he was not. Feeling totally and utterly helpless, he sat in his flat with a can in his hands and turned the situation over: The police believed Susan Oswald was telling the truth. Terry O'Driscoll believed Susan Oswald was telling the truth. The local press believed Susan Oswald was telling the truth. How could Mr Jeffries prove she was lying? He couldn't. Not until she'd had the baby. And if Susan Oswald was only three or four months pregnant, that meant she had five or six months to go before she had the baby. Mr Jeffries drained his can of lager and went and got another. How could he get through these months? He wasn't sure that he could. No job to go to each day. No Cerys. This flat. This can in his hands. He took another mouthful. He shut his eyes. He screamed. The sound of it bounced off the walls. It blended with the sounds of cars and lorries and life drifting in through the windows. Mr Jeffries felt soiled. He stood up. He went through to the bathroom. He stripped naked. He got in the shower. Hot water. Cold water. It didn't matter to him. He drank his super-strength lager and he turned and he turned in the spray.

Finally, it was the sound of his mobile phone that got him to step out of the shower.

Mr Jeffries staggered through to his bedroom. He picked up his phone and he said, 'Hello?'

A voice said, 'Is that Michael Jeffries?'

'Yes,' Mr Jeffries said. 'Why? Who's this?'

'My name's Lawrence Riden. I work for the *News of the World*.'

There was a moment of silence. Lawrence Riden waited it out. His job with the *News of the World* was on their Got A Story Hotline. Just over an hour ago, he had taken a call from Bob Oswald and taken notes about Susan Oswald. His notes read: *Fifteen. Pregnant. Alleges teacher. Teacher SUSPENDED. On police bail.* It was Bob Oswald who had given Lawrence Riden Mr Jeffries' mobile number. It was Susan Oswald who had given Mr Jeffries' mobile number to Bob Oswald. This, in turn, was Mr Jeffries' own fault, because he had given Susan Oswald his mobile number in the first place. Now Mr Jeffries stood cold and naked in his bedroom and said, 'For pity's sake. Are you a reporter?'

Lawrence Riden said, 'Yes. Why? Is that a problem for you?'

Mr Jeffries said, 'Why the hell should it be a problem for me? I haven't done anything wrong.'

Lawrence Riden said, 'You think it's OK to get a girl you're teaching pregnant? You think that isn't wrong?'

'I haven't got anyone pregnant.'

'So you don't deny the affair then?'

'What affair? For God's sake.'

'The affair between you and Susan Oswald.'

'There was no affair between me and Susan Oswald.'

'No? It was just a casual fling? A one-night stand? Did she try to tempt you with her body? Do you want me to tell your side of the story?'

'What side of what story, you bloody idiot? There isn't a story to tell. There wasn't any affair. Yes. There is a baby. Or at least, the girl claims she's pregnant. But it isn't mine. It's nothing to do with me at all. The girl came to me for advice. She told me she was pregnant. She said she wanted an abortion. I told her not to rush into an abortion. I told her to talk it through with her family. That's the only involvement I've had.'

'So you deny everything?'

Mr Jeffries said nothing.

'And the police have released you on bail?'

Mr Jeffries swore at Lawrence Riden and cut the call off. His heart beat hard in his chest. He swore at the emptiness around him, then raised the can of lager he was holding to his lips. It was empty. Mr Jeffries shook the last few drops into his mouth, then crumpled the can in his hand. For a moment, he considered getting another can and taking it back to the shower, but what he needed right now wasn't to get back in the shower and drink another can of super-strength lager. What he needed right now was to hear the voice of someone who believed he hadn't done anything wrong. Before he could stop himself doing it, he speed-dialled Cerys's mobile. She answered on the second ring. 'Mike. God. Are you OK?'

'I'm fine,' he lied. 'I'm fine.'

Cerys said, 'I'm so sorry about what's happened. We all know you never touched her.'

Mr Jeffries felt a rush of warmth despite the fact he was naked and cold in his bedroom. He said, 'I wish the police and the school could see that.'

'I'd tell them myself if I thought it'd do any good. Honestly. I would.'

The tenderness in Cerys's voice made Mr Jeffries shut his eyes and say, 'Cerys, can I come over and see you?'

'No.'

There was a moment's silence, then she said, 'I'm sorry, Mike. You can't.'

'I can't?' Mr Jeffries opened his eyes. 'Why? What's the matter?'

'Nothing's the matter. I just don't think it's a good idea.'

'As a friend,' Mr Jeffries said quickly. 'Not as a boyfriend. I won't try anything on.'

'I know that,' Cerys said. 'It's just now's not a very good time.'

'Any time, then. Any time at all. I mean, I haven't exactly

231

got a lot on till Susan's had her baby.' Mr Jeffries expected
Cerys to laugh at this. Instead, she started to cry. Mr Jeffries
could tell from the way she was breathing. He said, 'Cerys,
what's the matter?'

'I've been seeing someone else.'

The words were so unexpected they didn't make sense to
Mr Jeffries at first. Then, all at once, they clicked into place.
He took a deep breath and he said, 'How can you have been
seeing someone else? We've only been apart for a week.'

Cerys didn't answer. Mr Jeffries tried hard to keep his voice
light.

'Anyone I know?'

Again, Cerys remained silent. Mr Jeffries fell silent as well.
The two of them listened to each other's breathing until,
finally, Cerys said, 'It's Archie. I've been seeing Archie. Mike.
I'm sorry. I am so, so sorry.'

'Archie? You've been seeing Archie Cunningham? How long
for?'

'Mike . . . don't . . .'

'How long for? Exactly?'

'Please. Mike. Don't.'

'Longer than one fucking week then.' Mr Jeffries held his
phone very tight in his hand and thought back to the last
time he had seen her. Had she gone through to Archie's
bedroom after he'd left? Had they slept together that night?
That morning? That lunchtime? 'You back-stabbing two-faced
bitch, Cerys. I can't believe you've done this to me. On top of
everything else I'm going through right now. You back-
stabbing two-faced bitch.'

The sound of Cerys's sobbing grew louder. Mr Jeffries couldn't stand it. He killed the call and went to hurl his phone at the wall. It slipped from his grasp and fell pathetically to the floor. He stared at it for a moment, then headed towards the kitchen for yet another lager. As he did so, he caught sight of himself in the mirror on the back of his bedroom door. He was naked and dripping and held a crumpled can in his left hand. He stared at himself and imagined Cerys in bed with Archie Cunningham and remembered Archie Cunningham sitting beside him in that police cell and felt a wave of disgust for himself that made him see how everyone else must be seeing him now. Stupid, stupid, stupid. Behind him, his mobile phone began to ring. Mr Jeffries sank down to the floor and put his head in his hands and he wept.

Lawrence Riden tried to call Mr Jeffries three more times, then gave up and carried on driving. He was in Hedge End within the hour. It was the sort of place poor Londoners aspired to, tucked away between Southampton and Portsmouth, full of retail parks and hedgerows. Some of these Londoners even made it. They swapped the tube and the hassle for a ninety-minute each way commute and a house the size of a mansion. Lawrence Riden had often considered it himself. A nice house, a front garden, a back garden, sky that he could see. Then he met the Oswalds. If suburbia was full of people like the Oswalds, Lawrence Riden was staying in London. He sat at their kitchen table and sipped tea from an unwashed mug and watched female Oswalds run riot. One of them was Susan Oswald. Riden could see she was pregnant – hipster jeans and a crop top were not the things she should have been wearing. She shouldn't have been smoking either. Or playing on that rusty old swing. Lawrence Riden said nothing. It wasn't his place to judge. He looked down at his notepad and sighed. *Girl says teacher got me pregnant. Teacher says, nope, wasn't me.* Coming here hadn't exactly expanded the story. His editor was never going to run with this. What Lawrence Riden needed was an angle. He looked at Bob Oswald and smiled. 'Well, thanks very much for your time, Mr Oswald, but is there anyone else I could talk to? Anyone else who knows Mike Jeffries – anyone at all?'

Bob Oswald nodded towards the kitchen window. 'Try the Cunninghams over the square. He was knocking off the silly Welsh slapper who lives there. Number 29.' He drained his can of Stella and crumpled the tin in his hand. 'When do I get me money?'

Lawrence Riden shrugged. 'When my editor decides to run with the story.'

Bob Oswald went to the fridge and helped himself to another can of Stella, then opened the front door for Lawrence Riden to leave. 'Better get going then, hadn't you?'

Lawrence Riden nodded and got to his feet. 'Nice meeting you, then, Mr Oswald. Say goodbye to Susan for me.' He held his hand out for Bob Oswald to shake, but Bob Oswald just looked at it and did nothing. Lawrence Riden let it hang for a moment, then pulled it back to his side and turned and stepped out of the house. As Bob Oswald slammed the door behind him, Laurence Riden muttered *tosser* under his breath and made his way over to the Cunninghams'.

*   *   *

And as Lawrence Riden muttered *tosser* under his breath and made his way over to the Cunninghams', he walked past the Buckley place.

And as Lawrence Riden walked past the Buckley place, inside the Buckley place, a tragedy had happened, an ugly, horrible, irredeemable travesty of life.

Dillon lay still in Broken Buckley's wardrobe with his small bony hands clenched into fists and the hood of his pale pink hoodie pulled low over sightless blue eyes.

Broken sat uncertain before him. Dillon's stillness disturbed him. He wasn't sure where it had come from. He stared in silence for a long time, then pulled Dillon in towards him. Dillon lay with his head hanging back and his lips in a dry spitless line. Broken took a long deep breath and then pressed his lips to Dillon's. Dillon remained still in his arms. Broken continued to hold him. He breathed in, he breathed out, he breathed in, he breathed out, but there was nothing in Dillon to draw back on; there was nothing in Dillon at all. Digging fingernails into the swathes of Dillon's pale pink hoodie, Broken kept breathing in and then out, in and then out, but it was useless, pointless – innocence had gone, it had melted away.

And, still, Broken heard the laughter.

And, still, Broken heard the sound of a fist hitting flesh.

And, still, Broken heard his mother, insistent, from under the doorway: Rick, eat your lunch, please, baby, please, come out and eat your lunch, I've made you sausage sandwiches.

Broken turned and looked at the door.

You, he thought. It was you. You've stolen it. Innocence.
You've stolen it. I can hear it in your voice. I can smell it
in your cooking. I don't know how you did it. But I know
it was you who did it. I know it was you who did it. I know it
was you who did it.

And his mother said, Rick, please, eat your lunch, I've done
you sausage sandwiches with tomato ketchup. Please, baby.
Come out. Just for a little while. You know you love sausage
sandwiches with tomato ketchup.

And, finally, the door opened, and Mrs Buckley turned. She
looked up at Broken. She smiled. She said, Love, I knew you'd
come out, I knew, if I kept on trying, I knew it would all be
OK . . .

And Broken strode in a straight line towards her.

And he shouted LOVE at the top of his voice.

And he reached his hands out towards her.

And he pushed her in the chest so she fell down the stairs.

She screamed. Once. It was the last sound she ever made. It
echoed, quite a shrill sound. Cerys and Lawrence Riden thought
it was one of the Oswald girls. They both looked towards the
Oswald house on the far side of the square, then they both
looked back at each other. Cerys said, 'What's it to you?'

Lawrence Riden spoke calmly and clearly. 'I'd like to make
sure we get all the facts.'

Cerys stared, suspicious.

'Look,' Lawrence Riden continued. 'Like I said, I'm with
the *News of the World*. I've been over Mr Oswald's place with

his daughter and she's spilled her guts about Mike Jeffries. Where they did it. How many times they did it. What positions they did it in. A photographer's over there now, taking snaps of her in a bikini. Being honest with you . . . er . . . ?'

'Cerys.'

'Cerys? That's a nice name. What's your second name, if you don't mind me asking?'

'Hislop.'

'Well, being honest with you, Miss Hislop – it is Miss, isn't it? Thought so. I can usually tell – it's going in this Sunday's edition. My editor's gonna love it. But I'm not a monster. This Mike Jeffries won't talk to me. I can understand that. He's scared. He's been caught with his pants down. He's feeling ashamed. But I'm not out to demonise him, so what I'd really like to do is put a few things in from his perspective. What's he like? What motivates him? I'd like the viewpoint of one of his friends. According to Mr Oswald from over the road there, you and this Mike Jeffries are in a relationship? Is that still the case? Do you intend to stand by him? Have you forgiven him for cheating on you with a schoolgirl? How are you coping with the shame? The betrayal? Would you –'

Cerys stepped backwards and slammed the door in Lawrence Riden's face. He tried the doorbell a couple of times, but it was obvious he'd got as much as he could hope for. He sighed and pocketed his notebook, then made his way back to his car. It was parked in the lay-by to the left of the Buckley property. Lawrence Riden passed directly in front of a house that contained two corpses and considered his virtually non-existent story, then got in his car and drove away. As he did so, Broken Buckley made his way down the stairs and stood very close to his mother. Just the same as Dillon, she lay very still at his feet. He reached down and brushed her face with his fingers, then placed his hands on her cheeks.

'How?' he whispered. 'Why?'

No answer. Broken breathed in stiffly. He got down on all fours. He nuzzled his mother's cheek. Mrs Buckley's face lolled. Broken pulled it back towards him. He spoke very close to her mouth.

'How?' he whispered. 'Why?'

He stayed beside her all night.

Now she was suddenly silent, he didn't want to be away from her any more. There was an eeriness to her stillness. He prodded her. She refused to be roused. He circled restlessly around her. He cupped his hands to her ears and he whispered her name. She ignored him. Her lips grew blue. Spittle dried white on her chin. Broken shivered. He sobbed. He sat down close beside her. He tucked his knees into his stomach. His heart beat so hard in his chest. Shadows gathered and darkness fell. The evening turned into the night-time. The clock ticked on towards midnight. In the distance, Broken could hear the sound of boy racers along Bubb Lane and Tollbar Way. He rocked backwards and forwards, backwards and forwards, until three or four in the morning when, finally, the sound of screaming car engines died and only the indistinct hum of the motorway was left to float to him out of the darkness. Broken sat and hummed along with it. The night crawled on into dawn. Finally, the rattle of a milk float alarmed him. He got to his feet and stepped over his mother's body. He forced himself towards the front door. He stood with one eye pressed to the spyglass. The street elongated before him, all shadows and dew and empty grey pavements. Birds sang. A mist thinned and then melted away. Broken remained by the front door and saw Archie Cunningham set off to work and Mrs Weston take her dog for its first walk of the day. He saw a young girl go past. She was wearing a baseball cap. She had her hands in her pockets. She was dragging her feet. Broken wondered if it was Skunk Cunningham. He shut his eyes and breathed in. He opened his eyes and breathed out. He remembered days spent peering through the gap in his curtains, watching Skunk Cunningham skipping and riding her scooter. He remembered the sound of her laughter. These memories reminded him of the fact he had once been like Skunk Cunningham – once, it had been good to be him. Broken knocked his head against the door frame, then turned and looked down on his mother. She lay with her legs scissored and her hands splayed away from her sides. Her eyes stared up at the ceiling. Broken wanted to go to her. He wanted to pull her in towards him and breathe in, breathe out, breathe in, breathe out, but the last shreds of his sanity wouldn't let him do this. Better to go up to his bedroom and pull Dillon back out of the wardrobe. Broken shivered. He sobbed. What was the point in going up to his bedroom and pulling Dillon back out of the wardrobe? Innocence had left him. Broken had drained it away. Yes. That was how it had happened. Broken had drained it away. He turned and he turned in a circle. He slapped at his face with his hands.

And that was when he heard footsteps.

They dragged themselves through the gravel.

They made their way directly towards him.

Footsteps, outside the front door.

Terror. Panic. Fear. Broken stepped back. He stepped sideways. He stared through the frosted side panels and saw the distorted shape of a young girl wearing a baseball cap walking up the pathway. He pressed both his fists to his temples. He breathed in through his nostrils. He breathed out through his mouth. He crouched down. He stood up. He took a huge huge huge breath of air and made himself step forward and made himself open the door and made himself take hold of Sunrise Oswald and pull her inside the house. Her paper sack got stuck on the door jamb. Broken yanked it free then slammed the door on them both. Sunrise dropped the newspaper she had been about to deliver. It fell to the floor beside Mrs Buckley's slack-jawed face. Sunrise stared at her and screamed. A hand clamped over her mouth. Sunrise bit it. A fist punched her hard in the stomach. Sunrise squealed. She sobbed. Weight pressed down upon her. A mad, rasping voice yelled WHY DID SHE HAVE TO GO DO THAT? WHY DID SHE DO THAT TO ME? Before Sunrise could think of an answer, strong hands rolled her over. A mouth clamped tight to her own. Hot rank breath filled her lungs. Terror and horror and shock. Sunrise couldn't struggle. Sunrise couldn't breathe. The breath was being sucked from her. More breath was being pumped in. The taste of it made her feel sick. Sunrise wanted to vomit. She couldn't. Her throat had closed up. Still, Broken kept sucking breath from her. Still, Broken kept blowing breath in. Harder. Faster. More desperate. For a short while, the field sloped down to the south. For a short while, Broken could feel the soft breeze. For a short while, he could hear the sweet birdsong. But the image was fragile, fleeting. As Sunrise lay squirming beneath him, it drifted away into nothing and left Broken adrift in the hallway. He lifted his lips from Sunrise and stared blankly all around him. How had it all come to this? Broken didn't know. He couldn't think. He needed to get back to the field. But it was useless, pointless. This one. She wasn't like Dillon. She didn't have Dillon's innocence. She didn't have Dillon's sweetness. If anything, she reminded Broken of Saskia Oswald, but not like Saskia Oswald, because Broken had once loved Saskia Oswald. Now, though, all he could hear was the sound of Saskia Oswald's laughter as she walked away from his car. He lifted his head and he screamed, WHY DID SHE HAVE TO GO DO THAT? I DIDN'T DO HER ANY HARM.

Sunrise Oswald lay pinned underneath him and stared at the corpse of his mother and thought ohJesusChristyesyoudid.

It was almost three days before anyone noticed Sunrise was missing.

This was because of the chaos – not the chaos that was about to engulf the whole square, but the chaos of life in the Oswald house.

The Oswald house was always in chaos. There was no set time to have breakfast. There was no set time to have dinner. There was no rhythm to their lives whatsoever. Bob Oswald could be strumming his guitar at three o'clock in the morning.

241

Saskia and Saraya could be watching videos of *Trisha* as the sun came up over the pylons. Now that she was pregnant, Susan Oswald could be in bed for three or four days at a time.

Because of this unstructured lifestyle, there was no set time for the Oswalds to come together, and, as there was no set time for the Oswalds to come together, there was no set time for the Oswalds to notice Sunrise was missing. Two hours after being abducted, she came to her senses in Broken Buckley's wardrobe with the strap of her paper sack pulled tight around her neck and her mouth full of balled-up socks. She didn't know it was a dead body beside her. She thought the bundled-up pale pink hoodie was part of a larger pile of discarded clothing. She sat all alone in darkness and shouted Dad, Saskia, Sunset, Saraya, Susan, help me help me help me, but the only sounds she made were breathless little sobs. Finally, her throat hurt so much she stopped trying. She sat exhausted, hopeless, helpless, staring into darkness, until late Friday afternoon when Broken Buckley opened the wardrobe doors and removed the strap from around her neck and pulled her out and pulled the socks from her mouth and pressed his mouth to her mouth and breathed in and out and in and out until he gave up trying to get to the field through her and put the socks back in her mouth and put her back inside the wardrobe. As she fell against what she thought was a discarded bundle of clothing she saw eyes buried deep within them and screamed and screamed and screamed Dad, Saskia, Sunset, Saraya, Susan, help me help me help me, but her screams were no more than breathless little sobs. Still, though, she kept on screaming until exhaustion and terror and dread dragged her away into sleep. And, as exhaustion and terror and dread dragged her away into sleep, Susan lay in bed and smoked cigarette after cigarette, Sunset played all alone in the garden, Saskia and Saraya drank cider in front of the plasma, and Bob Oswald smoked dope and strummed his guitar. Poor old Sunrise Oswald. She simply fell through the cracks. The rest of Friday passed without anyone noticing. Saturday passed without anyone noticing. Then, on Sunday, the *News of the World* hit the shelves.

And Archie said, 'Fuck. Look at this.'

And Skunk said, 'Fuck's a bad word.'

And Cerys said, 'Oh fucking hell. I never refused to defend him. That fucking bastard reporter. How could he write so much shit? What the fuck will Mike think? What the fuck will Mike say when he sees this? On top of everything else?' She held the paper at arm's length, then dropped it and ran from the room. Archie got to his feet and followed her up the stairs. As Jed was already up there playing Xbox, Skunk was alone with the paper. She got up and walked towards it. The article Cerys and Archie had been looking at was tucked away on page 7. The headline screamed PERVERT TEACHER GOT ME PREGNANT. Beside it, there was a picture of Susan Oswald with her face pixellated. Skunk knew it was Susan Oswald, though, because there was a picture of Drummond Secondary School behind her and they had named Mr Jeffries by name:

Today, in Hampshire, a teacher is facing jail for bedding a 15-year-old pupil and getting her pregnant.

Michael Jeffries, 27, of Beavois Valley, Southampton, was suspended from his post as a schoolteacher at Drummond

Secondary School in Hedge End, where he would often be left alone with children as young as 11 years old.

Jeffries – who in a telephone conversation with our reporter protested there was nothing wrong with what he had done – has been placed on police bail following accusations of unlawful sex that came about after a 15-year-old pupil broke down and told her father she was expecting a baby. Her father, a lone parent struggling to bring up his five daughters on income support, complained to the school, who suspended Jeffries immediately. DS Jenks, from the specialist vice unit based in Southampton, refused to deny that investigations were ongoing into previously unreported complaints from other pupils.

The girl in question, Diana (not her real name, pictured here with her face obscured to protect her identity) is presently off school and receiving counselling for the ordeal Jeffries allegedly put her through. An everyday teenage girl who loves to play with her sisters and listen to Lily Allen, she at first tried to hide the identity of her lover in a misguided attempt to protect him.

'He was dead kind,' she told our reporter, 'always there, offering me lifts and sweets and complimenting me on how nice I looked and how grown up I acted. Now all I want to do is cry. I wish I'd never been born.'

Meanwhile, Cerys Hislop, Jeffries' ex-girlfriend, refused to defend him when given the opportunity.

There was more, but Skunk couldn't stand to read it. She dropped the paper and backed away. She sat down on the sofa. Upstairs, she could hear Cerys shouting and Archie trying to calm her down. Skunk stared up, at the ceiling, then down, at the paper. Above her head, Cerys's voice quietened, then footsteps descended the stairs. Archie walked into the front room and bent and kissed Skunk on the cheek.

'We're going out, little darling. Jed's going to look after you. You behave for him, OK?'

Skunk stared up at her father. 'Where are you going?'

'Just out, sweetheart. Just out.'

'Where?' she persisted. 'Why?'

Archie gave in with a sigh. 'To tell Mr Jeffries you love him. And to tell him Cerys does too.'

'Good,' Skunk said. 'I'm coming with you.'

'No, little darling. You're not.'

'Why?'

'Because,' Archie said. 'Final word.' He ruffled Skunk's hair. 'Try not to look so worried, little darling. These things, they sort themselves out.'

Poor old Archie. He really used to believe that.

Now he sits by my bed and clings to my hands and doesn't know what he believes.

After Archie ruffled Skunk's hair he ran out of the house and drove Cerys to Mr Jeffries' flat.

He drove Cerys to Mr Jeffries' flat because Cerys was worried Mr Jeffries had done something stupid.

Cerys was worried Mr Jeffries had done something stupid because he had sounded so sad and so desperate and angry after she'd admitted sleeping with Archie behind his back.

She had been trying his mobile ever since, but hadn't been able to reach him.

Now all this stuff in the papers.

So she sat beside Archie Cunningham while he drove her towards Beavois Valley and she tried Mr Jeffries' mobile number over and over again.

And Mr Jeffries did not answer.

Still, though, she kept on trying, until, finally, Archie found a parking space between a skip and a rusting transit van opposite the block of flats Mr Jeffries lived in. Then she stopped trying Mr Jeffries' mobile and the two of them jumped out and crossed the road and ran inside together. They climbed the stairs two at a time.

When they reached the door to Mr Jeffries' flat, Cerys pressed the buzzer on the wall to its right. It didn't make any sound. She knocked loudly on the door. Archie stared at her then at the door and then down at his feet. From inside the flat he heard nothing. Cerys kept knocking on the door.

'Mike,' she called. 'It's me.' She glanced at Archie then back at the door. 'Mike,' she repeated. 'It's me.' The sound of her knocking echoed around the stairwell.

Archie said, 'Try his mobile again.'

She pulled her phone back out of her pocket and speed-dialled Mr Jeffries' number. Moments later, Mr Jeffries' ringtone rang out from the other side of the door. 'Mike,' she called. 'Open up. Come on. Let me in.' She paused. She listened for the sound of movement. None came. She knocked on the door once again. 'Mike,' she shouted. 'Please. Let me in.' She breathed in, then began to shout louder. 'Mike. Open up.

I know you're in there. Come on. I'm worried about you.'
Nothing. Silence. No answer. Cerys stopped knocking on
Mr Jeffries' door and turned, instead, to Archie. 'Why isn't
he answering?'

'Maybe he isn't in.'

'But his phone's here. I can hear it.'

'Yes, I know. But he doesn't seem to be.'

'But he must be. He never goes anywhere without his
mobile. Why won't he answer the door?'

'I don't know, Cerys. I'm sorry. I just don't know.'

Cerys stared at Archie, then took a deep breath and made
herself say: 'What if he's done something stupid?'

'He won't have.'

'How do you know?'

'Because he won't.'

'How can you be so sure?'

'Come on, Cerys. Why would he?'

'Oh, I don't know, Archie. Maybe because the woman he
wants to marry has cheated on him with another man? Maybe
because he's on police bail for a crime he didn't commit?
Maybe because he's just been suspended from the job he loves
and his name's been splashed all over the papers? Any of those
reasons? Any one at all?'

Archie stared at Cerys.

She said, 'What if he's in there, dead?'

'He won't be.'

'But he could be.' Cerys looked at Mr Jeffries' front door,
then turned back to Archie. 'Do something,' she begged him.
'Please.'

'What do you want me to do? Kick his door down?' Archie waited for her to say no. Instead, she took a huge deep breath and said, 'Yes.'

'Cerys,' he said. 'Are you mad?'

'He's done something stupid. I know it.'

'You don't know any such thing. For all you know, he could be down the pub.'

'Archie, I hope he is. But what if he isn't? What if he isn't?'

Archie stared at her a moment, then turned towards Mr Jeffries' front door and kicked it as hard as he could. It only took one blow. Timber splintered. A hinge ruptured free. The door swung in and then outwards. The lower half came to rest at an angle. Archie stared in on Mr Jeffries' kitchen. Something in the air smelled dead. The kitchen itself, though, was empty. Archie looked over his shoulder at Cerys. 'Stay here,' he said. 'Stay here.' He walked from the kitchen to the hallway then on into the main room, where empty cans of lager lay strewn all over the floor. Mr Jeffries wasn't in there. Archie stepped back into the hallway. The next room along was the bedroom. It was dark and shadowed, the same as the main room. There were clothes scattered all over the bed. Mr Jeffries' mobile lay on the floor, but, again, Mr Jeffries wasn't in there. Archie stepped back into the hallway. He made his way towards the door at the end. It was closed. Archie took a deep breath and put a hand on the handle, then made himself push the door open. It knocked against the bath. Archie stepped in and stared at the shower curtain and knew what was waiting beyond it. He stood helpless, frozen, his mind full of the sound of Mr Jeffries' laughter and an image of

Mr Jeffries' face. Archie blinked. He swallowed. He didn't want to pull back the shower curtain and look down on Mr Jeffries' body. Instead, he stood paralysed with his hands clasped tight before him until Cerys came in and pushed past him and pulled the shower curtain aside to reveal the bath held nothing more than a crumpled can of super-strength lager and a dry bar of scented blue soap.

Still, though, they called the police.

Once they found the graph, they had to.

It was Cerys who found it. She held it out towards Archie.

'What?' he said. 'What is it?' He took the sheet of paper from her and saw the axis labelled TIME and the axis labelled ASPIRATIONS and the arc that started at zero, peaked at twenty, then descended to twenty-seven and the words DEAD, PROBABLY. Archie said, 'I'm calling the police.' He didn't have to. Cerys was already doing it. They arrived two hours later, one male officer, one female officer, their expressions fixed at a point between boredom and exhaustion. They took Mr Jeffries' details and listened to the background of his disappearance. The female officer made notes. The male one looked totally disinterested. Archie said, 'What are you going to do?' The two officers stared at Archie. They shrugged. What could they do? There was nothing in Mr Jeffries' flat to suggest where he might have gone, Cerys didn't have contact details for anyone he was close to, and, more importantly, no one knew exactly how long he had been missing or even if he was missing at all. As Archie had said to Cerys, he could simply have gone down the pub.

'But,' Cerys said, 'you have to do something. Look at this note we found.' She held the graph out towards them once more. The male officer and the female officer studied it then suggested Cerys and Archie phone around local hospitals. The female officer put a hand on Cerys's shoulder.

'Why don't you call us back if he hasn't turned up in two days?'

The male officer said, 'Yeah. That's the best thing to do.'

Then they made their excuses and left.

Alone in Mr Jeffries' flat, Archie and Cerys stared at one another without speaking, then Archie called an emergency call-out service to take care of the door and Cerys began to phone around local hospitals. By the time the handy-man had turned up and repaired the damage Archie had done, Cerys was still on hold to the last hospital listed in Mr Jeffries' copy of the Yellow Pages. Finally, she got the same answer the other hospitals had given her. No one answering to Mr Jeffries' description had been admitted in the last few days. She threw his copy of the Yellow Pages at the wall then stood with her head in her hands. Archie paid the handy-man then wrapped his arms around Cerys and pulled her in towards him. She shrugged him off. She said, 'Don't.' Archie stared at her back, then turned away and searched through Mr Jeffries' flat. He found a pen and paper and some Sellotape in one of Mr Jeffries' kitchen drawers. Struggling to know what to write, he scribbled a note to Mr Jeffries saying his new keys were with Cerys, then stuck the note on the mended front door. Then he went back to Cerys and wrapped his arms around her again. She stiffened for a moment, then turned in his arms and rested her head on his shoulder. 'Where is he?' she said. 'Where the hell is he, Archie?'

Archie didn't know. He stared helplessly at Cerys. She stared helplessly at him. Finally, he said, 'Come on. We can't do anything here.'

The two of them headed back to his car. As they drove out of Beavois Valley, Archie put a hand on her leg.

'Let's not mention this to Skunk. She's worried enough as it is.'

Cerys said, 'Aren't you?'

They drove back to Hedge End in silence.

I was waiting on the stairs when they got back. Did you see him? Is he OK? They answered yes to both questions. I followed them into the front room and bombarded them with more questions. Would he be back in school tomorrow? Had he come up with a way to prove Susan Oswald was lying? Had they come up with a way to prove Susan Oswald was lying? No? No? What do you mean, no? Why hasn't he come up with a way to prove Susan Oswald's lying? Why haven't you come up with a way to prove Susan Oswald's lying? There has to be a way, Daddy. There has to be. Just has to. Why can't you find one? Why, Daddy? Why, Cerys? Why?

I took Cerys's sharpness for impatience.

Archie, tell her, for God's sake. She's doing my bloody head in.

I took Archie's short temper for the fact it was a Sunday and he had to go back to work in the morning. He was always aggressive on Sundays.

Skunk, for God's sake, can't you leave it alone? Go play Xbox or something. Jesus. Jesus Christ.

But –

No buts. Go play Xbox with Jed. For God's sake. Leave us alone. Go away.

But I couldn't go play Xbox with Jed. I wasn't talking to Jed. I still hadn't forgiven him for punching me in the back and saying I was missing Dillon. He still hadn't forgiven me for annoying him so much he had to punch me in the back after I said he loved Susan Oswald.

That dumb lying trog Susan Oswald.

I'd only said he loved her because she'd been doing stuff to him at that party.

All of this was her fault.

I went up to my room and I sat and stared out on the square. I hated Susan Oswald with all of my heart. I loved Mr Jeffries with all of my heart. He made school time fun. He told me stuff I didn't know. There had to be a way to save him from her lies. I couldn't just sit and do nothing. I didn't know what I could do, though. I didn't know how I could help him. I couldn't think of a way. There had to be a way, though. Had to be. Just had to. I thought and thought and thought. I thought with all of my might.

And, as Skunk Cunningham thought with all of her might, Susan Oswald lay on her side in her bed. Her fingers were wet with fresh blood. She held them out towards Bob Oswald and said, 'Daddy, what's happening to me?'

Bob Oswald took hold of her fingers. He said, 'It's OK, honey, don't worry.' Behind him, Saskia sobbed in the doorway.

Susan said, 'Oh my God, it's the baby, isn't it? Oh my God, I'm losing my baby. Oh my God. Oh my God. Oh my God.'

Bob Oswald stared at his daughter and thought about his wife. He said, 'Saskia, call an ambulance.' Then he put his forehead close to Susan's and looked into her eyes. 'Baby, don't you worry. Things are going to be OK. We're going to get you to a hospital. We're going to get you seen to. You might not be losing your baby. And, if you are, it might just turn out for the best.' He put his arms around Susan's shoulders. He pulled her in. He held her very close. Susan curled up in his arms and cried into his hairy chest, though she wasn't sure why she was crying. She didn't want no stupid baby. She didn't want to be pregnant. She just wanted for this to be over. Poor old Susan Oswald. It had all got too adult for her. She pulled her legs into her stomach and enjoyed the sensation of having her father's arms around her. Bob Oswald put his face in her hair and ever so silently wept.

And, as Bob Oswald ever so silently wept, Broken Buckley sat on his knees in his bedroom.

He held Sunrise in his arms.

He leaned down above her.

He pressed his lips to her mouth.

He breathed in.

He breathed out.

He breathed in.

He breathed out.

But it was useless.

Pointless.

There was no way – through her – to the field.

Broken stuffed a pair of balled socks back into her mouth then stuffed her back into the wardrobe. He pulled Dillon's body out. He held it in his arms. Dillon's hoodie fell gently backwards. Dillon's eyes stared blankly at nothing. Broken prised Dillon's mouth open. He lowered his lips to Dillon's. He breathed in. He breathed out. He breathed in. He breathed out. But there was nothing. Nothing. There was nothing in Dillon at all. Broken sobbed. It was useless. Hopeless. Pointless. He put Dillon back into the wardrobe. He stared down on Sunrise Oswald. She was writhing, writhing, pulling at her bindings, screaming silently into the socks he had stuffed in her mouth. Broken swung the wardrobe doors shut. He fell in a heap on his bed. Voices. Swirling voices. Laughter. A fist hitting flesh. Rick. Eat your dinner. Voices. They swirled from under the door frame. They mingled with the sound of the doorbell. Broken heard this doorbell. He sat up. He got to his feet. He crept to his bedroom window. He reached a hand to the curtain. He pulled back the curtain. Downstairs, on the doorstep. Innocence. It had come. It had returned. Broken stared and stared. He put his hand to the glass. Then he let go of the curtain. He made his way down the stairs. He stepped over Mrs Buckley's prone body. He slid the chain off. He drew back the deadbolts.

He slowly opened the door.

And I said, 'Hello, Broken Buckley. Could you do me a favour, please?'

Because Broken Buckley could prove Susan Oswald was a liar. She had lied about him in the past. Just the same as she was lying about Mr Jeffries now, she had accused Broken of sleeping with her. Mr Buckley had said so to Bob Oswald: It wasn't my son who shouted rape, was it? It was your lying bitch of a daughter. It had been so long ago now, I'd almost forgotten about it, but sitting in my bedroom, trying to think about how I could help Mr Jeffries, I'd suddenly remembered. Poor old Broken Buckley. He hadn't always been broken. Once, he'd been the gangly teenager on the other side of the square washing the car his father had bought him as a present for passing his driving test.

And then Bob Oswald had walked up behind him and beaten him into a pulp.

And then the police had come and taken him away.

All because of Susan Oswald.

But, finally, the police had let him go.

Finally, the police had dropped all the charges.

Archie had said so. He'd shouted it at Bob Oswald after we'd seen Revenge of the Sith*: Open-and-shut case, considering the police dropped all the charges. Like taking candy off a kid, taking money off you.*

So, here, in the square, was someone who could prove Susan Oswald was a liar.

Here, in the square, was someone who could go to the police and tell them what Susan Oswald was really like.

And, once Broken Buckley had done this, the police would drop all the charges against Mr Jeffries.

And Mr Jeffries would come back to school.

All Broken Buckley had to do was come down the station with me and remind the police that Susan Oswald was a liar.

All I had to do was go over the square and ask him to do it. And, yes, I was scared. And, yes, I was terrified. But it was daylight. And the police had never come out and put a tent up, and the Oswalds had come back from the seaside, and, anyway, what did Jed know? I'd show him that Broken Buckley wasn't an axe-murderer-psycho-killer. I'd show him that Broken Buckley was nothing more than the man who lived over the square who could get Mr Jeffries his job back. All I had to do was go over and ask.

So that's what I did.

I walked out of my bedroom.

I walked down the stairs.

I walked out of the house and shut the door quietly behind me.

I walked across the square.

I walked up the Buckleys' front drive.

I knocked on the Buckleys' front door.

I waited for Broken Buckley to answer.

And, when he answered, I said, 'Hello, Broken Buckley. Could you do me a favour, please?'

And I held a hand out towards him.

And he thrust his hands towards me.

Broken Buckley grabbed Skunk Cunningham by the shoulders. He picked her up. He dragged her inside. The front door slammed shut behind her. Broken spun her round and screamed in her face. No words. Just noise. His eyes were wide.

They were bloodshot. There was snot and hair up Broken's
nostrils, snot and hair and darkness and his nostrils were wide
and his skin was yellow and his breath was damp like a grey
autumn day. His hands dug into Skunk's shoulders. He lowered
his face to her face. Skunk tried very hard to fight him. She
tried very hard to break free. But struggling was useless. Broken
lowered his mouth to her mouth. He blew sadness deep into
her throat. Skunk gagged. Still, she tried to break free. She
couldn't though. She couldn't. She could only stare into his
eyes. She hardly knew who he was. He was no longer the shy
gangly teenager she had once seen beaten up in the street. He
was no longer the person who could help her get Mr Jeffries'
job back. He was what Jed had said he was. A monster. A
monster. They danced like vampire and virgin. He sucked her
innocence out. He blew his misery in. But it was just breath.
Skunk's breath. His breath. Their moist wet mingled saliva.
Her terror. His terror. Her doom. His salvation. Broken shut
his eyes. He heard birdsong. He rubbed his face in dry grass.
He breathed in, he breathed out, he breathed in, he breathed
out, and, later, when he was calmer, while Skunk was dazed
and drifting and trying to work out what had happened, he
carried her up the stairs and tied her hands and feet with cord
from his mother's dressing gown and put her in the wardrobe.
Skunk sat dazed and disorientated, her head pounding, her
throat dry, her body shaking all over. Everything was dark.
Everything was spinning. The air smelled. Skunk didn't know
what of, but it gagged her, ripe, in the back of her throat. She
couldn't work out how she'd got here. Then, suddenly, she
remembered. She had been trying to help Mr Jeffries. She had

been trying to get Broken to help her. But Broken hadn't helped her. Broken had put her in here. Now, from beside her, to her left, she became aware of sound, of heat, of movement. She turned her head. She saw the outline of something in the shadows. She blinked and strained to see. She couldn't. It was hopeless. She could only hear. Schnumch. Schnumch. Whispered, over and over. Skunk sat very still, very quiet. Except she was shaking. She couldn't stop shaking. Schnumch. Schnumch. And she couldn't work out what that noise was. She only knew there was blood in her mouth. And socks. Schnumch. Schnumch. Skunk shivered. She breathed in through her nostrils. She breathed out through her nostrils. She couldn't get air down her throat. The socks. The smell. She pulled hard at her bindings. Her bindings were tight. They twisted her hands back behind her. Her shoulders ached. Her wrists ached. Her elbows ached. The small of her back ached. Her neck ached. Her head ached. Everything ached. And she was shaking all over. Schnumch. Schnumch. Skunk turned her head sideways again. Her eyes couldn't see through the darkness. She couldn't see what was there. And her neck ached too much to keep looking. She turned her head forward again. Darkness, stifling darkness. Then, without warning, the wardrobe doors opened and there was no darkness to protect her, only Broken Buckley, staring down, shifting from one foot to the other, his fists pressed close to his mouth. Skunk couldn't look at him. His wild hair. His staring eyes. His flaring nostrils. She turned and stared at Sunrise Oswald. Sunrise Oswald stared back at her. Sunrise Oswald was sobbing. Sunrise Oswald was saying Skunk's name. Over and over. Schnumch.

Schnumch. Skunk. Skunk. Like Skunk was someone Sunrise
Oswald was happy to see. Skunk stared at her, stared, then
turned away, towards Dillon. She knew it was him straight
away. It was the pale pink hoodie. It was the sightless blue
eyes. Oh. It was the sightless blue eyes. And the fact he had
never left her. The fact he had been taken away. Skunk stared
at his crumpled dead body and forgot all about Mr Jeffries.
She forgot all about Susan Oswald. She forgot all about everything except the fact Dillon was dead to her right and Sunrise
was tied to her left and Broken Buckley was leaning towards
her. She tried to squirm backwards. She sobbed. She screamed.
Nnnnnn. Nnnnnn. Nnnnnn. Broken reached in and seized
her. He pulled her out of the wardrobe. He took the balled
socks from her mouth. He placed a hand over her nostrils.
He placed his mouth over her mouth. Skunk screamed. She
writhed. She kicked. But her hands were tied. Her feet were
tied. She couldn't fight. She couldn't breathe. Broken Buckley
breathed for her. He breathed in. He breathed out. He breathed
in. He breathed out. Skunk stared up at him. His bulging eyes.
His tangled mess of hair. His wide mad staring eyes. She tried
so hard to fight him. But she had no air to fight with. She
had no air at all. And her hands were tied. Her feet were tied.
And she couldn't breathe. She couldn't breathe. Nnnnnn.
Nnnnnn. Nnnnnn. Dark spots danced before her. Skunk
slipped and slid within them, until darkness was all she
could see.

And, as Skunk slipped and slid into darkness, Susan Oswald
breathed in gas and air and stared wide-eyed at the ceiling
and watched it fade into black.

Asleep and dreaming of nothing, she was carried down the stairs on a collapsible stretcher and wheeled out into the square where a crowd had gathered, waiting. This crowd was small, pathetic. It consisted of Jed, Archie, Cerys, Mrs Weston from number 12, Mrs Weston's dog and two passing joggers. The Oswalds filed out to swell its numbers – all except for Sunrise – and, as this was their first time together since she had gone missing, this was the first time she was missed.

It was Bob Oswald who missed her. He climbed into the ambulance and sat down next to Susan and looked down on his other daughters and thought, where the hell is Sunrise? I don't think I've seen her in days. He thought back: had he seen her that morning? No. He didn't think so. Had he seen her the previous morning? No. He didn't think so. But then again, he couldn't be sure. Bob Oswald rubbed his temples. He couldn't think. He couldn't remember. He said to Saraya, 'Where's Sunrise?' Saraya shrugged. She didn't know. She couldn't think. She was still wasted on last night's cocktail of cider and dope. Bob put a hand on Susan's forehead. 'Find her,' he said. 'Susan will want us together when she comes home.' Saraya nodded. Bob gripped Susan's hands tight. One of the medics swung the ambulance doors shut. Sirens wailed. The ambulance drove out of the square. The crowd dissipated. The Oswald girls retreated.

Not to go looking for Sunrise, but to go and find Bob Oswald's drugs.

So even though Skunk went missing three days after Sunrise, it was her absence the world noticed first.

It would have been noticed that Sunday. On any normal weekend, it would have been noticed that Sunday.

Archie always looked in on his daughter as he made his way up to bed. He always had. He always would. He loved to watch Skunk sleeping. She looked so peaceful. She looked so happy. Jed never looked so peaceful or so happy. He tossed and he turned in his sleep and got himself lost under the duvet. Skunk, on the other hand, slept with her head in the one place on her pillow and her Jedi Knight duvet tucked neatly up under her chin.

On that Sunday evening, though, Archie didn't make it to bed. He sat beside Cerys while she kept phoning local hospitals again and again. What have we done? she kept saying. What the hell have we done? Nothing, Archie told her. We haven't done anything. Where is he then? she kept asking. Where the hell is he? I don't know, Archie kept saying. I'm sorry. I just don't know. They drank endless cups of coffee. They smoked endless cigarettes. Cerys sobbed. She was beside herself with worry. She was beside herself with guilt. She kept remembering the way Mr Jeffries had sounded on the phone when she'd admitted sleeping with Archie behind his back. She kept wondering if Mr Jeffries had done something stupid. She kept wondering if Mr Jeffries was dead. Dead. Mike, dead. It seemed impossible. Just a few weeks ago they'd practically been living together. Now, suddenly, she thought he was dead.

Finally, exhausted, she slept in Archie's arms on the sofa. He sat and held her and stared at the clock as it crept past 3 a.m., then 4 a.m., then 5. As he held her, he thought, if we can just get through this, we'll be happy. Me, Cerys, Jed, Skunk.

The four of us, a family. I know we'll be happy together. He looked at her shut eyes and her slack mouth and her nostrils. He held a hand before her mouth and felt the warmth of her silent breathing. He touched her soft stomach through the T-shirt she was wearing. He smelled her hair. She slept on, heavy on his chest, her bare feet tucked up on the sofa, one shoulder digging into his ribs. Once in a while, she twitched, or murmured. Archie said, It's OK, you're OK.

The first hint of daylight started to filter through the room at just before six. At seven, Archie shook her awake. 'Come on,' he said in a whisper. 'Let's get you up to bed.'

She stared at him. There was mascara on her cheeks and lipstick on her teeth. Her breath smelled of cigarettes and coffee.

'Come on,' he said again. 'Let's get you to bed for a few hours. You can get some more sleep while I get the kids off to school.'

'Aren't you working today?'

'No,' he said. 'I'm pulling a sickie. We can have a lazy morning then work out what to do about tracking down Mike. I was thinking we could go back over to his flat and see if there's an address book lying around. OK?'

'OK.'

He stood up. He pulled her to her feet. He guided her up the stairs. She leaned into him as he did it. His bulk was re-assuring. She liked the way being cared for by him made her feel.

Upstairs, in his bedroom, he laid her down on top of his duvet, then folded the other half across her. He knelt down by the side of the bed.

'Cerys,' he said softly, 'try not to worry. He doesn't strike me as the type.'

'What type?'

'You know what type.'

She nodded. She shut her eyes. She said, 'Archie. Thanks.'

The tone of her voice made him shiver. He got to his feet and made his way to Jed's room. It was just after seven fifteen. He knocked on the door then opened it. Jed was playing Xbox in the shadows, hunched up before the bright screen. Archie crossed the room and ruffled Jed's hair, then walked out again and made his way to Skunk's room. Here, he knocked on her door and waited. Skunk didn't answer. Archie waited a little longer, then knocked on the door once again. When, still, she didn't answer, he pushed the door open and peered inside. Skunk's bedroom was empty. The bed didn't look slept in. Archie walked towards it. He put his hand on Skunk's pillows. They were cold. Archie stepped away from the bed. He walked over to the window. He looked out on the square. It was quiet and empty. The sun wasn't yet over the pylons. Archie looked back at Skunk's empty bed. He swallowed. He rubbed his temples. Then he made his way back to Jed's room. 'Have you seen your sister this morning?' Jed frowned. He shook his head. 'When was the last time you saw her?' Jed shrugged. Yesterday morning? Archie thought back to the last time he'd seen his daughter himself. Yesterday afternoon. Late yesterday afternoon. After they got back from Mr Jeffries' flat. What was it he'd said to her? For God's sake. Leave us alone. Go away.

Leave us alone. Go away.

Archie stepped out of Jed's room and hurried through to

his own room. He shook Cerys's shoulder. He said, 'Cerys, Skunk didn't sleep in her bed last night.' Cerys woke up in an instant. She sat up. She drew her knees in under her chin. She said, What do you mean, she didn't sleep in her bed last night? Archie said, Her bed hasn't been slept in. Believe me. It hasn't been slept in. He kept a hand on Cerys's shoulder. He said, I told her to leave us alone. I told her to go away. Last night. Remember? I told her to leave us alone. I told her to go away. Cerys said, Have you called her mobile? Archie shook his head. He turned. He rushed out of his bedroom. He rushed down the stairs. He ran into the hallway. He picked up the phone. He called his daughter's mobile. She felt it vibrate in her pocket. She tried to move her hands. She tried to move her feet. She couldn't. They were tied with cord from Mrs Buckley's dressing gown. Sunrise sat beside her with her own hands and feet tied by the cord from Mr Buckley's dressing gown. She could feel Skunk's phone vibrating as well. Her eyes were huge dishes of hope. But Skunk's phone could vibrate all it wanted. Neither of them could reach it. Neither of them could move. They sat staring at each other and, between them, Skunk's phone vibrated, vibrated, then stopped. Still, they stayed staring at each other. Deep breaths. Deep breaths. Sobs. Across the square, Archie stood all alone in his hallway. He kept his hand on the phone. Finally, Cerys came down and joined him. She rested her head on his shoulder. He covered his face with his hands.

Skunk didn't see the sun rise up over the pylons. She didn't see Archie sitting all alone on the doorstep, his shirt hanging out of his trousers, his chin growing brittle with stubble, his eyes red and wet from lack of sleep. Cerys brought him a cup of coffee. He held it for a moment, then hurled it down at the ground. 'Where is she?' he screamed at his lover. 'Where the hell has she got to? Why is she doing this to me?'

It was Cerys who called the police.

Her call got put through to a switchboard. An operator who sounded hung-over took down her details and forwarded the call to the fire brigade in Glasgow. Cerys hung up in a rage. She tried a local number out of Yellow Pages. That station had been shut down last year. She phoned the Citizens' Advice Bureau. They gave her another number. Someone would come out shortly. When, she asked, exactly? Oh, the voice said, sometime soon. Archie took the receiver from her. 'You'll send someone out now,' he insisted. 'Within the hour. My eleven-year-old daughter is missing. You get me? My eleven-year-old daughter is missing. You'll get someone out here right away.'

Two and a half hours later, a squad car pulled into the square.

A young PC with bumfluff and a bored middle-aged overweight PC climbed out of the car. Archie, Cerys and Jed were already outside, waiting. They greeted the policemen under the porch.

'How old is she?'

'Eleven years old. She'll be twelve years old in July.'

'And has she ever run off before?'

'No. Never.'

'And your relationship to her is?'

'I'm her father.'

The younger policeman looked at Cerys's breasts. 'And you're her mother?'

A brief glance of unspoken contempt.

'Do I look old enough?'

'No, Miss. I'd say that you don't.'

Archie interrupted. 'Her mother and I are divorced. She lives in Majorca now. Sunning herself on my money.'

'I see,' said the bored middle-aged policeman. 'Could she have come back and abducted . . . er . . .' He glanced down at his notes. 'Skunk?'

'No,' Archie said. 'She didn't fight for custody. She hasn't tried to contact us since she left.'

'Is anything missing from Skunk's bedroom? More clothes than she would normally be wearing? MP3 player? Bedding? Anything like that?'

Archie stared down at his feet. 'No. Nothing. We've already checked.'

'And have you fallen out with her recently? Has anything upsetting happened?'

Archie drew his breath in. 'The last few days have been testing.' He glanced sideways at Cerys. 'We didn't have an argument last night, exactly, but I told her to leave us alone.'

The two policemen looked at each other, then the bored middle-aged one moved to one side and radioed it in. As he stood speaking into his handset, a taxi pulled into the square. Archie, Jed and Cerys watched as it parked outside the Oswalds' and Bob and Susan got out. Bob had his arms around Susan. She walked with her face buried in his broad chest.

Archie looked at Bob Oswald. Bob Oswald looked at him.

Archie made himself say, 'Everything OK, Bob?'

Bob Oswald shook his head. 'Susan lost the baby.' There were tears in his eyes. Susan's shoulders were shaking.

Archie made himself say, 'I'm sorry.'

Cerys said nothing. Jed stared at Susan, then looked down at the ground.

Bob Oswald pulled a face, then helped Susan into his house. Archie stared after them for a moment, then turned back to the two policemen. He said, 'What happens now?'

The bored middle-aged one said, 'I've radioed in an MPR. It's being escalated. Your daughter's description's being passed around all active units as we speak and a couple from CID will be out here as soon as possible. It'll definitely be today, probably within the next hour. In the meantime, we need contact details for your daughter's friends and a list of all her favourite places, plus as many recent photographs of her as you've got and an accurate list of exactly what she was wearing when you last saw her. If you've got any idea where she might have been heading when she disappeared, that would really be useful as well.'

The younger one said, 'Shall we do this inside?'

Archie nodded. He put one arm around Jed's shoulders and the other around Cerys's, then led the two policemen into his house. As he did so, Bob Oswald eased Susan down into her bed and pulled her duvet up under her chin. Behind him, Saraya, Saskia and Sunset stood sobbing in the doorway. Bob looked at them over his shoulder. 'Where's Sunrise?'

Saraya said, 'Dunno.'

Bob said, 'What do you mean, dunno? Have you seen her since yesterday evening?'

Saraya shrugged. Other than Susan losing her baby, she couldn't remember a thing about yesterday evening.

Bob Oswald straightened. He stared at his eldest daughter. 'Saraya,' he yelled. 'What did I tell you? When I got into the ambulance? What did I tell you to do?'

Saraya stared, defiant, because she had no idea what he had told her to do.

Saskia answered for her.

'You told us to look for Sunrise. So we did. We looked for Sunrise. We couldn't find her. We decided she'd gone off with you.'

'You useless fucking liars,' Bob yelled. 'When was the last time you saw her?' He looked from Saraya to Saskia. 'Either of you?' he demanded. 'When was the last time you saw her?'

Neither of them knew. Bob didn't know either. He looked down on Susan. 'When was the last time you saw her, honey?'

Susan said she didn't know.

Bob felt an emotion. It was fear. He turned back to Saskia and Saraya. 'Start looking,' he said. 'Turn this place upside down. She must be around here somewhere. Get going. I want her found.'

So Saskia and Saraya started searching, upstairs, downstairs, in the attic, under the stairs, while, back in Susan's bedroom, Bob called Sunrise's mobile, which rang and rang without being answered, and could never have been answered, because the battery was dead. Even if it hadn't been dead, though, Sunrise could never have answered. She was tied up. She was tied up in Broken Buckley's wardrobe. The wardrobe was dark and hot. In contrast, Dillon was cold, colder than anything Skunk had ever felt before in her life. His coldness had a strength to it that made his body feel larger than it was. It seemed there were rows and rows of Dillons all stretching off to Skunk's right, and each one was feeding off the sheer depth of chill in the other.

To Skunk's left, Sunrise wasn't hot or cold. She was luke-warm. Skunk could feel her breathing, but she couldn't hear her breathing. All she could hear was Broken Buckley, moving about in his bedroom, going to the window, going to the door. Once in a while he would come over to the wardrobe. He would open it up and stare down on his three captives. He would wring his hands together. He would turn his back. He would sob. Often, he was naked. His ribs bulged. His eyes watered. His thighs were starting to bow from malnutrition. The things he did made no sense. Why did he stand before them, cutting his arms with a knife? Why did he kneel before them, suck in their breath, blow it out? Why did he slap at his face? Why didn't he let them go? Skunk didn't know. She had no answers. But he did these things, and sometimes he did them while the wardrobe doors were open, and sometimes he did them while the wardrobe doors were shut. One time, he opened the doors and his mother's body was propped up in his bed. Broken had placed apple cores over her eyes. Juice stained like tears down the sides of her cheeks. Broken looked at her then his captives, looked at her then his captives. HOW AND WHY? he whispered. HOW AND WHY? OH HOW AND WHY? Then he shut the wardrobe doors. Skunk breathed a sigh of relief. It was good to be back in darkness. Sunrise breathed close beside her – weaker now, much weaker, something Skunk felt much rather than heard. Poor old Sunrise Oswald. She shuddered each time she breathed in. She shuddered each time she breathed out. And, as her breathing grew weaker, Skunk started to realise her classmate was dying. Quickly, horribly quickly, Sunrise was starving to death. Or dying of thirst. Skunk was hungry and thirsty as well, and she had only been in the wardrobe a matter of hours. How long had Sunrise been in it? Five days? Six days? Seven? Skunk didn't know. She tried to remember the last time she'd seen Sunrise outside of the wardrobe. Last Thursday? Last Friday? Had she seen her in the square on Saturday? Or Sunday? Was it two days ago? Three days? Four? How long could a person last without food? How long could a person last without water? Skunk didn't know. Archie had never told her. Mr Jeffries had never told her. No one had ever told her. She was afraid she was about to find out. She didn't want to. She didn't want to. She tried to stop thinking about it, but she couldn't stop thinking about it, she couldn't, she couldn't, because Dillon was huddled beside her, poor dead forgotten Dillon, and how long had he been in here all on his own? When had Skunk last seen him? She shut her eyes. She bit her teeth into the balled socks that were stuffed into her mouth. Almost a month ago now? Had it really been so long? Had he really been in here such a long time without her hardly ever thinking about him? Without her hardly ever giving him a second thought? Skunk squeezed her eyes shut tighter. She pictured Dillon's smile, Dillon's freckles, Dillon's bucky-beaver teeth. She sobbed. She made herself open her eyes. She made herself turn towards him. In the darkness, he was no more than a body, a still, cold, inanimate body, and there was nothing of Dillon inside it, there was nothing of Dillon at all. Skunk rested her head on his shoulder. She said, I'm so sorry I forgot you. And she sobbed through sheer grief for her friend.

How long was I in there? No clocks. No calendars. No school. No Cerys yelling up the stairwell: Skunk! You're late. Get a move on. No food. No drink. No hope. Just terror. My first real taste of starvation. My first real taste of despair. It felt like three or four months before my stomach started to hollow out within me. It was maybe just less than one day. It wasn't the hunger that hurt, though, it was the thirst. Within hours of being put in the wardrobe, my tongue seemed to swell as it rested against the socks that had been wet with my spit, but now seemed to suck all the moisture from me. The cramps in my legs and my arms were forgotten as my brain started to prioritise the two small things I needed to keep my heart beating. These two things never came. Not for me. Not for Dillon. Not for Sunrise. She died quietly in the darkness beside me. I knew it. The second she died. Not from any sound that she made. I knew it from her silence. It was sudden and swift and forever. I wanted to cry out, to murmur, but I was too scared to make a sound. She rested against me and slowly, ever so slowly, she grew as cold as Dillon, until it was like she had been mothballed in ice. I sat hunched up and shaking between them. I was the book between ends. They huddled so close against me, and the sound of their death was a roar.

* * *

271

The sound of Bob's grief was a roar. He threw an unopened can of Guinness at the living-room wall.

'Where is she? Where the fuck is she?'

Saraya shook her head. She didn't know.

Saskia shook her head. She didn't know.

Susan shook her head. She didn't know. She didn't have a clue. While Bob Oswald started to search through the house for himself, she lay on her side in her bed and stared out the window and clutched her stomach and thought, something was growing inside me. She remembered the white sheets and imagined the chill feel of cold metal as they scraped out what was left. She rolled over on her side and put her thumb in her mouth. She tried not to think of her poor unborn dead baby. Instead, she tried to think about Sunrise. She thought, Sunrise, come home, Sunrise, don't be dead, Sunrise, please, come home. But Sunrise was cold beside Skunk. Skunk felt cold as well now. How long had she been there? Four days? Five days? A week? It wasn't even close to one day. Every second stretched out, though, so it seemed like she'd been trapped in the wardrobe forever. Her legs and her arms had no feeling. Her stomach was empty of feeling. Only her throat retained feeling. It rasped with each breath that she took, except for when Broken was there, when it didn't rasp, it shuddered. Her whole body shuddered. His whole body shook. He bent down and reached out for her. He took the balled socks from her mouth. He pressed his mouth to her mouth. In and out. In and out. In and out. Poor old Broken Buckley. He believed doing this could save him. He never meant any harm. He never meant Dillon or Sunrise to die. He was a broken man. Life had broken him. His mother's love. His father's love. The brutality of his school friends, the indifference of his schoolteachers, the cruelty of people like Saskia Oswald, the violence of people like Bob Oswald, too many injections, not enough injections, too much time on his own, all alone. Broken sucked Skunk's breath in and out, in and out, in and out, then put the socks back in her mouth and put her back in the wardrobe. Dillon and Sunrise greeted her with indifference. The doors swung shut. Life went dark. Skunk breathed in. She breathed out. She breathed in. She breathed out. Where was Archie? Where was Jed? Where was Cerys? Mr Jeffries? Were they out looking for her? And, if they were out looking for her, how were they going to find her? How would they know she was here?

It occurred to her that they wouldn't.

It occurred to her that no one would know she was here, the same way no one had known Dillon was here, the same way no one had known Sunrise was here. The three of them were alone now, and nobody knew where to look, because Broken had slipped off the radar. He had his injections to suppress him and his family to keep him in line. He had his state benefits to feed him, so nobody worried, nobody cared, except for Mr and Mrs Buckley, but Mr Buckley was gone, and Mrs Buckley was dead, and Broken's file was gathering dust under a pile of other files on the corner of a desk in social services while his CPN was off sick and her colleagues were too short-staffed or too busy or too overwhelmed to realise it was there, so nobody administered injections, nobody came out to visit, nobody knew Broken was Broken, the same way nobody knew Dillon was in Broken's wardrobe, the same way nobody knew Sunrise was in Broken's wardrobe, the same way nobody knew Skunk was in his wardrobe as well.

She breathed in deep. And she screamed.

Nnnnnn. Nnnnnn. Nnnnnn. Her eyes were wide. Tears streamed down her cheeks. Her wrists struggled to break free of their bindings. Eight yards, nine yards from where she was, there was sunshine. Across the square was the pavement she had used to ride her scooter along, honking her horn at Jed. Next to that was the house she had grown up in; the window she had used to stare out of, Jed's room with its Xbox, the box room that was now empty, and the room Archie now shared with Cerys. He lay in there beside her. Just a couple of weeks before this, she had been all that he wanted. Now all he wanted was Skunk. 'Where is she? Where the hell is she?' The police had just finished taking statements. They were now checking with the school and all her classmates and hospitals and playgrounds. After that, they would make a decision: door-to-door inquiries, a press release, an appeal. If she hadn't been found by the morning, there was talk about searching with dogs. Archie couldn't stand it. He felt so frantic. So frightened. He wanted so badly to find her, but where the hell could he look? In the attic? He had looked there. In the garage? He had looked there. In the street? Across the road? In the roads that fed off the road he lived in? In every road on the estate where he lived? How many houses were there? And beyond that? How many garages? Attics? Bedrooms? Cellars? Car boots? And what if she wasn't somewhere nearby? What if she had got on a bus? What if she had got on a train?

What if she had accepted a sweet off a stranger and been bundled into a car or an MPV or a van? She could be anywhere. Nowhere. She could be alive. She could be dead. All the police in the world could make all the inquiries in the world and search all the playgrounds in the world and still they might not find her. All the prayers in the world might not save her. Archie sobbed. He covered his eyes. 'Where is she? Where the hell is she?' Cerys didn't know. Jed didn't know. The police didn't know. Bob Oswald didn't know. He'd turned the whole house upside down. He'd been through it like a cyclone. Beds were overturned. The sofa was on its side. There were boxes strewn all over the attic. The garage floor was a mess of tarpaulin and bits of wood and the box the plasma had come in. Now he was back in the front room. He was pacing backwards and forwards, backwards and forwards, and smacking a fist in a palm. Saskia and Saraya were standing anxiously in the doorway. Sunset was sitting with Susan. Time ticked on. Seconds. Minutes. Five of them. Ten. Bob Oswald kept on pacing backwards. Bob Oswald kept on pacing forwards. He kept on smacking his fist in his palm. 'Where is she? Where the fuck is she?' He turned. He pointed at Saraya. 'When was the last time you saw her?' Saraya didn't know. Bob turned. He pointed at Saskia. 'When was the last time you saw her?' Saskia didn't know. Bob yelled at them, 'Think, for fuck's sake, think.' But they couldn't think. They were too spaced out. Their days were too blurred to be certain. Bob couldn't think any better than they could: not about where Sunrise might be, not about what might have happened. All he could think about was the fact she was missing. Twelve years old. He couldn't remember seeing her since Thursday. Four days ago now. Maybe more than four days. Bob stopped pacing. He came to a halt. He pressed his fists to his face. 'OK,' he said. 'OK.' He looked up at the ceiling. He finally reached a decision. 'We're going out looking. We're going out knocking on doors. That's what we're gonna do.' He turned to his two eldest daughters. 'That's right,' he shouted. 'We're going out knocking on doors. We're gonna tell people Sunrise is missing. Your little sister, Sunrise. Twelve years old. We haven't seen her in days. She's out there, somewhere. You know what she's like. She won't have gone far. Let's just go knocking on doors. Let's just ask if anyone's seen her. Someone must have. She can't just have disappeared.' Bob Oswald blinked. He started to cry. Saraya looked sideways at Saskia. The two of them went outside with their father. Bob went next door, to the house on the right. He hammered on the door. Nobody answered. He stepped back. He looked up at windows that reflected blue sky. He went on to the next house. Behind him, Saraya crossed the square towards the side where the Cunninghams lived. Saskia worked her way left, towards Mrs Weston at number 12. Outside, in the sunshine, it was a bright day, it was a hot day, cloudless. There was a light, fresh breeze. Saskia rang Mrs Weston's doorbell. Mrs Weston answered almost straight away. She said, No, love, I haven't seen her, I'm sorry, really, I am. Behind her, Mrs Weston's dog barked. Saskia moved on without saying thank you. No answer at the next house. No answer at the one after that. Saskia looked up at the sky. She said a small prayer for Sunrise. Come on, Sunrise. Please. Be OK. But Sunrise wasn't OK. She was dead. Skunk was huddled beside her. She was huddled beside Dillon. The two of them were so cold. Skunk wished she was cold. She wished she was cold and still and silent. She wished she was dead like Dillon and Sunrise, with nothing to do but go cold. Then, when the wardrobe doors opened, she wished herself dead even harder. Broken Buckley reached in and grabbed her. He took the socks from her mouth. He pressed his lips to her mouth. He sucked her innocence out. He blew his misery in. Skunk struggled and struggled against him. Don't, don't, don't, let me go. He pinched her nostrils shut with his fingers. He shut off the air that she needed to fight with. He shut his eyes just as tightly. He looked for the grass and the slope. He breathed in, he breathed out, he breathed in, he breathed out. Skunk slowly stopped fighting against him. She grew still, very still, in his arms. Broken sat hunched over her body. He breathed in, he breathed out, he breathed in, he breathed out, but it was useless, pointless, he couldn't find his way to the field. He tried and tried and tried, but it wasn't there. There was only the sound of Bob Oswald's fists hitting flesh, the sound of Saskia Oswald's laughter. Broken sobbed. He sat back. Skunk's body was limp in his arms. Broken returned the socks to her mouth and returned her to the wardrobe. He shut the doors. He pressed his hands flat against them. He stood, staring at nothing, then heard the sound of the doorbell. He spun. He hurried across to the window. He stared through a gap in the curtains. Bright sunlight tortured his eyes. He squinted hard against it. He looked down on Saskia Oswald. He put his hands to the curtains. He breathed in through his nostrils. He breathed out through his mouth. No field. No safety. Just

Saskia Oswald, standing on his doorstep, staring up at his window. Broken heard the cruel sound of her laughter. He fell away from the daylight. He turned around and around and around. Downstairs, there was a knock on the door. The doorbell rang out yet again. Broken turned and turned. His mind was a whirl. *Don't laugh at me. Don't mock me. Oh my God I love you. WHY DID YOU DO THAT TO ME?* He made his way down the stairs. He undid the chain. He drew back the deadbolts. He yanked the front door open. He pounced, hands out, mouth gaping, fingers reaching. Saskia Oswald screamed. She staggered backwards. Broken fell against her. 'Why?' he screamed. 'Why did you have to go do that? Why did you do that to me?'

'What?' Saskia Oswald screamed back. 'You stupid fucking freak. Get your hands off me.' She reached up. She clawed at his face. Broken clawed at her face. He pushed her back. He put his hands around her throat. All this time. All this pain. The sound of this stupid girl's laughter. The thought of this stupid girl's little finger, waggling. The sneers. All those side-ways glances. Broken Buckley saw clearly. Not a field. Not a slope. He heard no birdsong. He felt no breeze. Just Saskia Oswald. She was all he could see now. And Saskia Oswald was ugly. Nasty. Hateful. He squeezed his hands around her throat. He tried to choke her to death. Saskia Oswald tried to stop him. She kicked at him. She lashed at him. She screamed. Her screams rang out, loud, in the square. Get off me. Get off me. Get off me. Saraya turned and saw her. She started screaming as well.

'Get off her, get off her, get off her.' She charged across the square. Her high heels echoed like gunshots. Bob Oswald heard the sound of her charge and turned away from the door he'd been hammering on. He looked across the square. He saw Broken Buckley. He saw Saskia, Saraya, a struggle. He yelled and ran towards them. Saskia was on her knees. Saraya was on Broken Buckley's back. The two of them were staggering. Broken Buckley was clinging to Saskia. He had his hands around Saskia's throat. YOU, he shouted. YOU, he shouted. YOU. Bob Oswald grabbed him from behind. He pushed Saraya out of the way. He dragged Broken Buckley off Saskia. He punched Broken Buckley in the back. He drove his knee into Broken's right thigh. Broken screamed. He staggered. Bob Oswald took hold of Broken's hair. He used it to yank Broken's head up. He wrapped an arm around Broken's neck. He used it to drag Broken backwards. Broken tried not to go backwards. He tried to go forwards, towards Saskia, the sound of her laughter. He kept shouting YOU, YOU, YOU. Bob Oswald yanked him back harder. There was the sound of a crack. Breaking bone. Bob Oswald didn't hear it. All he heard was the roar of his own blood in his own ears, the pounding of his rage. He spun Broken Buckley around and grabbed hold of his shoulders.

'You fucker,' he shouted. 'You miserable fucker. You touch my daughters again and I'll kill you. I'll fucking kill you.' He shook Broken backwards and forwards. Broken slumped loose in his arms. His head flopped left and then right. Bob Oswald shook him again. 'Don't try to shit me, you fucker. Open your eyes. Stop fucking around.'

Behind him, a police car pulled into the square.

Saskia yelled, 'Dad, what have you done? What the fuck have you done to his neck?'

Bob Oswald shook Broken Buckley harder. 'Nothing. I haven't done nothing.' He slapped Broken's face, open-palmed. Saraya screamed when Broken's head swivelled slackly towards her.

Across Drummond Square, two policemen climbed from the police car and made their way towards the Cunningham house. One of them looked towards the Buckley property to see what the noise was about. As he did so, Bob Oswald let go of Broken Buckley and Broken Buckley fell down at Bob's feet. The policeman touched his companion on the shoulder. Bob saw the two of them turn towards him. He looked down at Broken Buckley's body. He put his hands on the top of his head.

Before him, Saskia knelt down. She reached a hand towards Broken Buckley. Her fingers stopped short of his shoulder. She couldn't make herself touch him. He looked so pale. And so still.

Saraya said, 'Dad . . . fucking hell . . .'

Saskia pulled her hand away from Broken Buckley's body. She said, 'Why ain't he moving?'

Bob Oswald kept his hands on the top of his head. 'I dunno. All I did was pull him away. Fucking hell. Fucking hell. Fucking hell.'

Saskia kept staring at Broken Buckley. She couldn't seem to look away from his face.

'Jesus, Dad. I don't think he's breathing.'

Bob Oswald looked at her and then at the two policemen. He said, 'I didn't do this. Don't try to pin this on me.'

One of the policemen knelt beside Broken's still body. He took hold of Broken's thin wrist, then let it go and looked up at his colleague. He said, very simply, 'He's dead.'

'He can't be,' Bob Oswald shouted. 'You fucking idiot. He can't be.' He sat down on the ground. He stared at Broken Buckley, then looked up at the two policemen. 'That fucker,' he said, and pointed a finger at Broken. 'That fucker there, right. He attacked my two daughters. I ran over to pull him off. That's all that happened. I ran over to pull him off. I didn't attack him. I didn't even hit him. Saskia and Saraya will tell you. Saskia. Saraya. Tell them. I just tried to pull him off.' Bob Oswald stared at his daughters. They stared at him, open-mouthed. Bob shook his head. He looked back at the policemen. 'And anyway,' he shouted, 'don't go wasting your time on him. My little girl's missing. Sunrise. Sunrise Oswald. She's only twelve years old. She's been missing for more than four days.' He took a deep breath. He nodded. He kept his eyes fixed on the two policemen. He said, 'You two have got to help me find her. I haven't seen her in days.'

The policeman still standing began to read Bob Oswald his rights. The other one straightened and took his cuffs from his belt. Bob Oswald blinked as they glinted in sunlight, then raised his fists and tried to get to his feet. As he did so, he aimed a kick at the policeman holding the cuffs. The policeman saw it coming and stepped to one side. The other policeman kicked Bob's feet from beneath him. Bob fell down on his backside. He grunted and rolled on his side, then tried to get up on all fours. The policeman with the cuffs lunged forward and used his weight to force Bob down onto his stomach.

The other one grabbed hold of Bob's wrists. Bob tried to pull free. He tried to rise to his knees. He couldn't do it. The policeman on his back was too heavy. The other one still had hold of his wrists. Bob heard the jangle of cuffs. Again, he tried to rise to his knees, but, again, he failed to do it. Instead, he yanked one arm free and threw a punch over his shoulder. One of the policemen grabbed his hand and used it to twist his arm backwards. Bob Oswald cried out in pain. A cuff clicked shut on his wrist. 'Sunrise,' he shouted. 'You should be looking for Sunrise.' His other arm was twisted behind him. The second cuff clicked home on his wrist. The two policemen stepped clear and released him. Bob tried to get to his feet. He couldn't. He toppled helplessly forwards. His forehead smacked into the kerb. 'You fuckers,' he shouted. 'You miserable fuckers.' The policemen circled him, wary. There were sirens, far off, in the distance. Bob Oswald writhed like a fish on a hook. 'I'll kill you. You fuckers. I'll kill you.' He shook his head, side to side. 'I'm looking for my daughter. I'm looking for my daughter.' He nodded towards Broken Buckley. 'Forget about him,' he shouted. 'It's not about him.' He looked up at Saskia. He looked up at Saraya. 'Saskia,' he shouted. 'Saraya. Tell them. Tell them about Sunrise.' But they didn't seem to be able to hear him. All they could do was stand with their arms around each other and stare down on Broken Buckley's dead body. Saskia was shaking. Saraya's eyes were glazed over. Bob Oswald looked back at the policemen. 'It's not about him,' he shouted. 'You get me? It's not about him. My twelve-year-old daughter is missing. My twelve-year-old daughter is missing. Do you get me? Do you understand me? My twelve-year-old daughter is missing. This ain't nothing to do with him. Fucking hell. Let me go. You pair of fucking idiots. Let me go. Let me go. Let me go.' He pulled as hard as he could on his handcuffs. They bit into his wrists. They cut him. Bob Oswald pulled on them harder. The two policemen stood back and watched him. His fat head. His bulging muscles. His bulging eyes. 'Sunrise,' he shouted, 'Sunrise. Sunrise. Sunrise.'

He was still screaming her name when they took him away.

After they took Bob Oswald away, more policemen turned up in the square. Two were stationed over Broken Buckley's body. Two others escorted Saskia and Saraya down to the station to give statements about Sunrise and their father. Social services were called to look after Sunset and Susan. Officers put up scene-of-crime tape. Others started knocking on doors and taking statements. As more people realised something exciting had happened, a small crowd gathered and stared down on Broken Buckley's body. He lay on his side with his head turned at an angle. Staring down upon him, no one seemed to know what to say.

Once the senior investigating officer was satisfied he had all the pictures and measurements he needed, the ambulance crew were allowed to take over. The same as Bob Oswald before him, Broken Buckley was taken away.

In his dream, the field sloped down to the south and was full of the sweet sound of birdsong.

And when he woke up, it was real.

It was Monday. Late afternoon. He groaned and looked around him. The field he had fallen asleep in sloped gently southwards. The air smelled of the stream he had fished in when he'd been a child.

He lay face down for a long time, then rolled over, onto his back.

The sky above was a brilliant unspoilt blue. Staring straight up, with his arms and legs away from his body, he could imagine he was falling off the face of the earth.

It really did feel like he was.

Falling. Simply falling.

Mr Jeffries relaxed into the sensation, then ever so slowly sat up. Behind him, his two-man tent rippled in the breeze. Ahead, the fishing rod that had once been his father's still hadn't got a bite. He checked his watch to see what the time was, then reached for the pad that had slipped from his lap while he'd dozed. Squinting slightly in the afternoon sunshine, he read through six drafts of the letter he'd been struggling with since he'd arrived here, then made himself start on the seventh:

Dear Cerys,

I've no idea how to get this down on paper, but as I don't want to risk a repeat of last Thursday's phone call . . . well, I just want to wish you good luck. I won't pretend I'm happy with the way things turned out, but if you and Archie only went behind my back because you had feelings for each other, then I hope you'll be happy together.

I also wanted to let you know I won't be around for a while.

I'm going to take advantage of the fact I'm being paid to do nothing till Susan Oswald's had her baby. I'm not sure where I'm off to but if I'm allowed out of the country three or four months in Oz sounds better than hanging around Beavois Valley. If not, I might go to Scotland and do a bit of climbing. The fresh air should do me some good.

Anyway, hope there's no hard feelings. Say hello to Archie for me, and Jed and Skunk as well. With any luck, I'll see you all when I get back.

Mike

PS Had to ditch my mobile because the press got hold of the number. Here's my new one: 07796 345 201.

Mr Jeffries read and reread the letter, then started on draft number eight.

As Mr Jeffries started on draft number eight, the senior investigating officer found Mrs Buckley's body.

A small crowd gathered in Broken Buckley's bedroom. Photos were taken. Experts charged time and a half to do tests. Two community police officers searched the rest of the house for more bodies. Neither of them looked in the wardrobe. The children remained in the dark.

Across the square, a social worker carried Sunset Oswald out to a waiting car. Susan Oswald was already in the back. Jed sat alone at Skunk's bedroom window. For a long time he stared down on Susan Oswald, then the social worker's car pulled away and there was nothing for him to stare down on.

He put his hands to the window and said, 'I told you, Skunk. Didn't I tell you? Broken Buckley did it. Soon they'll come put up a tent.'

But no one came. No one put up a tent. It was an open-and-shut case. Broken Buckley killed Mrs Buckley. Bob Oswald killed Broken. It was as clear and as simple as that.

DCI Cunliffe stared at Mrs Buckley's body, the apple cores over her eyes. He said, 'You reckon he meant it?'

A pathologist peeled his thin gloves off. 'Who cares whether he meant it? He did it, didn't he? She's dead. He's dead. It's time to pack up and go home.'

They wheeled Mrs Buckley's body out two hours later. A constable slammed the front door as he left.

I was all alone then with Dillon and Sunrise and silence.

I drifted in darkness and waited to die.

How soon after that did they find me?

Soon? Not soon enough?

My body hasn't decided.

My brain hasn't made up its mind.

Skunk stayed missing until just after 8 a.m. the next day.

It was Mr Buckley who found her. The previous evening, he'd formally identified his son and his wife for policemen who didn't seem to care about the things he had lost. Now he needed to be alone in the house they had died in. Standing on the driveway, he stared up at his son's bedroom window for a long time, then pulled his key out of his pocket and opened the front door. He stepped into the hallway. Behind him, the breeze in the trees was a sigh. Mr Buckley pulled the door shut. He followed the same path Dillon had trod to his death; through all the downstairs reception rooms, the conservatory, the kitchen, then up the stairs, into the marital bedroom, then further along the landing, a pause, a sigh, a hand on smooth cold dust-laden wood. This, then, was where it had happened. This, then, was where the path led. Mr Buckley opened the door and stepped into his dead son's bedroom. It reeked of waste and death and anger. Mr Buckley's nose wrinkled. He very nearly stepped out and pulled the door shut. What would have happened then? An estate agent might have found them. Or a house-clearance worker. Or the proud new owners of the largest house in Drummond Square. Anything might have happened. Nothing might have happened. They might have remained in there forever, breeding their own maggots, feeding their own flies.

But Mr Buckley did not step out and pull the door shut. He stared at his dead son's stripped bed and remembered a cot. He stared at the neat nothingness the forensic team had left behind them and remembered a mess of clothes on the floor and the sound of his wife shouting down the stairs, Rick, come and sort this mess out, and his dead son shouting back, Oh, Mum, I'm watching telly, can't I do it later? He wasn't always mad then. She wasn't always cold. And Mr Buckley himself – he wasn't always defeated. He was once a chubby man approaching middle age with a miracle pressed to his bare chest and a stupid huge grin on his face. Oh my God. He's so perfect. Look at his fingers. Look at his toes. Mr Buckley screamed in a soundless vacuum of what it was to be the one left behind without reason. He wheeled round and struck a fist at a wall. Pain. Such pointless pain. He kicked the bed. He swept his hands through his thinning dark hair. He turned and punched the wardrobe. He kicked and kicked at the door. The door shuddered. It swung open. Skunk's almost lifeless body fell out. Supported by nothing but air now, Dillon and Sunrise fell inwards and collapsed over onto each other.

And Mr Buckley screamed.

And this scream had sound.

It pierced me. Not my body. My soul. I swirled high, free of the wardrobe. A cartwheel. A forward roll. I crawled up the walls and then over the ceiling. I stared down. I watched Mr Buckley drop to his knees. I watched him gather my body up. 'Skunk? Oh God, Skunk. Is that you?' He knew I wasn't dead. Of course he did. Mr Buckley knew death. He worked with it every day. The silent. The still. The whitewashed marble features of bodies that were empty of life. Poor old Mr Buckley. He knew the dead. And he knew Dillon. He knew Sunrise. So it was my body he went to work on. Fingers to my throat. Feeling. Feeling. His fingers felt warm. It was the first warmth I'd felt in too long. I hovered two metres above him and I blew kisses as thanks for his warmth. Did Mr Buckley feel them? I don't know. But he gathered me up. He carried me down the stairs. The shock of it almost killed me. Movement. The rise.

*The fall. I bobbled along behind him like a balloon tethered
too tight to float free. Down the stairs. Into the hallway. From
above, I watched my hair trail. I watched my lips part. Was
that a breath? I don't think so. Just a slight movement of teeth.
Mr Buckley sobbed softly. 'Skunk. Oh God, Skunk. Don't die.
Please God. Don't you be dead.' He pushed open the front door
and carried me into the square. I rose up into early-morning
sunshine. I swirled like a leaf on a dry breeze. Beneath me,
Mr Buckley fell down to his knees. He laid me down on dry
grass. 'Help me,' he shouted. 'Please. God. Somebody. Help
me.'*

*Along came Mrs Weston, happily walking her dog. What use
was she in a crisis? Did she have a mobile phone? No. Mrs Weston
did not. I did. I shouted, I've got a phone in my pocket. But
neither of them heard me. I lay still, on my back, on dry grass.*

*Mrs Weston ran over to our house. She beat her fists on the
door.*

It was Jed who answered.

It was Archie who ran over to claim me.

It was Cerys who dialled 999.

*I hung like a thin cloud above them. It was beautiful to be
out. It was beautiful to be free. Then Archie fell down by my
body and the beauty seeped out of the world. Skunk oh Skunk
oh Skunk oh baby please be breathing don't you be dead don't
you dare. He pulled my head into his lap and cradled me like
a baby. My hair fanned. My eyes stayed shut. Archie sobbed into
my throat. He rocked me backwards and forwards. And, in the
distance, sirens.*

Mr Buckley said, 'There are more bodies upstairs.' He looked back at the house he'd once lived in, then pressed his fists to his eyes. Beside him, Archie said, 'Hang on, Skunk. Come on, little darling. Don't you leave me. Don't you dare.'

Sirens wailed, growing closer.

Jed put his head in his hands.

Others gathered around. Timid. Like flies near a tail.

Is she OK?

Is she gonna live?

She looks dead already.

Mrs Weston's dog barked and barked and barked.

Jed kept his head in his hands.

Archie continued to sob.

Don't you die, Skunk. Please. Don't you dare.

I swirled, undecided.

Sirens grew closer.

The way that they do.

Still, now, I can't make my mind up.

It's almost six weeks later.

I'm in what they call a coma. Experts talk about suffocation, asphyxiation. They point to the bruises on my mouth and my throat and my nostrils. They stand around my bed and wonder out loud why Broken tried to throttle me, why he didn't simply leave me to die of thirst the way he did with Sunrise and Dillon. I stand in the corner with my hands pressed over my ears in a hopeless attempt not to hear.

In the bed, my body is very still. Tubes go in and tubes go out. Twice a day, nurses move me. For at least one hour a day, Archie comes in. Often, Cerys comes with him. Once – twice a *week if I'm lucky – Jed comes in as well. Cerys fusses. Jed fidgets. Archie clings on to my hands.*

Most of the time, though, I'm alone. Tubes go in. Tubes go out. My heartbeat flashes on black.

Sometimes, in the dead of night, I dream Broken Buckley comes in to see me. He drags himself over to my bed and takes hold of my hands. His thoughts pour into my mind and his thoughts are always jumbled: I see a green field, sloping. I hear Saskia Oswald, laughing. I see orderlies in lawn-green uniforms and hear the warm rush of breeze in the trees. How and why? How and why? Poor old Broken Buckley. He sits forward. His long blond hair hangs in his eyes. How and why? Oh how and why? Then Mrs Buckley comes in and puts her arms around him and gently leads him away.

Other times, it's Dillon I dream of. He sneaks into my room and asks me to die and go with him. Come on, Skunk. We'll run away. We'll get married. We'll live by the side of a stream. Whenever I dream about Dillon, his pockets are full of cold pearls.

Come with me, Skunk. Be my friend.

For a short time, I had this dream where Mr Jeffries came in to see me. I couldn't understand why he hadn't. Mr O'Driscoll had. And Mrs McCluskey. And most of my other teachers. Why not Mr Jeffries? Where was he? Why didn't he care? Then, five days after I was brought in here, he finally appeared in the doorway. He looked tired and his clothes were all crumpled. When he took hold of my hands, I understood why. He'd driven all the way down here from Scotland. As soon as Cerys had called him, he'd got in his car and set off. Other than for petrol and the toilet, he hadn't stopped once. Over ten hours of driving. Mr Jeffries barely noticed. He just had to be with me. He just had to pray for me to get better. When he took hold of my hands, it was like being held by my father. Wake up, Skunk, please, God, wake up. That first night, he stayed with me for over five hours. He's visited every night since. Sometimes he reads stuff to me. Sometimes he sits and thinks about Sunrise and Dillon. Other times, he fills me in on what's been happening at school. He's been back there for a month now. Not because of anything he did, not because of anything I did, but because Susan Oswald admitted he could never have fathered her baby. Poor old Susan Oswald. Now Sunrise is dead and Bob's in prison, she can't be bothered to lie. And, anyway, they were going to do tests on the foetus, so why bother denying the truth?

So Mr Jeffries is back in school. He stands at the front of his form class. He confuses them with the things that he says. For a few minutes every morning, he gives them updates on how I'm getting on. Class 7D sit in uncomfortable silence. Two empty chairs sit among them. Everyone stares down at their hands.

Once Mr Jeffries has finished unintentionally making the whole room feel awkward, he tries hard to make school time fun.

More often than not, though, he finds himself gazing at the empty desks Sunrise and I used to sit at. Where once he'd been able to see futures, all he can see now is space.

Still, though, every evening, he comes in here to see me. Like my father, he wills me to wake up. Come on, Skunk, open your eyes, get better, come back to school. It's not as much fun without you. Everyone misses you. He brings me the cards and the poems he gets them to write. He tells me about the things they're all *learning. As for Mr Jeffries himself, he still gets the odd paedophile comment, and there's graffiti all over the toilets, but he just shrugs and ignores it. What does he care? He's teaching again. He's back on good terms with Cerys. He hasn't had a drink for six weeks. Once, I would have loved this about him, but all it does now is make me feel sad. Poor old Mr Jeffries. I don't understand how he does it. How does he keep bouncing back? Every kick, every knock, every setback. How does he get up and start over again?*

My father's the same. Sometimes, when he takes hold of my hands and sends his love pouring through me, I don't hear his words. Instead, I see him pull over into a lay-by on his way into the office and rest his head against the steering wheel and dig his fingers into his scalp. He doesn't want to drive into work. He doesn't want to carry on as if everything's normal. He wants to curl up and die. He doesn't though. He takes deep breaths. He tries to pull himself together. He tries to be strong for Cerys, for Jed, for the day I might wake up and need him. I won't though. I don't have it in me. I'm not like my father. I'm not like Mr Jeffries. I'm just like Dillon and Sunrise. Small and cold and helpless. I wish I wasn't. I wish I could open my eyes and sit up and smile and make Archie and Cerys and Jed and Mr Jeffries and everyone else really happy. But I can't. I'm too tired. I'm too tired.

I never want to wake up again.

One day last week my heart finally stopped beating, just like that, without warning. The green line went flat on the screen. I felt such silent relief. Death's like that, I think – a whisper of powerful movement, like bicycle wheels turning on tarmac, or skis on powdery snow. After being stuck in that bed for so long, I felt a wave of weightless wonder. As nurses rushed in and buzzers went off, I floated dreamily above them, turning gently, staring down on my limp, lifeless body, the nurses and doctors around it. I circled them as they battled to save me. I could feel nothingness calling me on. I could feel electric pulses dragging me back. Don't, I whispered, don't, but the nurses couldn't hear me, the doctors couldn't hear me. All I could do was look down and beg them to fail.

I could have cried when they managed to get my heart restarted. It was like going down a water flume, slipping and sliding and falling, grabbing at edges that didn't exist. My body closed up all around me. There I was, in darkness again. Then Archie arrived and took hold of my hands and sent me his panic and fear: Skunk, Skunk, baby, don't die don't leave me so scared so scared so scared. All I could do was lie there. All I can do is lie here. Let me go, Daddy. Please. Let me go.

It's so hard. I don't want to leave him. I love him. I love Jed. I love Cerys. And Mr Jeffries. But love – it isn't a good thing. At least, it wasn't for Mrs Buckley. All the love she had for Broken. What good did it do for her? And Broken. Poor old Broken. He thought he loved Saskia Oswald. What good did love do for him? Love. It's just a four-letter word, a bad thing, nasty, destructive, like Bob Oswald's love for his daughters. Poor old Bob Oswald. Thanks to his love for his daughters, he wore handcuffs to Sunrise's funeral. Thanks to his love for his daughters, he had two policemen beside him throughout the service. I know because Archie shook his hand at Sunrise's graveside. I know because Archie embraced him. Then Archie came here to see me. I wanted to recoil. I wanted to scream. Bob Oswald's love swept through me. I saw how he beat up Broken Buckley because he loved his daughters. I saw how he attacked Mr Jeffries because he loved his daughters. I saw how he snapped Broken Buckley's neck because he loved his daughters.

And now he's sitting in a jail cell and mourning poor dead Sunrise Oswald. The fact he couldn't save her rips him apart day by day. The fact Susan and Sunset are in separate care homes rips him apart day by day. The fact Saskia and Saraya are out there struggling to get by without him rips him apart day by day. And, day by day, Bob Oswald paces backwards and forwards, backwards and forwards, and thinks to himself, so unfair, so fucking unfair, didn't mean it, stupid dumb fuck, stupid bastard, Sunrise, Sunrise, Sunrise, so unfair, so fucking unfair.

That is what love did to Bob.

And this is what love does to Archie. He uses the word like he's swearing. It runs around and around in his head: I love you, Skunk, I love you, I love you, Skunk, I love you. And each time he sends it coursing through me I flinch back and wish myself dead. Don't, Daddy, don't. Let me go.

Poor old Archie. He thinks I'm his little fighter. He thinks I'm hanging on in there. But what is there to hang on for? I don't know. I can't see it. I don't understand life. I used to. Or, at least, I used to think I used to. Life was playing Jed at Xbox. Life was dreaming about Mr Jeffries. Life was loving Daddy, loving Cerys. It was never mentioning my mother because it might upset my father. It was going to school and not getting killed by the Oswalds. It was riding my scooter, honking my horn at Jed. That's what life was. My life. But life, LIFE, life, what is it? Really? What have I got to wake up for? I don't know. I just know the life Archie wants me to wake up for won't be the life I was living. That life was happy and careless. I never needed to worry about depression, madness, starvation. I never needed to worry about how long a person can survive without water. But now, how can I not worry? How can I go back to that life? I can't. I've been locked away in a wardrobe. I've slept between silent dead bodies. I've seen my father park his car in a lay-by and rest his head on the steering wheel and dig his fingers into his scalp. When he finally arrives at work he washes his face in the downstairs toilet and goes up to his office and says there's no change, no change, no change. In his lunch break, he tele-phones my mother and begs her to come back to see me. He thinks she might make a difference. He thinks, maybe, if I hear her voice, I'll wake up, like a princess in a story, revived by the kiss of a prince. My mother won't come back though. And why should she? She didn't care about me when I was healthy. Why should she care now I'm sick? And anyway, I'd rather be held by Cerys. She's been more of a mother to me. But Archie can't see this. Poor old tired old Archie. He can't see anything any more. He comes in here every chance he gets. He holds my hands in his hands. He says, Come on, Skunk, wake up, beautiful darling, don't you leave me, please, don't you dare. He holds my hands to his forehead. I shy away in the darkness. His thoughts, they run through my body, but they're not the thoughts Mr Jeffries believes in – LIFE, ASPIRATIONS, DREAMS – they're the stuff of visiting hours and pulse rates and how did it all come to this? Day after day, nothing changes. Poor old tired old

Archie. What does he have in his life now? Nothing but an hour by this bed every evening and long lonely nights where he watches a video of me as a newborn and drinks and thinks, Nnnnnn. Nnnnnn. Nnnnnn.

If he sleeps, then he dreams I have died.

And the next day he does it again.

Why, Archie? Why?

I can't figure it out.

Archie can't figure it out either. He's so tired, so exhausted, so frightened. Cerys says to him, Come to bed, love, you're making yourself ill, then goes up and cries all alone. Across the landing, Jed hides away in his bedroom. He comes here less and less. He finds it too painful. He can hardly bring himself to touch me. Archie says, Kiss your sister goodnight, Jed. Come on. Tell her you love her. Jed takes a breath. He brushes my cheek, says goodnight. His life. It flashes through me: He plays Xbox. He studies. He watches our father come apart at the seams. He is silent, screaming. I am silent, screaming. What is the point? Why do we cling to our lives? I don't know. I can't figure it out. None of it makes any sense: Mrs Buckley falling backwards, snapping her neck on the stairs. Dillon, trying to steal that duvet, ending up dying of thirst. Sunrise, delivering her papers, delivering herself to her death. Why? What were their lives for, why did they struggle, why did they suffer, when all of them ended up dead?

I don't know. I don't know. I don't know.

But at least I know they are free now. No madness. No hunger. No thirst.

Only death. And death is silence. Death is darkness. Death is not having to face up to the fact that Dillon starved all alone in that wardrobe while I hardly noticed he'd gone. Death is not having to think about the moment Broken Buckley first grabbed me and covered my mouth with his own. Death is not having to think about the complete and utter silence that followed Sunrise Oswald's last breath.

Death is painless. Life is senseless.

I'm choosing death over life.

But I can't let go of this life.

Not while my father holds my hands and sends me images of myself as a newborn baby.

Wake up, Skunk. Wake up.

Wake up, Daddy. Wake up.

It is a battle of wills.

He refuses to let go.

I refuse to come back.

So tubes go in. A monitor beeps. A green pulse flashes on black.

Two months. Three months.

Four.

Finally, yesterday evening, he lifted his head off my shoulder and made his way out of my room. As the door swung shut behind him, I imagined him going home, sitting down, taking off his shoes, putting on a video – me, as a baby, on my back, tubes going into my nostrils, my small hands pawing the air.

I imagined him pouring a whisky, the sound of the rain falling, soft.

Cerys, in the doorway: Come up to bed, love. You're making yourself ill.

Archie, sitting in darkness. Wake up, baby. Wake up.

Me, alone, in blackness.

Let me go, Daddy. Please. Let me go.

He comes back again today. He sits down beside me. He is tired. He is all on his own. I think, today, I am going to leave you. Enough. I am going to die.

He takes my hands from under the bed sheets. He holds them tight in his own.

For the first time, I feel nothing.

No video of me as a newborn. No sadness. No hope for me. No pain.

For the first time in here, he cries.

Loud sobs. Choking. They shake him. He puts his head on my chest. When he looks up, he's still sobbing. I stare at him. I am frozen. This is Archie Cunningham. My father. A solicitor. A divorcee. He is balding. There are tears streaming down his pale face. I look at him, very closely. There are broken veins in his nostrils. His eyebrows have begun to go grey. His lips are cracked. There are sores there. His fingers feel thin, wrapped in mine.

Last night, Cerys told him she is pregnant. My father. A daddy again.

His fingers feel cold, holding mine.

He squeezes them, ever so gently.

Daddy, I think, you're so cold.

Daddy, I think, don't be cold.

He squeezes my fingers again. Pressure. Gentle pressure. I feel a flicker of warmth. I get a sense of something, coursing. It's not whisky. It's not a video of me as a newborn. It's an image of me, and I'm old. How old am I? Twenty? Possibly younger. I've just graduated from something. College? University? I might even have just finished school. Whatever it is, it's behind me, and I'm beautiful, all in white, and I'm walking – walking with Archie. We walk between old wooden pews. I don't know this church. Archie doesn't know it, either. He's dragged it up out of nowhere. His bricks. His choice of flooring. The bell-ringers are playing his tune. What else has he conjured? Flowers. Streaming sunshine. Pollen dust turns in the air. Cerys is there. So is the baby. She is a girl. She is eight years old. She is waving at me. She is smiling. She loves me. I'm her big sister. I babysit her at the weekends. I buy her cool clothes. I do her make-up. And Jed: he plays her at Xbox. He carries her high on his shoulders. He's here, in Archie's vision, standing beside Archie's eight-year-old daughter who hasn't even been born yet. Jed is in his early twenties. Tall. Dark-haired. Handsome. His wife, thank God, is not Susan Oswald. She is pretty, pretty and pregnant. Life. Like a dream. It goes on.

This is for me. It's from my father. But it's not a dream. He knows I'm not waking up. They told him last night. They've done all they can. In a few hours, they're switching the machine off. Without it, I'm slipping away. So here he is, my father. Jed and Cerys will arrive soon, but he wanted these last few moments alone so he could hold my hands and sob onto my chest and dream up this one final image. Dust motes captured in sunlight. My father and I, walking forward. My father and I, arm in arm. We walk, step by step, towards the end of the aisle, but there is no vicar, no pulpit, no crucifix, there is no groom who might tie me down or leave me or simply not love me enough. Instead of these things, there is a dense ball of light. It is bright and it is brilliant and there is somebody standing within it.

This somebody. She is all of the things I could have been.

I stare at her, almost blinded, then I look back at my father. His face is no longer buried in my chest. It is right above my own face. His tears stream. His body shakes. Life's painful. Love's painful. Love hurts, doesn't it? Get up in the morning. Go to work. Go to the hospital. Be told it's all been for nothing. Pull over in a lay-by. Cry for a daughter who's dying. Get home two hours later. Be told you're going to be a father again. Go to bed. Lie awake till the morning. Think and think about all the things your daughter could have been. My father. I never knew until this moment. He really thought I was special. I constantly surprised him. I was smart. I was funny. I was going to grow up and be something. He never knew what this something was, he just knew there was something out there for me, something brilliant, exciting, golden, something he could never have been. His Skunk. His little angel. No failed marriage for her. No single-parent family. No Sky+. No disappointment. I never knew. He never told me. He never said it could all be so bright. Mr Jeffries never said. No one ever said. But seeing it now, it is burning, it is brilliant, it is the most beautiful thing I've ever seen. And my father. He has created it for me. He has worked and struggled and saved and provided in the hope that I might grow up and study and learn and one day find my place in the world. This, for Archie, is what it is all about. Not a wedding. Not babies. Not a mortgage. But hope, possibility, choice. These are his DREAMS, ASPIRATIONS. Me, alive. Jed, alive. His unborn baby, alive. All of us happy. All of us fulfilled. All of us being whatever we have it within us to be. And it changes, it constantly changes, with each step we take down the aisle towards the person I might have become in the future, so one minute she's a teacher, like Mr Jeffries, then she's a solicitor, like my father, then she's a student, then she's a nurse, then she's a recruitment consultant, then she's a psychiatrist who helps people like Broken, then she's a singer on a cruise ship, then she's a volunteer aid worker in Africa, then she's a girl in a street selling flowers. And at all times, she is alive, and at all times, she is happy, and at all times, she is moving forward. And at all times, my father is thinking, come on, Skunk, come on, open your eyes, wake up, be alive, and at all times he is guiding me forward, showing me possibilities that bathe me in bright golden light, and at all times he is thinking and hoping and praying, come on, Skunk, wake up, we'll play Xbox on Sundays, I'll buy you that video phone you wanted, come on, Skunk, wake up, open your eyes, ask me an awkward question, ask me a million awkward questions, anything, I'll answer, I'll tell you, what do you want to know? Come on, Skunk. Anything. Anything. Just don't leave me. Don't leave me. Wake up, little darling, wake up.

He doesn't say it. He thinks it.

He doesn't think it. He needs it.

I stand behind him.

I could leave him. It's in the balance. My heart could quite easily stop. All I have to do is turn away. I could do this. It's in my hands. Darkness. Nothing. If I turn away from my father, I won't have to face up to what happened to Dillon. If I turn away from my father, I won't have to think about the silence that fell when Sunrise Oswald stopped breathing. If I turn away from my father, I won't have to think about Broken Buckley bending forward, his wet eyes coming closer to mine.

But if I turn away from my father, I'll never see him again.

Come on, Skunk. Come on, Skunk. Wake up. Wake up. Wake up.

His tears feel warm on my skin.

His breath feels warm on my face.

His hands feel cold, holding mine.

Come on, Skunk. Wake up, wake up, wake up. Please, baby. Please, baby, please.

How on earth could I leave him?

I squeeze his cold hands in mine.

I open my eyes, look in his eyes.

And I feel it all streaming back now. My life. My DREAMS. My ASPIRATIONS.

I'm going to wake up. I'm going to trounce Jed at Xbox. I'm going to be a big sister to Cerys's baby. I'm going to fill all the space I can in Mr Jeffries' classroom. I'm going to laugh and scream and cry and grow and learn and shift and change and strive and maybe one day I'll be a teacher who makes school time FUN, and maybe one day I'll be a mother who stays with her children, and maybe one day I'll be one of the things my father has conjured, and maybe one day I'll be none of the things my father has conjured, but no matter what I become in the future, I'm going to be twelve years old in a fortnight, and I'm going to wake up, be alive.

It's all coursing through me. It's all pouring in through my father. His hands. Wrapped in my hands.

Life.

Love.

Aspirations.

Dreams.

They all come in a jumbled rush of blood and warmth and Xbox summer picnics holidays abroad sunsets on a hot day white frost on a cold day nosebleeds toothache blisters laughter Christmas birthdays dull days all days these days my father's tears on my cheeks and his arms pulling me to him and his dreams wrapped in my dreams and yes it hurts and yes it is senseless but the breath in my lungs and the blood in my heart and the day that I die and the moment I sigh goodnight Daddy goodnight Jed goodnight Cerys and silent not even a whisper goodnight mother sleep tight sweet dreams I forgive you and pull my Jedi Knight duvet close to me. These moments.

Are why.

I'm alive.

Many thanks to Claire Gradidge, Anne Summerfield, Moira Merryweather, Virginia Warbey, John Barfield, Anne Sansome, Amanda Oosthuizen, Jan Moring, John Pemberton, and all others at Chandlers Ford Writers' for their advice and support over the years.

Yet more thanks to Richard Ashman, Allison Kirby, Penny Rudkin and Jo Smith of Southampton Central Library for much needed feedback on the first draft of *Broken*.

Even more thanks to Jonny Geller and Alice Lutyens at Curtis Brown, and to Annabel Wright at HarperPress: I don't think this novel would have been published without them. Also if I hadn't read Harper Lee's *To Kill a Mockingbird*, this novel would never have been written.

On a technical level, thanks to Chris Gaiger (who doesn't know what DNA stands for), Lisa Sarracini (soon to be a Dauncey) and Rob Barnard (the worst left-back in the world) for patiently answering my questions.

And finally – I promise – thanks to Claire Gradidge (again) and Mark Fowler, who have each read more than half a million of my unpublished words over the years and yet still return some of my e-mails.

P.S.

Ideas,
interviews
& features ...

About the author

About the book

Read on

Hi, I'm Daniel Clay

Author photograph by Jo Grant

HI, I'M DANIEL CLAY, and my editor has asked me to write a short piece about myself, which, I have to admit, seems a very strange thing to try to do.

Other than wanting to be a writer for as long as I can remember, I've lived a mostly dull and unremarkable life, so I've not really got much to tell you. At the risk of being boring, I'm going to start off with the facts.

At the time of writing, I'm thirty-eight years old. I was born in Buckinghamshire, and was brought up in a small town called Newport Pagnell, roughly halfway between

6 Other than wanting to be a writer for as long as I can remember, I've lived a mostly dull and unremarkable life. 9

2

London and Birmingham. You'll probably never have heard of it, so I shan't go into detail, but it's safe to say I had a standard working-class childhood; my dad worked as a coach-builder for British Rail and my mum, at various times, was a cleaner, a child-minder, and a lollipop lady as well as a housewife.

As well as a standard working-class childhood, I had a standard working-class state education and left school with very few qualifications. This wasn't because the schools I went to were bad or because I was particularly stupid or rebellious. It was more to do with the fact that I knew I wanted to be a writer from a very early age and, as creative writing wasn't taught as a separate subject in state schools during this time, my interest in what most of my teachers were telling me was pretty much nil. From the age of thirteen onwards I spent the majority of my lessons hiding away at the back of classrooms writing short stories, novellas and angst-ridden lyrics for a friend who played the guitar.

After I left school at sixteen, I drifted around without any real idea of what I should be doing with my life other than trying to be a writer. The problem was, I had no idea how to go about becoming a writer. No one in my family wrote and none of my friends wrote, either. In fact, I was in my mid-twenties before I finally started to meet other people who wanted to be writers. As crazy as this sounds with today's information highway and the massive boom in self-help books for writers, I didn't know who to send my stuff to, how to present it or have any real idea ▶

6 I was forced to do what most other people who can't control their own destinies do: I drifted through a succession of clerical and admin jobs, found myself studying in my spare time to be an accountant. 9

Hi, I'm Daniel Clay (continued)

◄ that things such as writers' conferences and creative writing courses existed.

Not being one to let a lack of knowledge stop me, I wrote novels all through my teens and early twenties, submitted them to publishers and agents and picked up a massive amount of rejections.

As there was no sign of any money ever coming in from my writing, I was forced to do what most other people who can't control their own destinies do: I drifted through a succession of clerical and admin jobs, found myself studying in my spare time to be an accountant, then met and married my wife.

My wife is from Winchester, so after we'd carried on a long-distance relationship for a couple of years, we bought a house in Chandlers Ford, which is a small town between Winchester and Southampton. We lived there for most of the nineties, then moved a few miles further south to Hedge End, where *Broken* is set and where we live now.

Although I was studying to be an accountant and holding down a full-time job, I was still writing as much as I could, which most times wasn't as much as I wanted. Back then, I really wanted to be a horror writer more than anything else. I loved Stephen King's early novels and was also a huge fan of James Herbert. Also around this time, I was starting to discover writing magazines, writers' circles and writing conferences. Although the time I had to write was restricted due to my day job and my studies, I was slowly developing

❛ In 1998, twenty-three years after writing my first-ever short story, I actually managed to get one published. ❜

as a writer: in 1998, twenty-three years after writing my first-ever short story, I actually managed to get one published.

This felt like a major breakthrough to me, so I immediately quit studying to be an accountant, just a year and a half before I might have qualified, and put as much time and effort as I could into writing. The first thing I wrote was a horror novel which attracted an agent's attention, but he said horror novels weren't selling and convinced me to switch to psychological thrillers. I spent the next three years writing psychological thrillers that didn't get published either, and ended up losing my agent. I then went through a bleak period, writing-wise, where not a lot seemed to get finished. Seven years after giving up studying, I was no closer to making the breakthrough, stuck in a dead-end job and feeling as if I'd allowed a huge chance to slip through my fingers.

As a weird contrast to this state of despair, my personal life was extremely happy. My wife and I had a strong relationship, a small mortgage on a house we were really settled in, decent cars, not bad incomes considering we'd both left school with few qualifications, and could afford to take half-decent holidays a couple of times a year. I had most of the things the majority of people from my background tend to aspire to, except for this one burning thing I was desperate to achieve in my life.

This was the situation I was in when I began to write *Broken* in May 2005. ▶

6 All in all, the first draft of the novel took me nine months to write. 9

Hi, I'm Daniel Clay *(continued)*

◄ All in all, the first draft of the novel took me nine months to write. It then went in a drawer for six months while I worked on something else. Then I had another look at it, decided I hadn't been completely insane to write it, and started to submit it to agents. The first six months were slow going as I approached agents who'd previously shown an interest in my writing on a one-to-one basis. For one reason or another, though, none of them felt able to represent me: some said they really liked what I'd written, but none of them could see who they'd sell it to.

Once this list of sympathetic rejecters was exhausted, I simply started working through the *Writers' and Artists' Yearbook*, sending off a covering letter, the first three chapters and the opening pages to as many agents as I could afford to. I was still in my dead-end day job at this time, and it became a mini-adventure to come home every night and see just how many rejections I'd been sent through the post. I think sixteen at once was my record, after a two-week holiday abroad. Our poor postman must have hated my guts.

By the time Jonny Geller at Curtis Brown e-mailed to say he'd really enjoyed the opening pages and would I please send him the rest, I'd collected more than thirty rejections for *Broken*. Jonny loved it, though, and after a three-week rewrite, when I addressed some concerns we both had, it quickly sold in the UK, the US, Canada, Italy and Holland. This all took place in the summer of last year.

❝ I'd collected more than thirty rejections for *Broken*. ❞

Right now, November 2008, I'm currently working full-time on a new novel, *Swap*, which is (among other things) about the repercussions of a wife-swap that goes wrong, and, like *Broken*, set in Hedge End. My wife and I are also about to take up jobs as chalet hosts in France over the winter ski season, something that will be a complete departure from any sort of work we've ever done before, and an experience we're both really looking forward to. After that, I've no idea what the future holds. Definitely more novels, but outside of writing, I don't really have much of a clue what I want to do on a day-to-day basis.

And that's it, really. Fifteen hundred plus words on all there is to know about me. I hope you enjoyed reading *Broken* more than you enjoyed reading this, because I definitely got more out of writing my novel than I did out of recapping my life.

Best wishes,
Daniel Clay

A Conversation with Daniel Clay

***Broken* is a hard novel to bracket. What inspired you to write it?**
I'd just given up on a novel that, for one reason or another, had been refusing to get off the ground for nearly three months, when I read a newspaper article about Harper Lee's *To Kill a Mockingbird*, which was celebrating the novel's fiftieth anniversary. There's an interesting back-story with the fact it's Harper Lee's only published novel and in the rumours Truman Capote actually wrote it, plus the character Dill is supposedly based on Truman Capote, who Harper Lee knew as a child.

The article also went into Harper Lee's background. When I'd read the novel, I'd assumed it had been written by someone who'd enjoyed a literary upbringing and a long publishing history before sitting down to write it: there's such a superior quality to the writing style and the voice. I probably had a bit of a chip on my shoulder about my own lack of publishing success and the fact I was from a working-class background, so the fact this stunning novel had been a debut by someone with an everyday upbringing made me realise the only thing stopping me from at least trying to write something special was my own lack of ambition, not where I came from myself.

Something in my mind also started to wonder how the characters in *To Kill a Mockingbird* would cope with life in the society we live in today, as times have changed so much in the eighty or so years since the events in that novel took place yet, as basic human beings, I don't think we've moved on a great deal at all. Once I started thinking about it, I couldn't let it go. Although I don't think my characters and plot resemble *To Kill a Mockingbird*, this train of thought and the family structures Harper Lee used in her novel were my starting points, which is why I have Skunk for Scout, Jed for Jem, Dillon for Dill, Archie for Atticus, Broken for Boo, etc. I really can't stress enough that I would never have sat down to write *Broken* had I not read *To Kill a Mockingbird* or the newspaper article about how *Mockingbird* had come to be written.

Did you draw on anything from your life as you developed the characters and events in your novel?
Yes. For Bob Oswald and Broken Buckley, there was one particular event that really shaped both of them. It happened years ago – I was in my early twenties and my wife and I were living in Chandlers Ford, which is quite close to where we live now in Hedge End and a relatively nice suburban area. It was a Sunday lunchtime and I'd driven to the local video shop to get a movie (which shows how long ago it was), and the drive back took me past a pub called The Halfway Inn. There was a fight going on outside, but it wasn't a fight, it was a beating. Quite a short guy had knocked down a much ▶

A Conversation with Daniel Clay
(continued)

◄ bigger guy and was standing with his hand in this bigger guy's hair, just punching him in the face, over and over again, and the bigger guy was just sprawled in a heap staring up at him with his mouth hanging open and his eyes all glazed. A couple of Oswald-like girls were standing around watching but not doing anything to intervene. I really wish I'd intervened myself, but I'd driven by before I'd realised what was happening. Even though I only caught the scene for a matter of seconds, I just couldn't shake the image of this beaten guy staring up at this other guy and I kept thinking about the back-story – were the two of them friends who'd fallen out? Were they strangers who'd never seen each other before? Did they ever cross paths again, and how did they feel about themselves when they woke up the next morning? When I sat down to write *Broken* ten or so years later, memories of this definitely inspired the scene early on where Bob attacks Rick, and I drew on how upset I'd felt at the time to help get into Rick's mindset once the humiliation of his beating set in.

What, outside of your life and other novels, did you draw on for inspiration?
Funnily enough, in terms of structure, I was probably influenced much more by TV and film than any novels I've ever read. I absolutely love the film *American Beauty* and I'm also a huge fan of *Desperate Housewives*. Both of these use the omnipresent voice-over to great effect to

6 Funnily enough, in terms of structure, I was probably influenced much more by TV and film than any novels I've ever read. 9

link all the action, and they also centre around different dramas in different households, which is something I was very keen to do with *Broken*. Skunk's coma voice came from my desire to have a first-person narrator linking everyone together the way these two programmes do.

When thinking of how to tell the story, I was also strongly influenced by three epic sagas that probably seem a million light years away from *Broken* – *Star Wars*, *The Lord of the Rings* and J. K. Rowling's *Harry Potter* series. For me, in all of these plots, the action starts at a point where you quickly know something major has already happened and something precious has been lost or destroyed – possibly forever. The compulsion to find out what happens comes from a desire to know what has already happened as much as it does from the need to know how everything is going to be resolved. *Broken* isn't an epic in terms of length or scope in the way that these three stories are, but they did play a significant part in my decision to let the reader know straight away that Skunk is in a coma and that the main thrust of the novel is going to show how she came to be in it.

How similar is the Hedge End described in *Broken* to the Hedge End you actually live in?
In terms of street names, it's a mish-mash. There is no Drummond Square, but the place where I imagine Drummond Square to be does exist – it's called Drummond ▶

A Conversation with Daniel Clay
(continued)

◄ Community Centre, and the grounds and car park are large enough to hold the houses described. The local rubbish tip the Oswalds' house backs onto really is next door to this place, and the One Stop is just over the road as well. (It's where I buy the lager that helps me keep writing.) Late at night, when I tend to do most of my writing, I can hear the boy-racers tearing it up along Bubb Lane and around the car parks of McDonald's and Burger King as well.

When I wrote the first draft of *Broken*, I did imagine the three main families living in the street I actually live in, which goes around in a sort of crescent shape, with the Cunninghams in my house, the Buckleys in a larger house that's off to the right on the opposite side of the road and the Oswalds in one of the terraced properties a little further over to the left, but my wife put her foot down and said I wasn't allowed to do this. It wouldn't have been technically correct anyway, as none of these properties are Housing Association (and the people in the terraced houses seem very nice and polite), so I came up with Drummond Square instead.

Your descriptions of the Oswalds and Southampton paint a bleak picture of life in England. Do you really see life like that?
Not all of the time, no. But sometimes, yes, I think life in England can leave you pretty shaken, as I'm sure it can anywhere else in the world. Kids do sometimes hang around outside the One Stop in large gangs late at night, and although I'm sure they're all

6 The local rubbish tip the Oswalds' house backs onto really is next door to this place, and the One Stop is just over the road as well. (It's where I buy the lager that helps me keep writing.) 9

mostly harmless middle-class kids who are just discussing their homework, they can often seem pretty intimidating.

I've never met a family like the Oswalds, thankfully, but they are out there somewhere, and the situation in *Broken* is based on a scenario someone told me about friends of theirs who scrimped and saved to afford a mortgage only to have a family move into the Housing Association property next door and completely ruin the neighbourhood. None of the private residents could afford to move out because no one would put in an offer on their houses, so everyone was just stuck with each other. For a long time after I heard this, I couldn't get it out of my head.

On top of the stuff in *Broken*, some things I see every now and then just leave me with a sense of despair. My wife and I were shopping in Southampton over Christmas, and Southampton's got a really nice shopping centre right next to a major port, so it can feel quite cosmopolitan and vibrant. We were walking from one shop to another when I saw three teenage boys walking just ahead of us. One of them turned his head and sneezed – all over his friend. The sneezer didn't raise his hand to cover his mouth or try to avoid his friend at all. He didn't even say sorry or act as if he'd done anything wrong. So, without breaking stride or making any comment, his friend turned and spat in his face. Then the three of them carried on walking. The two who'd exchanged mucus didn't even bother ▶

❝ On top of the stuff in *Broken*, some things I see every now and then just leave me with a sense of despair. ❞

13

A Conversation with Daniel Clay
(*continued*)

◄ to wipe their own faces. As a writer, I can't get images like these out of my head. I try to (believe me) but I can't help imagining what their girlfriends or mothers must have thought when they turned up like that – or, if they were prepared to treat their friends this way, what would they be willing to do to their enemies?

Seeing things like this is, luckily, pretty rare, but once I've seen them, like the fight in Chandlers Ford, they stick in my mind, and I guess that comes out in my writing.

The character Dillon is obviously inspired by Dill in *To Kill a Mockingbird*. Why is he a gypsy in *Broken*, rather than simply a close neighbour's distant relative as he is in *To Kill a Mockingbird*?

It's because there actually were gypsies living in the Halford's car park around the time I started writing *Broken* – maybe three months before, in fact. Our local Halford's had just moved from one retail park to another one a few streets away. Within a few days of the old store shutting down, its car park was full of caravans. I think they were there for about a month before the council moved them on. I used to drive past every day on my way into work and there would be makeshift washing lines and rubbish and second-hand cars all over the place, plus a few kids just hanging around staring at the traffic going by. That's where Dillon came from. I wouldn't have thought up that scenario all by myself. ■

Author's Picks: Books that Shaped Me

I WOULD SAY the following books have shaped me as a writer for all sorts of different reasons, and would highly recommend them to anyone who loves a great read.

....

To Kill a Mockingbird
Harper Lee
Scout Finch tells the story of growing up alongside her brother, Jem, and friend, Dill, in Depression-era America. It's a study of life and relationships set against the backdrop of Scout's father, Atticus, defending a man who has been falsely accused of rape.

As I said earlier, this novel set me off on the path to writing *Broken*, but even without that link it would still be very high on my list. It's a beautifully crafted novel that moves at its own pace and demands you slow your own life down to enjoy it. Also, does it have the most subtle title ever? It's certainly the title I've always been most impressed with.

....

One Flew Over the Cuckoo's Nest
Ken Kesey
A battle of wits between Nurse Ratched and R. P. McMurphy, the newest inmate on the psychiatric ward Ratched is in charge of, has disastrous results for some of the more established inmates and uplifting results for the others. Narrated by Chief Bromden, ▶

Author's Picks: Books that Shaped
Me *(continued)*

◀ Kesey's novel leaves you wondering
exactly who's mad and who's sane, and
questioning whether being sane really
makes that much of a difference when all
else is said and done.

This, for me, was just such a moving
story told in such a fantastic style. My only
regret with this book is that I saw the
movie before I picked the book up. I've
watched and read both time and time again
since. The scene where the patients are
having a party and have to hide in a store
room, only to discover the security guard
they've bribed to look out for them is
hiding in there with them, is probably one
of the funniest I've ever read.

Jaws
Peter Benchley

A man-eating Great White shark terrorises
the inhabitants of Amity, leading to the
beaches being shut, small-town political in-
fighting, the chief-of-police's wife having an
affair with the college boy her husband
brings in to help fight the monster and a
gripping finale between the shark and three
men who really did need to find a bigger
boat.

This was one of the first 'grown-up'
books I read. I got it for about twenty-five
pence in a second-hand book store when I
was eleven or twelve. I couldn't believe the
bloke behind the counter sold it to me. It
had sex scenes and everything. I'd been
desperate to see the movie for ages but it

was rated too high for my age, which was what drove me to buying and reading the novel. When I finally did get to see the movie, the shark on the screen just didn't compare to the shark Peter Benchley had put in my head. This, more than anything else, really got me into reading and affirmed my desire to be a writer as well.

As an aside, I think *Jaws 2*, by Hank Searls, is an equally excellent read. Just when you thought it was safe to go back in the bookstore!

Boy A
Jonathan Trigell
Meet 'Jack'. He's twenty-four years old. He's just chosen his name out of the Big Book of Boys' Names. He's also just been released from prison for a crime he and a friend committed against a young girl when they were just children themselves. Now Jack, who has spent his formative years in juvenile detention centres and prison cells, has to integrate himself with a society that would condemn him if it ever found out who he is and what he has done. Rightly or wrongly, he's been given a new job, a new identity and a chance to enjoy the sort of life he and his friend took away from their victim. Can Jack find the future he's not even sure he deserves himself?

A searing debut novel that draws parallels with the ongoing debate over the release of Jon Venables and Robert Thompson following their conviction for ▶

Author's Picks: Books that Shaped Me *(continued)*

◀ murdering two-year-old Jamie Bulger in 1993, when they were just ten years old themselves. This won the World Book Day 'Book to Talk About' prize in 2008 and has since been adapted into an award-winning Channel 4 film. For me, there's so much to admire in the pace and style of the writing, but I feel the novel's overriding strength is the way it humanises a character the vast majority of us would instantly dismiss as inhuman. A thought-provoking read that is gripping and moving as well.

Girl with a Pearl Earring
Tracy Chevalier
Set in Delft, Holland, in the 1660s, *Girl with a Pearl Earring* tells the imagined story of how the anonymous girl in Vermeer's revered painting came to pose for him in the first place. After her father is injured at work and loses his sight, Griet becomes a housemaid for the artist's family. As well as helping with general household chores, she has to clean Vermeer's study with methodical care, replacing everything exactly as she found it. Displaying a rare competence, a tense form of respect builds between the artist and the maid, culminating in Griet becoming more and more involved in his work. Tensions in Vermeer's large household, particularly the pecking order between his wife's mother, his wife, his many children and the staff, not to mention the painter himself and those who commission work from him, are expertly

explored as Griet finds herself buffeted from maid to assistant to model in what becomes an increasingly manipulative and dangerous game for a housemaid to be involved in.

As soon as I knew that *Broken* was going to be published and that I had to start work on my next novel, I began looking out for second novels that had been at least as successful as the debuts they had followed. Although, being a contemporary writer myself, I rarely read historical fiction, the fact I was being represented by the same agent and published by the same publishing house as Tracy Chevalier convinced me to give this novel a try. I was instantly glad that I did – Chevalier's eye for detail is amazing, not just in bringing 17th-century Holland to life but also in creating pitch-perfect characters whose motivations are complex and yet, thanks to the way they are portrayed, instantly recognisable and easy to grasp. A great read, highly recommended.

....

The Curious Incident of the Dog in the Night-time
Mark Haddon

Told through the eyes of Christopher Boon, a fifteen-year-old autistic boy living with his father, the incident of the title is the murder of Wellington, a neighbour's pet dog. Christopher is wrongly arrested for the crime and, upon his release, sets about solving the mystery as his personal hero, Sherlock Holmes, would have done. This, ▶

Author's Picks: Books that Shaped Me *(continued)*

◀ in turn, leads him to discover some surprising truths about his mother, his father and the dog's owner, not to mention his own place in the world.

Although a lot is made of the unusualness of the narrator's condition and, therefore, his outlook on life, for me this book is the sharpest depiction of a contemporary English upbringing I've ever read. No heroes, no villains, just a lot of muddled-up adults trying to do the best that they can. I loved the dialogue and Christopher's narrow view of what was going on around him, and don't mind admitting that the style was a huge influence on me at the time I sat down to write *Broken*.

....

God's Own Country
Ross Raisin
Martin Martin's on the Other Side
Mark Wernham
In *God's Own Country*, we see our world through the eyes of Sam Marsdyke, a young man who has recently been expelled from school for what may have been a clumsy sexual advance – or may have been something more sinister. Tending his father's flock on the brooding Yorkshire Moors, Sam slowly becomes involved in the rebellious life of his new-to-the-countryside neighbours' teenage daughter. As the novel progresses, our perception of who is using who rapidly shifts as the relationship between the two disintegrates

into the novel's studied and chilling climax.

In *Martin Martin's on the Other Side*, we see a version of our world set in the near future through the eyes of Jensen Interceptor. Jensen's busy trying to pay off his life debt by working for the Department of Media and Culture. When he's not running focus groups, Jensen's also busy snorting boris and going to Starfucks. He then has the misfortune to stumble across Reg in one of his focus groups. Reg is a Martin Martinist – someone who believes that Martin Martin, a TV psychic who was assassinated by the state in 2008, was actually the saviour and a prophet. Encouraged to infiltrate the 'dangerous' Martin Martinists by his boss in return for having a large chunk of his life debt paid off, Jensen's life is about to be totally changed – and probably not for the best.

I appeared on a panel with Ross and Mark at this year's Edinburgh Festival and read their debut novels back-to-back in preparation, which is why I've put them together here. Both are very different novels and superb reads on their own merits, but what struck me was the strength of the first-person narration in each novel. Both Sam Marsdyke and Jensen Interceptor have their own unique vocabularies, but the strength of each character and the choice of language used by each author was so faultless that I was never in any doubt what each one of them was saying. Great debut ►

Author's Picks: Books that Shaped Me *(continued)*

◀ novels, and I can't wait to see what these two writers do next.

As there are so many novels out there that I've loved reading but nowhere near enough space here to go into detail about more than a few of them, here's a list of authors whose work I've really enjoyed in the past and whom I would recommend as worth reading if you've not yet had the chance to discover them: Jodi Picoult, Lionel Shriver, Robert Harris, William Boyd, Kazuo Ishiguro, Clive Barker, Chimamanda Ngozi Adichie, Alice Sebold, Kem Nunn, Rupert Thompson and, last but most definitely not least, Thomas Harris' supremely fantastic Hannibal Lecter books, *Red Dragon* and *The Silence of the Lambs*. (Jed Cunningham might know his stuff about serial killers, but it was Thomas Harris who taught him virtually all he knows!) ■